Catherine Fox was educated at Durham and London Universities. She is the author of four adult novels: *Angels and Men, The Benefits of Passion, Love for the Lost* and *Acts and Omissions*; a Young Adult fantasy novel, *Wolf Tide*; and a memoir, *Fight the Good Fight: From vicar's wife to killing machine*, which relates her quest to achieve a black belt in judo. She lives in Liverpool, where her husband is dean of the cathedral.

UNSEEN THINGS ABOVE

Catherine Fox

Marylebone House

First published in Great Britain in 2015

Marylebone House
36 Causton Street
London SW1P 4ST
www.marylebonehousebooks.co.uk

British Library Cataloguing-in-Publication Data
A catalogue record for this book is available from the British Library

ISBN 978–1–910674–23–9
eBook ISBN 978–1–910674–24–6

Typeset by Graphicraft Limited, Hong Kong
Manufacture managed by Jellyfish
First printed in Great Britain by CPI
Subsequently digitally printed in Great Britain

eBook by Graphicraft Limited, Hong Kong

Produced on paper from sustainable forests

For
Margaret, Maeve and Gill,
for being fabulous

Dramatis personae

Bishops

Paul Henderson	Former Bishop of Lindchester
Bob Hooty	Suffragan Bishop of Barcup
Harry Preece	Acting Bishop of Lindchester
Steve Pennington	Bishop of Aylesbury
Rupert Anderson	Archbishop of York

Priests and deacons

Cathedral clergy

Marion Randall	Dean of Lindchester (the boss)
Giles Littlechild	Cathedral Canon Precentor (music & worship)
Mark Lawson	Cathedral Canon Chancellor, 'Mr Happy' (outreach and matters scholarly)
Philip Voysey-Scott	Cathedral Canon Treasurer (money)

Lindchester clergy

Matt Tyler	Archdeacon of Lindchester
Martin Rogers	Bishop's chaplain
Dominic Todd	Rector of Lindford Parish Church
Wendy Styles	'Father Wendy', Vicar of Renfold, Carding-le-Willow, Cardingforth
Virginia Coleman	Curate to Wendy Styles
Veronica da Silva	Linden University chaplain, assistant priest of St James' Lindford
Geoff Morley	Vicar of St James' Lindford
Ed Bailey	Rector of Gayden Parva, Gayden Magna, Itchington Episcopi, etc.

Other clergy

Johnny Whitaker	Vicar in Bishopside, married to Mara Johns
Guilden Hargreaves	Principal of Barchester Theological College

People

Cathedral Close

Gene	Husband of the dean
Timothy Gladwin	Cathedral director of music
Laurence	Cathedral organist
Iona	Assistant organist
Nigel Bennet	Senior lay clerk
Freddie May	Choral scholar in Barchester/probationary lay clerk in Lindchester
Miss Barbara Blatherwick	Cathedral Close resident, former school matron
Philippa Voysey-Scott	'Totty' wife of the canon treasurer
Ulrika Littlechild	Precentor's wife, voice coach
Felix Littlechild	Younger son of precentor
Helene Carter	Diocesan safeguarding and HR officer
Penelope	Bishop Paul's PA

Beyond the Close

Dr Jane Rossiter	Lecturer at Linden University
Danny Rossiter	Jane's son
Neil Ferguson	Father Ed's fiancé
Andrew Jacks	Director of the Dorian Singers
Becky Rogers	Estranged wife of bishop's chaplain, mother of Leah and Jessica
Leah Rogers	Older daughter of bishop's chaplain
Jessica Rogers	Younger daughter of bishop's chaplain
Janet Hooty	Wife of Suffragan Bishop
Susanna Henderson	Wife of former Bishop of Lindchester
Mara Johns	Artist
Dame Perdita Hargreaves	Guilden Hargreaves' mother

APRIL

Chapter 1

I n homage to our esteemed forerunner, we commence this ecclesiastical tale with the question: Who will be the new bishop?

Back in the year of 185— when this same puzzle absorbed the good folk of Barchester, appointing a new bishop appears to have been a pretty straightforward affair. To be sure, there was some Oxbridge High Table-style manoeuvring behind the scenes. There were raised and dashed hopes, with the press confidently (and, for the most part, wrongly) naming names; and then the prime minister made his choice. Dr Proudie, we read, was bishop elect 'a month after the demise of the late bishop'. A month! I fear, by contrast, we will still be asking, 'Who will be the new bishop?' for a long time to come, while the Crown Nominations Commission ruminates.

Ruminates? Dare I apply so bovine a metaphor to this august body? Do I wish my reader to picture jaws rolling, rolling, strands of saliva swinging, heads turning ponderously this way and that as the process of discernment toils on? And how – if we pursue this alimentary metaphor to its logical conclusion – are we to characterize its outcome?

No, we had better eschew rumination.

And anyway, they are not an august body. They are just a bunch of ordinary Anglicans operating as best they can in this awkward limbo that C of E senior appointments currently occupies (somewhere between 185— and the real world). These days it takes a very long time to appoint a new bishop. It feels especially protracted for those caught up in the process and zipped by oaths into the body bag of confidentiality.

So who will be the new bishop of Lindchester? I have no idea. If you're keen to know early, your best bet is to keep an eye on Twitter. It is possible that someone will award themselves a smiley sticker on the wallchart of self-aggrandizement by being the first to blab what others have appropriately kept under wraps.

We rejoin our Lindcastrian friends the day before Low Sunday, that is, the first Sunday after Easter. In parishes across the diocese this collect may be said:

> Risen Christ,
> for whom no door is locked, no entrance barred:
> open the doors of our hearts ...

It *may* be said; but it is not, of course, compulsory. Gone is the golden age of Book of Common Prayer uniformity, the days of 'Here's a digestive biscuit, take it or leave it.' Gone, too, are the late unlamented days of the Alternative Service Book. ('Here's a choice: digestive, Lincoln, rich tea or garibaldi.') We now inhabit the age of the biscuit assortment. ('Here, have a rummage.') Heck, we are pretty much in the age of the liturgical bake-off. Provided *some* of the right ingredients are used, frankly you can go ahead and make your own. Anything, provided there are biscuits to feed the hungry people of the UK!

Like the risen Christ himself, this narrative will find locked doors no obstacle. The hearts and homes of our characters stand ajar to us. We may slip in and snoop around. Let us set out now to walk the joyful road of sacrifice and peace in their company as far as Advent, the Church's New Year. New Year at the end of November? Yes, there it is again, that strange tension between the two realms we inhabit: the Church and the world, with ever and anon the tug of homesickness for the home we have never seen.

Come, reader, and dust off the wings of your imagination. Fly with me once again to the green and pleasant Diocese of Lindchester. Ah, Lindfordshire, from you we have been absent in the spring! Even now, as the month draws to its close, proud-pied April is still dressed in all his trim. Look down as we glide upon polite Anglican wings, and see how every road edge is blessed with silver and gold. Daisies and dandelions – no mower blade can keep them down. See where eddies of cherry blossom, pink, white, swirl in suburban gutters.

Hover with me above parks and gardens. The horse chestnut candles are in bloom, and the may blossom authorizes the casting of clouts. Sheep and cattle graze in old striped fields. Listen! A cuckoo dimples the air, and for a heartbeat, everything stands still. The waters have receded, but signs of flooding are everywhere across the landscape. Even now, the distant cathedral seems perched like the ark on Ararat, as rainbows come and go behind the cooling towers of Cardingforth.

We will head to the cathedral. I'm pleased to inform you that the spire has not crashed through the nave roof in our absence. The historic glass of the Lady Chapel has not slipped from its crumbled tracery and smashed to smithereens. Restoration work is under way on the cathedral's south side, where a vast colony of masonry bees has been ruthlessly exterminated. Dean and Chapter (how can they call themselves Christian?) were in receipt of letters from single-issue bee fanatics. A reply drafted by the canon chancellor, referring them to Our Lord's brusque treatment of swine, was never sent.

It is Saturday afternoon. Gavin, deputy verger and closet pyromaniac, is mowing the palace lawn before the rain starts. All downhill now till Advent, he thinks. The triumph of the Easter brazier still glows in his mind. New paschal candle lit first go. Cut-off two-litre Coke bottle, that was the secret. Stopped it blowing out. Up and down goes Gavin. Keeping things under control lawn-wise during the interregnum.

Ah, but the garden misses the touch of Susanna, the former bishop's wife. Bleeding heart plants nod in untended borders. Roses shoot unpruned. The laburnum walk is unforbidden, poised to rain its deadly Zeus-like showers on nobody at all. Everything waits for the new bishop, whoever he may be.

As you may have seen in the press, there was a brief outbreak of squawking in the ecclesiastical henhouse back in February, when it was (wrongly) rumoured that the Church Commissioners had decided to sell the palace and stick the next bishop of Lindchester in a poky little seven-bedroomed house in suburban Renfold. Indignant petitions were worded. SAVE LINDCHESTER PALACE! The bishops of Lindchester had *always* lived there, since ...

It emerged that the bishops of Lindchester had, in fact, only lived in this particular house since 1863, when a vigorous and godly Evangelical bishop sold off the other two palaces. The Rt Revd William Emrys Brownlow used the money to clear the city's slums, provide clean water and good housing for the impoverished leatherworkers, build a hospital, schools and a theological college. Prior to that, no bishop of Lindchester had ever lived in the Close in such proximity to his clergy and people. It would have been tactless to do so, since they could not have afforded to ape his gracious lifestyle. No, far kinder to retreat to Bishop's Ingregham and eat quails in aspic with a clear conscience.

Shall we pause to lament the passing of those glorious historic palaces from the Church? Ingregham Palace is particularly lovely, with its mellow sandstone walls, its acres of Capability Brown landscaping, the deer park, the lake. What was Bishop Brownlow *thinking* of, selling off the family silver like that? These treasures are not ours to dispose of – we are but custodians! Selling off property is only a short-term solution, a crass attempt to throw money at the problem.

As is so often the case when the problem is 'lack of funds', the throwing of money at it turns out to be the solution. A great many runty little leatherworkers' children failed to die of cholera. Many were educated. Scores of earnest young Evangelicals were trained and sent to work in places of great danger and deprivation across the Empire.

Ah, but the palace *is* very lovely. It's a shame the Church no longer owns it.

We will leave the garden in Gavin's care and swoop gracefully to earth outside the deanery instead. Come with me, on tiptoe, to the old scullery, where the Very Revd Marion Randall (just back from a post-Easter break in Lisbon) is standing amid open suitcases. She is discussing the identity of the next bishop with her husband. Or rather, *not* discussing it.

'There's nothing to tell. And even if there was, I wouldn't tell you. We take oaths, you know.'

'Oaths! How Shakespearean. Ods bodkins! By my lady's nether beard!' he declaimed. 'Like that?'

'Funnily enough, Gene, nothing like that.'

'How dull. But can't you drop a tiny hint? In passing. I can infer. I'm an excellent inferrer.'

'Yes. And you're also an inveterate gossip. Which is why I'm not going to tell you anything.'

'Aha! So you admit you *do* know something!'

The dean continued to sort and toss dirty laundry into heaps. 'Of course I know *something*. Look, we're only at the consultation stage. People have been invited to submit suggestions, that's all. We'll get a long list from the Washhouse, which we'll sift, then decide who we want to mandate.'

'Ooh! Who's on the long list?'

'You're not actually listening.' She bent and began thrusting a lights load into the machine. 'Nobody yet.'

'But who's *likely* to be on it?'

'Anyone whose name has come up.'

'Literally anyone? What if some bonkers old trout suggests her parish priest because he does a lovely Mass?'

'Then I suppose he'll be on the list. Hence the sifting process. No.' The dean held up her hand. 'That's it. Shut up.'

'At least promise me it won't be another swivel-eyed Evangelical pederast with a muffin-making wife.'

Silence.

'Not funny?' he enquired.

'No.'

'But quite clever?'

'No.'

'Oh.' Another silence. 'Well, let me go and choose us a homecoming wine. I am confident I can get *that* right, at any rate.'

My readers will see from this that Gene's character has undergone no reformation in the last few months. He remains the same disgraceful reprobate. His mission is unchanged, too: to cherish, divert and pamper his beloved wife, and make the task of modern deaning more fun than it might otherwise prove, were he not on hand (at all times and in all places) with the right wine and the wrong remark.

Marion sets the machine running, then gazes round her. The overhead airer, the Belfast sink, tiled floor. This was where staff of former deans presumably toiled with their washboards and goffering irons. She thinks about the old servants' bells still there high up on the deanery kitchen wall in a glass case – BED RM 3, DRAWING RM, TRADES. ENT – though they no longer work. Fell prey to health and safety regs when the deanery was rewired ten years ago. There is a button in Marion and Gene's en-suite bathroom (formerly DRESSING RM 1). She imagines her predecessors summoning a valet to bring up a hip bath and pink gin. Gene, no doubt, would recreate this scenario with enthusiasm, were she to mention it.

Dear Gene. She smiles. But the brief holiday is already retreating from her mind. The thought bailiffs shoulder their way in to repossess the unpaid-for happiness. The spire. The stuff coming out about the school chaplain from the 1970s. The new bishop of Lindchester – would it be uncomplicated; someone she could work with and not be forever thinking, *You are younger than me, less gifted, less experienced* . . .? How wearing it is, all the nuisance of being one of those tipped to be the first woman bishop. To know you're being talked about. Folk speculating: would she be suffragan somewhere, or was she holding out to be the first diocesan? She shakes her head. Come on, you're still on holiday till Monday.

She casts her mind back to Lisbon. That basilica. Was it only this morning they were there? Muted palette of browns and terracottas. Easter lilies, a CD of plainsong alleluias playing. High above in the dome, blue sky glimpsed through glass. Peace, beauty. And then to emerge into the big bright spring world! Dazzled by full sunlight, buffeted by the wind, the whirl of life, the vast dome of the sky above. If the inside was the only thing you knew, how could you guess at all this? And yet it made perfect sense. Of course, *of course*! Would it be like this – resurrection?

She goes through to the kitchen and puts the kettle on.

Gene emerges through the cellar door. With a fey flourish, he presents the wine. 'Nineteen-ninety-six Chateau Latour.'

'Lovely.'

He sees from her face that his magic words have conveyed nothing. 'Bless you, my darling, I know you love that vinho verde.' He gives a dainty shudder. 'But some of it was *so* young, drinking it was practically a safeguarding issue.'

And now it is Low Sunday. Where shall I take you today, dear reader? I know that you are eager for news of our various friends. How is Father Dominic faring in his new parish, for example? And what of our lovely Bishop Bob, shouldering the weight of the whole diocese during the interregnum? To say nothing of our stout hero, the archdeacon, last seen haring off to New Zealand in pursuit of his lady!

You must be patient. I am going to introduce you to a new character, one I fear you may not find it in your heart to love, but Veronica plays an important part in our tale. There are times when we must stoically eat our plate of school liver (horrid tubes visible) before we are allowed out to play.

Come with me now to a church in Lindford. Not the parish church (where Father Dominic now serves), but one nearby with a Gothic revival building of the type that looks as though it might soon be cut loose by the evil archdeacon, Matt the Knife, and turned into a supermarket. Or more likely a nightclub called Holy Joe's. It is in the clubbing district, such as it is, of Lindford. Beside the church is that narrow alley where, last year – you may remember the incident – two men picked on the wrong faggot. A CCTV camera now keeps watch. Every Friday and Saturday night the church pitches its gazebo in the little yard behind the railings, and from here the street pastors operate, dispensing love, hot chocolate and flip-flops to the lost souls of Lindford.

We will pop in now and see what's going on in St James' Church this Low Sunday morning. The first thing you will spot is the lack of pews. The Victorian Society took a tonking here, all right. There are cheerful banners. Someone plays thoughtful music on an electric piano. Can this be another Evangelical stronghold? By no means! This is an inclusive church, my friends, where God is mother and father of all, in the *commonwealth* not the kingdom of heaven. It is Bishop Bob's kind of a place. Change from the bottom up, not the top down. They do good work here in their rainbowy way.

Veronica wears a simple cassock alb and Peruvian stole in bright colours. Lent is now over, so she has laid aside her equal marriage campaigning rainbow dog collar. She is not the incumbent, she's a university chaplain. Here comes Geoff the vicar now. It's a baptism, so he's wearing a stole with Noah's ark animals on. I believe somebody made it from upholstery fabric. It would cover a nursery chair very nicely. The baptism will move seamlessly into the Annual Parochial Church Meeting (getting in before the end of April) and be followed by a shared lunch.

I don't suppose you want to stay for a church AGM, do you? No. Let us 'risk the hostile stare', and tiptoe back out as the congregation stands to sing 'Will you come and follow me if I but call your name?' (tune: Kelvingrove).

A glimpse of Veronica is all I vouchsafe you this week, dear reader. Instead, I will whisk you back to the Close and into the study of the Revd Giles Littlechild, the canon precentor. The Littlechilds have just returned from holiday in Heidelberg, visiting in-laws and older son (Gap Yah). Giles has read somewhere that you should do one thing each day that scares you. Opening his work emails surely qualifies!

He scrolls through, delicately, like a bomb disposal expert. Excellent. Nothing too dire. But then a new email pings in.

Oh, God. A last-minute application for the post of tenor lay clerk. They can't *not* interview him, can they? And then they'll have to appoint him, because he'll be the best.

Lord have mercy! Frankly, Giles would rather have a tone-deaf moose on the back row of *dec* than Freddie May.

Chapter 2

hy hadn't they worded the advertisement more carefully? *The successful candidate will not be hell on wheels.* Lindchester Cathedral's music department had been complacent. It had placed its trust in Mr May's legendary powers of self-sabotage. To be sure, the application bore signs of having been submitted in panic, but it had arrived with two whole hours to spare. What was wrong with Exeter? Or Truro? thought Giles. Or Christchurch New Zealand? Why couldn't you apply for *those* when they came up, you little horror?

Oh, well. Giles supposed it was inevitable that Freddie would be drawn back to the place where he was known and loved, and where that little hiatus in his CV ('gap year' indeed!) required no mumbled explanation. And who could say, perhaps the stint as choral scholar in Barchester had steadied him? Of course it had. No awful rumours had reached Lindchester. If one discounted getting banned from Tesco Extra for skateboarding down the travelator. And the midnight Buff Run incident. But streaking round the Close was a historic tradition for choral scholars! Pure bad luck to collide with the precentor's wife.

Giles skimmed the references. Look at that: Freddie had been gainfully employed as a cocktail waiter for the last six months. 'Cheerful.' (Stoned.) 'Reliable.' (Consistently stoned.) His boss at the Cuba Club had 'absolutely no hesitation in recommending Frederick for the position he was applying for'. Neither had the director of music at Barchester Cathedral. *Take him! Someone, anyone! I'll pay you!* screamed the subtext. Or was Giles just imagining that?

'Darling, some lovely news!' he called.

Ulrika appeared in the doorway with the bottle of Mosel she was opening (decent stuff, not the crep they exported to the ignorant Brits). 'What?'

'Our beloved Frederick has applied for the lay clerk post after all!'

I will not enlarge your vocabulary of German profanities by recording her reply.

How on earth had Freddie mastered his terror of forms sufficiently to fill in the application? The answer is not far to seek. It is Monday morning. Miss Blatherwick is hanging up the birdfeeder she has just refilled. The finches rely on her this time of year, with young to feed and no ripe seeds in the hedges and fields yet. Ironic that spring should be the season of starvation. She ought to have done this yesterday really, but it was getting dark by the time she returned from her little mission to Barchester. Couldn't really trust herself in poor light. Balance not what it was.

Amadeus the cathedral cat, sleek on his diet of donated Sheba and goldfinches, watches from the top of the wall. Miss Blatherwick gets carefully down from her stool. She gives Amadeus the look that quelled generations of naughty choristers. He flicks his tail and gazes back, all innocence. She can't stand guard for ever.

This being Monday, the canons have gathered for their weekly meeting, which for historic reasons is referred to as 'Canons' Breakfast'. Dean Marion is away on a conference in Derby with her fellow deans. Derby lies beyond the borders of the diocese, so an indistinct idea must suffice that they are conferring on matters germane to the office and work of a dean in God's Church. In her absence, the meeting is taking place at the precentor's house, and the precentor is chairing, because he is the first canon. Let's slip in behind the latecomer (Mr Happy, the canon chancellor) and eavesdrop on the mice at play.

'To be honest, it's a right chuffing mare.'

I am sorry to disappoint the reader, but this was not our friend the archdeacon speaking.

'We're up to our axles in the whole interregnum malarkey, and now the volunteers are going tits up on us,' continued Philip, the canon treasurer. He had his feet up on the precentor's dining-room table. His chair was tilted at a rakish angle, as was the precentor's son's pork pie hat, which was perched on his head.

The precentor handed him a mug of coffee. 'Thou look'st like antichrist in that lewd hat.'

'You're conflating antichrist and archdeacon, there,' said the chancellor. His voice quavered.

'Well, to be fair, I *am* the chuffing arch-antichrist of Lindchester, so you can do one, you nob.' Satisfied that Mr Happy was now helpless

11

with mirth, the treasurer removed the hat from his head and his feet from the table.

The precentor's phone buzzed. 'Ha! Text from Mrs Dean. She hopes our meeting goes well, and they're off on a coach trip to Chatsworth House,' he said. 'Oh, that's nice. The deans of the Church of England are off on a jolly, while the lowly canons keep the show on the road.'

'Just think,' said the chancellor. 'If the coach driver misjudges a bend and they all go over a precipice, the archbishops' appointments secretary is going to have a very busy year.'

His colleagues both stared at him.

'You have a ghoulish imagination, Father,' said Giles. 'I like you!'

'Well, gentlemen, we have a lot to get through,' chided Philip in Marion's voice. 'Let's make a start, shall we?'

And so the business commenced. Visitor donations, coach parking facilities, volunteers' job descriptions, major art exhibition planned, big service to celebrate the twentieth anniversary of the first women priests in Lindchester diocese, rewiring of properties in Vicars' Yard, fresh wave of allegations involving the Choristers' School in the 1970s, and (on a happier note) the successful fundraising effort to cover Amadeus the cathedral cat's vet bill!

'So, my suggestion is this,' said Philip, 'that we produce a document outlining the grave danger to Amadeus from falling masonry if the restoration work on the spire is not undertaken immediately. We'll have the 7.8 million in two weeks.'

'Get the cathedral architect on to it at once,' said Giles.

'Don't forget FAC,' said the chancellor.

'FAC!' shouted the precentor. 'Great facking FAC, man!'

The Fabric Advisory Committee's acronym was among chapter's favoured expletives. We will tiptoe away as the treasurer launches into his cathedral architect impersonation and the chancellor weeps with helpless laughter again. I won't apologize for their behaviour. It is gallows humour. If clergy could not assemble now and then to ridicule their congregations, colleagues and senior staff and generally make light of their lot, I doubt they would survive.

I am now going to introduce another new character. I know, I know. You are impatient to hear about the archdeacon and Jane. But I think you will like Pedro. He's out for a walk with our lovely friend Father Wendy. Let's leap forward now to Wednesday morning, and join them on the banks of the Linden.

'Well, Pedro, isn't this a lovely morning?'

Pedro makes no reply.

'Look! Red campion – not to be confused with ragged robin, which is this one here. And that's stitchwort. Isn't the may blossom glorious?' Wendy stops and takes in a lungful. 'We could cast a clout, if we felt like it, boy.' She unzips her puffy gilet as a token.

Pedro is wearing a jacket. He is also wearing a muzzle. Wendy still isn't sure how he'll behave round other dogs. It's been less than a week. He's in a harness, because she was warned about his Houdini-like escapes from collars to chase small furry things. He's still fast, even on three legs.

'Listen! Willow warbler.'

Pedro walks on. So different from Lulu. But she will get used to this lurching silky gait. This quivering shyness. And Pedro will get used to her plodding, her non-stop nature documentary and tuneless singing.

> Glad that I live am I,
> That the sky is blue.
> Glad for the country lanes
> And the fall of dew.

And she *is* glad! 'Twenty years, Pedro. Can you believe it? At Petertide I'll have been a priest twenty years! Oh, and by the way, this Saturday I'm off to London to the big celebration in St Paul's, so it'll be Doug taking you for your walk, all right? You like Doug, don't you? Yes, you like Doug.' She bends down and massages the greyhound's neck and ears.

Pedro does not know yet that he is safe; that from now on he will be loved lavishly and unconditionally.

Who else is glad to be alive this spring morning? Why, Dr Jane Rossiter! Here she is, waiting for the lift in the ground floor of the Fergus Abernathy building. She might get into the lift, begin her ride up to the sixth floor, only for the cable to shear off. The lift will then plunge down the shaft in a few endless seconds of screaming terror, followed by a blaze of mangled pain, then death. So yes, because the alternative would be worse, Dr Rossiter is glad to be alive.

Happily, she arrives safely at her office door and rummages in her satchel for her keys. Jane was forced to come in by train today because the car's out of commission. Why are keys so hard to find? She puts down the bunch of papers and bulging files (Poundstretcher, a paper-less university! my bottom) and has a proper hunt. Why do handbags have so many effing compartments? She hunts in her pockets. She hunts in her bag again. She hunts in the files. In her bag. Files. Bag pockets files. Now what? Punch door. Set fire to building.

Because the fecking keys are at home.

Which means she'll have to go back down to security and sign out the spare set. And now, joy! Another hot flush. She rips off her jacket with a snarl and blots her face with it. Then she gathers up her stuff and stomps back to the lift, scanning round for someone to blame.

Doors closing! says the voice primly. Jane shuts her eyes and leans her head back against the lift wall. She can feel the cold film of sweat on her face, but she's taken a vow never to fan herself. Kill people, possibly; but never fan herself. So this is the end of project fertility, is it? Hoorah. Do I get my pre-adolescent body back? Do I get to be lean and lithe again? Will I be able to shin up trees and run naked without my arms folded? No? So what do I get? A beard, you say? Yeah, thanks for that, Nature.

The lift stops at Floor 3 and some undergraduates get in with their phones and tattoos and water bottles and hangovers and deadlines. Jane doesn't kill them. She's decided to kill the archdeacon instead. For not sorting her car out for her. He offered to sort her car out, but she informed him that she'd been looking after a car all by herself for over thirty years, thank you very much, so he can stop bloody patronizing her.

Oh, Jane! Why are you being beastly to the poor archdeacon? Is he not devoted to you? Was he not, only last night, steadily insisting that yes, he *does* want to come with you to New Zealand at the end of the summer term, to tie the knot? You can go ahead, crack on with the paperwork, book the tickets, everything's peachy.

But *is* everything peachy, though? This is what Jane is wondering as she crosses the foyer to get the spare keys. She's not a stupid woman. She worked out many years ago how to decode what men actually mean when they say something: they actually mean *what they say.* That's the secret. Women are from Venus, men are from Ronseal. So why is she fretting that he's got cold feet? Was there ever a sweeter, more uncomplicated bloke in the world? Maybe hormones are doing her head in. She should probably go home and wash down a handful of black cohosh with some Jack Daniels and get a grip. Sort it, go to New Zealand, return as civil partners and move in together at last. Stop having to creep about being *discreet* the whole fecking time.

Oh, God. Just to make the morning perfect, here comes the bouncing bomb in her dungarees and dog collar. Jane is a sitting duck by the Security window, while Mike searches ponderously for the spare keys to FA 609. She whips out her phone and pretends to check her emails.

14

But Veronica gets her phone out too! Maybe she hates me back? She can hear Veronica approaching the revolving doors, talking away. Either it's a genuine call, or she's making good use of her drama workshop skills. In comes Veronica.

'Well, anon for now!'

Jane directs her sneer at an imaginary email. This is the crucial moment. She can feel Veronica's gaze like a loopy searchlight sweeping the foyer for pastoral possibilities. But it passes her by. When Jane next sneaks a glance, Veronica is heading towards the student cafeteria.

The cafeteria has been redesigned, and is currently waiting for a new name. Suggestions have been sought, but as far as Jane knows, people aren't getting behind her own idea: the 'Give us lecturers a fucking pay rise instead of tarting up the cafeteria' Café.

As Jane is signing for the spare key, it crosses her mind that she's locked out of her house as well. Who can she blame now?

The archdeacon. Why hadn't he accepted that spare set of house keys when she offered them, eh? Sanctimonious nob. All this was his fault.

We will don our Anglican seven-league boots and stride over the intervening days until we arrive at Saturday evening. Where normal mortals are opening their second bottle of wine, clergy who have sermons to finish for the morrow are being more abstemious.

Father Dominic, for example, is being very abstemious indeed. He normally favours something of an extempore style of preaching, but he finds himself required to prepare notes so that the gist of his sermon at tomorrow's Eucharist can be translated in advance into Farsi. He is looking now at the passage about the Road to Emmaus, and forbidding himself to open that nice bottle of Chablis until he's finished his preparation.

Let me explain. Quite without any growth strategy or effort on his part, the congregation at Lindford Parish Church has grown. Three months ago some asylum-seekers were housed in the Abernathy estate, which is in Dominic's patch. Four of them arrived at church and asked to be baptized. Cynics might suppose that this was a ruse to strengthen their claim to asylum. And maybe he was being taken for a ride; but Father Dominic had more sympathy with homeless refugees than with middle-class parents strategically attending church in order to wangle little Oscar into the nice C of E primary school.

And the group of four has grown to nearly twenty! He's scrambling each week to prepare Enquirers' sessions. If it carries on like this, he'll end up running an Alpha course! He reaches out instinctively for his non-existent wine glass.

Focus. Dominic rereads tomorrow's Gospel. He's always loved this story. He thinks of the Caravaggio painting, that moment of stunned recognition as Christ blesses the bread. This is what it's like, he thinks. The truth bursting in. And then the thought, *I knew it!* Did not our hearts burn within us as he talked to us along the way? It was him all along.

He starts making notes, but then his phone rings. He checks. Jane. Goody-good! This will be the dates for the civil union! And about time, too!

'How's tricks, you old tart?'

'Not so good, Dom.'

'Oh, no! What's wrong, darling?' There was a silence. 'Janey?'

'I think Matt's gone off the idea.'

'No! Really? Have you tried asking him?'

'Yes. He says he hasn't.'

'Well then.'

'Well then, it's probably all in my head. I lost my keys earlier. Do you know where they were? In the fridge. I'm at an interesting age. Do you find me interesting?'

'Darling, *endlessly*. Do you need wine and a shoulder to cry on? Is it urgent, or can I quickly finish my sermon?'

'I'll help. What's it on?'

He tells her.

'The disciples didn't recognize him because he had no beard,' she says. 'Check out the Caravaggio. There will be no beards in heaven. So unless you shave yours off, you're stuffed.'

'I *could* score a cheap point about facial hair here,' says Dominic. 'But I'm too mature. Listen, give me an hour, and I'll be round with a bottle of Chablis. All right? Byesy-bye, darling.'

He hangs up. Oh, Lord. Please let this be OK. Dominic sighs, and gets back to his sermon notes so that poor old Ahmad has something to go on tomorrow.

At another desk in another part of the diocese another clergyman is sighing. It is the archdeacon. He's a bastard. He should tell her. More than happy to zip off down under for the old civil union. But what about when they get home? He can't see a way round it. If the Church requires gay clergy in civil partnerships to be celibate, the same applies to him.

MAY

Chapter 3

Marion the dean wakes with a jolt an hour before dawn. There's some payment she wrongly authorized years ago. Money has been going out of her account ever since. A vast debt has built up. Thousands, millions! For a few terrible moments she nearly remembers what it is. Slowly reason regains its grip: no, nothing's amiss. It's just a dream. She waits for the panic to recede. Beside her Gene snores. The cathedral clock chimes. Quarter past four. Well, that's all hope of sleep gone for the night.

Five minutes later she's out walking in the deanery garden, wellies on, coat over her pyjamas. On the far side of the Close a lone blackbird whistles in the dark. Bank holiday Monday. It has rained in the night. She can smell the wet lilac, the dirty sweetness of rowan blossom. All is still.

From the deanery rooftop, another blackbird tunes up. For ten minutes he duels with his rival on the opposite side. Like the *can* and *dec* sides of the cathedral choir, thinks Marion. The sky is lightening now. A great tit calls, *teacher, teacher!* Then three quacking ducks fly over in a line, like Beswick wall ornaments. The last bats flitter home just as the first rooks start to caw from the cathedral spire. With each passing moment the sky gets lighter and more birds join the chorus. Robins, wrens, wood pigeons, thrushes.

Marion walks round and round the lawn, leaving dark footprints in the dew. Colour seeps back into the flower beds. Bluebells, red roses, tints in a sepia photo. Then an old gospel song plays in her mind:

> I come to the garden alone
> While the dew is still on the roses
> And the voice I hear falling on my ear
> The Son of God discloses.

Extraordinary! How on earth does she know this? She can even hear a tinkling piano accompaniment. It must have been those holidays with Granny, being taken to the chapel. 'Women's Bright Hour', that's what it was called! All those ladies in Sunday hats, who she was to call 'auntie'. It was Auntie Ivy who used to warble the solo. Dreadful saccharine stuff, but sung with total heartfelt seriousness.

> And He walks with me, and He talks with me,
> And He tells me I am His own;
> And the joy we share as we tarry there,
> None other has ever known.

Mary Magdalene, presumably, on that first and best of mornings, coming to the sepulchre while it was still dark. Hearing the beloved voice saying her name. *Mary*. Marion feels tears rise, as though she'd just heard her own name called. This story never fails to move her. Mary Magdalene, chosen to be the first witness of the resurrection, the first one to see the risen Lord. Commissioned by him, apostle to the apostles. Marion half laughs. And here we are, over two thousand years later, still arguing about whether women can be bishops.

She is there a long time tarrying in the garden, walking, praying. The cathedral, the school, those poor kidnapped schoolgirls in Nigeria, her colleagues, family, Paul and Susanna Henderson in South Africa. The clock chimes five. Her thoughts turn to the new bishop of Lindchester. Well, this won't be the diocese where the stained-glass ceiling is first broken. The vacancy came up too soon. But what about the *pink* stained-glass ceiling? thinks Marion. Maybe we can be the first diocese to appoint an openly gay bishop? The Principal of Barchester Theological College's name has already cropped up several times. Can she ensure Guilden is mandated? Oh, it would be so good not to have *another* Evangelical bishop! To have someone who speaks the same language. Is she just being selfish? Historically, Lindchester has never been an Evangelical diocese. So Paul was an anomaly, really. She'll have to sound out the other members of the CNC.

And a lot will depend on the new Archbishop of York, of course. Yet another Evangelical. Marion catches herself and smiles. I'm not prejudiced: some of my best friends are Evangelicals! Oh, dear. Well, she'll be meeting him later this month, when he comes to lead their service to celebrate the twentieth anniversary of women priests. How conservative will Rupert Anderson turn out to be? Then she remembers: he used to be Bishop of Barchester. So he must know Guilden well. His mind will already be made up. And that will be that.

Stop it! A lot also depends on the Holy Spirit, Marion reminds herself. Your job is not to scheme and manoeuvre. It is to stand aside and try not to get in God's way too much.

She goes back inside, has breakfast, then comes back out with her second mug of coffee. It's light now. The clock chimes six. Cars start to arrive on the Close. She hears voices, poles clanking. The May Fayre. Gene has promised to whisk her away, unless it's all cancelled owing to an outbreak of good taste. She pauses under the cherry tree. On the grass, among the fallen pink blossom, lie half a dozen dead bumble bees. Poor things. Is it that virus? Hasn't she heard that our bees are all dying? (Another pang of guilt over the masonry bee colony.) But as she stoops in pity over the closest one, she hears a faint buzz. And then, slowly, slowly, as the sun's rays reach them, they all begin to vibrate. One by one the dead bees come to life and stagger up into the morning air. Not dead but sleeping! There they go – dazed – another, and another. She watches in wonder as they fly away.

A noise rouses her. She turns and looks up. The bedroom window opens. Gene appears on the wrought-iron balcony, stark naked. He raises his hand and bestows a pontifical blessing.

'You're up early,' he calls. 'Dabbling in the dew?'

'Couldn't sleep. Bad dream.'

'Poor you! Did you wake with a terrible jerk again?'

'I always do, darling. Unless you're away or I'm off on the Deans' Conference.'

He bows. 'Ba-dum-tish!'

It's now eight o'clock. Over in Cardingforth a sporty black Mini pulls up outside number 16, Sunningdale Drive. The archdeacon kills the engine, takes a deep breath. He has the breakfast kit: croissants, freshly squeezed orange, posh coffee. He has the bouquet of lilies and roses. He takes another breath. Dons his mental flak jacket. All righty. Let's get this over with.

'Flowers!' said Jane. 'Because I'm worth it, or because you're feeling guilty about something?'

'Mmm. Both.'

'Oh, Jesus.' Jane put the bouquet down on the kitchen counter. Her hands trembled. So she hadn't been imagining it. 'Well, let's have it then. You've gone off me?'

'No!'

There was a silence. Bonked another woman. New job in London. Terminally ill. 'Well? What is it?'

'OK. Look. You're going to be seriously pissed at me.'

'*Don't* tell me how I'm going to react. Tell me what's wrong.'

Matt rubbed his hands over his face. Laced his fingers behind his neck. Looked up at the ceiling. Took another deep breath.

'For God's sake, get on with it, Matt!'

'OK. Here's the thing: current regs say clergy in civil partnerships have to be celibate.'

'Is that all?' Jane laughed in relief. 'That won't apply to us!'

'Why won't it?'

'You're serious?'

'Yes. Why should there be one set of rules for gay clergy, and—'

'There already *are* two sets of rules! Duh. The Church is institutionally homophobic.'

'That's not fair.'

'Of course it is! Gays are second class – they can't get married, if they want a top job they have to pretend they're celibate.' She gave his shoulder a shake. 'Come on, don't be ridiculous! Who cares if we ignore some blitheringly stupid, totally unjust rule?'

'*I* care. How can we ask the gay clergy of this diocese to play ball if the chuffing *archdeacon* won't?'

'Jesus! I don't believe this! I thought we had a solution, Matt.'

'I know. I'm really sorry.'

'Just a second.' Jane narrowed her eyes. The archdeacon took a prudent step back. 'When did this *scruple* first occur to you?'

There was a very long silence.

'From the start? Excellent!'

'I'm sorry. I'm sorry. To be honest, Jane, back in December I'd've said yes to an Elvis wedding in Vegas.'

'Oh, and now you've got your rocks off, you've cooled down and remembered sex is *verboten*? No, get off me!'

'But I've made you cry.'

'So what? Get off! Listen to the words, not the tears: fuck you and your fucking Evangelical conscience! Fuck the Church of England. Oh, Jesus.' Jane grabbed the kitchen roll and tore off a strip. 'Don't you dare say you love me, Matt.'

'I love you.'

'You thought I'd come round, didn't you? You thought you could wear me down!'

'I hoped I could, yes.'

'You total shite! So now what? What happens now? You seriously think I'm signing up for celibacy? What kind of relationship is that?' She blew her nose. 'Oh, don't you start crying too, you big girl's blouse.'

They stood helpless. Jane blew her nose again. 'Well. I'll bung the croissants in the oven.'

'I'll do it.'

'I'LL DO IT!'

'OK.' He retreated, hands up. 'Look, I'm not giving up on this, Jane. If I have to, I'll jack in the job.'

'Oh, fuck off.' Jane slammed the oven door. 'Get off the moral high ground. Ooh, look at me, prepared to give up my job, while you're not even prepared to re-examine your views on marriage!'

The archdeacon flushed. He had a long fuse, but Jane had lit it now. 'That is *not* what I'm saying. But now you mention it, I've spent the past six months re-examining my views from every conceivable angle. Would it kill you to do the same?'

'Oh, so you think I haven't?'

'OK, then let's google it right now, shall we?' He grabbed his iPad. 'You talk me through the registry office marriage vows and explain exactly what your problem is. I've got them right here.'

'My "problem", you twat, my "problem" is that it's *marriage!*'

'No, it's a legal contract. Here. Look. Will you just chuffing *look*, Jane!'

'I *am* looking! It says "Your MARRIAGE Vows" in big fucking letters.'

'Here!' He stabbed at the screen. '*Declaratory* words, *contracting* words. "Are you free lawfully to marry Matthew John Tyler?" "I am." "I take you, Matthew John Tyler, to be my wedded husband." That's it. No rings. No white frocks. Nobody giving you away. Just two adults entering a legal contract. Sorted. Is that so impossible for you?'

'Yes! Because it's still *marriage*, you moron! And marriage institution- alizes female subordination! Everything about it, all the symbolism—'

He snapped his iPad cover closed. 'Fuck you and your fucking feminist conscience.'

She stared in shock.

'I'm off.'

And he went.

I am afraid we too must leave Jane, and wend our way back to Lind-chester. We will calm our nerves by taking the scenic route across green and pleasant prebendal lands, the historic rights and appur-tenances whereof belong to the cathedral prebends. The village names are carved on the canonical stalls in the quire: Bishop's Ingregham, Cardingforth, Gayden Parva, Gayden Magna, Carding-le-Willow. Glide with me over fields of rape, and railway woodlands, where silver birches stand like ghost trees in a green gloom, and a haze of bluebells ravishes the eye. We pass a meadow, which last month was a shimmering lake. White geese graze. One beats its wings, then refolds them. Below us now lies the Linden. Grown-up ducklings, their yellow down browned over, tack upriver in groups. A woman walks with a three-legged greyhound. Green regrowth now reaches halfway up last year's dead rushes. There's the cathedral on its mount. For a while some tricksy optical illusion makes it seem to grow smaller as we approach.

Off to our right, roads meander between hedges. Trees and lamp posts bear placards. Local elections loom. Every so often a vast UKIP poster assails the motorist round some bend in a country lane, promising to 'give Britain its voice back'. What, had it been taken away? Not round here. The voice of Little England is generally audible in Lindfordshire without too much straining. 'I'm not racist, but.' 'Run by Brussels.' 'Supposed to be a Christian country!' Cathedral clergy hear it at annual dinners. And when they do, they have to choose between schmoozing that wealthy patron and living with themselves afterwards.

Are we still a Christian country? Maybe our sword has slept in our hand! The church year no longer governs the national calendar, that's for sure. In 1971 parliament cut the 'late May bank holiday' loose from its Whitsuntide moorings and fixed it in the last week of the month. But Easter is still a movable feast. It was late this year, which is why this bank holiday follows so hard on its heels. Historic Christian outcrops remain, like stubborn features in the landscape that the new motorway must go round.

May Day bank holiday never was Christian, though. It smacks faintly of communism and was only foisted on us in 1978. We have yet to settle into it properly. Can't we switch it to St George's Day – yes! How come we don't commemorate the day of our national patron saint (whenever that is)? The campaign comes and goes, and in the meantime we must make the best of it. Here in Lindchester the city council has gone down the Merrie England path. Perhaps we can cement it into our tradition if we trowel on enough mirth of a maypole and madrigal type? And where better to attempt this than under the shadow of a medieval cathedral?

We will do a quick fly-past. Red, white and blue bunting is strung from tree to tree. I believe it was left over from the Jubilee. As Dean Marion is whisked away from all this foolishness by her shuddering husband, little stalls go up. Soap stalls, local honey stalls, pottery stalls. A splat-the-rat stall (run by the choristers). A splat-the-chorister stall (run in the precentor's imagination). Morris dancers arrive with fiddles and accordions, ready to clack a stick and jingle a leg. A hog roast lorry toils up the steep cobbled road. The falconer unloads hawks and owls. A maypole stands proud, right smack in the middle of the cathedral lawn. Coloured ribbons trail in the grass.

A maypole? Oliver Cromwell would turn headless in his grave! But we are all staunch Royalists here in Lindchester. The Royalists were the good guys: they didn't try to close the theatres and ban Christmas. Down with the tyrannical Parliamentarians, imposing their Puritan political-correctness-gone-mad! Huzzah for King Charles I, gentle martyr, who never imposed anything on anyone, apart from illegal taxation, ship money, the divine right of kings and eleven years of personal rule without calling a parliament! Give Britain its voice back! And another thing, the Cavaliers had nicer hats.

The flag ripples and snaps on the cathedral flagpole, and carried on the wind – like rumours from outlying villages – comes the smell of rape fields. The sky is blue. Will it stay blue? Let it stay blue! People consult their weather apps to see if it's worth packing the kids into the car and heading to Lindchester. And if they don't like the forecast, they consult another app, and another, until they find one that promises fair weather this May Day bank holiday.

Jane no longer cares about the weather. They were going to plant roses today. Book the flights. Go for a walk in the bluebell woods at Gayden Parva. But let it rain. She sits in her kitchen weeping and eating too many croissants. The archdeacon drives to the Peak District so he can climb a very high hill. He will climb it, stand there and look out at the view. Get a bit of perspective. Sort his head out. And try not to cry like a big girl's blouse.

It's now ten o'clock. Back in the city of Lindchester, another couple is quarrelling this May morning. Shall we listen in?

'Well, my darling, I think it's safe to say this car park is full. But by all means carry on with your man thing, and drive round three more times looking for a space.'

'Look! They're leaving.'

'No, they're just putting something in the boot. I hesitate to mention this for the *fifth* time, but that multi-storey we passed ...?'

'And for the *fifth* time I reply, it's a bit of a hike up to the cathedral from there, Mother.'

'I am not as frail as you think, my young whippersnapper. By the way, isn't this the place where there was all that nonsense about the bishop? Didn't he leave under something of a cloud?'

'He left, certainly.'

There is a silence. 'Darling, we're not having a little snoop around *with a view*, as it were?'

'Of course not! I am taking my dearly beloved mother to visit the historic cathedral city of Lindchester. Because she adores that kind of thing!'

'Indeed I do! Why, I even have my trusty Pevsner guide here in my handbag! I shall stay unwaveringly in role.'

'Look! They're leaving. No, no, they really are this time. See? My man thing is rewarded.'

'I retire abashed.'

They wait as the car reverses out of the space.

'Darling, aren't you worried someone will recognize you, and guess why you're snooping around?'

He laughs. 'They will be far too busy recognizing *you* and wanting autographs, Dame Perdita!'

'So I am your decoy. Cunning!'

'No, no! You adore cathedral cities, remember.'

'That I do – to the point of dangerous obsession!' She places a hand on his arm. 'My darling boy, as you know, nothing would thrill me more than to see you in gaiters. Think of the scope for actress and bishop jokes at clan reunions. But . . . oh, oh, oh. You aren't going to get dreadfully hurt, are you? The Church is still so beastly about gay people.'

'Well, perhaps the tide is turning?'

'Oh, I do hope so! Hey! Well, I like that! He's pinching your space! Barefaced piracy!'

'I know – what about that multi-storey car park? I can't *think* why you didn't suggest it earlier, Mother,' says the Principal of Barchester Theological College.

Chapter 4

oday is Vocations Sunday. Clergy in their pulpits strive to impress upon their congregations that *all* the baptized have a vocation. Lay people ought not to regard ordained ministry as special, or as the only 'real' vocation. No, their *own* vocation to be God's people in their homes, their workplaces, their communities, is equally important, in some ways *more* important! Whether congregations fully believe this message I leave for my readers to imagine; coming as it does from the mouth of someone carefully selected and trained, in receipt of a stipend, living in tied accommodation, addressed by an honorific title, and clad in the distinctive garb of their non-special vocation.

In the cathedral, the diocesan director of ordinands preaches. She reiterates this message. All the baptized have a vocation ('Christ has no hands but yours'). Then she adds that perhaps some of you here this morning are wondering whether God is calling *you* to explore a vocation to the ordained ministry?

We will leave the cathedral folk to mull this over during the offertory hymn ('Is it I, Lord?') and pay a visit to Lindford Parish Church, where Father Dominic has invited an old friend to preach about vocation.

Father Ed is a vicar over on the other side of the diocese. He looks after a group of rural parishes, including the Gaydens, both Magna and Parva, and the wonderfully named Itchington Episcopi. Ed and Dominic go way back. They were at theological college together. In fact, there may once have been a bit of a thing between them, but that's really none of our business. I will just mention that Ed was the other bearded man in the infamous snogging incident on Latimer Hall lawn that shocked Jane so much (even though she didn't actually witness it).

The service is over now, and they are back at the vicarage. The lamb is roasting, the Pinot Noir is open. Ed and Dominic are wandering in the back garden in the sunshine drinking Prosecco. Dominic's lawn is large, mown every fortnight by the firm who come in to do the churchyard. It is shaded by mature trees which screen off the tower blocks of the Abernathy estate, but between which the spire of the parish church is visible. Hardy vicarage garden perennials – cranesbill, Canterbury bells, columbine – flourish in overgrown beds. Rambling roses riot unchecked. The air is sweet with their scent. Birds sing. A cabbage white flutters by. This is truly a classic of the vicarage garden genre: charming at this season of year, but requiring more time, money and horticultural passion than most clergy have at their disposal.

The two friends look faintly comic, I confess, rather like an animated Spy Cartoon, as they stroll in their clerical black. In a bygone era their hands would have been clasped behind their frock-coated backs, and Father Ed's hunter would have been in the stable, rather than his silver Skoda Fabia on the drive. Father Ed is tall and slender, beardless these days. He inclines his head as he converses with his shorter, stouter companion. Dominic will shortly be re-entering the final phase of his three-year dieting cycle, I fear.

'I told Jane one o'clock,' said Dominic. 'You remember Jane Rossiter? Trained at Latimer, but jacked it in.'

'Tall? Played rugby? A bit scary?'

'That's Jane. She's a history lecturer at Linden Uni now.'

Ed stared. 'Did you just say "uni"?'

'Yes. I'm down wiv da yoof.'

'Oh, stop embarrassing yourself, Father.'

They walked in silence for a while. Before long Dominic's pastoral antennae sensed the approach of an important conversation. The antennae passed the message on immediately to conscience. Conscience did a quick scan and issued the all-clear – along with a brusque memo that everything wasn't always about Dominic Todd.

'Can I run something past you before Jane gets here, Dom?'

'Yes, of course.'

'Neil and I are thinking of getting married.'

Silence. A blackbird sang, gloriously unconcerned. 'Congratulations!'

'We've been together nearly eighteen years.'

'Eighteen years! Gosh! Can I be chief bridesmaid?'

Ed looked down at him over his glasses. 'Are you still a maid, Father?'

'Oh! You can't ask me that! I've "embraced a vocation to celibacy"! You aren't allowed to ask prurient questions about my "friend" prancing about the rectory in his cowboy chaps!'

Ed laughed and shook his head.

They took another turn about the lawn. Then Ed stopped. They faced one another.

'Look, Dom, I know you can't really approve. That's OK, I don't expect you to.'

'We-ell. Personally I'd find it hard to square with my oath of canonical obedience, but it's not me, it's you, and that's fine. I mean ... Oh, Ed, I thought you'd got your civil partnership all lined up for the autumn!'

'We had, but look, "all things lawful and honest". *Is* it lawful — to forbid us to marry, when the law of the land says we can? More people have got to stick their necks out and challenge the status quo, or it'll just be allowed to carry on.'

'Mmm.' Dominic believed he could discern the influence of a short grumpy Scottish atheist hovering here. 'Is this your idea, or Neil's?'

Ed did not reply.

Dominic let the silence do its work.

'God, I hate this so much!' Ed burst out. 'I've never been a campaigner. I just want to be left alone to get on with being a priest. I've always tried to accept the discipline of the Church, even when the bishops treat us like ... Oh God, am I just being a coward?'

'No, of course you're not!'

'I am. I'm a total coward. I don't want to end up in the press as a cause célèbre.'

'OK, well, what about the timing?' asked Dominic. 'Is an interregnum a good time? Who'll end up having to discipline you? Poor old Bobby Barcup?'

'I know, I know! I can't bear the thought of dragging him into the crossfire. Paul Henderson, mind you—! But anyway, he's gone.'

'So you'll wait till we've got a new bishop?' asked Dominic.

'I don't know. Is it fair to spring it on him the moment it's announced? Neil— He's got nothing invested in the Church, as you know. It's not tangled up with actual people for him.'

'Yes, well, Neil's an actual person too, though. And so are you.'

They walked again in silence.

'What am I going to do, Dominic? Obviously I want to marry the man I love. The law says I can. I think the Church should be able to bless that. I used to think civil partnership was enough, but ... I genuinely don't know what's right here.'

'Mull it over a bit longer, maybe?'

'Yeah. Probably.'

'After all, Father, marriage is not something to be taken in hand unadvisedly, lightly or wantonly, is it?'

'Or to satisfy men's carnal lusts or appetites, Father. So no more cowboy chaps for you.'

'If only!' Dominic sighed. 'Oh, well. I wonder if the archdeacon will be witch-finder general during the vacancy?'

'Yes, Evangelicals certainly have a special talent *there*.'

'Now, now! He's an *open* Evangelical, remember.'

'Open! To what?'

'To the idea of being nicer than God,' said Dominic. 'They'd be in favour of equal marriage if only God wasn't a nasty old bigot. But sadly, *the Bible says* . . . Actually, I have a lot of time for Matt. He got me this parish.'

'It was all part of his evil-gelical master plan! If you'd stayed in Renfold, you'd be on the CNC. You'd have influence!'

'I know I would!' wailed Dominic. 'Oh, and by the way, don't mention the archdeacon when Jane gets here. Slightly a sore point. He's just dumped her.'

'No! They were an item? Seriously? *No!*'

We must leave them now to finish their Prosecco and gossip in their cattily catholic way, while we attend to important matters of process.

I have been remiss, dear reader. I have made casual reference to the CNC (Crown Nominations Commission, rather than Civil Nuclear Constabulary) without clarifying what it gets up to. Briefly, it is the body that chooses new bishops.

So what does their work involve? How are bishops chosen these days?

If you are the kind of person who likes to curl up with a mug of cocoa and a bunch of standing orders, then I refer you to the Church of England website, where you may consult a vast document called *Briefing for Members of Vacancy in See Committees*. For ordinary mortals, here's what you need to know about the process at this point in our tale:

(1) Bishop retires/resigns/moves/falls under a bus: there is a 'Vacancy in See' (see = diocese). (2) A 'Vacancy in See Committee' is formed in the diocese, of lay and ordained people. (3) The Vacancy in See Committee has two tasks: to draw up a 'Statement of Needs' (what we want from the new bishop) and to elect six of its members on to the Crown Nominations Commission. (4) The two 'appointments secretaries' (one for the prime minister, one for the archbishops) visit the diocese for two days and consult widely with local civic and

church figures. (5) CNC meets twice, to draw up a shortlist, then to interview the candidates (21–22 July).

Compared with Trollope's day, this is – as Wikipedia notes – 'a somewhat convoluted process'. The first meeting of the CNC for Lindchester will happen in Bishopsthorpe (home of the Archbishop of York) on 11 June.

This information conveys little of what it *feels* like in a diocese when a vacancy occurs. You are probably already skimming ahead to find the next interesting bit. As the interesting bits generally involve people not processes, I will tell you instead who some of the members of the CNC are.

Dean Marion is one. This means (paragraph 5b: 'not more than one of the members elected shall be a member of the bishop's senior staff') that the archdeacon is *not* a member of the CNC. Matt, therefore, has no finger in the biggest pie currently on the church table. He's not happy, I can tell you, but he bowed to the inevitable.

If we do the ecclesiastical maths ('not less than half of the members elected shall be lay members of the Committee') this leaves only two places for clergy of the diocese. As Father Ed pointed out, if only Dominic hadn't just moved from the parish of Renfold, he would doubtless have been on the CNC as the longest-serving area dean in the diocese. He would have been able to influence the choice of new bishop. He might even have formed a little alliance with the dean, and tried to ensure Guilden Hargreaves was appointed.

This is sad indeed, but I hope my readers will be cheered to know that one of the other clergy members is our good friend Father Wendy.

Right now Father Wendy has more pressing things to think about than the CNC. She's at Cardingforth primary school.

'Gooood *moooo*ming, Mist-er Crowth-er. Gooood *moooo*ming, teach-uz. Gooood *moooo*ming, Revrun-Dwendy.'

'Good morning, boys and girls. It's lovely to be here with you again. I've brought a friend along with me today. His name's Pedro. Here, boy! That's right. Come and say hello. This is Pedro.'

'It's a dog!'

'Cool! It's a dog!'

'Miss, Miss! Revrun Dwendy, why's he only got three legs?'

'Why's he got that cage over his face?'

'He's soooo-oo cute!'

'Why's he shivering like that? What's wrong with him?'

'Miss, Revrun Dwendy, Miss! Can I stroke him? Oh, pleeeee-ease?'

Mr Crowther stands up. 'All right, simmer down, children. Jack, sit down, please. I'm sure Reverend Wendy is going to tell you all about him. QUIET!' Pedro flinches. 'Now then. I want to hear a pin drop.'

Somebody says, 'Boing!' Mr Crowther eyeballs the individual concerned, but lets it go. When the hall is approximately silent, he sits down again.

Wendy tells the children all about Pedro. Poor Pedro, he used to be a champion racer, he could run like the wind. Who here likes running races? Good! Pedro loved racing too, but he got cancer on his leg, and they were going to put him down. Does everyone know what that means? That's right, he was going to have an injection that would put him to sleep, so he would die peacefully without suffering. But he was rescued by a greyhound charity. He had to have an operation, and sadly his leg could not be saved. But he's learned to run on three legs, haven't you, boy? For a while nobody wanted to adopt him, but then Wendy came along.

Two hundred and eighty-eight children stare, rapt, devouring every word. Or rather, two hundred and eighty-seven. One child rolls her eyes. She provides a little commentary of her own, which is just audible to those sitting nearby:

'But in *Jeee*-zuz' race you don't have to be fast, *everyone* can take part. *Jeee*-zuz wants to rescue *everybody*, because *everybody's* special! *Everyone* can be a winner, even if they've got no legs!'

I'm afraid this rather pre-empts Father Wendy's moral.

Mrs Fry, seated at the piano, sees a bout of giggling taking a grip in the Year 5 section. She leans forward and hisses: 'Leah Rogers, go and stand outside Mr Crowther's office.'

Leah is still standing outside Mr Crowther's office when the school scrambles to its feet to sing 'One more step along the world I go'. Mr Crowther will come any minute and tell her he is Very Disappointed. Apologize to Revrun Dwendy for being silly and rude. Sorreeee, Revrun Dwendeeee.

But Wendy comes along the corridor without Mr Crowther. Pedro bobs along beside her on his three legs. Leah pretends she hasn't seen them. She stares at the Year 3 'Healthy Eating' wall display, which is so *lame*, with lame drawings of fruit stuck on paper plates.

'Hello, Leah! What are you doing here all by yourself?'

Yeah. Like you don't know. 'Mrs Fry sent me out.'

Wendy laughs. 'Oh, dear! What for?'

Leah doesn't answer. *Eat your Five a Day!*

'Oh, I was *always* getting sent to the head for talking!' says Wendy. 'And once because someone put a plastic dog poo on Mrs Curzon's chair.'

Leah turns and stares in surprise at Father Wendy's round, beaming face. There are little tiny veins all over her cheeks. 'Was it you?'

'No. It was Colin Beasely. But it was my plastic dog poo, so nobody believed me.' Wendy laughs. 'I *still* feel outraged after all these years.'

Leah spots her chance: 'Well, life isn't fair.'

'No,' said Wendy. 'No, it's not, I'm afraid.'

'But Jeee-zuz makes *everything* fair.'

'Not in my experience.'

Leah blinks, then looks away, shocked.

'Anyway, I'd better be off. Goodbye, Leah. Come along, Pedro.'

Leah carries on staring at the crappy lame Healthy Eating display, so she won't have to watch Pedro limping away on his three legs, or think about how they were going to throw him on the rubbish heap because he couldn't win any more races.

Now the assembly's out of the way Wendy can turn her thoughts to the CNC, and pray for the next bishop of Lindchester – whoever it turns out to be – in fact, she can surround the whole process in prayer. They'll be getting the *long* longlist soon. Who will be on it? Guilden Hargreaves! She laughs. 'Oh dear, Pedro! I still can't believe we nicked Dame Perdy Hargreaves' parking space! It was an accident – Doug didn't realize they were waiting. Do you suppose she's forgiven us yet?'

Pedro makes no reply.

And now it's Saturday evening. We will pay a visit to the third clergy member of the CNC. We glimpsed him once before. Perhaps the tenor of this narrative seemed a little disparaging of Geoff, Vicar of St James' Lindford, when he appeared in his Noah's Ark stole? I wish to clarify that we have nothing but respect for him. He is in his study, staring at his computer screen. Please admire the painted cross on his wall. It's from South America.

Right now, the Revd Geoff Morley is questioning his fitness to be part of the CNC. His style is collaborative, he values unanimity. He instinctively plays down his own role, seeks to abstain from personal prejudice. But the ground has just shifted under his feet.

He clutches an old prayer in panic: *Be a bright flame before me, O God.*

He ought to have spoken up. But there was nothing he could put his finger on. And apart from him, it was unanimous. Veronica's paperwork was stellar. Her performance at interview blew the other candidates out of the water. So he hesitated, doubted, and remained silent. After all, it was a university chaplaincy appointment, really.

What's he going to do now?

A guiding star above me.

'We have no record of a student of this name on our files.'

If he carries on checking, what else is he going to uncover?

A smooth path beneath me.

What if she's a complete fantasist? What if everything on her CV is fake?

A kindly shepherd behind me.

Is the Revd Dr Veronica da Silva even ordained?

Chapter 5

I n all this hoo-ha about equal marriage and the vacancy in the See of Lindchester, we have rather lost sight of another important question: what's going on in the women bishops debate?

Lindchester diocesan synod was among the first to vote in favour of the draft legislation back in early March – hoorah for Lindchester diocesan synod! It was not unanimous. But never fear; voting is by secret ballot, rather than a show of hands. There was no risk of the nays being pelted with stale rich tea biscuits by an angry Yes 2 Women Bishops mob.

Thus far, the proposal has been carried in every diocese. So unless one of the few remaining synods (who need to get a move on before the deadline at the end of the month) astounds us by voting against the measure, we will have unanimity ahead of the important vote in General Synod this July. What could possibly go wrong?

The same thing that went wrong on 20 November 2012 – the measure might once again fail to reach a two-thirds majority in the House of Laity. It will be the same bunch of people voting, after all. A bemused outsider might assume that members of the House of Laity are there to carry out the clear wishes of their local synods and vote in favour of the measure. (Short pause for hollow laughter.) I'm afraid it is entirely possible that they see themselves as conscientious objectors and will vote as they jolly well see fit.

How has this situation come about? Well, the C of E is at least partly governed by those who turn up. May I whisper confidentially that most clergy secretly regard deanery synod as 'a bunch of people waiting to go home'? It attracts the type of parishioner who would rather be at a great long tedious meeting than in bed with a good book. At the very least, this has what we might call a skewing effect on synod composition. No use moaning now, is there? You should have got off your backside and stood for election if you wanted to head the nutters off. We will just have to wait and see what happens in July when General Synod meets.

Hang on, though, don't we live in an enlightened twenty-first century society? asks the same bemused observer. What possible reason can you have for opposing women bishops? Are you all *mental?* Briefly, the objections are these: (a) 'If Jesus had wanted women bishops, he would have ordained the Virgin Mary' (Anglo-Catholic, on grounds of Apostolic Succession); and (b) 'If Jesus had wanted women bishops, St Paul would not have said, "I do not permit a woman to speak or assume authority over a man"' (Conservative Evangelical, on grounds of Male Headship).

And yes, we are a bit mental, I'm afraid.

Here might I stay and sing; but I am sure my readers are fretting about poor old Jane, so ruthlessly dumped on bank holiday Monday by the Archdeacon of Lindchester. We will pop across to Cardingforth at once.

It is the marking season. Jane is wading through final year history dissertations. She is relieving her feelings somewhat by cracking down on students who don't adhere to the MHRA referencing guide. They were warned! In among all the marking, she has to find time to wrestle with funding bids for research projects, the details of which need not trouble us here. I'll tell you what, though: if someone popped a swear box in her office or on her kitchen table (where she is sitting at this moment), her funding issues could be addressed promptly and effectively.

Fuck you, Mr Archdeacon and fuck the Mini you drove in in. Duplicitous bastard!

What if it's me, though? Is it *me* being the unreasonable one here? No, it's bloody not. It's him. Letting me believe we'd found a way through this problem, while knowing all along we hadn't! And fuck you, Church of England, with your interminable twaddly 'how many gay women bishops can get married on the head of a pin' debates. And while we're at it, fuck your hand-wringing 'don't ask, don't tell' hypocrisy.

Yeah, Matt, why don't you fuck all *that*, instead of trying to lay it at the door of my feminism? Arsehole. Dump me, would you? Come here NOW, so I can dump you right back! Jane glares out of the kitchen French windows. Overgrown lawn. Ground elder and brambles taking hold again in the beds. All Freddie's hard work last summer, wasted.

But *is* it me, though? Have I ended up quibbling over mere words? Is there really no way I can bring myself to say, 'I take you to be my lawful wedded . . . *aargh!*'? No, there isn't! Oh, *why* can't we do it the New Zealand way? Yep, I'm the real Jane Rossiter. Yep, I'm entering this union freely. Yep, happy to sign here.

But no use crying over that particular carton of spilt milk, is there? Not if the House of Bishops (fuck them too, especially fuck *them*) says we'd still have to be celibate! *Celibate!* What am I − a nun? I'm not an Anglican, I'm not even a *Christian!* Don't fucking dictate to me how I conduct my sex life!

Anyway. Marking.

She makes herself open the next electronic submission on Turnitin. At least this year she's not having to cart a suitcase full of hard copies to and fro. Come on, cheer up, gal. But then her jiggered thermostat decides that now's a good moment for another heatwave. She rips off her top layer. Jesus! My own personal climate change. Please consider the environment before having a hot flush.

She tries in vain to engage with the dissertation. Not fair on the student. Go for a run, you silly bag. Sort your head out.

Quarter of an hour later she's squishing along the banks of the Linden. A grey day. Grey and green, that gobsmacking green of mid-May foliage that crowds in on all sides. The child botanist in her reels off the names of plants: cow parsley, buttercups, speedwell. It's still muggy out, despite last night's storm.

She should Skype Danny and tell him it's all off. No new stepdad. Won't be seeing you in June.

God, I can't stand this! There's nobody around, so she just lets the tears fall. Love and marriage! Horse and carriage! If we're going to be together, one of us is going to have to give way. But why does it have to be me? What if I'm already too late? Over two weeks since he walked out, and nothing. Maybe I should make the first move? No, *he's* the one who behaved badly! Oh God, Matt. Is it really over? Because I'd run all the way to Lindford in high heels and a strapless wedding frock and marry you right now, you bastard, you total and utter bastard, I love you so much.

For Jane's sake, we will pretend we didn't hear that momentary lapse from feminist orthodoxy. She will finish her run, have a shower, and knuckle down to her marking like a sensible person. Tonight she will ring Dominic and repeat her rant about what an obdurate shite the archdeacon is; then hang up rudely when Dominic points out that she would not be interested in a bloke she could shove around, she prefers obdurate shites.

The obdurate shite is not aware that he has dumped Dr R. All he's aware of is how badly he has behaved towards her. Stringing her along all these months. Losing his rag and swearing at her. Storming out. Days later, he was still too livid to apologize. Eventually, he calmed down and texted: 'Sorry for getting mad, any chance of a chat? Xx'

And he's had zip in return. Unsurprisingly.

Basically, he's completely stymied. He's already offered to jack his job in – and had that flung back in his face. What more can he do? Found himself googling '100 red roses' on Interflora last week. But £349.99 is a lot to shell out for the privilege of getting a luxury hand-tied bouquet shoved up your jacksie.

Meanwhile, he's having to keep the diocesan plates all spinning, with no fellow archdeacon to share the load. Employment tribunal looming, which means hauling Paul all the way back from flipping South Africa. Keeping the in-box down to under 200 emails is a daily challenge. Archbishop of York due in a couple of weeks. Ordinations looming. Rogue priest apparently not been declaring his funeral fees for yonks – there's twelve grand the diocese can kiss goodbye. CNC. Question mark over whatsername, uni chaplain's, CV, *must* get on to that. Choristers' School scandal brewing. Something's bound to go belly up at some point.

Now it's Thursday morning. Matt is standing in the churchyard of St Michael's, Gayden Parva. With him are a churchwarden and the rector, Father Ed. Matt is here for a spot of gentle chivvying. The PCC has been dragging its feet, and it needs to deal with the dangerous monuments before a stone angel flattens some youth as he innocently vandalizes the graveyard.

''Fraid you can't just do that,' said Matt. 'You need to rope the area off and stick up a waterproof notice.'

'Yes, I meant to—' began Father Ed.

'Notice affixed to the gates, Mr Archdeacon,' interrupted Duncan. 'As per instructions.'

Tricky pause.

'Must've missed that.' Matt didn't catch Ed's eye. 'Well, let's take a quick shufty, then.'

Duncan led the way along the mowed path – Matt was betting this had been speedily done for his benefit, too – past toppled monuments and drunken crosses, to the wrought-iron gates at the far side. Sure enough, there was a handwritten notice taped there, in a suspiciously pristine document holder: DUE TO AGE AND DETERIORA-TION, SOME HEADSTONES HAVE BECOME UNSAFE. THE PCC HAS TAKEN ACTION BY LAYING FLAT IN THE CHURCHYARD.

The archdeacon banished a surreal image from his mind. Out of the corner of his eye he sensed Father Ed quiver with stifled laughter. 'Okey-doke. Well, next step is to get some rope up.'

'All in hand, Mr Archdeacon.'

'Public liability insurance all in order too? Good. You're probably aware that laying them flat is only a temporary solution. Basically, we need to draw up a proper plan of campaign for repairs. Good. I'll whizz the latest guidelines over to you.' He got his iPad out. 'Got an email address?'

'I'm sorry to say I don't, Archdeacon. I'm a bit of a Luddite.' Duncan laughed proudly. 'You'll have to write me an old-fashioned letter.'

'Luddite! Like my dad,' said Matt as he and Father Ed walked back to their cars. 'Bought him a mobile phone two years back, showed him how to use it. Total waste of time. Never switches it on.'

Ed laughed. 'Well, it's for emergencies. He's conserving the battery, isn't he?'

'Yep, that's what he says. OK if I email you the bumf to pass on? Cheers.' Matt scanned round. Clocked the mature trees. Couple of big ashes, but no sign of dieback so far. Rape fields beyond. Pretty idyllic, really. 'Lovely spot, but these old churchyards are a right mare.'

'That's for sure. Nobody told us about *this* in theological college. Sorry I've not got on top of it,' said Ed. 'We're trying to chase up the relatives, and see if we can pass the buck to them.'

'Good luck with that. How's tricks otherwise?'

'Oh, you know. Ticking over.'

'How's Neil?'

'He's fine.'

Great. Matt always tried to ask after the family. But Ed had closed down, bam, like this was the chuffing Canterbury Inquisition. They walked on in silence for a moment. Here we go again. The old balancing act between pastoral support and toeing the party line. Did his head in, sometimes, but you had to at least try.

'Look. Ed. I've been doing a spot of thinking in recent months. About what's asked of you folks by the Church. Completely sympathize with your situation.'

Ed's colour rose.

Matt hesitated, then decided he may as well keep shovelling. 'We've got our knickers in the mother of all twists on this issue. In an ideal world, we'd spend another twenty years finding a way forward, try and take as many with us as possible. But we haven't got that luxury. It's a PR disaster. Missionally speaking, it's a disaster. I'm a pragmatist: let's get this sorted ASAP. My sense is that you folks won't have too long to wait, is what I'm saying. That's the way the wind's blowing. My impression. For what it's worth. So hang on in there.'

They passed a stone cross standing in relief against a yew: *God is Love*. Nettles sprang up at its foot.

'It would help,' said Ed, barely able to get the words out, 'if you didn't frame everything in terms of "we" and "you folks". Like I'm somehow not part of the Church.'

The archdeacon did a quick recap. Good going, Matt. 'Fair enough. I hear you. Apologies.'

Ed tilted his head but made no reply.

Oh, Lord. Couldn't get anything right at the moment, could he? Maybe he'd better go and lay flat in the churchyard with the PCC, see if that helped.

Ed held the lichgate open for him and they went out.

'Well, I'll email those guidelines,' said Matt. 'So yes. Well, thanks for all your hard work out here in the sticks. Much appreciated.'

'Oh, that's . . . Thanks for making the time.'

They dithered a moment. Handshake? No.

'Well.' Matt made a vague salute with his iPad and got into his car. 'Bye for now.'

'Bye.'

'Thanks again. Bye.' I'm not the enemy, I'm really not. I'm just a bit of a tit sometimes. Couldn't really say that.

He drove all the way back to the office wishing he had, though.

Let us follow the archdeacon's Mini through the lanes and fields of rural Lindfordshire. You will spot that someone has added a moustache to the giant UKIP poster, using little strips of black electrical tape. A timely reminder. People of England, don't forget to get off your backsides and vote, if you want to head off the nutters.

Posters of a different flavour deck the historic city of Lindchester. *Souls and Bodies*: a major art exhibition opening in the cathedral in a fortnight's time. This is the culmination of over a year's hard work by the canon chancellor. Hours well spent, if he has seen off for ever the local art clubs with their watercolours of cats and teapots, and terrifying portraits of Princess Diana. But he desperately needs this ambitious project to go well, so he will be vindicated.

Until last month, everything was on track. He met the artist, a tall, frightening woman with zero small talk. He has seen JPEGs of all the canvases and cleared a couple of nudes with his clergy colleagues (the exhibition is now referred to informally as 'Cocks in the Cathedral'). The publicity material looks stunning. But there are delays with the specially commissioned new display boards. If they don't arrive in time, what the hell's he going to do? Bang picture hooks into the medieval masonry?

The canon precentor is also stressed. Shortlisting for the post of tenor lay clerk has taken place. They are down to four. Three appointable candidates with appropriate experience and solid references. And one Freddie May.

After evensong Giles invites Timothy, the director of music, along with Nigel, the senior lay clerk (a sort of shop steward cum supergrass figure) back for a glass of Mosel and a little conflab.

'Nigel, tell me candidly and completely off the record: can you bear the thought of Mr May standing next to you at every evensong for as long you both shall live?'

'I'd rather that than have him dep for me,' says Nigel. 'My cassock was impregnated with weed and Le Male for *weeks* after he'd worn it.'

'Olfactory objections aside, you'd be happy?' says Giles.

'Of course. He's a major talent. We did all the hard graft when he was the chorister from hell. Are we seriously going to let someone else poach him now?'

'Yes, but let's be frank: he's a liability. Potentially.'

'Never fear, Mr Precentor. We'll make sure he lives a godly, righteous and sober life.'

'Of course you will, Mr Bennet. The gentlemen of the choir are famed for their godly sobriety. Timothy, what do you think? You'd be his line manager.'

Timothy hesitates. 'I wonder whether we could identify someone to mentor him?'

'Don't look at *me*,' says Nigel.

'Unless you're offering to pay me extra?' suggest Giles.

'Are you?'

'No.'

'Well then.'

'I was thinking we need someone completely outside Lindchester circles,' continues Timothy. 'Someone he'd look up to, respect, who's au fait with the choral tradition. Who could offer him support. And the occasional ... er, steer, when necessary.'

Mr Dorian? wonders Giles. Or would that be like making Vlad the Impaler school javelin monitor? 'We're getting ahead of ourselves. Let's see if he manages to turn up for the interview clothed and in his right mind first. We can worry about mentors later.'

It's day off eve. Away on the far side of the diocese, in the rectory of Gayden Magna, Father Ed puts a bottle of champagne in the fridge.

Hang on in there. Ed got the message all right. That little pep talk was a 'friendly' warning not to break ranks and get married, wasn't it? There are no words for how deeply, bitterly, Ed resents the archdeacon's patronizing interference.

His heart judders like stumbling feet.

When Neil gets in from London, he's going to tell him, 'Yes.'

Chapter 6

Another bank holiday. Our good friend Bishop Bob is sitting in his back garden with a cup of coffee this morning, enjoying the fine weather and a rare break from the burdens of office. It is upon his shoulders that the pastoral weight of the diocese currently rests. He is praying for the CNC, and for the next bishop of Lindchester, whoever that might be. Poor Bob is horrendously busy, and this lends his prayers a real poignancy. I won't say urgency, as that suggests a directness that is not characteristic of Bob's spiritual style. He is not one to request parking spaces of the Almighty. Nor is his wife, Janet. But this is because she's afraid that the Almighty might grant her one, and then she won't be able to manoeuvre into it. Blunt though her prayers usually are, it seems a bit cheeky to pray for fifty yards of clear kerb just because you are rubbish at parallel parking.

Later, when Bob has finished his meditations, they will go house-hunting. Bob is only two years off retirement. He could stay in office until he's seventy, but being a bishop isn't that much fun these days. Far too much work, and not enough executive power. He can't move his clergy about the diocese like chess pieces, or foster favourites and give them plum livings. Nor can he spend his days harmlessly fly-fishing and writing learned monographs, and leave the running of things to his chaplain. He does not even have a chaplain. He has an inefficient but well-meaning PA inherited from his predecessor and who he didn't have the heart to sack. So Bob will retire at sixty-five.

Where will they settle? Somewhere very ordinary. They hope to find a bungalow. Walking distance to shops, library, bank, GP's surgery. On a bus route to the hospital. He and Janet don't intend to move again after this. They've observed too many people retiring – hale and hearty in their sixties – to gorgeous properties up steep village streets and precipitous steps, with no downstairs bathroom; then having to relocate in their eighties when they can no longer cope, to an area where they don't know anyone. Where they are just old, lonely people, whose history and achievements nobody cares about, driving their poor children frantic with worry. The Hootys don't want to be a pest if they can help it.

We must shortly wave them off, since their search today will take them beyond the borders of the diocese. Bob has no desire to lurk in the region and haunt the scenes of his former glory. That would be terribly bad form. There's an unspoken rule in church circles that you shove off and leave room for your successor, and never allow yourself to become an alternative focus of power for the disaffected. Bob isn't in the least bit tempted to find another cathedral city to settle in, either. This is unusual, for cathedral cities attract retired bishops. They are like purple moths around a flame. What are they to do? Can't help it.

Bob drinks his Fair Trade instant, and admires the lovely garden. None of it is his work. He mows the lawn, that's all. But Janet is a born gardener. She's pottering now with her edging tool. One of the things he's most looking forward to about retiring is Janet having a garden of her very own. All these years she'd been pouring her resources into something that didn't belong to her. Yes, like me and the Church, thinks Bob. Good to keep that in mind. *All things come from you, and of your own do we give you.* Won't do to get too used to it. He wants to be able to hand his pastoral charge over graciously.

'Ready when you are,' says Bob, to give Janet a chance to do the five last-minute things she always does, while he sits waiting in the car. He probably has time for another coffee, actually.

'OK. Five minutes?' says Janet, meaning fifteen. No point hurrying. She knows from experience that she'll rush around, only to find he's gone and made himself another coffee.

What Bishop Bob does not know is that his name has appeared on the list now being circulated among the members of the CNC. When the two appointments secretaries visited the diocese to consult with the locals, several people mentioned Bob as the man they would like to see as the next Bishop of Lindchester.

Ooh! Ooh! Who else is on the list? It's a secret, I'm afraid. I need to protect the identity of the candidates, and the privacy of their families. Actually, I shouldn't even have told you Bob's name is on the list. I'm counting on your discretion here.

We leave him in his sunny garden, with the interesting thought that he might unwittingly be praying for himself.

I will not pretend to you that Father Ed is having a nice bank holiday. In a fit of righteous rage at the archdeacon, Ed had allowed the wedding camel's nose into his tent. He woke the next morning to find the camel with its feet up smoking a fat cigar, and the tent transformed into a silk-swagged marquee complete with chandeliers, champagne fountains and a forty-piece Cuban dance band in pink tuxedos.

'Neil, I really, really do *not* want a big fancy wedding.'

'No? Then don't marry a designer.'

They were standing on the rectory drive.

'Neil . . .'

'It's got to be-e-e-e-e-e—' sang Neil.

'No! Promise me we'll keep it low key?'

'—*per*-fect! You leave the planning to me, big man. All you have to do is turn up on the day, in the suit I choose, and do as you're told.'

'But—'

'Ah, ah, ah. In the car, now. Not *your* car. We've got smart venues to check out. We're not pulling up in a wee Skoda looking like vicars. Anyway, will you look at this gorgeous weather!' Neil flung his arms wide as though Gayden Magna were alive with the sound of music. 'It would be rude not to.' He zapped the car with the remote. 'In.'

Ed folded himself into the front seat. The roof hummed back. Neil adjusted his Ray-Bans and programmed the satnav. He was still singing the 'Perfect' song. Ed hated perfect. Perfect meant demanding to see the manager, sending starters back, getting bespoke shirts adjusted three times. It spelled a million minor mortifications to Ed's English temperament. Excuse me? This isn't chilled. That's never eau de nil. I've been waiting fifteen minutes. Wipe that table first, young man!

'Where are you taking me, exactly?'

'On a voyage of mystery and adventure! Oh, stop that. It'll be fun!'

'Right.'

They drove the first mile in silence. Then Neil sighed.

'Eds, do you want to marry me or not? Actually *me*, just as I am, with all my endearing ways?'

'Yes, of course, but—'

'Low key! Do I look like a low-key person to you? I'm not having some hole-in-the-corner wedding, like we're *ashamed*. I know you: always the path of least resistance. If you could, you'd go through your whole life without upsetting anyone. Well, hello? You can't.'

'I realize that.'

'Good. So here's the choice: you can either upset the archdea-con – and isn't *he* a sweetheart? – or you can upset me, the love of your life. Path of least resistance? Hmm, tough call.' Neil drummed his fingers on the steering wheel. 'Which one has more power to give you hell on a daily basis, I wonder? Wait. That would be ME. Heh, heh, heh!'

'No question. It's just— Look. I don't want to look like we're being . . . needlessly provocative.'

'Really? You really think that if we do smart casual and only invite three people, then somehow we can stay under Church radar and the haters will give us a free pass? Eds, they're going to be pissed whatever, so let's have us a big fat gay wedding, OK?'

'Neil—'

'No. It's a no-brainer. We're doing this, we are *so* doing this.' He turned and flashed Ed a smile. 'Hold tight, preacher man.'

With a roar the sports car leapt forward and burned off up the country road. Ed knew from experience that remonstrating just upped the ante. All he could do was hold tight, confess his sins, and pray they didn't meet anything coming the other way.

Martin, driving at a sensible 58 mph, watches his rear-view mirror in disbelief. Some *lunatic* in a black Porsche is overtaking four vehicles! Idiot! A lorry crests the hill ahead. He'll never make it! Martin slams on the brakes. The Porsche cuts in across him. Just! The truck's horn yowls as it passes them. Thank God Martin's reflexes are sharp. He leans on the horn now disaster's averted, heart thundering.

'Wanker!' shouts little Jessica Rogers from the back of the car.

'*What* did you say?' demands Martin.

There's a silence. The Porsche snarls off into the distance, a finger flourished aloft through the open roof.

'That's what Mummy always says when someone's driving badly,' explains Leah. 'She says "wanker".'

'I see,' says Martin. 'Well, it's something we try not to say.'

'Why?' asks Leah. 'What does wanker mean?'

'It's . . . like idiot, only ruder.'

'Yes, but what does it *mean*?' persists Leah. 'What's a wanker? Wanker, wanker, wanker.'

'Wanker, wanker, wanker!' sings Jess.

'Just – will you *stop* saying it! Both of you!' snaps Martin. 'It's a bad word, and I don't want to hear you using it.'

'But *Mummy* says wanker.'

'I'm warning you, Leah.'

46

They are going to Chester Zoo. It is just possible that Daddy might explode – *That's it! No zoo for anybody!* – and turn the car round and drive them straight back home.

Leah mouths it at the back of Daddy's head for the next mile.

'It means "con-tempt-ible per-son",' reads Jessica.

'STOP USING MY PHONE!' shouts Martin.

Dreadful silence. Leah hugs herself with glee. For once Jess is in trouble. YES!! It's even worth not going to the zoo!

'You'll make yourself car-sick,' he adds in a calmer voice. 'Put it away, please.'

Leah thinks about whispering to Jess, it means a boy rubbing his willy. But then Jess will tell on her and Leah will get in trouble. Daddy will be Very Disappointed.

Oh, boo-hoo, Daddy's disappointed! Who even cares?

But Leah does care. She tries to imagine that just for once Daddy says, 'Well done, Leah.' But even thinking about that makes her nearly cry. He should *stop* being disappointed if he wants her to be good! It's *his* fault. Because sometimes when he's Very Disappointed she accidentally hears a lie coming out of her mouth before she can help herself: 'It wasn't me, it was *her*.' 'It was *him*.'

And then she can't stop the consequences. It's like the sorcerer's apprentice, when he casts a spell and it gets out of control. Leah can't bear to watch that bit of *Fantasia*. The bit where Mickey Mouse chops up the broomstick, and he thinks it's all over, only then the bits of broomstick all come to life and turn into *more* broomsticks. Hundreds of broomsticks all carrying buckets of water! Even though she knows the sorcerer will appear and put everything right in the end, Leah can't bear to watch it.

It's just, why does *everyone* always like Jess best? It's like Jess is the class hamster and Leah is the class stick insect, and everyone in class always wants to take Hammy out of his cage and play with him because he's so-o-o-o cute. But they're all, ew, gross! with the stick insect.

To be fair, stick insects are totally boring.

But if Freddie had been *nice* to her that time, instead of always playing with Jess and her stupid Barbie, then Leah would never've told that fib. It was Freddie's own fault. He only had himself to blame. He had to learn.

Anyway, he's moved away now so she won't ever have to see him again. Plus she never got into trouble about it. She never got found out. (Mummy doesn't count.) Daddy never said, 'Why did you lie to me about Freddie? Why did you tell me a pack of lies, Leah? I'm Very Disappointed in you.' So it's all OK. It's not like she even cares about it any more.

'Leah, will you *stop* kicking the back of my seat, please. It's very distracting when I'm driving.'

Martin is not enjoying his bank holiday, either. He has enough on his plate, frankly, without having the girls dumped on him at two hours' notice by their mother. He's still technically 'the bishop's chaplain' during the interregnum, but the next bishop will naturally want to make his own appointment. Martin has an important interview tomorrow, and he ought to be preparing his PowerPoint, not going to the zoo. He's trying not to take his frustration out on the girls, *but*. Clearly the girls' mother is incapable of setting them proper boundaries.

It's Wednesday. Dr Rossiter is invigilating an exam. 11.02. Rain drums on the roof of the Luscombe sports hall. Most of the desks are empty. Just the two exams, history and politics. After a brief spike of panic, when 9.25 came and the entire politics cohort had failed to appear for their 9.30 exam (discovered outside, smoking), the morning has passed without incident. They're in the home straight now. The other invigilators prowl the rows. She suspects them of playing Pac-Man.

11.03. Jane yawns. She'd sneak her phone out and read the news, but it's all too depressing. French far right. English far right. The Resistible Rise of Nigel Farage. Forty years from now, will they be setting exam questions on him? God, I hope not. She decides to while away the last 27 minutes pretending she's casting director for a *Lord of the Rings* remake. She divides the students into orcs, hobbits and elves. She will take the role of Gandalf herself. Then she can shout, 'YOU! SHALL! NOT! PASS!' into the microphone at the end of the exam. This may well prove true of the ones who left an hour early.

She looks at the electronic clock again. 11.06. Through a slice of reinforced window she can see someone running on a treadmill in the gym. Someone else does press-ups. Other worlds. Still 11.06. Will this never end? She stares at the green swags of net hanging from ceiling to floor. The rain rains. She thinks of all the exam halls she has sat in. School, university. The grinding tedium of revision, the cliff falls of dread. And then the final day of Finals. Walking out and thinking: That's it. I will never sit another exam again, ever. From now on, freedom!

Yeah, right.

11.07.

Ring him, you idiot. Today. The minute you get out of here, just ring him and say *Yes*. Don't waste the rest of your life. You know now that the whole New Zealand thing was just a pipe dream. Not legally valid back in the UK. (Text from Dom: 'Woman's Hour, now. Civil Unions.') At least we didn't waste the airfare, eh?

But he hasn't been in touch. Is he trying to outwait her? Or was it actually over? Final. Him walking out and thinking, I will never see her again, ever. From now on, freedom from the nightmare of Jane Rossiter and her fucking feminist conscience.

No, she can't ring him. Wouldn't he have been in touch by now if he was still interested?

Thursday is Ascension Day. But it is half term. There are no overexcited choristers up on the tower first thing. No wafts of incense or choral praises sung seraphic-wise; just said services. Elsewhere in secular Lindfordshire, who would even know to hail this festival day? It comes and goes in Britain like Labour Day, Waitangi Day. At dawn in the silent cathedral a robin sings. A pair got in through a tiny broken pane last month and built a nest behind the high altar. Sometimes the male perches on the marble pinnacle of the altar screen and carols with the choristers, adds his ornamentations to the Tallis setting. This Ascension morn, rain at the windows, and his sweet thread of song echoes round pillar and vault. The world sleeps, but God is gone up with a merry noise.

All week long the local members of the CNC brood over the *long* longlist. They will meet soon to whittle it down to the names they want to see mandated on to the long list, from which a shortlist of three or four names will be chosen for interview. Who should they choose from this list? Marion wonders. The archdeacon (astute strategist that he is) pointed out to her that if the Lindchester half of the CNC vote en bloc, they can pretty much ensure the outcome. But that feels too hard-nosed for Marion. Although the Principal of Barchester Theological College's name is there ... And Marion knows that neither Father Wendy nor Father Geoff would be hostile to Guilden Hargreaves as bishop. But what about the lay members of the CNC – would they be averse?

Father Wendy chats it all over with Pedro as they walk along the banks of the Linden.

Father Geoff prays in a Celtic manner for the names on the list. For guidance. *Christ on my right, Christ on my left.* He banishes his fears about Veronica da Silva's CV (he's informed the archdeacon, he can leave it in the archdeacon's hands). Patiently, he sets those fears outside the circle of Christ's light each time they obtrude.

I'm sorry to say that the archdeacon has not given Geoff's concerns another thought. That email is now buried. Maybe later Matt will remember with a jolt. But right now, he has something even more horrible to contemplate. It's Friday. He's just checked his phone. That texted apology to Dr R from weeks ago remains 'undelivered'. Crap. She'll think— No-o-o! He clasps his hands behind his neck and gazes up to heaven in despair. This is a Total. Mare.

With all this on his mind, it's probably just as well he has no idea his name is on that CNC list too.

JUNE

Chapter 7

'Fly, my pretties! Fly!' whispers Gene. He gives the departing guests one last royal wave, and shuts the door.

Post-evensong Sunday tea in the deanery drawing room has just finished. The real deal: silver teapot, bone china service, linen napkins. He wheels the detritus back through to the kitchen on an antique wooden trolley.

'So, what are the archbishop's views on our next bishop?' he asks.

'We didn't discuss the CNC,' says Marion. 'This afternoon was all about Lindchester celebrating twenty years of women priests.'

'Do you think he'd try to block Gilderoy Lockhart's appointment?'

'His name's Guilden Hargreaves, you horrible man.'

'I'm aware that Gilderoy's your preferred candidate.' Gene holds up a hand. 'It's fine – no need to confirm or deny. Maybe he'll meet someone, then his boyfriend and I can run the diocesan clergy spouses programme together? At last, an end to aromatherapy awaydays! My masterplan enters its final phase – to turn the diocesan retreat house into a Texan bordello! Dame Perdy could be the Madam! Ooh, will I need to apply to the archdeacon for a faculty?'

'You're hopeless.'

'But I behaved myself impeccably all afternoon!'

'You did not. You were doing your Eugène Terre'Blanche impression.'

'Oh, phoo! Only the mild version. I doubt if anyone noticed. But go on: what do you make of our new archbishop? Quite the handsome devil, isn't he? In a faded Biggles kind of way. But is he a weeny bit starchy? He looks as though he keeps a WWJD biro clenched in his butt cheeks.'

'*Thank* you for that image, Gene.'

'Speaking as an unreconstructed old lecher, though, I like his wife! But tell me the truth' – Gene drops his voice – 'do you think she had any idea *quite* how much cleavage she was blessing us with?'

A diplomatic pause. 'Oh, I'm sure Cordelia . . . These wrap dresses can be a bit tricky to pull off.'

'Tricky? Piece of piss. One quick tug . . . Shall I buy you one? Would you like that?'

'You can load the dishwasher and shut up,' says Marion. 'I'd like *that*.'

'I'm yours to command, Deanissima.'

If Marion had asked him, Rupert Anderson might have given the following opinion. The time to object to gay bishops was *before* the ruling about celibate partnerships came into force. Now it *is* in force, like it or not, there ought to be no more nonsense. If people still have objections, they need to lobby for a rule change, not campaign to prevent legitimately appointed priests taking up senior posts.

Such is the opinion of the Most Revd Rupert Anderson. And he is right, surely? Whatever we may believe personally on the issue, he is correct as regards proper process. So far he has only voiced this in private conversation. Bishops – let alone archbishops – are reluctant to stick their necks out here, because they are nervous that wealthy Evangelical congregations (for whom celibacy is not enough, repentance is required) might take their ball home and refuse to pay their parish share. This has an inhibiting effect on episcopal candour – as does a fear (valid or not) of unleashing a wave of persecution upon Christians living under intolerant regimes. Will Rupert Anderson boldly state his opinion in public? We must wait and see.

I wonder what Paul Henderson would have said on the subject, had he become archbishop instead of Rupert? But no, we must resist the temptation to speculate about the narrative door we never opened into the rose garden. (Except to observe that Susanna Henderson would not have fallen out of her frock at a deanery tea party, thus Gene would not now be googling 'Diana von Furstenberg wrap dress' with an eye to the dean's approaching birthday.)

Marion is pondering neither gay bishops nor wardrobe malfunctions at this moment. She's thinking about the Chaplain of Women. 'Well, I imagine she must be a real asset to the diocese.' That's what the archbishop said, a question mark hovering. In a moment of blank panic, and not wanting to look like an idiot, Marion made a noise that implied assent. Rather than saying: 'What? But I thought she was with you!'

Marion frowns. Better ask the precentor and see if he can clear this mystery up. Because who the hell *was* she? Late thirties, dark, tallish, possibly an American accent? Sweeping in with the archbishop's party, robing up, joining the procession, networking afterwards in a high-powered way. Chaplain of Women! There's no such thing in the Diocese of Lindchester. Or is there? The archdeacon will know.

We have reason to believe there are limits to the archdeacon's omniscience. He still does not know his name was on the CNC's long longlist. And he will never know, unless someone blabs. Neither he nor Bishop Bob made it on to the whittled-down list agreed by the Lindchester CNC when they met a few days ago. After discussion and prayer, it was felt that Bob and Matt had been nominated out of strong local prejudice: 'better the devil you know'. The list of ten names fixed on consists of deans, theological college principals (including Guilden 'Magical Me' Hargreaves) and assorted area bishops from around the country. The Lindchester CNC will horse-trade with the national CNC members on 11 June and come up with a shortlist.

So relax, O readers worried about how Jane might fare as a bishop's wife! You are getting way ahead of yourselves. Why, he and Jane have yet to speak after their big bust-up! They both think that the other would have got in touch by now if there was any future for their relationship. They are both sunk in despair. Honestly, I am tempted to wash my hands of them sometimes.

It is Friday and it's all happening at once on Cathedral Close. Tonight is the private view of *Souls and Bodies*. Those who love the canon chancellor will rejoice with him that the new display boards arrived. There was a tense couple of hours yesterday afternoon when the artist paced the south aisle grinding her teeth and excoriating the poor chancellor with her pale, mad stare. I will shield you from the details, and assure you that the boards did eventually arrive and all is now well. The artist has brooded over which pieces to hang where, so that the exhibition coheres. She is now overseeing the proper fixing of canvases to display boards (screws and mirror plates, for insurance reasons).

This is also interview day for the post of tenor lay clerk. Three candidates have already been auditioned. It is now 3.28, and the interviewers are waiting in the Song School for the final candidate to present himself for his three o'clock audition. The panel consists of the director of music, Timothy; the canon precentor; Nigel, the senior lay clerk; and the cathedral organist, Laurence. Also present is Iona, the sub-organist. She is here to accompany the audition pieces and facilitate the aural tests, but visibly wishing she were elsewhere.

We join them as they grow restive, and lapse somewhat from the impeccably professional standards we expect from Lindchester choral foundation.

Giles checked his phone again. Nothing. Maybe Freddie had got the wrong day.

Iona played an angry chord. 'Can I go now, please?'

'Shall we give him till quarter to?' asked Timothy. 'I'm feeling a bit unenthusiastic about the three we've heard so far.'

'Although, notice how they managed to get themselves here on time,' muttered Iona.

'I vote for waiting,' said Laurence. 'We all know Freddie has "time management issues", but we also know how gifted he is. I'm told he was called "the boy tuning fork" when he was a chorister.'

'Really?' said Nigel. 'I seem to remember we had other names for him.'

'Like freak?' suggested Iona.

'Well, tart, mainly,' said Nigel.

'He has a freaky memory,' said Iona. 'He's got entire operas and oratorios down, all the parts, everything. But when you try and have an actual conversation with him—' she crossed her eyes. 'Hello? Anybody home?'

'Oh, Mr May is by no means as thick as he'd have us all believe,' said Giles.

'Right.' Iona played another grumpy riff. 'He's a musical idiot savant.'

'Is that a thing?' asked Nigel.

'I don't know if it's a *thing*. It's what he is,' said Iona.

'Wait!' Giles cupped a hand to his ear. 'Do I hear the scamper of tiny feet? Positions, everybody.'

The door burst open.

'Oh, my God, sorry, sorry. Phone's dead. Missed my connection? Totally ran. All the way. Up here? Shit. Sweating like—' He peeled off his suit jacket, tossed it aside.

The panel recoiled.

'Argh!' cried Giles. 'Is that a gunshot wound?'

'Nah! Minute. Get my breath.' Freddie panted, hands on knees.

They watched in fascinated horror.

'Sorry, yeah, no, this massive. Nosebleed. On the train? Whoosh. No kidding, everywhere? I mean, look.' He straightened and plucked at his white interview shirt in despair. 'Got nothing else appropriate. Sorry. Mind if I—?' He pulled off his gory tie and dropped it on the jacket. Undid some buttons.

'Are you in a fit state to continue?' asked Giles.

'Sure. I'm good.' He took a couple more deep breaths. 'It just kinda happens? Whoosh. No warning. Since I got my nose bust that time?' He swigged from his water bottle. 'Yeah, so anyway, relax, people, at least it's not the blow, yeah? Ha ha, in case you were thinking! Not done any for like, *ages*?' He ran a sleeve over his face. 'Awesome. Ready when you are.'

Silence.

'What? Aw, c'mon guys! Properly ages? I mean, like it must be a year?'

They were staring, open-mouthed.

'Not good?' Freddie tugged his hair. 'Unnhh. Probably don't raise the drugs thing on interview, right?'

Gavin the deputy verger carefully mows the labyrinth on the cathedral lawn. Round, back again. Week five of the project, and it's coming along nicely. Foot-high purple grass heads nod. Got the idea from Freddie May, mowing a big heart on the bishop's lawn last year. Obviously, they had to get rid of that, but it got him thinking. Went on the internet. Him and the canon chancellor mapped the labyrinth out last month, cricket stump and washing line to get the circles accurate, set it all out with tent pegs. Tourists love it. Simple Chartres job, but next year, who knows? Maybe octagonal? Nine-petal vesica, even?

Leah Rogers storms out and sits on the wall in front of the palace. *If you can't be nice, go outside.* FINE. Who even *wants* to be nice? Leah scrapes the backs of her school shoes against the wall hard, to ruin them. Stupid boring Fridays, waiting after school for Daddy to finish his stupid work.

'*God!*'

She waits, tense, in case God heard her shout his name in vain. A stupid bird sings in the big tree. The weirdo's mowing the grass.

Nothing happens. Which just *proves* there isn't a God. She opens her copy of *Northern Lights*. This is the third time she's read it. Every bone in her body yearns to be Lyra, with a daemon and an alethiometer. Because who'd be all pink-tastic like Jess, with her lame princess Barbie Hello Shitty crap, when you could be Lyra?

Whoa! Freddie hurtles down the Song School stairs and into the cathedral. Total endorphin rush?

He throws his bag and jacket down. Then turns two cartwheels and a back flip in the crossing – he actually does that! – lands, flings his arms wide like a gymnast rounding off. Ta dah! He looks high up into the vault and laughs. The pleasure of God. He totally feels it. Like he could dive up, up, right now, and bury himself in joy, in God himself? For one second he nearly launches into that aria again.

A woman stares.

He comes to with a jolt. Sees how it looks. Yeah – they'll think he's on something. Plus the shirt? It's gone kind of stiff. And he smells rank: blood, sweat. Gah! He grabs his stuff and heads down the aisle before he gets himself thrown out.

Exhibition going up. He sees the big canvases as he passes. Splashes of colour, white, grey. Abstract, except *almost* you can see stuff – archways? and pillars? Wait. No way! They're by the same artist, the one whose painting he used to stare at in the chapel in YOI! Oh man, it totally has to be the same guy. I am so going to find him and say thank you. But the shirt situation? Yeah. Clean up and change first. Maybe Penelope will let him in to use the office cloakroom?

He leaves through the west door and he's out in the sunshine. The rush wears off, he's coming down now. Ah, cock. They are *so* not gonna offer him the job. Arriving late, covered in blood? Then the PhD level self-sabotage? He smacks his forehead. No-o-oo, why does he *have* to do that? Why's he always, loaded gun – foot – wahey!

Only— It felt like when you screw up your driving test and you're all, that's it, I've failed, and then you relax and actually, you drive better? That's totally what it was like. He saw their faces and knew: OK, game over. Nothing to lose.

May as well crash and burn in style, no?

The artist closes her eyes. She waits motionless in the crossing until she's sure the image is burnt on to her memory. That glimpse of quivering communion. Coiled tension in his every muscle. He is edged with light. She thinks: prey, waiting for his god to seize him. Ganymede. Then she pulls out a pad. Her pen scratches in the silence. But no. She gives up in disgust. It's gone, the ecstatic martyred moment.

Leah heard the footsteps and looked up from her book.

Him!

Her heart bumped like she was about to start a race. He's not supposed to be here! There was blood all down his front. He stopped right in front of her.

'Go away!'

He stared. Mad scary eyes. Then slowly, slowly, he raised his hand and aimed two fingers like a gun.

She started to shake. 'I'm telling my dad!' But the gun came down level with her forehead. 'I mean it. He's watching. He's just in there.'

'Hmm.' Freddie tilted his head. 'Nah. I forgive you.' Then he grinned, dropped his arm.

'You psycho! I'm still telling.' Her voice came out squeaky. 'You're gross, you've got all blood on you.'

'No shit, Sherlock.' He turned and walked off.

'I hope someone punched you. I hope it hurt!' she called after him.

He stopped, turned round again and came back. 'Really?' His eyes had gone scary again. 'That's really what you hope? Well, guess what? Last year two guys started on me. Broke my nose. I still get nosebleeds. Know why they did it?'

She shook her head.

'Coz I'm gay.'

She blushed. 'Well, you should fight back, shouldn't you? I would. I do karate. I'm a yellow belt. With two stripes. You should take up karate.'

That made him smile. 'Did a bit of that, back in the day. Show me *Pinan nidan*?'

She hesitated. 'What, like . . . now?'

'Yeah! C'mon.' He dropped his bag. 'Let's do it!'

She jumped off the wall, and they did that whole kata together on the palace drive. She remembered every move. Well, sometimes she had to sneak a look and copy him: blocks, strikes, turns. She tried to do her *kiai* in all the right places.

'Hey! Nice one.' He bowed, stuck out a hand. She shook it. 'You rock, girlfriend.'

'Huh.' Her face went bright red, so she picked her book up and pretended to look at that. 'What belt are you?'

'So I got my second dan?'

'You're a *black belt*? Why didn't you hit them back, then? I would if I was a black belt. I'd totally make them sorry for starting on me. You should teach them a lesson.'

'Ya think?' He picked up his bag. 'Well, catch you later.'

'You should *make* people be sorry!' She could feel herself crying with rage. 'You can't let them just get away with it. They've got to learn!' She watched him walk off towards the office door. He was about to go in. 'Sorry!' she yelled at his back. 'I'm sorry, OK?'

He turned and smiled. 'Hey. All forgotten, babe.'

Lighten our darkness, we beseech thee, O Lord; and by thy great mercy defend us from all perils and dangers of this night . . .

Timothy raises his hand discreetly as Giles intones the third collect. Three fingers, final amen, in case the lay clerks haven't been concentrating. Men's voices only tonight. Plainsong, Victoria. There's a new face on the back row of *dec*. Well, an old face. Freddie May, on a try-out. This is his chance to prove he's a team player as well as a total flaming divo. (That aria – good grief!)

Giles announces the anthem: ' "If ye love me, keep my commandments". Music by Thomas Tallis.' He sits.

In the moment of silence before the first chord, the robin flits down the length of the quire and lands on the altar screen. Giles sees Freddie's gaze following it, his face alight with joy. Concentrate, you little tyke! Don't make me come over there!

Oh, Lord. Are we mad to take him on? *If ye love me . . .*

Giles waits – please, no showboating – focused on the tenor line. *And I will pray the father . . .*

Ah, he's blending in perfectly, thank God.

No, we'd be mad to let him get away. Three months' probation period. Mentor. What could *possibly* go wrong? Provided the dozy sod doesn't get himself arrested, or fall into a threshing machine.

Leah is crying in bed. Because she's a bad person. Someone should punch her and break her nose. She can't stop crying.

'What's the matter, darling? Can you tell me what's wrong?'

She stays hidden under the duvet. Daddy sits on the bed. She kicks him, but he doesn't go away.

'Is it something to do with Freddie?'

Leah tries to shout, *Go away!* But it comes out all strangled.

'Look, you'll feel better if you tell me about it. Is there something you need to own up about, sweetheart? You can tell me.'

She flings back the duvet and shouts, 'I said sorry! And he – he—' The words were jammed in a clump of hiccups.

'I know, Leah.' He reached out and hugged her. 'Freddie told me it's all forgiven and forgotten. It's all OK now.'

'I said sorry!'

'I know.' He hugged her tighter. 'It's sometimes a very hard thing to do. Well done, Leah. Well done.'

Chapter 8

It's all kicking off in Lindchester Cathedral. There was a whole string of complaints about the nudes in the *Souls and Bodies* exhibition. By 'whole string', I mean two. But one of them was in the form of an email to the local paper, and I'm afraid somebody there was unable to resist a naughty item on the website about 'Bare Faced Cheek in the Cathedral'. The church press and one of the national papers got hold of the story and little storm in church tea urn was brewed up. The dean defended the exhibition. 'This is a major new exhibition by an artist of national standing. We are privileged to host it.' The Archbishop of York, who attended the private view, granted his imprimatur: 'Nonsense. This is serious art.'

The clergy of Lindchester Cathedral addressed this in their customary thoughtful way at canons' breakfast while they waited for the dean to arrive.

'Mr Chancellor, people should be able to attend a place of worship without having male genitalia shoved down their throat!' boomed the treasurer.

'Won't somebody PLEASE think of the children?' warbled the precentor.

'Obviously, we love our graphic life-sized models of somebody being brutally tortured to death, but we cannot allow small children to see naked men!'

'You'd think it was Gilbert and bloody George!' The chancellor had not yet been coaxed into finding the whole thing hilarious. 'I can't *believe* we're even discussing this!'

'But here we all are!' said the treasurer brightly.

'The dean's asked me to put up a warning notice at the entrance,' said the chancellor. 'But I'm not prepared to insult the artist by even *considering* anything further.'

'"Warning: this Major Exhibition of Serious Art contains willies",' said the treasurer.

'You said willies!' giggled the precentor. They nudged each other and snorted like schoolboys.

'Oh, for God's sake, you two!' But the chancellor was weakening.

Seeing a smile lurking, the precentor burst into a rousing rendition of the Monty Python penis song and the treasurer joined him. The chancellor had never heard this before and in a moment he was weeping with helpless laughter. Mainly because his colleagues hadn't noticed the dean enter the room and stand behind them, arms folded.

The song finished. 'Thank you, gentlemen.'

'It's the House of Bishops' school song,' explained Giles. 'We were teaching it to the chancellor.'

'Well, let's hope they're working on an inclusive language version,' the dean replied.

The treasurer and precentor are disposed to take the matter lightly – in order, perhaps, to help their angry colleague gain a sense of proportion. But it is an interesting question: what is appropriate in a sacred space? When we cross the threshold, do we enter another holier realm? A place where voices must be hushed, hats or shoes removed, and bare shoulders and legs covered?

> Let all mortal flesh keep silence
> And in awe and trembling stand.
> Ponder nothing earthly minded.

What counts as earthly minded? Is mortal flesh and human sex inherently sinful? Unfortunately, that's the message the Church has been broadcasting down the centuries, consciously or not. That human flesh might be redeemed and glorious, and the whole of creation a sacred space – really *not* what people think the Church says.

Souls and Bodies engages with this question. The chancellor is right to be impatient with that combination of prudery and prurience the work has been subjected to. Come with me now, and see for yourselves. Go bravely past the sign: 'Parental Guidance Advised for Children under 16'. These huge canvases are explorations of light falling through stained glass on to ancient stonework – floors and archways and pillars. They hover just at the point where representation breaks down into abstract. And now we come to studies of the human form, where light illuminates the architecture of the body.

This large nude is the piece at the centre of the fuss. A man lies on his back on what might be a white sheet (a shroud?) with his arms spread. Notice that broad diagonal stripe of light from an unseen source, which falls across torso and groin. The head is in shadow. Are we seeing this from above, like flies on the ceiling? Is it meant to be a crucifixion? Where is the viewer standing; who is the viewer? Is the man dead, or just sleeping? Does the light imply resurrection? Take a moment to look at the preparatory sketches too. In another setting they might simply have been appraised as studies of the male form. But in a cathedral, it would seem that they take on another set of connotations.

The chancellor has no need to worry about the artist. She is not insulted. She finds the fuss revelatory. Would there have been a rumpus if she'd exhibited pictures of naked breasts? Possibly. But she suspects there's something particularly troubling in the public's mind about adult male sexuality. Why is the penis so unacceptable in a sacred space? (Even one so small, as she remarked to the model himself on the opening night.)

And so Lindchester ponders what is appropriate in a cathedral. It is a debate Freddie May inadvertently strayed into, when he ran back to the exhibition last Friday afternoon to find the artist and thank him.

He'd grabbed a shower and was now in busted-knee jeans and his scarlet 'Suns Out, Guns Out' vest. Seriously, he loved wearing this in cathedral circles, because literally every second person stopped him to say there was an apostrophe missing? It totally killed him.

Freddie went back in through the south door, and there he was, the artist, screwing a picture to a board. Gotta love a guy with a tool belt. Freddie made his way along the aisle. Guy looked round, eye contact. All ri-i-ght. Tall, dark, earrings, tats, in his fifties, and a total *fox*.

'Hey.'

'Hiya, bonny lad.'

Oh man, the accent? I'm in love. 'Are you the artist?'

'Nah, I'm just here to do the heavy lifting.'

'Yeah?' Freddie came closer; hit him with the slow smile. 'So when you're done with the lifting, wanna get a drink? Or something?'

The guy did a mock gasp. 'Ee, you cannot ask me that in church! Jesus is watching!'

'Dude, he's always watching? He's cool with it.'

'Is that right?' The guy stopped what he was doing and leaned a hand on the pillar. Checked Freddie out properly. 'So anything goes, does it?'

'Hell, yeah!'

'What, there's no rules?'

'Yeah, no, I mean, yeah there's *some* rules.'

'Such as?'

'Don't be mean to people?' Hhnnn. He tugged his hair. This wasn't going so well.

The dude laughed. '"Thou shalt not be mean to people."' He ran his eyes over Freddie again. Like he found him hilarious? 'What if we are mean to people?' Freddie shrugged. 'What would Jesus do?'

'He'd be all, du-u-ude, how could you even do that? After everything I've done for you?' Hello? I'm trying to hit on you here, case you hadn't noticed?

'What's he done for you, then?'

Nuts. I totally do not *believe* this, I'm welling up. 'Not saying.'

'Haway, why not?'

'Coz?'

Then – what the?! – the guy reached out and put a hand on his head. Freddie nearly ducked out from under. Everything stood still. The guy was only *praying*! Like a priest giving you a blessing when you're only a kid and not allowed to take communion yet? Freddie closed his eyes. And he could feel it, literally? Like heat, running down his neck, shoulders, all down him?

Then the guy rumpled Freddie's hair for him, took his hand away. Smiled. 'There you go.'

Freddie blinked. 'Whoa. Are you like a priest, or something?'

'Why aye. A big old married priest.'

'Man! No fair. You were totally flirting with me back there. You so were.'

He laughed. 'It's my factory setting. I was flirting with the pillar before you got here.' He slapped the stonework. 'Anyway, did you want to meet the artist? Here she is.'

We will leave Freddie to blurt out his admiration and thanks (and affront the artist's feminist sensibilities by saying he totally thought she was a guy?), because there is somebody we must revisit. We will make this transition seamlessly, by reminding the reader that Freddie May himself once tried his hand at portraying the male member. It is above this character's bed that his (painted-over) masterwork still proudly stands.

How this year has flashed past! Virginia cannot believe that it's less than a week till her priesting. Her ordination retreat starts tomorrow, led by the Principal of Barchester Theological College, and then the service itself will be taken on Saturday evening by Bishop Bob. A year! How is this possible? And a year from now she'll be starting to look for a parish of her own.

'Come along, Pedro.'

Father Wendy is away at Bishopsthorpe for the first meeting of the Lindchester CNC, so Virginia is looking after the dog. Virginia is not really a dog person, but she's doing her best. They make their way along the bank of the Linden. Pedro knows things aren't quite right. Virginia is a city girl, and she does not tell him that the elder is in flower, or point out the ox-eye daisies, or urge him to smell the wild roses that mass in the hedges.

Rushes hiss softly beside them. This season's new growth has almost overtaken the old now. Only the dead feathery heads nod above the green blades. Virginia and Pedro pass under a huge willow. Fluff from the seeds drifts on the wind. Somewhere high up a willow warbler drips a silver trickle of song. It is one of those grace-filled June days of sunshine and cloud, when rain threatens, but at this moment, *this* moment, it is not raining, and even the white plastic ice-cream wrapper spindling on the breeze is lit up and lovely.

Something of this seeps into Virginia's soul, and she leaves off her lists of bullet points she must action. It's actually quite warm. She struggles out of her raincoat – not easy, when you're trying to hold a dog lead – and even contemplates flinging the coat on to that bench and collecting it on the way back. Except someone might pinch it. Although there's nobody about. But no, it *is* Gore-Tex.

She casts her mind back over the last year. Odd to be looking back on something that for years had loomed so large. A portal large as marriage – as death, nearly! – that she had to pass through. And now ordained ministry is just my life. Just ... normal, she thinks. A Bible verse pops into her head: *I am going ahead of you to prepare a place for you.* Or is it two Bible verses merged together? Virginia looks along the bank towards the distant bridge, as though she might glimpse a figure glancing back and waiting for her. Calling: 'Come along, Ginny, it's fine!' And hadn't it always turned out to be fine? Even when things hadn't gone according to plan – like ending up as Wendy's curate. She can barely remember how dismayed she was, or how wonderful she had pictured the alternative at Risley Hill parish being.

Yes. She looks down at Pedro, bobbing along with a curious grace on his three legs. 'It's actually all right, isn't it?' she says. 'This life?'

We cannot join Father Wendy and the rest of the CNC as they deliberate in secret, I'm afraid. But for the purposes of our tale, I will confide that one of the men on the shortlist will be Guilden Hargreaves, the Principal of Barchester Theological College.

By the end of the priests' ordination retreat, he will have been informed of this. He accepted the invitation to lead the retreat over a year ago, without the faintest notion that there might be a vacancy at Lindchester. And now look! I bet he will survey the cathedral with keen interest this Saturday. He may even glance out of the corner of his eye at the huge throne. And I am prepared to guess that his famous mother, Dame Perdy, will suddenly decide that she would like to attend the ordination service after all. She will, of course, drive ve-e-e-ry slowly past the palace to refresh her memory – nice, oh *nice*! – as she heads round the Close to park. An extra place will be set for her in the deanery dining room, and the meal will be conducted without reference to the elephant in a pink mitre in the room (although Gene will smirk with glee). But all this understandable excitement and speculation must be reined in by the knowledge that Guilden's undisguised orientation will be a stumbling block to some of the good folk of the Diocese of Lindchester.

Who else is on the shortlist? Don't ask. It's confidential. They are simply three clergy who have been on the preferment list for quite a while.

Hold it: the preferment list? What preferment list? I didn't know there was a preferment list! cries the reader. Aha, that's because *this* is confidential, too. Or semi-confidential. I believe it's been rebranded the 'Senior Appointments' list. Just think of it as a holy head-hunter list.

But how do you get on The List? Your diocesan bishop is the one who will nominate you. So don't fall out with your diocesan bishop. There are those who get on The List, and for several giddy months they believe they have been given a significant nod and wink. And then nothing ever comes of it. Off you go, back to parochial obscurity. God speed! Whether this system is any better than the old one, where you simply got a phone call from the prime minister out of the blue, asking if she/he can suggest your name to the Queen, I leave for the reader to decide.

Tomorrow is Pentecost Sunday. Our good friend Father Dominic is hurriedly finishing off his homily so that he can email it to his ever-patient Farsi translator. This will mean that his Iranian parishioners can sort of follow what he's saying when he gets into the pulpit. I'm afraid Dominic tends to stray from his prepared script with off-the-cuff anecdotes. The rest of the congregation laughs, and this leaves the Iranians studying their photocopied sheets in perplexity. But they love Father Dominic. Five more of them will be baptized this Sunday, and then all eleven will be confirmed by Bishop Bob immediately afterwards. How high the stakes are for them. Dominic thinks about the pregnant woman sentenced to death for converting to Christianity. Jesu mercy. And people call it persecution if they aren't allowed to turn gay couples away from their B&B!

He looks at his watch. Jane will be here in an hour, then they're off out for a meal. Better crack on.

Jane parks outside Matt's house. Come on, you silly mare, you know he's not in, he's at the ordination service. But all the same, her heart pounds as she scurries up his drive and slips a card through his letter-box. Aargh! It's like playing knocky-nine-doors! She runs back down the drive, leaps into her car and drives away, heart still thumping.

It's evening. Back in the cathedral, the vergers shift chairs ready for tomorrow's Pentecost service. The Flower Guild has been busy. Do admire the fiery red floral displays on the pillars.

Up in her loft, Iona launches into tomorrow's volley (Kyrie: *Gott, heiliger Geist*, Bach). Laurence has gone down with a bug, so she will be on duty instead. The precentor has just challenged her, and she categorically denied it. No, she did *not* include a phrase from the Harry Potter theme tune in the fanfare as Guilden Hargreaves mounted the pulpit steps.

Giles stomps back down from the organ loft. Unless he wants to get locked in a did-didn't-did-didn't argument, there's nothing he can do.

Bloody organists.

But apart from that, the ordination went smoothly. The mystery Chaplain of Women didn't rock up, anyway. Giles heads back home for a well-earned glass of wine. As he approaches his drive, he spots flags protruding from his car roof. How unspeakably vulgar. Both English *and* German flags. Once again he will have to be neutral – Switzerland, as it were – for the duration of the World Cup, while his wife and son slug it out.

Just then, his phone rings. He checks. And about time too. 'Well hello, queenie.'

'You called?' drawls a voice.

'I did, actually, Andrew. Repeatedly. How lovely of you to take time out of your busy schedule. Did you manage to catch a word with Mr May at the private view?'

'Yes.'

'And? Is he happy to be your mentee?'

'He is – I quote – totally happy, fuck yes, to be my anything, literally, in a heartbeat.'

'Mmm. Yes, I'll talk to him about boundaries. Are you going to be OK with this?'

'Well, it should be interesting. I've never had an ingénue of my very own to torment before.'

'I'm not sure you've *quite* grasped what mentoring entails. Be nice to him.'

'Nice *is* my middle name, as you know. Was that everything? Good. Ciao, ciao.'

Ought he to feel bad about inflicting Freddie on his oldest friend? Or vice versa? Giles really cannot decide.

The archdeacon gets home from the ordination to find a card on his doormat. He recognizes the bold black italics on the envelope and his poor heart cartwheels. *Hi Matt. I think this is about when that employment tribunal is due to take place. Just wanted to wish you good luck. Hope all's well with you. J x*

Our big, strong, fearless archdeacon sits down on his stairs and cries like a little boy.

Chapter 9

ane was correct. This is the time when the employment tribunal is due to take place. The former Bishop of Lindchester will fly back from South Africa next week. It's been a right old headache keeping up to speed of the whole legal malarkey; liaising with the diocesan bods, barristers and whatnot, on top of everything else. And for nothing, in all probability. Matt has a gut instinct that the sewer (Dr R's word for the litigious priest) knows he has no case. Having failed to intimidate them into settling out of court, he is now just maximizing the amount of hassle and expense he can cause, by withdrawing at the last possible moment. True, it would have been cheaper for the diocese to settle, but Matt was damned if he was going to roll over for this pillock, and leave everyone with the impression the Church had behaved badly. You might cost us a packet, but it's game over for you, matey Joe. You won't be pulling this stunt again.

But anyway, who gives a monkey's? Matt is smiling as he tootles along through the country lanes of Lindfordshire. *For a tender beaming smile . . .* Now what was that from? Oh, yes. Matt chuckles. Choir. His house sang it in the school music competition one year: 'The Lark in the Clear Air'. Lovely piece, no doubt, when sung by the likes of young tarty-pants. Less so when it's being murdered by two hundred sweaty adolescent boys, creaking and squeaking their way through it. Matt's voice is nothing special, but he can hold a tune. Nobody listening, is there? He gives it another whirl this June morning.

> Dear thoughts are in my mind
> and my soul soars enchanted,
> As I hear the sweet lark sing
> In the clear air of the day.

The reader will have inferred from this that Matt and Jane have finally found a way of talking to one another again. That good luck card Jane slipped through his letter box did the trick. She returned from her meal with Dominic to find the archdeacon sitting on her doorstep like a waif. A very large waif, admittedly. Being a charitable woman, she invited him in for coffee. This all went off fairly smoothly, although Matt knocked a pile of books over and banged his head on a cupboard door, and at one point Jane couldn't find the kettle – simply couldn't find it at all, search though she might. (It turned up on the work surface by the toaster, of all places.) They stood tongue-tied, then blurted out simultaneously what a miserable time they'd been having of it, how they'd been convinced they'd blown their last chance, that the other would have been in touch by now if any hope had remained. Matt showed Jane the undelivered message on his phone, and they laughed at themselves, although their laughter wobbled on the edge of tears.

'Matt, what are we going to do?'

'I don't know. If I knew, I would've done it by now. Nearly sent you a hundred red roses.'

'You did? What stopped you?'

'The cost, really. Over three hundred flipping quid.'

'Ah, you romantic devil!'

'And obviously, I didn't want to come across as a patronizing male chauvinist. Knew you'd be insulted.'

Jane nodded. 'Deeply. Nothing says "Get back in the kitchen, you castrating feminist harridan" like a hundred red roses.'

He smiled. 'Oh, Janey, I can't tell you how much I've missed you.'

'You could try.'

'Am I allowed to show you instead?'

'Have you brought along a visual aid?'

'No, but I could do you my PowerPoint presentation.'

Jane laughed her filthy laugh. 'I bet you could, Mr Archdeacon.'

This, then, is why our hero is singing happily in his car as he drives to a remote parish to take a look at their plans to remove a couple of pews from the back of the church and put a new loo in the vestry. His route lies through Gayden Magna. For a mischievous moment he contemplates popping in on Father Ed. He could stick on the old leather gloves like the archdeacon in *Rev*, put the fear of God into him over his engagement. But no. Matt's a tad on thin ice here himself (ahem). And to be honest, the way he's feeling this morning, Ed and Neil could prance up the aisle in Village People costumes and Matt would give them a blessing. Senior Staff team have discussed the situation, obviously. You can't not. They are minded to take no action during the interregnum. Keep an eye on developments in other dioceses where it's cropped up, see what they do. In any case, Father Ed hasn't actually got married yet, has he?

High above as he passes Gayden Magna a skylark sings. Below lie the rape fields, the silage fields, mown too soon, too often. The old pastures over-grazed, the acres of winter wheat too dense for nesting. Decline, decline; half our skylarks gone in less than a lifetime. Our children grow up never hearing its dare-gale poetry, that blithe spirit spilling rubbed and round pebbles of sounds, and showering music on upturned faces in the morning of no man's land.

But today a lark sings above a Lindfordshire meadow. Maybe its nest is on the ground of some neglected strip, some wilder, unprofitable spot. Or perhaps some good-hearted farmer misses that song, and has set aside both land and best interests to coax it back?

The wedding plans in the vicarage of Gayden Magna grind slowly, but they grind exceeding small. You would not believe the colour swatchery, the micro decisions about things which to the mortal eye appear identical. Abdication is not permitted. Father Ed is trapped in an endless optician's appointment. Is it better like *this*, or like *this*? It is the worst of both worlds: to be consulted, yet granted no executive power. He must share the racking anguish over infinitesimally fine gradations of card texture for the invitations, then have his opinion slapped away. Mere acquiescence is not an option. He must actively want what Neil wants.

'You said I could leave all the planning to you,' protests Ed.

'I *am* doing all the planning, you useless bugger. You can't even decide what you want for an engagement present. The party's next week.'

'I don't *need* an engagement present.'

'But *I* want to give you one, and you agreed. We've been through all this, remember? Did you have another think about that painting?'

'It's not for sale.'

'It might be. I can make them an offer. Let me find out who owns it. Come on, Eds. I want to buy you something you really want.'

'But I liked all the paintings. Any of them.' Oh, pathetically, amateurishly cavalier! Neil demands hard-core specificity. A decision has to *hurt* before it's worth something. 'The one with the sunlight on the stone steps,' Ed tries. 'Remember? All those radiant colours?'

But Neil is shaking his head. 'You said the nude.'

Ed curses himself. He'd let his guard slip and expressed an opinion at the private view. Neil is now locked on to his target like a smart missile.

71

'Look, I'm having doubts. It'll be too big for the vicarage. Think about it, Neil. Where would it go?' He's on firmer ground here. 'It would totally diminish the piece if we just stuck it in the hallway.'

'Hmm.'

Ed did not like *Hmm*. *Hmm* meant things like, why don't we buy a property in the Dordogne and hang the painting there? Sometimes he wished Neil was a lowly curate, an out-of-work model, dog walker, anything, just so long as he had no money.

'I'd really love one of the sketches, actually,' he says. They'd been small, hadn't they? Less expensive?

'Really? Well, they *are* gorgeous. Maybe a set of three? Properly framed, not that IKEA tat. Or all six? Ooh, yes. For the dining room? Had any of them been sold, did you notice?' Neil has his phone out. 'What's the number for the cathedral? Actually, you know what, it's Friday. I may shoot across and refresh my memory.'

Oh, God. Ed knows that look, that tone. Impeccably casual, like an over-rehearsed actor. 'He was just visiting, you know. He won't be there now.'

Pause. 'Sorry? Who won't be there?'

'The blond. The Swedish porn star.' Why is he doing this? Why does he have to torment himself and his beloved with his scab-picking jealousy?

'Him? Och, he's nothing. Just a freeloader. A pretty wee freeloader trading on his looks.'

Ed makes no reply.

'Oh, what? Stop that, Eds. Did you see me leave with him? Was I out of your sight for even one second?'

He feels ugly. 'No, you weren't. Ignore me. Just having one of my wobbles. Sorry.'

'Och, Eds.' Neil takes Ed's hand and gives it a shake. 'Come on, big man. I'm marrying *you*. I love *you*.'

'I know. It's just, I can't think why you would. Sorry. That came out all needy. I'm fine, darling. You go and look at the sketches again. It's fine.'

'Yes, it *is* fine.' He raps on Ed's forehead with his knuckles. 'I'm all yours. Got that?'

'Yes. Sorry.'

'Look at me.' Ed looks. 'Boys like that, they see me and think "meal ticket". Whereas you.' For a second Neil nearly chokes up. Tears sting in Ed's eyes as well. 'You look at me and see the man you love. You know I'm a total shite, but you love me anyway.' Neil wipes his eyes with a fingertip. 'Can you even *think* how many years it would take me to train up another one, if I lost you? Exactly. So

72

let's have no more of this. Go and write a sermon or something, Vicar.'

Neil gets in his Porsche and heads for Lindchester.

Ah, the Calvinist conscience! You never can give it the slip. Auld John Knox, popping out like a jack-in-the-box. Puff of hellfire: *I saw that, laddie!* Pulling your old trick back there, making Ed feel bad for something that's your fault. Neil hits the steering wheel. Bad man. Poor Eds, he's the dumb, loyal friend at school you abandon by the broken window, holding your catapult.

Neil knows deep down that marriage won't stop him straying. So why's he insisting on it? All the hassle, the expense, the professional grief it'll cause with the powers that be? What's the point of standing up in front of those gathered here today, just to make a vow he knows he can't keep? Is he trying to convince Ed that though he strays, he has a homing device? Yes! He *wants* to forsake all others. He wants to say loud and clear: I love you. You are my choice. I will be true to you, as true as I have it in me to be. You are everything in the world to me.

Except *new*.

Aye, bad man, Ferguson. What's your *problem*, eh? You've got wholesome home cooking, haven't you? So why the Big Mac? Why those trashy empty carbs you regret even as you stuff your face in a layby? Before you've wiped the grease off your chin you're sick of yourself. It's never worth it. But my *God*! Those Pavlovian Golden Arches . . .

Still, maybe he's mending his ways? He'd been a good husband-to-be that night, hadn't he? He'd not slipped out for a breath of fresh air with yon wee slut. *Boing!* Here's Revd Knox again. Ah, come *on*! Gimme a break here! Neil pounds the steering wheel again. Fine, then, so it wasn't the thought of Ed.

Neil had caught the stranger watching. Older guy, tall and lean, like a stoat in an Italian suit, watching, watching, across the crowded exhibition while young Happy Meal cruised him. Boyfriend? Boss? Case worker? Neil has no idea. But he can still feel that psychotic stare trained on him. Red laser sights dancing on his forehead. Hey, no worries. He's all yours, pal.

The fuss surrounding the *Souls and Bodies* exhibition has died down now. There were a few tense phone calls, but none of the local school groups pulled out. Each day the vergers lay polythene sheets on the floor, and the cathedral rackets to the sound of children making their own abstract stained-glass art out of tissue paper and cardboard. The far end of the exhibition is now roped off – much to the chancellor's disgust, but the dean is the boss – and volunteers in blue gowns step forward to alert parents, and prevent unaccompanied small children from entering and having their innocence smirched by a glimpse of penis.

Willies. Huh. Leah Rogers has seen willies before and they're lame in her opinion. Daddy is lame for bringing her to this lame exhibition of paintings that aren't actually *of* anything. The only good thing is that Jess isn't allowed to come because it's Parental Guidance Advised. There are some Grown-Up pictures, but because Leah is a sensible girl, she is allowed to see them.

Huh. Like she *wants* to see them. She only tried to get into the exhibition in the first place because she was bored waiting for Daddy to finish work. Well, *and* because the lady in the blue gown said she couldn't enter without a grown-up. So she pretended she was all, 'Oh, I'm so disappointed, but I will obey your stupid rule.' Then she went round the corner and ducked under the red rope, only they caught her. And then, worst luck, Penelope came along and said, 'Let's go and find Daddy, shall we, Leah, he's in the office!' in her smiley-sticker voice, like a Reception teacher going, isn't this exciting, boys and girls! Well done! Have a smiley sticker!

So now she's got to look round the exhibition, saying, oh, this is so interesting, another giant painting of NOTHING, while Daddy reads bits out from the leaflet to her like she's got Special Needs. And now they've come to the willy section, which is really inappropriate, she has no interest in it whatsoever.

'Now, Leah, this piece is a bit controversial. Some people have been silly about it, because it's a painting of a naked man. Or a nude. That's the proper word if it's a painting.'

Really? Because it looks like NOTHING with a great big stripe of more NOTHING going across it.

'But it's an important piece of serious art. It's called "That time will come and take my love away",' reads Daddy.

Leah looks at the label. '"That time will come and take my love away", Shakespeare, Sonnet number sixty-four.'

'It's a quotation from Sonnet number sixty-four, by William Shakespeare.'

Leah rolls her eyes. I can actually *read*, for your information, Father.

Next to it there are some proper drawings. These *are* of a naked man. Leah just glances. Boring. Someone else is in the exhibition too, worst luck. A man wearing black clothes. He has diamond earrings and a leather bracelet on and a gold watch and dark spiky hair. She can smell his perfume. He's talking on his mobile while he looks at the pictures, which isn't allowed, you aren't meant to use a mobile in the cathedral. Please, please, *please* don't let Daddy tell him off. Then he puts his phone away and walks out. Phew, because it's embarrassing enough with Daddy reading out stuff from the leaflet in his totally embarrassing way like a vicar doing the Bible reading.

'"This is an exploration of the architecture of the human frame."' Blah blah. Leah wanders round pretending to look where Daddy's pointing.

The man comes back with the lady in the blue gown. Very, very slowly the lady peels tiny round red stickers off a sheet and starts sticking one on each label beside the willy pictures.

'The potency yet vulnerability of. Brushwork. Death. Incarnation. Blah blah.' Shut up, shut up, shut UP! Why do you have to be SO embarrassing?

She walks off and lets her eyes sneak a longer look at the nearest drawing. It's nothing like the giant sausages the boys at school scribble on the whiteboard, like that's really clever. The willy sort of drapes itself there on the man's leg, like a pet animal or something.

Then she sees the man with the diamond earrings watching her. She goes red. He makes a pretend shocked face and puts a hand over his mouth, like the girls at school. This makes Leah do a great farting snort. Like she's blown a giant raspberry. Honestly, it explodes out of her and echoes round the cathedral. Immediately the man looks away and stares at the big painting with a fake 'I am an angel, I didn't do anything' expression. Leah just cannot, *cannot* stop laughing.

'Leah, if you're just going to be silly, I think we may as well go.'

'FINE.'

The man shakes his head like he's Really Disappointed in her. She checks Daddy's back is turned, and swiftly sticks her middle finger up. The man does it back! A grown-up!

'Come along, Leah.'

She looks back one last time, but the man is talking to the lady now and doesn't see.

Coincidentally, Father Dominic is also out trying to find an engagement present. The gift needs to tick three boxes: something Ed will like, Neil won't despise, and Dominic can afford. He is nearing despair as he walks through Lindford's biggest mall, the Abernathy Centre. Debenhams? He pictures Neil's curling lip, before which Dominic's confidence in his own taste quails and everything seems naff. He surveys his options. Maybe he should abandon this and head off out to some craft place. Pottery, bespoke ebony and silver napkin rings. Something camp and antique? But what? He looks round for inspiration. He's woefully behind on his Trinity Sunday sermon. H & M, Whittards, Thorntons? I think not.

By the big chrome waterfall he notices a dark-haired woman in a hoodie with 'CHAPLAIN' on the back. She's handing out leaflets.

Ex-*cuse* me? Dominic has a complete Lady Bracknell moment. Last time he looked, *he* was chaplain to the Abernathy Centre.

Chapter 10

I t's the green that strikes him. How green everything is this mid-June in Lindfordshire! It crowds in, assails, assaults him.

And the faces. He had forgotten how pale Caucasian skin is. His own reflection jolts him these days; but to be surrounded by white faces suddenly— He realizes he can no longer gauge attractiveness. Is this flattish young woman pretty or plain? And that sharp-featured man – handsome? His scale has been recalibrated to African standards.

Paul Henderson smiles. At least he will be able to wear shorts in Lindfordshire without small curious hands gently exploring the hair on his legs as he stands talking to people. The hire car crosses the border into his old diocese. He must relearn punctuality, reacquire a sense of dissatisfied entitlement and view his glass not only as half empty, but old and considerably smaller than the one in the advert he clearly deserves. He need no longer be struck by the reckless grace of clean water gushing from a tap.

A memory ambushes him. He's back in his office in the palace. He can hear a voice through the door, singing: *What can wash away my stain? Nothing but the blood of Jesus.*

Freddie. Freddie. Of course he's going to find himself thinking of Freddie, as each passing mile takes him closer to his former life. There's a pulse of lust he must acknowledge – this is me, I am attracted to my own sex – then set aside. Where is Freddie now? That choral scholarship must be nearly finished. Has he got something lined up? Is someone keeping an eye on him? Keep an eye on him, Lord; keep him safe from the likes of me!

As he drives, he conjures a paler, angrier version of himself in a parallel universe: the Most Revd Paul Henderson, Archbishop of York. He knows he would have told himself that he needed a chauffeur, that Freddie needed a job, that it made sense to take him with them to Bishopsthorpe. He sees himself denying everything to the very last, even as the tidal wave of scandal broke over him. Well, at least he'd been spared – he had spared everyone – all that. Through the severe mercy of God.

Paul is still married. His marriage is tender and intimate, physically affectionate, though not sexual. He has not surrounded himself with beautiful African youths and told himself they are pastoral assistants. Suze is flourishing. Yes, yes, she is: happy and occupied with her mama bishop role, using her nursing skills once more. When he asks, she claims her needs are catered for. (But when would Suze admit otherwise?) This is as valid a marriage as many a middle-aged marriage, surely? Faithful, companionable. True, not all his needs are catered for. But nor are those of plenty of married people. And single people. Are we any less human than those fortunate enough to find sexual fulfilment? (*Is* this truly a marriage?)

Paul has not made sense of last summer yet. But he has made peace with it, or nearly. It is no longer *sins* that trouble him. A sin is a sin, get over yourself. There's provision for that. Clean water laid on for every life. What racks him is the *condition* of sinfulness, that web of finitude, of fallenness we are all tangled in, thrash and struggle though we might. A tug here sends shivers across the whole matrix. A wrong done cannot be undone; it must run its course. And wrong will come of it and go on coming of it, for generations, maybe, individual repentance and forgiveness notwithstanding. How can this growth be cut out, now it's wrapped round all our vital organs? (A white man in South Africa – how can he not wrestle with this?)

On some self-aggrandizing days he feels as though he embodies all the Church's conflict on the gay debate. The full, irreconcilable spectrum is incarnate in Paul Henderson. Save me, *Kyrie eleison*, I'm sinking! On other days he remembers John Newton. Amazing grace? But what can wash away the sins of a repentant slave trader, when his legacy is with us to this day? He thinks of Newton on his deathbed, with just these two things left: I am a great sinner, and Christ is a great saviour.

Is there provision for the sins of the whole world, not just the sins of John Newton, of Paul Henderson? Can everything be put right? It cannot be so. It must be so. Paul never hears the words of the Agnus Dei nowadays without weeping. *He himself bore our sins in his body on the tree.* The intellect balks, but here we are, all sharing the same broken bread, the same cup. Great sinner, small sinner. The ground is level at the foot of the cross.

Well, look at that – he's gone into automatic! He's driving towards Cathedral Close, not to the Lindford Travelodge. Paul slows and finds a place to turn round. He's halfway through the manoeuvre when he recognizes it: that layby. The place where he had to pull over and stop, after he'd dropped Freddie off. Heart breaking. Wind stirring bleached grass. Blond, blond.

A white carrier bag snagged on thorns inhales, exhales, as the wind passes over it. Paul waits a moment, heart fracturing all over again. *Thou best of dearest.* But the grass is green now. Roses trail. Brambles are in bloom. This might be another place entirely.

The bishop checks his mirrors and starts off again in the right direction.

'Tell me a bit about your uni chaplain,' Dominic says to Jane on the phone.

'Veronica da Silva! Hah!' It's Monday, and she's eating a doughnut at her desk. 'Can't stand her. She's like a keen drama student honing her trendy chaplain role by staying in character twenty-four seven. Why?'

'I met her in the shopping mall last Friday,' says Dominic. 'Are you eating something?'

'Nope.'

'Good. Well, she was wearing a chaplain hoodie and handing out leaflets!'

There's a pause. 'OK. Which part am I meant to be indignant about?'

'*All* of it. *I* am chaplain to the Abernathy centre!'

'Oh, I *see*! And did we come over a tiny bit territorial?' Jane takes another bite.

'I fear we did. Possibly because— would you *stop* chomping in my ear? It's disgusting. *Possibly* because I feel guilty for not making more of the chaplain role. Be that as it may, there she was. In her hoodie.'

'Never mind, sweetums, I'll buy you a chaplain hoodie of your very own.' She finishes the doughnut and wipes her fingers on her jeans. 'Did you publicly denounce her?'

'I went over and introduced myself.'

'In all your queenly splendour.'

'Flouncing *may* have occurred, yes. But we soon cleared up the silly misunderstanding. *Uni* chaplain, not mall chaplain! "Oh, Father Todd, I've heard *all* about you!" Eurgh! She's one of those women who *adores* gay men. Because we're endlessly available to listen to their man troubles and help them choose curtains.'

'A fag hag like me!' Jane stands up and brushes sugar off her front.

'You? You're a rubbish fag hag! And she *prefers* the term "ally". She told me she's an LGBTQIA *ally*.'

'Did you say you self-identify as a big ponce, and it's LGBTQIA*BP* these days?'

'See? You're rubbish. Why can't you adore me properly, you cisgendered old trout?'

'Adore, adore, adore. There. So what were these leaflets about, poncykins?'

'Oh, the food bank. She's on the staff of St James', which I'd forgotten. Is she American, by the way?'

'God knows.'

'She sounds vaguely transatlantic. Apparently she trained at some American seminary or bible college I'd never heard of. Slight sense the goalposts kept shifting when I tried to home in on the facts, though.'

'Ooh, interesting! PhD from the University of Narnia, you think? Internet ordination?'

'We-e-ll. The thought hovers.'

'Poundstretcher will have chased up her references and asked to see her degree certificates,' says Jane. 'So she's unlikely to be bogus.'

'True. But I'm telling the vice chancellor you call it Poundstretcher.' Jane laughs. 'Bring it.'

'My, aren't *you* chirpy today!'

'Ha ha! That's because I'm getting some hot archidiaconal action.'

'Ew!' cries Dominic. 'I'm very happy for you, darling, but ew. I take it you have birthday plans, then? You won't want to come with me to this engagement party on Saturday, after all?'

'Sorry, no. It's the solstice. We'll be frolicking naked in the woods, wearing antlers . . .'

But Dominic has already hung up.

Late that afternoon, Dean Marion stands with Gene in the deanery garden by the high sunny wall. A clump of bees droops there. Thousands, tens of thousands of honey bees, a mass of seething amber, like an enchanted velvet pouch. Earlier the air was peppered with them, as though the deanery had been struck by a freak black blizzard; but they've clotted round their queen now. Marion watches. The world is dizzy with their thrumming.

A local beekeeper has been summoned.

'Tell him he owes you a silver spoon,' says Gene. 'That's the traditional worth of a June swarm, I believe.'

'I wish there was a way we could keep them. Lindchester ought to have its own hives,' says Marion. 'Why not? Other cathedrals do.

Even Southwark has bees. If they can keep them in central London, we can keep them here.'

'Ooh! We could sell Lindchester Cathedral honey! And beeswax candles!'

'We could!'

'What a shame you slaughtered all those poor innocent masonry bees,' mourns Gene.

'Thank you for the reminder.'

'Did you know that during her mating flight, the queen is serviced by seven to ten drones?'

'Strange to say, I didn't know that, Gene.'

'It's true. After ejaculation, the drone pulls away from her and his tiny bee member is r-r-ripped from his body. He dies, his function fulfilled. Sometimes you can even hear the little *pop!* on a quiet sunny day.' Gene sighs a wistful sigh, as if of golden summers remembered.

'Well, that sounds like a sensible system to me,' remarks Marion.

He bows. 'Just a little thought to cherish at General Synod next month, during the debate about women bishops.'

It's Wednesday. Martin is nervous. He shouldn't feel nervous. Paul isn't his line manager any more. They are just going to have a pub lunch together. Martin had tried suggesting that Penelope joined them, so it wouldn't feel like a PDR. But it turned out that Paul had already arranged to meet up with his former PA for afternoon tea.

If only the employment tribunal was still going ahead! Then Paul wouldn't have all this spare time on his hands to catch up with old colleagues. But the ex-vicar of Lindford (not wishing to judge, but a truly horrible human being, in Martin's humble opinion) withdrew his case on the very morning the tribunal was due to start. Hadn't Martin been saying all along this would happen? But nobody listened. The diocese has wasted thousands on legal costs. Martin rather questions the archdeacon's judgement here. On the other hand, there *is* a principle at stake.

He enters the village and makes for the canal-side pub. His heart does a little panicky flip. Paul's bound to make friendly enquiries. How are you doing? How's the job hunt going? And Martin's going to have to find a positive way of dressing up the bleak truth: I keep applying for incumbents' jobs and being rejected. I was even interviewed for one post, but then I didn't get it.

Horrible though this topic is, Martin would rather discuss his failure than stray into other more awkward avenues of conversation. The ghastliness of last summer will hover all the time, he knows it will. He won't be able to banish the thought of Paul's wrecked career. Worse, Paul might confide toe-curling things about his newly discovered orientation. His *boyfriend* ... Not that Martin's homophobic. It's just that nobody wants to have to imagine other people's relationships.

Here's the pub. Martin pulls into the car park. Obviously it would be inappropriate to discuss the CNC and Paul's successor. But Martin can ask about theological formation in South Africa and how Susanna is faring, can't he? He can enquire after Paul's daughters and grandchildren. Yes, so long as they steer clear of Freddie May, everything will be fine.

It's now mid-afternoon. Jane is back in her office trying to sort out next year's units and she's thinking about coffee and cake. There's a knock at her office door. Oh, good, she thinks. That will be Spider, coming to rescue me from MOODLE hell.

It is not Jane's poet friend. It is the uni chaplain. I regret to say, we are about to witness Jane at her worst. Or possibly her best? I leave it for the reader to determine. Part of me thrills with admiration, I confess. Jane violates the first rule of being English, which states we must suck up any amount of inconvenience, pain and insult rather than be rude to someone we neither know nor care about.

'Come in.' Well, if it wasn't the fag hag. In her half done-up dungarees (bib and one strap dangling) and rainbow clerical shirt. How old? Thirties? No, early forties, but dressed too young.

'Hi!!! Janey!? I'm Veronica Da Silva!? A colleague of Father Dominic!? He's a friend of yours, right!? Hi!'

Good grief. 'Hi.'

'Am I innerrupting?'

'You are, actually.' Jane gestured at her desk.

'No worries. I can come back. When's a good time?'

'For what?'

'I was thinking we should grab a coffee and chat? Being as we both work here and we have a friend in common and all? Dom said to look you up. So, coffee?'

'No, thanks.' Dominic Todd, I'm going to kill you.

The woman blinked. 'Cool. That's cool. Work/life balance. I get it. You've set your personal boundaries. I totally respect that.'

Jane tilted her head.

'Well, it's so GREAT to meet you at last!!! I've heard so much about you from Dom! And I've seen you round the campus? I was always, who is that striking woman with the awesome haircut? She looks so awesome, who *is* she?'

Jane tilted her head awesomely.

'Hey, and I've just been reading some of your work on gender and the Victorians?' Another head tilt. 'I am in *awe* of your scholarship and publications?' The chaplain's awe unfurled into several paragraphs.

Fuck this head-tilting shit. Get out of my office.

'A-a-anyhoo. I was gonna ask, would it be OK if I sat in on your lectures this semester?'

'That won't be possible. For pedagogical reasons.' Plus this is starting to feel a bit *All About Eve*. Jane waved at her desk again. 'Sorry, I need to press on.'

'Cool. Oh, can I get you a coffee? I'm heading to the bistro, maybe I can bring you one back up, save you going all the way down? Man, it's a long, long way, isn't it, especially when the elevators aren't working. So what can I get you? You normally drink double espresso, right?'

Jane felt a chill creep up the back of her neck. *I'd like a martini, very dry . . .*

'Nothing for me, thanks.' She turned to her computer and started tackling her in-box. 'Bye.' Eventually the burbling ceased with a cheery 'Anon for now!' and her office door closed.

Jane grabbed her phone and left an almighty bollocking on Dominic's voicemail.

The England football flags have vanished from the precentor's car. Brazil flags now flutter beside the Germany ones. The precentor's son switched allegiance once England were knocked out, to wind his mother up. 'You're *half German!*' shouts Ulli. 'Doesn't that count for anything? Why don't you support Germany? You can't support sodding Brazil, for God's sake!'

Iona climbs up to the organ loft to practise for Sunday. At least she won't have to accompany that bloody Tchaikovsky Hymn again till next Trinity. Some Vierne, to cleanse the palate. As she adjusts the stool height she finds herself thinking of Freddie May. His audition. Blowing them away with that *Il Trovatore* aria. Bloody hell. Like he suddenly had four extra ranks of pipes nobody knew about. Pity he was so thick, really. *Actively* thick. Talking to Freddie was like being smacked round the head with short planks. Bless.

The summer solstice approaches. As good Anglicans, we have no truck with all this New Age Stonehenge druidery. There will be no church-sanctioned Fresh Expression of naked cavorting and phallus worship in the Diocese of Lindchester. We might go a bit Celtic, but in the

C of E that tends to mean saying some nice circling prayers and singing Iona worship songs, rather than burning Calvinists in wicker cages. In any case, attempting to burn Calvinists is a theological nonsense. If they are meant to burn, they will.

You will be alarmed to hear, then, that our friend the archdeacon rises stealthily on solstice morn while it is still dark, gets in his car and drives off on a secret mission. Elsewhere in the diocese, midsummer frolics will be held to celebrate the engagement of Father Ed to his partner Neil. Hmm. Now I come to think of it, I cannot put my hand on my heart and promise there will be no phallocentric pagan cavorting in the vicarage of Gayden Magna tonight. But we will retain our customary practice of averting the narrative gaze and leaving such things to the reader's imagination. I will just confide that after a happy evening of internet research, Neil hired some scantily clad cocktail waiters. Like a good husband-to-be, he scrupulously refrained from hiring anyone he thought he recognized. (Though it's *possible* he's now following @choirslut90 on Twitter.)

Jane wakes on her birthday to find her doorstep piled with big flat cardboard boxes. The pile is taller than she is. What the hell? The boxes contain long-stemmed red roses from Covent Garden market.

A thousand of them.

Chapter 11

O h, to be in England, now that June is there! (*Pace*, Robert Browning – surely June is our loveliest month of all?) Mock oranges flower in gardens across the Diocese of Lindchester. Pale pink peony bowls slump and dash themselves in smithereens on pavements. Swifts circle, young magpies churr and chase through treetops. The nights are a-murmur with insects, busy in the honeysuckle and jasmine and nicotiana. Privet hedges bloom. Plane trees scent the towns with a rakish Parisian note. At dusk you may glimpse the eerie ghost moths as they flicker over meadows; while barn owls – like larger ghosts – hunt white and silent along the margins of fields. Who knows? Between English earth and sky, in doorways and under railway arches, in steamed-up cars in abandoned places, perhaps the homeless can sleep a little less clenched these perfumed June nights? (In England – now!)

Petertide. Frantic painting and decorating is going on. There will be eight men and women ordained deacon in Lindchester Cathedral next Sunday.

'Can you believe, Pedro, a whole year has gone by since I was in such a flap about my new curate's house?'

Pedro makes no reply as he bobs along beside Father Wendy. He has seen something small and furry on the bank ahead. Every nerve quivers for the chase.

'I don't know how we ever got it done in time! And that naughty boy the archdeacon sent us! He just lay around smoking dope and painting rude pictures on the bedroom wall!' Wendy laughs. 'Poor Madge was at her wit's end— Whoa there, Pedro! It's just a little vole. We don't need to chase brother vole, remember?'

Father Wendy spares a prayer for the naughty boy, and for all the parishes across the diocese who are in a flap this week about curate accommodation.

It's not just the Diocese of Lindchester that is in a flap. You may be surprised to learn that there will be a thousand #NewRevs ordained priest and deacon this year. What, a thousand rats *boarding* a sinking ship? That's very altruistic of them. Unless the good ship C of E is not quite ready to go down yet after all. I dare say the press will be inclined to dismiss our efforts as rearranging the deckchairs on board the *Titanic*. But we could always ask them how their circulation figures are holding up.

Bishop Bob drives to the cathedral for the senior staff meeting. It's like the beautiful Junes of childhood, he thinks; editing out the misery of exams and sports day. He rounds a bend, the one where the distant cathedral spire on its mound first becomes visible on the road from Martonbury. A shadow falls across him, like the thought of school blighting August. My word, but the diocese is a heavy burden! Each day he must draw a deep breath to steady himself, before once again shouldering the load. Still, the CNC meets to interview the shortlisted candidates in less than a month. We'll have an announcement before the end of the year, God willing.

His thoughts turn to his former bishop. Well, South Africa certainly seems to suit Paul! He looks comfortable in his own skin at last. Really touching that he should make time to visit like that. Quite a big detour on his way to his daughter's. Bob's happy he can now erase the image of Paul, broken and weeping, at his farewell service only six months before. Perhaps – is it fair to speculate? – perhaps in policing himself so fiercely, Paul had appeared to be policing everyone else as well? Is that what caused the air of taut disapproval, and earned him his 'Mary Poppins' nickname?

Then again, it might simply have been the pressures of the job. Bob has gained some insight into that during the last months! He's weary, bone weary. Janet has started nagging him to visit the GP. Yes, he rejoices for his brother Paul in this evident new lease of life.

Oh, but poor Paul, all the same! Bob was surprised and honoured to be confided in yesterday. They had never achieved much rapport as colleagues, after all. How hard Paul's life must have been. Back when we were growing up, sex was in the very air. Short skirts, free love! But our parents belonged to an earlier era. How did we timid, nicely brought up boys ever find out anything? Headmaster giving a pep talk? Biology lessons? Perhaps an awkward conversation with Dad, and a Ladybird book called *Your Body* (too babyish, but what else was there?). And later on – oh dear! – smutty giggling over *Playboy*. A battered copy of *Fear of Flying* passed under the desk.

Well! If it was difficult for me, what must it have been like for Paul? Where on earth would a clean living Evangelical boy turn to try and make sense of his feelings? No wonder it was a relief to be told this was just an immature phase; that he should marry and put it behind him. Because there would have been nothing else, no other source of knowledge, apart from public toilets and the Jeremy Thorpe case. Though at a private school there might have been a coterie of boys calling one another by girls' names, and so on. Bob frowns. His grammar school imagination fails him here. But anyway, boys like that would only have revolted someone like Paul.

Boys like that? Someone like Paul? He's slipping into generalizations. There is nobody like Paul, he reminds himself. Nobody like me, for that matter. We are all quirky one-off originals, infinitely precious to the Creator.

He drives up cathedral mount. A procession of 4×4s streams out through the great arch of the gateway: the school run. He pulls courteously to one side to let them past, although technically, they are supposed to make way for him. (Yet another reminder was issued last week by the head of the Choristers' School, after complaints from angry Close residents.) But Bob waits. Hasn't he dropped children off for school himself in years gone by? Yes, he's probably blocked drives and been a nuisance in his time.

He opens the car windows. It's so warm. He finds his hanky and blots his face. The first wafts of lime blossom are in the air. Heavenly smell, but tree pollen does trigger his hay fever. Seems to be worse than ever this year. Can't stop coughing. So long as he doesn't splutter all through the ordinations this Sunday!

The last car passes, and he trundles through the gatehouse on to the Close. He's not looking forward to this senior staff meeting, to be honest. He fears the upshot will involve him having to take a course of action that will satisfy nobody, least of all his own conscience.

What is the issue that exercises our poor friend Bob so sorely? We will speed ahead a few days to find out. It will involve another visit to the vicarage at Gayden Magna, to call on Lindchester's tumultuous priest. He is not willingly tumultuous. I am sure my readers know by now that Father Ed would kneel quietly throughout compline on drawing pins sooner than instigate a tumult.

87

It is late evening when we call. Neil has just returned from London, surfing on a successful business wave (he has just schmoozed a new and very wealthy client). It is a while before poor Ed can get a word in.

'...I kid you not. I was on *fire!*'

'Well done,' says Ed yet again. 'Um, but listen, I'm afraid I've had a phone call, Neil. I've got to discuss "the status of our relationship".'

'Are there any Gordal olives left? Discuss? What's to discuss? Tell them to feck off and mind their own business. Oh, here they are. Want some?'

'Thanks.' He takes one. 'But anyway, I've got to sort out an appointment.'

'Oh yeah, these are *the business!*' Neil eats olives with an urgent Capital City edginess. Can't keep still. Edgy-edgy. 'Just refuse. Make the buggers come to you. Seriously, I won't have you summoned to the head's office like a naughty wee schoolboy. I mean it. We'll take the fight to them. I've got journalist friends. Let's get our story out there.'

Great. Ed takes Neil by the shoulders and checks his pupils. Yes, those London edges have been pharmaceutically bevelled.

'Oh, stop that.' Neil bats him away and heads over to the big American refrigerator. 'It's just nicotine gum.'

'Of course it is, Neil.'

Neil takes his U'Luvka vodka out of the freezer, oily cold, the way he likes it. 'So who called you? The arch-demon?'

'No, it was Bishop Bob's PA.'

'Och, Bob's a pussy cat.' He gestures with the snakey bottle. 'Join me?' Ed shakes his head. 'Seriously, is this because of the party? How the fuck did they hear about it, anyway? It was a private party!'

'The whole world heard about it. You swore it would be a quiet affair.'

A pause. 'Yes, well, and *why* aren't the vodka glasses in the fridge where they belong?'

Ed points to the vodka glasses in the fridge.

'There they are! I'll let you off.' Neil pours himself a large shot in an icy glass. 'And? Can I help it if things got a bit out of hand? It was the solstice.' He takes a mouthful of vodka. Savours it. 'Ah, that's better. Good. Want me there for the Spanish Inquisition? For moral support?'

'No!'

'Oh, what? Why do you always think I'm going to pee in your pool?'

'Because you always pee in my pool. Off the top diving board, usually.'

Neil cackles. 'Come on, Eds, man up. You've got to take the bastards on some time. You're just exercising your legal right to marry. Got that? Your *legal right*. We'll take this to the European Courts if we have to. No omelettes without breaking eggs, big man.'

'I notice it's only *my* eggs that are getting broken here.'

'Excuse me?' The air quivers. 'Are you sure you want to have this conversation? Because I am more than happy to have this conversation right *now*, about how your God-bothering has consistently fucked my life up over the last eighteen years.'

'Yeah, and talking of fucking your life up, maybe we can have the "nicotine gum" conversation too.'

Neil narrows his eyes at Ed. Then he pours more vodka. 'Did the buggers from the cleaning firm do a proper job with the party clear-up?'

'Yes.'

'Let me rephrase that: if I go and check, will *I* think they did a proper job?'

'No. But I was answering like a normal person.'

We will leave them to their fencing match. They know all the steps these days, how to feint, how to parry the other's thrusts; it's well choreographed after eighteen years. The vicarage will be the fraught interface between Lindchester and London for a few more hours, until Neil once more satisfies himself he's the boss, and Ed allows him to believe it.

Ed's parishioners adore Neil, by the way. 'Ooh, you're so naughty!' they tell him. They view him as a flamboyant and rather wicked parrot, and long for him to squawk *Fuck off!* during a big service, so they can be scandalized all over again. As interested onlookers, they believe they have a pretty clear idea who wears the trousers in the vicarage. Poor old parrot-pecked Father Ed, they think.

The truth, of course, is much more interesting. It usually is. Personally, I am not a big fan of trouser-based reductionism as a basis for understanding human partnerships. Perhaps in a simpler age – when one stout pair of leather britches was handed down, father to son, for fourteen generations – we might profitably have asked who wore them. But is it still that simple? Well, some argue that it is, rooting their theology of trousers in creation (it being clear from Genesis that Adam wore them, Eve didn't, and there was no such thing as Steve). All the same, I find it hard to avoid the impression that even in traditional circles, trouser-wearing in twenty-first century relationships is a complex and nuanced thing. We might as well ask, who wears the buskins in Shangri-La? Oh, slippery-slopery thin-end-of-wedgery! We'll have donkeys in kilts before you know it!

Then again, we are all just people; and people are not so very weird and frightening once we get to know them. The same rules apply as ever did, and they have already been summarized for us by that noted theologian, Freddie May: *Thou shalt not be mean to people.*

Helene, head of HR for Lindchester Diocese, comes into the archdeacon's office and parks her bum cheekily on the edge of his desk while he's on the phone. He finishes his conversation and hangs up.

'Your bum's invading my personal space,' he says. 'That's sexual harassment in the workplace. I'm reporting you to my HR lady.'

She taps her pen on her clipboard and waits.

'Woman. I meant HR *woman.*' He smiles disarmingly.

'How long have you known me, Matt?'

'Just over a year now, Helene.'

'And you still haven't noticed I don't find you amusing?'

'You don't?' She shakes her head. 'Dang.'

'Re Bishop Bob: I want to flag up my concern. How does he seem to you?'

'Well, I'll be honest with you: he's looking a bit under the weather,' says Matt. 'Had a quiet word at the staff meeting, as a matter of fact. He tells me he and Janet have got three weeks' holiday in Brittany lined up. Says he can hang on till August.'

'Hmm. I'm not happy.' Helene taps her pen some more. 'He's not taken any annual leave since Christmas.'

'Not sure you're right there, Helene. He had a bit of a break after Easter.'

'No, Matt, I'm not talking about that. I mean, he hasn't taken any leave over and above the inside of the week after Easter, which he's entitled to anyway.'

'Mmm.' Matt is not on firm ground himself here. But then, Helene doesn't quite get the whole stipend/salary distinction.

'Correct me if I'm wrong,' says Helene, 'but essentially, Bob's acting CEO of a medium to large organization, with all the extra time commitments and responsibilities that entails. But without the appropriate support and admin structures you'd normally get in an organization this size.'

'Fair point. But it's temporary. That's the way it goes in an interregnum, I'm afraid. We'll all be spread a bit thin for the foreseeable.'

'Both,' she says. 'Not all, *both*.'

Matt remembers in time that he isn't amusing. So he doesn't tell her his strength is as the strength of ten because his heart is pure.

'Basically, you and Bob are trying to keep on top of the port-folios of *four* full-time members of staff. Two bishops, two archdeacons. Yes? Yes. It's not sustainable, Matt. How many hours did you work last week?'

'Ooh. Forty-ish?' Give or take fifty. 'Point taken. Why don't I have another word with Bob? Suggest he takes a bit of time off next week, once the ordinations are out of the way?'

'Good. I'll email his PA, and cc Martin and Penelope in the bishop's office. Oh, one more thing: I don't seem to have a record of your annual leave on file, Matt.'

'You don't? Hmm.' He frowns as if this is a bit of a conundrum.

Helene leans forward and raps him smartly on his bald head with her clipboard. 'The new rules apply to *all* diocesan employees,' she says. 'Understood? Good. Just to keep you in the loop, I'm intending to contact the archbishop. He needs to second some staff to this diocese to provide cover.'

'Hah, ha ha!' guffaws the archdeacon. 'Oh. Sorry. Thought you were kidding.' He flashes her another disarming smile. 'That was aggravated assault and battery back there, by the way.'

'Was it now? Well, why don't you keep a log of each separate incident, and lodge a complaint with your HR lady? She'll tell you what to do with it.' Helene gets up off his desk. 'King's Head after work some time?'

'Oh, go on then.' He checks the diary. 'Next Wednesday? Cheeky pint. Don't tell the missus.'

'Not if you don't tell mine.'

The day for the ordinations comes. Too hot for those new robes! Thank goodness we've got service booklets to fan ourselves with! But by the end of the service the pristine clerical shirts will be wringing wet. Dean Marion watches Bishop Bob anxiously through-out. Twice she almost beckons the verger (poised to bring a chair), so Bob can sit as he ordains the remaining candidates. But it never quite gets that bad. The heat, he says afterwards. I'm fine. Don't worry about me, Mrs Dean.

Helene watched the bishop too. Not good. The archdeacon can laugh, but she's definitely contacting the archbishop about this.

You might be wondering why Helene was at the ordination service. Her missus, Kay, is a priest in the diocese. Kay is a member of the Cathedral College of Canons. She and Helene fly below the radar, but Matt is aware of the situation.

And Helene is aware of the archdeacon's situation. This is why she has suggested a drink after work, to drop a hint. Yes, the gossip mills are churning out rumours about the archdeacon's steamy affair. If Matt wants to brush it off, that's fine by her. But Helene has familiarized herself with the details of the Clergy Discipline Measure 2003 (as amended by the Clergy Discipline (Amendment) Measure 2013). She can see that it's not beyond the realms of possibility that someone with an axe to grind might file a letter of complaint against the archdeacon for 'engaging in conduct that is unbecoming or inappropriate to the office and work of the clergy'.

JULY

Chapter 12

Marion listens to the news over breakfast. Lord have mercy. Where's this going to end? Will every celebrity from her youth end up being arrested?

The early 1970s creep into the deanery kitchen, as though the radio were dispensing clouds of Aquamanda. 'Well, just keep out of his way then, dear.' Back then it was funny, it was 'wandering hand syndrome'. Only an uptight prude complained. Sometimes it was friends of your parents, the ones you were meant to call 'uncle'. Arm crawling round your waist, gathering you too close. 'Well, hello! Where have you been hiding? What about a kiss for uncle?' Whisky breath in your face as you tried to shrink away without looking rude.

Rude! Marion wonders now how many women her age ended up in genuine danger by obeying the 'don't be rude' rule. It was *rude* not to accept unwanted dances, kisses, drinks, lifts. What a pity that the confidence to deal with dirty old men is only gained in proportion to our lack of need, she thinks. These days, now that pestering is rare, Marion can wither a pervert with a single look. She'd love to parcel up this power and bestow it on her helpless fourteen-year-old self. She really hopes that the young women of today aren't expected to put up with it. She hopes nobody tells them it's rude to demand respect.

Enough. She turns the radio off. A peach-coloured rose nods outside the kitchen window. Gene potters at the stove. She hears the cathedral clock chime quarter to eight. She reminds herself: *The steadfast love of the Lord never ceases . . .*

Oh, but all those children! She can't banish them from her mind. Those poor preyed-upon children. How many more are out there, adults who have kept silent and felt dirty for decades? Yes, and how many men in their eighties live every day in dread? Waiting for that knock on the door that is surely coming; tomorrow, next week, next year. Do they sit rehearsing their statement? *Utterly refute. Witch hunt. Completely without foundation.* Do they protest that the rules have changed? Ask why are they being hunted down and punished for the slap-and-tickle of yesteryear? They had no idea it was wrong! Everyone was doing it!

Perhaps they genuinely think like that? Marion wonders whether she ought to feel pity for these frightened old men. These bewildered grandfathers crying out that things were different back then. Hmm. Maybe she's taking her habit of empathy too far. Except, how far ought mercy to extend? Is it wide, like the wideness of the sea? *Thy knowledge is the only line to sound so vast a deep!* Ah, but nobody can survive the terrible pressure of the ocean's deepest depths. So could mercy and judgement be the same thing in the end?

She shakes her head. And now her thoughts turn closer to home, and the investigations into the Choristers' School in the 1970s. What can she say? Was there a big cover-up? Was the Church just looking after its own, avoiding scandal? Marion doubts it was that cynical. She can picture the clergy Chapter meeting. Yes, what those individuals did was deplorable; but surely this did not negate (so the argument would have gone) all their *other* contributions, their long years of faithful ministry? And let us not forget that we are all frail and sinful human beings. (Article XXVI of the 39 Articles: *Of the Unworthiness of the Ministers, which hinders not the effect of the Sacrament*.) Nobody's interests would be served by pursuing this any further. Yes, Marion's fairly sure it would have gone something like that. The men should be confronted, but given a fresh chance. Wasn't that the heart of the gospel? Of course, there had to be an understanding that in future they would never be appointed to any post with responsibility for children ...

Oh, Lord. And now it was clear they'd gone on abusing for years. We knew what they were; we could have stopped it, and we didn't – through ignorance, through weakness, if not through our own deliberate fault. What now? Two of the men are now dead. The third, the former chaplain, is in his eighties. He has been arrested but released on bail. Lindchester Cathedral was to blame, yes. We failed to safeguard those boys. Better that it comes to court at last, so the victims feel listened to, so they see justice done—

'Oh!' Marion stares at the plate Gene has just put in front of her. 'Thank you. What's this?'

'French toast. Made by your chef, with fresh orange zest and the merest dash of *triple sec* and dusted with cinnamon. Crème fraiche drizzled with maple syrup. Sliced banana, and raspberries from the deanery garden,' says Gene. 'Two of your five a day.' He leers.

'Er, you do know that refers to fruit and veg, don't you?' She starts eating. 'Delicious. Thank you, darling.' Gene pours her some more coffee. 'Do you think they had any idea? Back then.' She waves at the radio. 'Those men, I mean?'

'Oh, yes. They knew, all right,' says Gene. 'We know the difference between welcome and unwelcome. The question is whether you think you can get away with it.' He puts a foot up on her chair rung and angles his groin at her. 'Now, about your five a day, you minxy little minx, fnurr fnurr ...'

Marion grinds a raspberry slowly and viciously with her fork. The juice oozes. She stares up at Gene. 'Yes?'

He removes his foot. 'Oh, nothing.'

It's Monday evening, and Giles is on the phone to the lay clerk elect of Gayden Parva, trying to firm up his accommodation for next year.

'No, of course you don't *have* to live in Vicars' Court, Freddie. But why wouldn't you? The rent's subsidized, it's handy.'

'Meh.'

'So where *are* you going to live?'

'Oohhh. I'm like, y'know?'

'No, Freddie, that doesn't actually convey anything.' Giles considers running headlong into a tree trunk for a bit of light relief. In the memorable phrase of the sub-organist, this is like trying to stir pigshit with two short planks. 'Tell me your plans.'

'Yeah, no, it's fine, only it's kinda like ...Aah ... It's all the stuff, y'know?'

Giles bites his own hand. 'Once again, Freddie, I have *no idea.*'

'Aw. It's just ... Me? Yeah?'

A flash of inspiration: 'Is it something you might find helpful to discuss with your mentor?'

'NO! No way. Dude, he scary!'

'Then concentrate, and tell me your plans. Or I'll get Dr Jacks to ring you. Where—' Giles breaks off. 'Did you just scream?'

Freddie clears his throat. 'Yep, wa-a-ay up in my falsetto range for a second there. *Man!* So listen, all I'm saying is, I'm not sure I can cope with the whole living by myself ... thang, OK? The bills, the rent, yeah, the whole being responsible for shit? *Man*, that's so lame. Gah. Don't make him ring me. Begging you?'

'All right.' Interesting! Mr Dorian as crowd control. Must make a note of that. 'Good. And for the third time I ask: what are your plans?'

'Ooohhh. Um. Maybe lodge with someone? Like I did with the Hendersons?'

Well, not *quite* like that, preferably, thinks Giles. 'With whom?'

'Anyone? I'm easy.'

'Yes, try not be. And when are you planning on moving up here?'

'Um. End of term?'

'In a *fortnight*?! Were you just going to turn up with a suitcase and see who took you in?'

'Yeah. Pretty much. Hnhnn. Not good? Yeah. Probably should've planned that a bit better?'

'You are a prize wazzock, sometimes, Mr May.' Giles sighs. 'I'll ask around.'

'Can't I crash at yours till I get sorted?'

'If all else fails, yes,' says Giles, resolving to move heaven and earth.

He rings off and gazes through his study window to the front garden where two different colours of bunting vie. From his bedroom window hangs a Germany flag the size of a tablecloth. It is half obscured by a Brazil flag the size of a tennis court, which hangs from the attic.

He goes through to the kitchen where his wife and second son are bickering.

No booze on school nights, no booze on school nights! he recites.

Giles opens the fridge. Unless you've just been talking to Freddie May? No, that is *not* sufficient reason. Anyway, look, there's some delicious lemongrass and ginger cordial. Right there. Beside the open bottle of Chablis . . .

'No, hear me out, Mother.' Felix has his hand raised. 'Hear me out, please. For every goal Germany scores—'

'You will tidy your room, empty the dishwasher and take the recycling out for a month! Which, notice, ARE YOUR CHORES ANYWAY!'

He presents his middle finger. 'And for every goal Brazil scores, you are not allowed to say anything at one banquet or annual dinner. Instead—'

'Pscha!'

'No, hear me out. You can only make noises. But they have to be based on . . . wait for it . . . farts you have previously made. OK? Like, the questioning fart' – he demonstrates – '*Hmmm?* Or the total disagreement: *Pah!*'

'Hey, I like your thinking!' says the precentor's wife. 'These banquets are full of old farts anyway.'

A brief exchange of conversational flatulence ensues.

'You *disgust* me, the pair of you!' Giles grabs the Chablis (it needs finishing) and a glass and escapes back to his study. They say you get the children you deserve. Unfortunately, he appears to have the children his wife deserves.

There are tears after evensong on Tuesday. Timothy has announced which boys will be head chorister and deputy next year. Even if all have done well, not all can be awarded this special prize. Hence the tears. It is not always the boy with the finest voice who is given the role. The head chorister must also be a good leader and set a proper example to the other choristers. Freddie May was not head chorister.

Miss Barbara Blatherwick dealt with those disappointed tears in her day. And other tears besides. Oh dear me, yes! She is a sensible woman. She knows that times have changed. One cannot simplistically judge the past by the standards of today. But all the same, her hand trembles as she pours her second cup of English breakfast tea. Ought she to have done more?

I can tell you, reader, that Miss Blatherwick has no need to accuse herself. It was she who blew the whistle and released those little boys from their nightmare – and probably prevented many others from suffering the same fate. At the time she was young and the newly appointed matron at the Choristers' School. But she realized what was going on and did not turn a blind eye. She was not held back by fear of being rude, or of causing trouble for important men who were respected and loved, or of bringing a venerable institution into disrepute.

She sits at her kitchen table now, with no appetite for her porridge. Outside in her yard the goldfinches flutter at the feeder. Amadeus the cathedral cat won't be far away. It feels to her, with the advantage of hindsight, that she was part of the cover-up; that she colluded with the system that allowed men like that to move on and repeat their pattern of offending elsewhere. How could she have been party to that?

The parents. Yes, that's what decided it. They were adamant: no police. Their sons had suffered enough. How could one argue with that?

Oh dear, what a mess we make of things, even when we act with the best of motives. Miss Blatherwick blows her nose on her pocket handkerchief, then gets on and eats her porridge like a sensible woman.

It is early on Wednesday evening. The archdeacon leaves the King's Head and sets off back up the steep hill towards the cathedral. He stomps past the little shops selling their posh tat; wooden seagulls, driftwood mirror frames, cushions like faded deckchairs – as though Lindchester was a chuffing seaside resort. We'll have chuffing winkle stalls next.

Oh, dear. Our hero is not happy. If a thought bubble like a helium balloon bobbed along over his bald head, I fear it would say *Bloody bossy women!* His life is overrun with bossy women! As a good modern archdeacon he cannot permit himself to articulate this thought; so he takes it out on the knick-knack shops instead. For chuff's sake! All this girly clobber. All this retro bollocks. Fancy jam-pot covers and flipping peg bags taking over the entire world!

Matt is mad because he's in the wrong and he knows it; but there isn't time to process this before the next thing, which is prayer vigil in the cathedral for the new bishop of Lindchester. Bloody Helene. Interfering again. Are HR managers this proactive in other dioceses? He bets they bloody aren't! Should've bloody blocked her appointment when he was on the interview panel. *Of course* I'm aware what the Clergy Discipline Measure says! I'm the chuffing *archdeacon*!

Matt pauses at the gatehouse to get his breath back. For a wild moment he longs for a fag – and Matt has never smoked. That tells you how hassled he is! He takes a big lungful of lime blossom scent instead. Better cool his jets before the vigil.

Right, so fair enough, it's *possible* he's left himself a tad open here. But conduct unbecoming? No way! He and Janey are consenting adults, they're not married to anyone else, both are seriously committed to the other. Plus they're discreet. Not like there's an open scandal here. Not like she stands on his porch in a marabou trim dressing gown every morning smoking a cheroot, is it? Conduct unbecoming would be a pretty hostile interpretation to place on his domestic life!

'Methinks the archdeacon doth protest too much,' was what Ms B. Boots from HR replied. 'Does anyone bear a grudge against you, Matt?'

Ha! Do they ever! How do you want the list: chronologically, alphabetically, or in degree of toxicity?

He turns into the Close. Ron the constable sticks his head out of the lodge. Matt spots that someone has kindly tacked a bell rope sally to the low stone lintel, the one he's forever cracking his skull on.

'All right, Mr Archdeacon?'

'Fine thanks, Ron. You?'

'Ooh, not so bad, thanks.'

Matt crosses the cobbles past the entrance to Vicars' Court. He catches himself wondering whether there was something a tad knowing in Ron's manner. *All right, Mr Archdeacon, getting your end away, are you?* No, don't be daft. Ron's always like that.

Isn't he?

Great. Getting paranoid now. Thanks for that, Helene.

Suddenly Matt thwacks his archidiaconal thigh. OK, let's stop being a big girl's blouse, shall we? Helene's a force for good. Truth is, she's right: he's in a bit of a bind here. He daren't raise it with Janey. Doesn't want to rock the little boat of happiness they have both managed to clamber back into. In his own mind he's settled it. He's as good as married. There's no other gal for him. He'd rather have Jane in his life on her terms, than not at all. He grimaces. Ah, if only he could put his hand on his heart and say he's 100 per cent squared the situation with the good Lord! Sorry, sorry, sorry. He needs to get down and have a good pray about this.

He pushes open the cathedral north door. Takes another deep breath. About eight centuries' worth of prayer greets him, and his blood pressure drops. Yes, the good Lord has been pretty patient with him over the years. He heads for the William Chapel, far end, behind the main altar, where the vigil is due to happen. A flock of little lights flickers at the shrine. He scans the congregation with an expert eye. Situation normal: more than he feared, fewer than he hoped. 'Twas ever thus. Cathedral Chapter clergy. Scattering of good-egg vicar types have made the effort: Dominic, Ed, Wendy, Geoff (of course, both on the CNC).

Matt tunnels into the robes he's just been handed. Having ticked Bishop Bob off, and made him take a couple of days' leave, Matt's ended up holding the baby. Not that onerous, no preach, just a question of leading. Good, here's the precentor now, with the order of service booklet (*Vigil for the Appointment of the New Bishop of Lindchester, Followed by Night Prayer*).

'Everything under control, Giles?'

Everything was not quite under control, as it turned out. But the archdeacon was in no mood to listen patiently to yet another bossy woman demanding that half of the vigil be given over to praying for the upcoming debate about women bishops in General Synod. Organize your own vigil, lady (he managed not to say). This is the cathedral. We've already printed the liturgy. The precentor can't do spontaneity at this kind of notice.

Instead, he fobbed her off with a polite suggestion that a further hour of vigil might be added after compline, if she cleared it with the precentor. No, sadly, he himself would not be able to stay and demonstrate his solidarity. Important though this issue undoubtedly was. She turned and stalked off. There you go. No such thing as strangers, Matt, just enemies you haven't made yet. Who the chuff was she? Chaplain of something, going by the hoodie. Uni? Now why was that ringing a faint alarm bell?

But by now the precentor was twitching and looking at his watch, so Matt let it go.

After the vigil was over, our weary friend got in his Mini and drove off to his lady, to spend (tell it not in Gath!) the night over at hers. He had a lot on his mind; but all the same, you'd think a former police officer would have clocked that he was being tailed all the way there by a silver Skoda Fabia.

Chapter 13

'No, you should definitely apply for the BLO job,' says Penelope. 'You'd be ideal.'

Martin – uncharacteristically – finds himself in some difficulty here. We join our two friends in the bishop's office. PA Penelope no longer has a bishop to manage, so she is making do with managing Martin. He composes his features. 'Well, that's very kind of you, Penelope. But there's another parish job I'm weighing up, too. Look.' He passes her last week's *Church Times* with an ad circled.

'But that's in the Chester Diocese! You'd have to move. You don't want to move away from your girls, do you? No, no, you should definitely go for the BLO job. You'd enjoy it!'

A spasm crosses Martin's face again. 'Yes, but look,' he taps the advert with an Ecclesiastical Insurance pen, 'it's only just over the border, so the girls could still spend every weekend with me. If I took Friday as my day off, I could pick them up from school.'

'Yes, well, maybe.' She still hasn't really looked at the advert: *A prayerful and energetic priest with a passion for the gospel, who enjoys being visible and engaged.* 'Bishop Paul thinks you'd be perfect for the Borough Liaison post. Oh, he told you that, did he? Well, there you are! You know the agencies and funding bodies, you have links with the churches. Talk to the archdeacon. Matt's desperate for you to get the BLO job!'

This time it's too much. Martin snorts.

'What?'

'It's just, you keep saying . . . Um.' Martin purses his lips and regains control. 'I wish they'd called it the Borough *and Churches* Liaison Officer job, that's all.'

There's a long silence. Penelope frowns. Then she suddenly leans over and paffs him over the head with the *Church Times*. 'Oh, honestly, Martin!'

'Sorry!' No, he's lost it. The bishop's chaplain slides down in his chair and laughs till it hurts. When did he last laugh like this? He can't remember. Oh, let it stop! Let it go on for ever!

Now he's infected Penelope. They sit in the bishop's office rocking with laughter. They are still whimpering when the precentor appears in the doorway.

'Knock, knock!' Giles enters. 'Oh, dear. Been raiding the diocesan whippits supply again, have we?'

'It's Martin!' weeps Penelope. 'He's being very silly. Tell him, Martin!'

Martin can only wave his hands in despairing apology.

The precentor surveys them for a long moment. 'A-a-nyway. I just popped in with a request. Mr May's looking for digs. Just over the summer, in the first instance; but long-term from the autumn. So if you could put out feelers, I'd be grateful.'

Penelope sits up straight and wipes her eyes. 'But I thought – *stop it, Martin!* – I thought accommodation was part of the deal? Isn't there a sweet little house in Vicars' Court?'

'There is indeed. But Mr May' – Giles strikes a fey pose, back of hand to forehead – 'will have none of it. He prefers to lodge with someone.'

'Honestly! That boy,' says Penelope. 'He just wants someone to run around after him and do his laundry. Susanna *completely* spoiled him when he lived at the palace. Well, we'll put our heads together, won't we, Martin?'

'Thank you,' says Giles. 'He intends to bestow his lovely presence on his new landlord in around two weeks' time. Yes, I know! But this is Freddie we're talking about here – who thinks that remembering to get dressed in the morning constitutes being organized. Well, bless you, my dears.' He sketches a cross. 'Please enjoy your nitrous oxide responsibly.'

The office door closes.

'Oh, dear!' Penelope wipes her eyes once more. 'Whatever must he think of us?'

'I think I'd better get a breath of fresh air,' says Martin.

The air outside is not fresh today. We are due a thunderstorm, I think. Martin's new light blue clerical shirt clings to his back. He aches as if he's been doing stomach crunches.

Laughter aside, he's pretty offended, actually. Nobody seems to rate his pastoral abilities. Maybe they're right? Maybe he'd be a disaster as a parish priest these days? There's clearly something about his personal statement that's putting people off. Probably his failed marriage. He's going to carry the blame for that for the rest of his life! He catches himself, and tries not to think this is unfair. Paul's voice comes back to him, something he said at their pub lunch a few weeks back: *In the end, you can only live as you can, not as you can't.*

Is that what I'm trying to do? wonders Martin. To be something that is impossible for me to be? But what room does Paul's maxim leave for the transforming power of God? Surely we are called to live *better* lives than we can, assisted by the Spirit?

Bees drone above his head in the lime trees. The whole Close is giddy with scent today. He passes the school. It's playtime. There's the usual racket of screams and shouts. A football comes sailing over the high wall.

'Bianchi, you dickhead!'

Martin catches the ball awkwardly on the second bounce and lobs it back.

'Oh, thanks!' pipe several treble voices in surprise.

Martin's pulse races a little. He still gets flustered by hurtling balls. *Hurr hurr, Rogers throws like a girl!* But nobody saw. He dusts his hands together and walks on. The cathedral clock chimes. On cue, an old-fashioned school bell is rung vigorously: *Ker-dang! Ker-dang! Ker-dang!* The screams and shouts are doused as though someone has clapped a mute over the playground.

'*What* does the bell mean, Harry Bianchi?' demands a voice in the silence.

'Sorry, sir!'

Martin continues on his circuit of the Close. He passes William House, and slips into the alley that leads to the narrow way off the Close. There should be a breeze there. Yes. He unsticks his shirt and stands looking out from his dizzy perch across the lower town. From up here you get a real sense of the old medieval fortifications. He brought Leah here recently, to help bring her *Horrible Histories* to life. That hadn't gone well. He can't seem to get anything right with that girl! He's tried cracking down on her rudeness, he's tried ignoring it.

He certainly ignored her comment last weekend about his trousers! He's a bit self-conscious about them. Linen. A new venture, and with Becky gone, there's no authority to give him a ruling: 'Definitely yes' or 'Definitely no'. Penelope hasn't commented. He fears this means '*Definitely* no!' Are they an inch too short? (*Dad's got jack-ups!*) Maybe he should have opted for the longer length, and then tried to find a seamstress to turn them up? He tuts impatiently at this endless loop of fretting. So what? Does anyone even care about your trousers? (Ah, if there were someone to care!)

There's the Linden down there among willows. He can just hear the kerfuffle of incompetent punters. His gaze follows the river's meanders out to the ancient water meadows, then further off, to where the cooling towers of Cardingforth plume out steam columns like Old Testament pillars of cloud. He thinks of the relentless bombing of Gaza. Place names escaping – bang! – from Bible pages into headlines. *How long, O Lord?* Will the conflict never end? How can it ever end, after so many centuries of tangled wrongdoing and blame and hate?

The wind flutters the lime leaves. Somewhere behind him he can hear a clarinet. Martin is not musical, but even he recognizes this: Mozart's Clarinet Concerto. The slow movement. His sister learned to play it for one of her grades. And here comes the bit she never quite mastered, a downward squiggle of notes that launches back up into another slow, soaring phrase. He holds his breath . . . a-a-and the unseen player nails it. Martin leans both hands on the wall and bows his head.

It's back again, isn't it, that quiet question mark?

Oh, please don't ask me to do this!

A whole-body flush creeps over him. How he burned with hatred this time last year! Martin has not yet taught himself that he's forgiven for his treatment of Freddie May. Forgiven by the good Lord, forgiven by Freddie himself. And now, as if by some stealthy plan, along comes an opportunity – like treasure stumbled upon in a field – for Martin to make amends. He could offer Freddie a home for the summer. Couldn't he? The question shimmers on the edge of his vision, like the first warning of a migraine. As if divine prompting were one long nagging headache!

Martin can see how neat it would be: a year on, to invite into his home the very man he had maliciously dumped into a safeguarding case. To say loud and clear, 'I trust you with my daughters.' His heart thumps. I should do it.

I *could* do it, couldn't I?

I *will* do it! And then, like a little tumble of dominoes, come two more decisions. He will agree to those sessions of Family Therapy the children's mother has suggested, and he will apply for the BLO job after all.

(Mirth cramps his stomach again. If he gets the job, his first act will be to adjust the title, that's for sure.)

Yes. He grips the wall top. He will action these three points. Good. He turns and heads back towards the palace, completing his lap of the Close. He passes under the high window where the clarinettist is still practising. The phrases spool out with an effortlessness that floats on years and years of diligent practice.

*

It is Wednesday evening. Dr Jane Rossiter has a problem: what to do with a thousand dead roses? Her house smells like a compost heap. If she were a thrifty homebody like Susanna Henderson she might have planned ahead and made a hundred jars of rose petal jelly. She might have dried the flower heads for potpourri. As it is, she failed to press even a single bloom in the pages of the family Bible (which she does not in fact own, so I suppose we must excuse her).

The very best she can salvage from the situation at this late stage is to recycle them all conscientiously in the brown wheelie bin. Ah, sorry end to the archdeacon's grand gesture! We see her now, making repeated trips down her overgrown garden path, scattering wizened petals behind her and shoving armfuls into the bin amid much swearing. What a churlish woman you are, Dr Rossiter! Yes, a hundred red roses *would* have been easier to cope with. And true, a thoughtful lover *might* have augmented the gift of a thousand red roses with the gift of, say, fifty vases. But wasn't it exuberantly romantic to have your shabby house – every vase, bottle, jar, bowl, jug, mug, sink, bath, loo cistern even – bursting with glorious roses for ten days? And still to have so many spare you could strip petals to make paths over worn-out carpets up your tatty stairs, and so to rose-strewn bed? Wasn't that a tiny bit fun? Shame on you for muttering, 'Yes, but who's the one bloody clearing it all up, though?'

Jane leans her weight on the bin lid, to crush in the final dead bouquet. Swifts circle overhead. She stands there for a moment, hands on the bin. Smell of dead flowers. Rank wafts of buddleia and privet blossom on the breeze. The rowan berries are already turning orange. A year, nearly, since she and Matt first got to know one another. Where's this all heading? She looks at the bin and it strikes her as depressingly symbolic: he's offering her more than she can possibly cope with. He has said nothing further about getting married, he's agreed to her terms; but she knows that marriage is what he wants. So is this what his love is like? A thousand red roses: appearing on her doorstep undeserved, astounding while they last, but in the end destined for the wheelie bin? Dear Matt, dearest Matt, what in hell's name am I going to do with you?

Oh, she may as well go and get that daft bit of paper and be done with it.

Yes, why doesn't she?

Because every single time she runs this idea past herself, she gets the same answer: a marriage certificate is not just a daft bit of paper. Even at its most minimalist and non-bridal, the ceremony still represents something Jane's deepest being recoils from. She just cannot abide the thought of being *someone's wife*.

She stomps back into her dreary house to hoover up dead rose petals.

Somebody else is doing the recycling tonight. Yes, it is Felix Littlechild, son of the canon precentor. He up-ends the big green box into the wheelie bin. A vast crash of shame echoes round the Close, broadcasting this week's alcohol consumption. The giant Brazil flag has vanished from the front of the house. Felix will be taking out the recycling for the next seven months, I'm afraid. Seven fucking one! How was that even possible? Please let Argentina win, please, *please*, or Mother will be impossible to live with. He closes the bin lid on all the tragic Brahma beer bottles.

The only silver lining is the thought of Mother attending the Cathedral Patrons Dinner in September, and conversing with the old farts in their own language. She'll do it, too. Ha ha! Legend! Dad will go *mental*, but there's nothing he can do. There's a Total Frickin AWESOMENESS to how embarrassing Mutti is. Seriously, he's in *awe* of it these days. Felix walks back to the house, kicking the recycling box across the drive in front of him.

Across the Northern and Southern provinces suitcases are being packed ready for General Synod, which meets this week for its July session in York. Bishops, archbishops, and all the company of Anglicanism. Some have booked train tickets, some have had train tickets booked for them, some will drive, some will be driven; but all shall pack cases. Yes, in these austere days clergy no longer have servants to fill carpetbags with port, Macassar oil, monogrammed shoe-trees and I know not what frippery pertaining to a more gracious era.

As you are aware, we cannot concern ourselves with suitcases outside the Diocese of Lindchester; nor will I detain the reader with detailed lists of synod members and the clothes they are packing. Let generalizations suffice here. The clergy must decide whether to go in mufti, the lay members must pack something a bit posh to wear to the Minster on the Sunday, and everyone is wondering what they did with all the bumf about fringe events; oh well, never mind. I suspect all the members are pretty tense about how the crucial vote will go on Monday. The debate about women bishops is being served up again, to see if the House of Laity manage to eat their swede this time, so everyone will be allowed out to play.

Actually, I think it must be a pretty lonely business to find yourself in the position of opposing the measure. To be the 'one or two individuals spoiling it for everyone else', and getting shouted at by the whole school. And now the governors are threatening to come in and knock their heads together if they don't play the game.

Oh, dear. Let us pray that the debate will not be framed in these playground terms. Let it be gracious and generous. But oh, let right prevail!

Such are the prayers of the Dean of Lindchester as she packs her case for synod; but that is what we have come to expect of the Very Revd Marion Randall. Though she has strong feelings on this issue, she remains doggedly courteous in the face of even the most outrageous misogyny. Well done, Mrs Dean! That said, Marion has no need to be obnoxious. She has a man to do that for her.

'What's this?' asked Marion.

'This, your deanship, is a magnum of Veuve Cliquot La Grande Dame rosé, nineteen-ninety. In case you have reason to celebrate on Monday. Or in case you don't. On the grounds that there is no situation in life which cannot be improved by a bottle of champagne.'

'Except possibly an AA meeting,' said Marion.

'Oh, tilly-vally! Even an AA meeting. These recovering alcoholics are such dull company. Here. Pop it in your case to share with your fellow top lady clerics on Monday night. You can get shit-faced, and lay bets about who gets to be bishop first.'

'Thank you, darling.' Marion hefted the bottle in one hand. 'But I'm not sure it'll fit. It's very big.'

'As the chauffeur said to the bishop.'

Marion levelled her headmistress stare at him.

'Still not funny?'

'Still not funny, Gene.'

'Oh.' He watched as she tried nestling the bottle among her clerical shirts. 'On another topic entirely, ought we to volunteer one of our many spare rooms to lodge the lovely Mr May?'

'No.'

'Just for the summer? I'll undertake to wield the riding crop if he misbehaves.'

'I dare say. But he'd drive me bananas. I question the wisdom of appointing him, frankly. But that's Giles's call, not mine.'

'Oh, he'll run off and join the opera before long, never fear.' Gene watched her futile packing efforts. 'May I make a tiny suggestion? If you turfed the pious paperwork out – which you won't find time to read – you'd have room for the fizz. However, I will leave you to weigh those priorities up for yourself, Deanissima.' He planted a kiss on her forehead and left.

Maybe I need a bigger case, thought Marion. Now *there's* a metaphor for my life. She was going to need a steamer trunk at least to accommodate the great burden of stuff she was going to end up carrying in the coming months. All the nonsense about who'll be the first woman bishop. Not to mention the CNC.

Could we really take that step? Appoint an openly gay bishop? Is Lindchester ready for that? Is the C of E ready for that? But perhaps those were the wrong questions. Maybe she ought to ask, 'If he performs best at interview later this month, how can we *not* appoint Guilden Hargreaves?'

Oh, Lord. The women bishops debate is just the knuckle-cracking before the real fight, isn't it? Marion evicts the paperwork and sticks the champagne in her case instead.

Chapter 14

hen it came to it, Father Wendy couldn't stand the tension, so she went for a walk. She was sitting on a bench beside the Linden when her phone buzzed late on Monday afternoon. A damselfly hung, then flickered away, then hung once more over the water's edge, like a strand of turquoise electricity. Wendy fondled Pedro's silky ears. The phone buzzed again.

'That'll be Doug texting me the results, Pedro. Is it "Yes" this time?'

It's already decided, she thought. And I'm still sitting here, suspended in a bubble of not knowing.

'This is Schrödinger's text message, Pedro! Until I check, it's both "Yes" and "No", isn't it?'

As usual, Pedro had nothing to contribute to Wendy's philosophical musings. He was focused on the rushes, and the rustling there that seemed to promise a water rat, or a coot; something to chase.

'Well, let's find out, shall we?' Her hands were trembling.

'YES. Passed in all 3 houses. So pleased for you darling. xx'

The message wavers. Twenty-two years since synod voted in favour of women priests. She texts 'Thnx. Bless you xx' and puts her phone away.

'I watched that vote on TV,' she told Pedro. 'Well, half watched it.'

November. Her sitting room was the high seas. Three kids under five. How endless those afternoons seemed, waiting for Doug to come in and take over the childcare, so she could snatch some sermon preparation time! Little Laura, sitting round-eyed in a cardboard box on the big blue blanket. Wendy still has a photo, with the bulky old TV on in the background, broadcasting church history in the making. Her two little boys in their pirate hats and eye-patches, rowing their box galleons with plastic tennis rackets and wooden spoons across the powder blue main.

Ahoy, ahoy! Why are you crying, Mummy?

It's happy tears, because it's good news. Mummy can be a vicar now.

I don't want you to be a vicar, I want you to stay Mummy!

Oh, don't worry, I will never stop being your Mummy.

That's what she told them. Oh, dear. If Lulu were still alive, she'd be crying with me, thought Wendy. She wiped her eyes and reached down to stroke Pedro.

'But here we both are, boy.'

And if Laura were still here, I'd be texting her to say 'Hooray!' Reminding her of the vote she was too little to remember. A short lifetime ago. Maybe Wendy should take a selfie? Then she'd have a photo of this moment to go alongside the other. If I could time-travel, I would go back with this picture and show it to that hassled young deacon, run ragged by small children and parish duties. Look, look at this plump, white-haired woman, late fifties now, sitting on a bench with her three-legged rescue dog. Do you recognize her? What would you do differently, if you could have known this was what lay ahead?

What would we all have done differently? Was that the golden era – the wall down, apartheid ending, the towers still standing – and we blinked and missed it? Or is this the golden era? The wall dividing men from women broken down, and (despite the prophets of doom) the poor old Church of England still standing. Ah, let every moment be golden! Every moment that we still have left.

Father Wendy got to her feet. 'Come along then, Pedro.'

A swan glided by with five big, scruffy, fluffy cygnets. Pedro leaned stealthily on his harness, to test Wendy's reactions. She laughed. 'Well, unless you can walk on water, I don't rate your chances, boy.'

They made their way back along the riverbank, both limping, Pedro on his three legs, Wendy on her dodgy knees. 'Oof! What a couple of old crocks we are!' And because there was nobody about, Wendy began to sing:

> O Jesus, ever with us stay,
> Make all our moments calm and bright.

All along the water's edge damselfly filaments zizzed in the sun as though already arcing with holy light.

You may have been there at synod for the announcement, or perhaps you were among those following the debate on Twitter. (Oh, that heart-thumping hiatus when everyone was #praying!) Most of you will have seen the news coverage. The eagle-eyed may even have spotted the Very Revd Marion Randall in the background of one of the interviews, celebrating with her fellow top lady clerics –

something she later regretted, because it looked a bit gloaty. (And because Gene caught her on national TV pouring unchilled Veuve Cliquot La Grande Dame rosé 1990 into plastic tumblers.)

The cathedral precentor followed the synod debate. His loyal wife was beside him, to cheer loudly (from the diaphragm) a second great victory in as many days. She took the opportunity to remind him that the Lutheran Church in Germany had appointed its first woman bishop back in 1992, which meant that in ecclesiastical terms, as in all matters footballing (and let's face it, in just about *everything*), Germany ruled. YESS!!

He evicted her from his study on the grounds that he had intercessions to write for evensong. She left. Then she stuck her head back round the door to add: 'And I can't believe we *still* don't have girl choristers here in Lindchester! What the bloody heck is going on, you load of sodding dinosaurs? Sort it out, please!' She closed the door, then burst back in abruptly to check that Giles was not doing a Nazi salute.

The idea! Brr! Giles regarded her blandly, and pushed his glasses back up the bridge of his nose with his middle finger.

How will the news of women bishops be received across the Diocese of Lindchester? In general, with bemusement and vague good will; for in general they are not practising Anglicans, and don't really care that much. It is hard for me to bear this in mind, viewing the world as I do through my stained-glass spectacles.

People under the age of thirty would doubtless greet the news with a 'Well, durr.' Of course women can be bishops. What's your problem, exactly? Older Lindcastrians, who have some nostalgic memory of traditional churchgoing and an all-male priesthood, may wonder with a pang where this modernizing will end. God forbid we should rip the pews out of the church they never attend! Can't the dear old place stay the same as it's always been, so they can go on singing 'Morning has broken' and 'Lord of all hopefulness' whenever they turn up? Obviously, women should be allowed to become bishops. Except . . .

It's tricky to articulate this tiny snag of resistance out loud. But won't the mystique go out of things if someone like your mum, your sister, like a girl you were at college with, becomes a bishop? Think of the captain of a large ship in dress uniform – doesn't masculinity still add a *je ne sais quoi* to the image that would be fatally undermined by, well, bosoms?

In that world-within-a-world which is the C of E, how will the news be received? The Diocese of Lindchester is a moderate place, a landscape of gentle fields and hills, seldom very high, or very low. It has its Evangelicals, but they are of an open and charismatic kind. It has its Catholics, but we know Father Dominic, don't we? He likes women. It seems to him that the Virgin Mary had a priestly role in being the god-bearer.

The Diocese of Lindchester lacks mighty bastions of GAFCON-flavoured Conservative Evangelicalism; it lacks spiky high parishes wobbling on the brink of the ordinariate. Opposition to women bishops exists, but it is not concentrated, it is not militant and organized. There are members of the Prayer Book Society, but they are not armed and dangerous (think of them as the Anglican wing of the Sealed Knot). Witness the reaction to Dean Marion's appointment a few years back. A lot of people were not happy. Some left the cathedral, others stayed away on the Sundays when she was presiding. There are a handful of conservative priests who still do not recognize her authority, and refuse to turn up at the Maundy Thursday Chrism service in the cathedral, despite the episcopal three-line whip (i.e. 'I will be jolly, jolly, jolly annoyed if you don't come'). The Choristers' School chaplain famously swept out to another job ('Goodbye, Father! Don't forget to write!'). But overall, people have come round to the idea. In fact, the good folk of the diocese rather wish that Bishop Paul could have hung on another year, then Lindchester would be in the running to be the diocese with the first woman bishop.

Does this give us grounds to suppose they would welcome Guilden Hargreaves as their bishop? I honestly do not know the answer to that. The CNC will be interviewing the shortlisted candidates on Monday and Tuesday of next week. This means we can look for an official Downing Street announcement in, ooh, about four or five months.

Bishop Bob is rejoicing quietly about the vote as he gets on the train home from York. He sleeps on the journey, poor man. If someone hadn't woken him at Manchester to change trains, I fear he would have slept all the way to Liverpool. The burdens of high office take their toll. Not long now till he's on holiday, though. Obedient to his wife, he's made a doctor's appointment for early next week. The biggest shadow left on the horizon before France is that horrible conversation he must have with the vicar of Gayden Magna on Friday morning. Oh, Lord! Bob respects Ed, and his heart bleeds for him. If he could, he would bless his marriage in a second; but what about the unity of the Church, the concerns of the wider Anglican Communion? The pain and tension here are truly heartbreaking.

Neil cuffs him. 'Oh, *what*? It's not like you're having to do anything! *I'm* doing it all.'

'Sorry. Things on my mind today.'

'Right, like what?' There's a pause. 'Feck. That's today? The bollocking's today? Ah shit.' He bumps his head against Ed's shoulder. 'Sorry, big man. Totally forgot. When do you have to set off?'

Another pause. 'He's coming here, remember?'

'He is? The bishop's coming *here*?' Neil snatched the mug out of Ed's hand and clattered it into the dishwasher. 'Look at the floor! Where's the mop?'

'Stop it! The floor is *immaculate*! Idiot.'

'Yes, well. And *why* is he coming here, I should like to know?'

Ed draws breath. At *your* insistence. Make the buggers come to you. I won't have you summoned to the head's office like a naughty wee schoolboy. 'Well, never mind, he is. He'll be here in any minute.'

'Good.' Neil folds his arms. 'I want to be there.'

'No.'

'Yes. Hell, yes! If he's going to pass judgement on my "lifestyle", I want to be there.'

Ed meets the mental blue-eyed glare. Sparks spike from his fiancé's hair, pure electric rage glints off diamond ear studs. O-o-o-Kay. Not this battle, then. 'Fine. But I need you to be polite, and let me do the talking. Promise? Don't pick a fight.'

'Pick a fight? Who's picking a fight? They're the ones picking a fight! With their fecking "clergy discipline"!' He stabbed each word into Ed's chest with a finger. 'And you can go and iron that shirt properly, it's a disgrace.'

'See? This is why I don't want you in the room! You're picking a fight with me, now! Oh God, he's here. Just behave, OK?'

Ed brought Bishop Bob through to the kitchen for a glass of water.

'This is my fiancé, Neil,' he said. 'He'd like to join us, if that's OK with you, Bishop.'

'Of course. I'm glad you're here, Neil.' Ed passed him the glass. The bishop half-raised a hand. 'I'm so sorry. I need to . . . sit. Sorry . . .'

I'm glad Neil was there, too. I'm glad that when he was a boy he was packed off to Boys' Brigade, where, aged eleven, he took a first aid course.

How it all came back to him, who knew? But Neil was there in that church hall again, kneeling on the dusty wooden floor with the dummy. Lads all sniggering, 'Gi'e him a snog, Fergy!' St John Ambulance man, big, red hair gone grey. Check the airways. Feel for

117

a pulse. No heartbeat? Don't worry if you break a couple of ribs. Put your back into it, laddie! Aye, that's it.

Sure and stedfast. Sure and stedfast. That was the motto.

Aye, he was a goner, the bishop. But Neil kept on. Sure and stedfast, sure and stedfast.

> Will your anchor hold in the storms of life,
> When the clouds unfold their wings of strife?
> When the strong tides lift, and the cables strain,
> Will your anchor drift or firm remain?

Neil could hear the old BB hymn pounding as he pounded and prayed and pounded and prayed, until at last the paramedics were there and took over, and the bishop was driven away in the silent ambulance, blue lights licking round, across the gentle landscape of Lindfordshire.

AUGUST

Chapter 15

I t's late July in Lindfordshire and there's willowherb like pink smoke over railway embankments and beside canals. Holidaymakers in striped Breton shirts steer narrow boats under humpbacked bridges, where naughty children pelt them with unripe crab apples. The wheat fields are edged with poppies frail as Bible pages. Look – cabbage white and tortoiseshell. Brimstone, red admiral, peacock. All the butterflies of childhood, as if we've opened our old copy of *What to Look for in Summer*, and out they all fluttered.

The train to London clatters past the cooling towers of Cardingforth. Along the river orange and turquoise damselflies still glint. A monstrous dragonfly copters past; then a pair of them manoeuvre in formation, up, up, round, loop the loop, whisking away quicker than the eye can follow. Midges yoyo in clouds above the rushes.

Stand still in any wooded place and you will hear a single bird call, *tweep, tweep*. No carolling now, that's all done with, apart from thin bursts of wren song, like the tiniest of organ pipes played by furtive virtuosos. Listen. Somewhere a bird knocks, knocks. A nuthatch, perhaps, or a woodpecker? How still it all is. Waiting. The landscape gathers itself for harvest, plumping up, dozing. Sheep graze the white clover fields beside the Linden, where mirror trees quiver in the water. They fragment as the wind picks up and rushes in the willows like a downpour. And then the silence creeps back.

I will not toy with you any longer, reader. The good bishop is now recuperating after heart bypass surgery. He owes his life to the NHS and, indirectly, the Boys' Brigade. Were it not for the prompt and vigorous action of Neil Ferguson, Bishop Bob would have died on the quarry-tiled floor of the vicarage of Gayden Magna.

Janet Hooty, being a medical woman, knows a thing or two about your survival chances if you go into cardiac arrest when there's no defibrillator handy. I doubt a day will go past without her offering a prayer of gratitude for Neil. If she were Susanna Henderson, she would have baked Neil a lavish (artery-clogging) cake of some kind. Instead, she had an orchid in a mauve pot sent to the vicarage. An orchid in a mauve pot! But, no, Neil would not have a *word* said against it, despite his well-documented scorn of orchids encountered outside rainforests or the lobbies of exclusive boutique hotels.

More interestingly, Neil will not hear a word said against Bishop Bob now, either. Neil, whose contempt of Anglican bishops was so scathing, his rage so molten! Because it was all *his* fault that poor old Bob had a heart attack. Dragging him all the way out to Gayden Magna on a hot day, stressing him out by putting him in an intolerable position! Fracturing his sternum!

'Yes, and saving his life!' said Ed, who for once felt like rapping on his fiancé's forehead to emphasize his point. 'Why are you blaming yourself? Why not blame the C of E for putting him in an intolerable position?'

'Yes, well, and *why* haven't you been to visit him? Go visit him,' Neil ordered. 'I'll buy some flowers. Dark calla lilies. No, too funereal. I know, spray roses! Those green-tinged ones? You know the ones – what are they called? Anyway, them. And— Oh, what? Of course you can take flowers! What do you mean, you're not allowed to take flowers? Everyone takes flowers to hospital! Really? Fascists. Well, chocolates then. Wait, no, should you eat chocolate after a heart attack? Dark chocolate, that's got antioxidants in, that's healthy. So, some nice single origin seventy per cent cocoa . . . Wait! Will it need to be Fair Trade? Is he one of those? Better get grapes instead. Please tell me they've not banned grapes? Oh, and he's probably only got that nasty antibacterial NHS sheep dip, so I'm thinking maybe some nice toiletries? Aye. We'll make him up a wee hospital survival kit, and you can take it. No, I'm not going. I'm allergic to hospitals.'

Ed knew better than to try and check Neil. He was in 'it's got to be perfect' mode. Any attempt to remonstrate would trigger escalation, and then the hospital visit would resemble the arrival of the Queen of Sheba, with camel trains of hand-polished organic grapes and Nubian aromatherapy masseurs laden with oil of pure nard.

'Well? Don't just stand there. What do you think?'

'I think I love you,' said Ed.

'Och, stop that. What should we get him? I don't know anything about bishops, for fuck's sake. Help me here! I want to do the right thing.'

'Just a get well card. That would be the right thing.'

Neil sagged against him. 'Really?'

'Truly.' He wrapped his arms round Neil, and they stood there in silence for a while. 'John Knox giving you a hard time again?'

'That fecker. I save someone's life and now I feel like a bad person! What's that all about?' Neil wiped his eyes. 'Och, well. I'll get him a card, then. Or I could design him one.'

'He'd like that.'

'Should it have a religious theme?' worried Neil. 'How should I sign it? Kind regards? No, *warmest* regards? Is that better? Warmest regards?' Cheered by the fresh vistas of complication opening out in front of him, Neil hurried to his computer.

The days pass, and now it is August. BACK TO SCHOOL! We are in that brief retailing window between beachwear reductions and Halloween masks. Back to school? Half of us haven't even been on holiday yet! There will be a reward for those still waiting for their two weeks in Portugal: the nice weather here seems to have vanished. They will be able to enjoy the treat of coming home and complaining that the temperatures were in the thirties. What is the point of going somewhere hot and returning to find there's been a heatwave in the UK in your absence, all your neighbours are tanned, and your hanging baskets dead? To the English, a holiday without meteorological gloating is no holiday at all.

Bishop Bob is out of hospital now. The Hootys will not be spending two weeks in Brittany after all. Bob sits in the lounge (his study is off limits to him), gazes over the garden, and thinks of how he'd longed for that holiday. If I can just make it through till August, then I'll be able to slump, he'd kept telling himself. Back then, back in his old life. This is how he thinks of it: before, after. Old life, new life. Like his Evangelical brothers and sisters giving their testimony. Everything has changed. His former life looks misty to him now, especially the last weeks before his heart attack. He has no real recollection of that visit to Gayden Magna, cannot even picture the man who saved his life. He did not go down a long tunnel and find Jesus waiting for him. He did not reluctantly agree to return, because his work here was not yet done. All he has is a few vague memories, blurred sepia shots. He has no energy to put them in the right order and they are fading fast.

I was dead, but now I'm alive. I'm saved. Born again.

He trembles with gratitude for everything he once took for granted: the steady miracle of pulse, the fleshware the mind rides on. He has been cracked open like a pistachio. His heart has been rebooted and mended. A wild bird roosts in his ribcage. One day it will take flight for good. But for now, for now, it roosts in him. He places his hand on his chest. Welcome, dear guest. He feels the staples through his shirt. Thank you. For every new breath. For creation, preservation, all the blessings of this life. He rolls on a wave of sleep. It's a dove he's nursing, plump breast under his fingers. It broods over him, spirit, breath, wind, over the chaos . . . Blessings. All the blessings.

Janet comes in to check whether he needs anything. Sees him slumped in his chair! She speeds to his side, bends over him to check that he is still breathing, the way she hung over the children's cots all those years ago. She holds her own breath, waits. Yes, he's still here, you dope. She breathes out. Her eyes brim with tears and she sits on the sofa to watch him, just to watch him while he dozes. Cots in dim rooms, animal mobiles circling, Brahms Lullaby tinkling slowly, more slowly, into silence. Keeping watch after the nightmare was over. There, there. Everything's all right.

The lounge is full of flowers and cards. Outside the soft rain falls. A mother blackbird runs across the patio. Stops. Checks all round. Runs on. Janet hears the flap of the letter box. Envelopes skim on to the hall floor, but she makes no move. Rain taps. Before long he will wake and give her a sweet smile. Until then, she will watch.

But who is watching over the Diocese of Lindchester? Is our poor friend the archdeacon lamenting, like the prophet Elijah, that he alone is left? My readers will be relieved to hear that the Archbishop of York has heard the cry of his people (as articulated by the diocesan HR manager, Helene) and has sent aid. If you go on the diocesan website you will see that there is now an acting bishop of Lindchester, appointed for twelve months, or until a new bishop arrives, whichever is sooner.

Am I alone in being amused by the term 'acting bishop'? To me it conjures up the image of His Right Reverence doing voice exercises in the vestry and accidentally including his agent in the General Thanksgiving. Check out the diocesan website, and you'll find a picture of the acting bishop, the Rt Revd Harry Preece, sitting at a desk in the office, with Penelope handing him a mug of Fair Trade coffee in a Lindchester Cathedral mug. Martin is in the photo too. *Not* in the photo is Freddie May, although he was present in the office. (The diocesan communications officer was not prepared to pixilate his T-shirt.)

Bishop Harry, you will learn, took early retirement from his suffragan bishop's role earlier this year, when a handful of small dioceses were merged into one super-diocese, and they ended up with more bishops than they knew what to do with. Harry is married to

Isobel, 'who is also ordained'. The couple have two teenage daughters. Harry looks like a fairly ordinary bloke in the picture. He has a nice smile. Are we going to like him here in the Diocese of Lindchester? A quick Google search outs him as another Evangelical, which in cathedral circles means he's guilty of being a prat until proved innocent. We shall, of course, reserve judgement; but, wincingly, as though we can already hear the strains of Slane in four/four playing in the background.

Everyone is curious about this incomer. Quite right. Curiosity may account for the massive turnout at the service to commemorate the centenary of the outbreak of the First World War. Afterwards the cathedral floodlights, and all the old-fashioned Narnian lamps round the Close, were turned out and the congregation departed in darkness and subdued silence. The cathedral Chapter verdict was that Bishop Harry acquitted himself well; that is, he did exactly what the precentor told him. Nor did he commit that most heinous of Evangelical crimes: interlarding the liturgy with helpful little explanations.

But that is enough of Bishop Harry for the time being. He will be around for several months, so we will have ample opportunity to get to know him and scorn his taste in music and wine, and lament afresh the ghastly protestantizing of the C of E – without which, frankly, there would *be* no C of E, but no matter. At present all I wish to say is that Captain Harry will be at the helm of the good ship Lindchester until the new bishop arrives.

Any news on that front? Or failing that, any rumours? The CNC met back in June. Surely by now *someone* will have tipped a tiny wink? Someone will have said, 'I'm afraid I can't comment,' in answer to the question, 'Is it X?'; which any Anglican worth their salt will know is code for, 'Yes, but you didn't hear it from me.'

I am sorry to disappoint you. There is no news. There are rumours, of course, and these may be plotted somewhere along the spectrum between 'informed deduction' and 'wild speculation'. Close to the latter end was the rumour going round a week ago that the archdeacon had got the job. He knocked that idea on the head so firmly that nobody believes it any longer – apart from those cynics who will always detect a tacit admission lurking in a categorical denial. Let them have their fun.

I can assure you it is not Matt, but further than this I cannot go. My lips are sealed; as sealed as though I were a member of the CNC. All I can tell you is that a common mind was reached and one of the candidates has been chosen. He – yes, it must be a he until the legislation has passed through parliament allowing the C of E to appoint women bishops – must now submit to a medical and obtain a fresh DBS check. His name may then go forward to Her Majesty, who is currently at Balmoral, and when in Scotland she must make like a Presbyterian, and refuse to believe in the phenomenon of bishops.

Once the Queen is back, an announcement can be made. You might think it will then be done and dusted – but not so hasty, if you please! A series of letters couched in gracious archaisms laced with medieval menace must be issued. Marion, as Dean of Lindchester, will be instructed to summon the College of Canons for the purpose of electing a new bishop to the See of Lindchester, made vacant by the resignation of our beloved in Christ, right trusty and well-beloved Paul Henderson &c &c. Hot on the heels of this epistle comes another saying: 'Oh, and by the way, here's who you have to elect.' Then comes the Confirmation of Election. Once all these hoops have been jumped through in the proper stately manner by a bewigged gentleman in sparkly-buckled shoes, there can be a formal announcement of when the enthronement service will take place.

In the meantime we must watch and pray. As the announcement approaches more and more people will quietly be admitted into the knowledge of who is to be the next bishop. This will greatly enhance the possibility of the news being leaked. For now, the members of the CNC are keeping schtum. So unless somebody hacks into one of their email accounts – and who would do a thing like that? – the secret is safe.

Gene would not *dream* of snooping around in the dean's inbox. He is not above trying to sneak a read over her shoulder, however. We will join them for his latest attempt, which was on Saturday night.

'How was your Day of Rage?'

'Oh, all right, thanks.'

'Day of Rage! It's never really going to be a Day of Rage in a cathedral city, is it? It's more "A Day of Being Jolly Cross about Gaza". How many turned up?'

'It was in Lindford not Lindchester, actually. We were about a hundred.'

'How thrilling! Any *foreign* people?' He slid round behind her and began solicitously to massage her shoulders.

The dean sighed and closed her email. 'There's no point even trying, Gene.'

'I have no idea what you're talking about. So what did you chant in your rage?'

'Never mind. It all sounds silly out of context.' She hesitated. 'Darling, you will confine this kind of cynicism to me, won't you?'

He bent down and kissed the top of her head. 'It is for your ears only, Deanissima.'

'Good. Because otherwise folk will get upset, and then I will have to defend you by revealing your heroic anti-apartheid past.'

'Fie! You would destroy my reputation as a heartless sybarite? Just as well I've got a dozen oysters and an exceptionally good 2010 Meursault in the fridge. What say we get pissed?'

'Nice idea. Let me finish my sermon first. But even pissed I won't be telling you who the next bishop is.'

'Curses!'

Our good friend Father Dominic was among those marching through Lindford. I'm afraid he allowed himself to get distracted from Rage by something less noble. He found it almost impossible to join in with the chants 'Two, four, six, eight, Israel is an apartheid state!' while the megaphone was being wielded by the Revd Dr Veronica da Silva.

'Oh, Father Dominic,' she gushed when it was over, 'it means so much to me that you were able to join us!'

Join you? Fuck off, he told her back in its black chaplain hoodie as she got into her silver Skoda.

I'm allergic to her, he thinks when he's back in his study. I can't bear to be within twenty feet of her. He shakes his head. Lord have mercy.

The archdeacon was not on the march. He was spending a day with his lady. They parted with a certain coolness when he declined to spend the night over at hers. Had to ration his visits and be discreet. If she was fed up with that, she knew what she could do. He was therefore alone when he got in and flipped through his post.

Just as well. Not every day you got asked to apply for a suffragan bishop's job at the other end of the country.

127

Chapter 16

I t feels like autumn. It's August, but it feels like autumn. The tail end of ex-hurricane Bertha lashes Great Britain. The Linden rises. Red triangles appear in country roads saying 'Flood'. In the Diocese of Lindchester, clouds hide the supermoon. The Perseids shower away out of sight and the International Space Station goes by like a silent star, unseen.

I am not fond of August, personally. Lassitude is laced with dread as the new academic year looms. On the whole, not much happens in church circles. Brand-new curates bomb about their parish like bluebottles banging into windows. 'Help! Where am I? What am I meant to be doing again?' In time they will learn that this is normal for August. Clergy with any sense do not waste annual leave by going away now, because (*ssh!*) you can be *semi* on holiday at home. Unless you are an Evangelical, of course. The higher your doctrine of grace, the greater the drivenness of your works.

The cathedral choir is still on vacation. Visiting choirs come and go. Some of them camp out in the Choristers' School and get in touch with their boyhood experience, though without the cod-liver oil and corporal punishment. The presiding canon thanks them each week for their 'invaluable contribution to our worship'. Last Sunday the canon chancellor was heard thanking them 'for leaving our worship', but he denies this slip.

August would normally allow hours of excited speculation for anyone shortlisted for a suffragan bishop's job. Our friend the archdeacon does not have that luxury. Acting Bishop Harry has not been here long enough to have made a significant difference to Matt's workload. In any case, excited speculation is best shared with another person. And call Matt a coward, but he hasn't dared broach this new development with Jane. Trying to get his own head round the implications first. Plus there's no guarantee he'll get the job, so no point frightening the horses at this stage. Then again, he can picture her face when he finally has to admit he's been keeping her in the dark for weeks. So: not fair to keep her in the dark, or not fair to worry her unnecessarily?

No need to decide yea or nay yet. He 'updates his paperwork'. Tarts up the old CV, hones his personal statement. Sends the lot off. No time to worry about it during the day, but the minute the old head hits the pillow he can't chuffing sleep for thinking about it. How will it play out? Does he really want the job? Is he effectively going to end up choosing between the job and his Jane?

Yes, but what if the boot was on the other foot, and *she* got offered a promotion in the back end of beyond? He'd want her to go for it; not be held back by the thought of him. Then he'd move heaven and earth to get a job in her neck of the woods. Course he would. But is she going to think the same way? Oh Lord, if only they could get married, how much simpler it would all feel!

Which gets his pulse up. Still not squared the old domestic situation with his conscience and the good Lord. Helene's warning rings in his ears, if he's honest. *Do you have any enemies, Matt?* It's no way to live, is it? Wondering when you're going to be exposed? Because essentially, he's pretty much a hypocrite. Publicly upholding the Church line on gay priests, yet secretly living – to use the good old-fashioned phrase – 'in sin'.

Nope. No good. Matt gets up and plays a few games of Spider Solitaire to unwind. Then seeing as he's up, he may as well whizz through a few work emails. Next time he looks it's 3 a.m. and he really should get some sleep! But now his head's buzzing with naughty priests and dangerous tombstones and all that malarkey. Which is why he finds himself doing his tax at 4 a.m. Horrible. He'd drive over to Janey's and blurt out the whole sorry business. Except she's off in France with Father Dominic. Got fed up with kicking her heels waiting around for him to clear a bit of holiday space.

And who can blame her?

Can he wangle a couple of days when she's back? Surely! He looks again at his diary. Chocka. The archdeacon sinks his head into his hands. Lord, get Her Maj back from Balmoral, and let's crack on with the appointment of the new bishop, pronto.

If he weren't such a big tough bloke, he'd be saying, I'm not really coping here, am I?

Our archdeacon is not the only one battling with dread. If we could invent an anxiety-detecting device, and fly by night across the Diocese of Lindchester on our fictional wings, we would pick up hotspots in every second household. See those splashes of fiery red throbbing in bedrooms on the third Wednesday of August? School children waiting for A and AS level results. They believe their futures hang in the balance. And those blotches nearby are the anguish of their ever-loving parents. By tomorrow evening the worst will be over until the following week, when our device will register spikes of GCSE dread blipping across the region.

Ulli, the precentor's wife, makes her penultimate grim trip to school on results day (parking at the required distance for embarrassing parents). Felix is collecting his AS level results. They will be terrible, because he has farted about all year, and Ulli has yet again failed to beat him about the head with a spätzle-maker and *force* him do his coursework properly, like a good mother. For someone so bossy, it's amazing how lax she has been. Sometimes she just doesn't understand herself.

Here he comes now. With a long face. *Ach Gott!* He really has failed them all! He climbs in and pulls his hood up and hides. She snatches the sheets of paper. *Scheisse!* Her eyes hunt through. Different exams, different exam boards.

Then he laughs. 'Fooled ya!'

The grades spring into focus: A, A*, A, A.

A perverse rage seizes her. She swats him with the crumpled-up pages. 'If you only *worked*, you'd get straight A stars! You'd get into Cambridge, even!'

'What?! First off, Mother, fuck Cambridge, I'm going to drama school, and secondly, hello? What happened to "well done, Felix"?'

She claps a hand to her mouth. 'Well done, darling! Brilliant! I'm so sorry. I didn't mean – forget I said that, *ja*?'

Get in! he thinks. She'll probably pay for my trip to Ibiza now, ha ha!

Ah, *das wohltemperierte Mutterklavier*! Played here with the virtuosic skill only a last-born son can master.

Exams are not even a wrinkle on the brow of Mr Happy junior. It is a long time since we last glimpsed him, a squalling scrap draped over his dad's shoulder. Reader, I have been remiss. He is now mobile. Has been for ages. Oh yes, indeed. After many an important agenda and Bible commentary was annotated in yogurt, the chancellor finally worked out a formula for calculating how high a toddler can reach: X plus six inches (where X equals how far you *think* they can reach).

We join them now on the cathedral lawn, where Master Happy is toddling round the labyrinth that Gavin the verger mowed earlier in the year. There are those who are inclined to disparage the Lindchester Cathedral labyrinth as 'a complete disgrace'. True, the unmown parts are now tall and shaggy. When it rains, the purple seed heads lie prostrate like an infinity of despairing bishops. The Chartres beauty of the maze is difficult to discern, except (sermon illustration klaxon!) from high above on the tower, when the incomprehensible mess emerges into perfect sense. Emails of complaint have been sent to the dean. I will not trouble the reader with Gene's drafted reply.

Master Happy remains a stout labyrinth fan. He insists on visiting it every day. Come and watch him now, as he trundles round its curves, cornering occasionally on two wheels. The chancellor looks on. Anyone watching the Revd Canon Dr Mark Lawson's face at this moment would be puzzled to explain his reputation for irascibility. See how he melts in a syrup of paternal doting? He's on childcare duty so that his poor wife Miriam gets a rest. Yes, she's expecting again. Argh! Just when they were all emerging into post-partum normality, and Junior is showing signs of becoming an interesting conversation partner. Oh, well.

Junior— Stop. *Junior?* Does he not have a name? Of course he does! This is young Chad William Lawson. He stops in his tracks. 'Wabwin!'

'Yes, it *is* a labyrinth. Clever boy.'

Chad William points up at the sky, beside himself with excitement, and shouts, 'Am-nair!'

His dad looks. 'Yes, there's an aeroplane! Clever boy.'

The chancellor has been granted the interpretation of tongues. Nobody else has a clue what young Chad William is on about.

He points again, like Adam in the garden naming everything for the first time: 'Yagy!'

The chancellor turns. Her! Fuck, she's early! 'Oh, hi there!'

It is the artist, come to take down the *Souls and Bodies* exhibition.

'YAGY!' insists Chad William, astounded to receive no fatherly approbation.

For a second the chancellor is torn between applauding his son and appeasing the artist, who will surely object to being called a lady.

She looks at Chad William.

He stares back solemnly. He points at her nose: 'Zat?' he enquires.

'This?' She points at her nose too. 'Nose stud.'

'Notud.'

A smile dawns on her face, then vanishes. Like sunshine crossing a dour Welsh hillside, or the back parts of R. S. Thomas's absent god passing by. Her own baby is six foot four and twenty years old these days.

'Clever boy,' she says.

By the end of the day, the canvases are suitably cushioned in bubble wrap and stowed in the hired van. Freddie May was summoned to help carry the 'sold' work across to the palace where it will be stored until the purchasers collect it. Would he help? Hell, yeah! (To his disappointment the Flirty Vicar Alert proved groundless: the artist was alone.)

I dare say my readers are curious to know how Martin is getting on with his lodger. Very well, thank you. Martin was rather buoyed up by being appointed to the BLO job. This has not been announced yet, but he has a spring in his step again, I'm pleased to say. He is still a bit flinchy in Freddie's presence, mind you. It's as though he has invited a big cat into his home. A friendly one, but anarchic, like the tiger who wreaked such havoc when he came to tea, in the bedtime book Martin's girls used to love.

The girls are on holiday in Portugal with their mother, so it's just Martin and Freddie. They don't see that much of one another, however. Freddie is out most evenings (Martin makes no enquiries). During the day Freddie works in the bishop's office if he's not off doing gardening jobs or casual labouring for the Choristers' School maintenance team.

Out of sheer nosiness we will join them in Martin's car on the way to the Close. The tyres splosh through puddles. There will be no gardening today.

'Omigod, I am totally *in love* with Bishop Harry! Shame he's married to death.'

No response suggested itself to Martin. For a moment, the events of a year ago tainted every possible avenue of conversation.

'Oh, been meaning to say, Marty, I appreciate how you trust me?'

'Well, good.'

'Coz the Hendersons – don't get me wrong, love those guys to bits – but the minute I arrived they were all, here's the House Rules? Seriously, they had this actual fucking list? Yeah, whatever, guys, your house, your rules. Except, wahey! Got a rule against skateboarding in the kitchen? No? Got a rule against answering the door in my underpants? So my whole time there, The List is getting longer and longer? But in my head I'm, why are you even doing this? These totally nice people have taken you in, why do you have to be such a tool?' He fell silent. 'Yeah. So, basically, awesome? I totally did not think you'd be this relaxed. Thanks, man.' He reached over and squeezed Martin's knee.

'You're welcome.' Martin's knuckles were white on the wheel.

'Hey, look! A fair! We could go to the fair!'

Martin drove resolutely past the fair. He could still feel a phantom hand on his knee. The car was full of Freddie. Bursting with Freddie. He knew he would be able to smell his aftershave in here for days.

'Listen, Marty, you would like, *tell* me if I was doing your head in? Coz probably I won't notice unless you say something.'

Martin inhaled deeply. He rehearsed the formula he'd learned at family therapy. When you do *that*, it makes me feel *this*. 'Well, there's one thing. It's just, for example, when Harry arrived, that T-shirt you wore—'

'Gah! My bad. I should totally not have—'

'—it makes me feel—'

'—worn it, coz I know you don't approve?'

They stopped talking over one another. There was a silence.

'So yeah,' concluded Freddie. 'Sorry.'

Martin tried to relax his hands on the wheel. 'It's not that I don't approve. It's more, it made me feel how I felt last year, when—'

'Na-a-w! Last year was last year, yeah? We've both moved on.'

'It just makes me feel that you're attention-seeking. Being deliberately provocative. That's all I'm saying. Sorry. But you wanted to know if there was anything . . . Sorry.'

'Yeah, I meant, like leaving towels on the floor?' He slumped down in the seat and put his headphones on. 'Jeez.'

Out of the corner of his eye Martin could see Freddie's leg jiggling. Well, he'd misjudged *that*, hadn't he? But hang on, was he responsible for Freddie's reactions?

They drove the rest of the way in ghastly silence, apart from the music leaking from the headphones. Martin parked on the gravel drive of the palace. Freddie disentangled himself from his technology. Still not talking.

'Look, I'm sorry if I hurt your feelings, but—' Martin stopped aghast. 'What's wrong?'

'I'm lonely.'

'But you have lots of friends! You're out every night!'

Freddie shook his head. Wiped his face on his sleeve. 'Dude, I'm so fucking *lonely*.'

Martin felt tears rush up. 'Freddie!' He reached out a hand and nearly touched him. 'I'm really sorry to hear that. I'm sure it's only temporary. People love you. You're always so popular.'

'Nah. Everyone's hey, cute dog! I wanna stroke the cute dog! But nobody's like, y'know? Wants me? Gah. Sorry.' He sniffed. 'Got a tissue? Thanks. 'Kay, let's go.' He got out of the car and crunched off across the gravel.

Martin followed. 'Look. We could go to the fair after work. If you want.'

Freddie spun round. 'Seriously? Aw, sweet man! We should totally do that? Yeah.'

He's just a little boy inside, thought Martin. How can I not have seen that before?

The days are drawing in now. It's getting dark by nine o'clock. Tonight, and for the rest of August, the floodlights will not shine on Lindchester Cathedral. Visitors to the Close will see instead a simple light installation projected on to the west front. It is red. It looks almost like a smiley face with only one eye. It's an Arabic letter 'N' for Nazarene. Sprayed on Christian doorways in northern Iraq, so that the angel of death will stop here, not pass over.

In windows all around the darkened Close, in vicarages and churches, in Christian homes across the diocese, across the nation, there are black posters with the same symbol. One by one the Twitter avatars are dimmed and replaced. We are all Ns. The cathedral shop sells candles with the N symbol. Pray. Pray. Pray. Give. Give. Give. The money saved by switching the floodlights off (£30 an hour) will be donated to relief work for fleeing Christians and other persecuted minorities.

The lamps are going out across the Levant, thinks Marion. It is nearly two in the morning and she can't sleep. She stands alone in the dark gazing at the symbol. A red brand of anguish. Jesu, mercy. The clouds part. A few stars glint. Somewhere a car alarm goes off. The cathedral clock chimes two.

Do they feel our prayers? Marion shivers. There's an autumn chill tonight. The clouds cover the few faint stars again. Is there a communion of saints, a web of souls? Are we all one? Is there a heaven? Is it right there, a hand's width away, a breath away, a parallel universe in another dimension? Are those terrified martyrs bursting through, even now, as the blade butchers them? Are they stumbling through and plunging into glory? Oh, catch them, please catch them all.

Footsteps in the distance. A figure passes under the shadowy lime trees. Another restless soul? Ah, it's Gene. He must have heard her leave the house.

He doesn't say anything, just comes and drapes a coat round her. She leans her head on his shoulder. He wraps her in his arms and they sway together, back and forth, gently, very gently, as she sobs bitterly in the dark.

Chapter 17

oldenrod droops in the unkempt vicarage gardens of Lindchester Diocese. Water cascades over clogged vicarage gutters. Oh, well. The diocesan housing officer's probably on holiday. And anyway, not much point him sending someone to clear the gutters now, when before long all the leaves will fall and it will need doing again. For the most part, clergy just shrug and put up with it. They know the diocese is strapped for cash, that there are probably more urgent repairs to attend to elsewhere. And so the old wooden fences wag and knock in their concrete posts when the wind blows. The kitchen sink doesn't drain properly. Cables snake from five-gang extension leads because there aren't enough sockets. But vicarage families live with it. One day their turn may come for a new kitchen, or sealed double-glazing units, and that will eat up the budget for three normal vicarages. So for now, water crashes from the blocked gutter. It's not as though they own the house, is it? No, or they'd make sure the job got done properly, rather than put up with the cowboys the diocese sends because their quote came in cheapest.

The gutters are not blocked in the vicarage at Gayden Magna, no siree. Neil gets them cleared twice a year and sends the bill to the diocese. The housing officer coughs up without a murmur. Please pretend I didn't tell you that, and hold fast to the belief that work done on Lindchester vicarages is governed by a strict and fair schedule of repairs, rather than a league table of how big a nightmare the clergy spouse is. But the squeaky wheel gets the grease even in the Church, I fear.

The Gayden Magna wedding is now officially postponed until the New Year. Neil can't bear the thought of distressing poor old Bishop Bob any further. No, not a word please. Bishop Bob is off limits. But the new bishop? Hah! The new bishop is going to get it with both great big gay barrels.

'Yes, but what if the new bishop's a nice guy too?' asks Ed. 'What if it's Guilden Hargreaves?'

'Who?'

'Guilden Hargreaves. You know. Principal of Barchester Theological College.'

'What, him with the big hair? Wait! Isn't his mother Perdy Hargreaves? Oh my God! Dame Perdy? So *he's* the new bishop! Does that mean you won't get defrocked for marrying, like the others?'

'Nobody's been defrocked. They've been disciplined, or had their permission to officiate revoked.'

'Whatever.' Neil swats this casuistry away. 'But Guilden will back you up, so excellent, about time! Let's invite him to the wedding.'

'Hold on, hold *on*, it's just a rumour. Rupert Anderson' – he pauses while Neil delivers an opinion on the archbishop – 'has just gone on record saying there's no reason why a gay priest—'

'Pff! We've heard *that* before.'

'Yes, but why would he emphasize it again now, if it's not a signal?'

'You know what, Eds? I have no idea. I have no *idea* what goes on in their heads. He's probably got some Brazilian boyfriend stashed away somewhere. Half of them have. The last guy was a closet queen.'

'We don't know that.'

'Oh, really? Talk to Roddy Fallon some time,' says Neil. 'Last summer he was *that* close to breaking the story, but then the fecking church Gestapo moved in and his source went to ground. Fine, don't believe me then. You carry on thinking if we all just pray and wring our hands the haters will go away.' He does his annoying knuckle-rap on Ed's forehead. 'Hello? You've got to *campaign* if you want anything to change. Roddy would do a feature on us in a heartbeat. Yeah, yeah, fine, I understand, Mr Nice Vicar. But for my money, it's time to stop being nice. Let's out those hypocrites who keep voting against equal marriage, I say.'

Ed sighs. 'I've got a funeral to take. Can you rant at me later?'

'What about that replacement bishop you've got?' Neil calls after him. 'Where does *he* stand?'

'Later.'

'Fine.'

Where does the replacement bishop stand? He's currently staying by himself in the vacant house in Vicars' Court (the one Freddie turned down). His teenage daughters are off at some dangerous charismatic festival, the damaging effects of which will manifest themselves later in extreme helpfulness round the house. There's no sign of a Brazilian boyfriend, but Harry Preece is a bit camp. We all know that doesn't necessarily mean anything. Camp doesn't equal gay. Freddie May is totally in love with him. Which doesn't mean anything either. Freddie May would fall for a saltwater crocodile if it smiled at him sweetly.

So, Harry Preece remains a bit of a puzzle. We need to solve the puzzle. Because how can we possibly know how to behave towards someone unless we know what they *are*? Are you male or female, posh or common, gay or straight, saved, not saved, one of us, not one of us? And in Anglican circles, we would also like to know where to place you on the churchmanship spectrum, so that we know whether we agree with you. Harry is from an Evangelical stable, but is he an *Open* Evangelical? If so, how open? Flung wide (*Accepting* Evangelical)? Or simply ajar (OK with civil partnerships provided there's no mincing)? We will not quite relax until we know where the bishop stands.

He does not on his dignity, anyway. Unlike Bishop Paul, Harry leaves the office door open. Every time Penelope or Martin tactfully close it for him, Harry opens it again. They have been forced to conclude that he wants it left that way.

It's Wednesday morning. Martin has just made a big cafetière of Fair Trade coffee and is checking on his Swiss Railway watch to see if it's ready to plunge. Uh-oh. Freddie has just popped in to scrounge a coffee and smoulder at the bishop. He's taking a break from painting radiators at the school. He sits on Penelope's desk in his undone painty overalls, swinging his feet in his undone work boots. Straps trailing, laces trailing, pheromones trailing. He looks (in Iona the sub-organist's memorable words) as if he's just had a swift shag in a broom cupboard. There's a fresh tattoo on his inner forearm – a rainbow ichthus – still covered in clingfilm.

We will sneak in and eavesdrop.

'Yes. Yes, of course. Someone will be here to help you. Bye bye.' Penelope put the phone down and stuck her tongue out at it. 'Honestly, there's no pleasing some people! Freddie, a gentleman's coming this afternoon to collect the pictures he bought from *Souls and Bodies*. I don't know where you put everything.'

'Hnnh? Oh, it's all in the palace dining room with labels on, Mish Moneypenny.'

'Well, can you show me? He's been a pain in the bottom about artwork being stored in an empty house,' fretted Penelope. 'The temperature and humidity, for heaven's sake!'

'Want me to deal with him?'

'Would you? Oh, thank you, lovely boy.'

'No worries. Text me when he comes.'

The bishop appeared in the doorway. 'I smell coffee. Is it elevenses?'

Martin checked his watch again and carefully plunged the cafetière. 'May I pour you a coffee too, Bishop?'

'Yes, please!' He beamed round at them all. Then his gaze focused on the prize Freddie had won at the fairground rifle range. 'Why is that large pink bear wearing my mitre?'

'Coz he's a bishop? Gotta love a right reverend bear.' Freddie swung his feet and lolled his tongue out.

Penelope swatted him.

'That bear's an imposter!' cried Harry. 'He's never taken holy orders in his life! Where did he train?'

Martin pursed his lips. He crossed the office, removed the mitre and handed it to Harry.

'Thank you, Martin. Now, about tonight, Penelope,' said the bishop. 'I notice I'm down to bless a window out in the sticks somewhere. Hmm. "Bless this window to our use and us in your service, amen." That should cover it. Could you print me off some directions?'

'Certainly. But aren't you taking Martin?'

'Should I?'

'Well, he *is* the bishop's chaplain,' said Penelope.

'Gosh, I've never had a chaplain,' Harry said wistfully. 'No, don't worry. Seems a bit daft for two of us to trek out there.'

'More than happy to come with you,' said Martin.

'Hey, lemme drive you?' said Freddie. 'I totally know this entire diocese coz I was Paul's chauffeur back in the day?'

'I think you'll find you're no longer insured,' muttered Martin.

'And? Not like I've forgotten how to drive.'

'That's not the point.'

'Yeah? Screw you, Marty.'

'Please don't fight over me, darlings,' said the bishop. 'You're both very kind, but why don't you take the evening off? Penelope, if you could print off those directions, I'm sure I can manage. Thanks for the coffee.' He took it back to his office.

Martin returned to his computer.

There was a silence.

Then Freddie yawned massively, stretched and rumpled his hair. 'Laters, guys.' He slouched off like a rough beast, towing laces and paint fumes and Le Male in his wake.

The holiday season speeds to its close. After the bank holiday we will no longer be able to pretend there's anything left of the summer. Once again there will be meltdowns in Clark's shoe shop. Good mothers will sew Cash's nametapes into new uniforms. Bad mothers will scrawl their child's name on the labels in Biro. Academics will ask themselves how the vacation has fled with so little writing getting done. School leavers prepare for uni by rewatching the entire Harry Potter oeuvre. Apples ripen and fall un-scrumped.

Martin's daughters will be home tomorrow from their fortnight in Portugal. Jane and Dominic will shortly return from France, having eaten and drunk not wisely but too well. The archdeacon will collect them from the airport at some ungodly hour. Father Wendy is back from two weeks in Northumberland, where Pedro has run free on miles of sand.

He sits at her feet now in her study, as she talks to her curate Virginia. They have just done a belated end of first year review thingy. Not entirely a comfortable experience, because Virginia kept having to put her vicar right on points of process; but there, it's done, and they are now eating cake. Gluten- and lactose-free cake, which Wendy has made specially, because she's so lovely.

'So, is there anything else?' asks Wendy. Oh, no. Eek. There's something horrid.

'It's awkward. Please don't think I'm trying to angle for information about the new bishop. But there's a rumour that it's Guilden Hargreaves.'

'Mmm,' says Wendy.

'Personally, I have no problem with that. But there are a lot of people in this diocese who aren't happy with the way the Church seems to be going on the gay issue,' says Virginia. 'So if the rumours are right, there's going to be a lot of protest and opposition. Including in our own congregations, Wendy. I know he's single now, but he used to have a partner. People just aren't comfortable with that. Do we have a statement prepared?'

'Um, not as such, no. I think we can play it by ear, can't we?'

Virginia frowns. 'We need to be proactive. As a member of the CNC who made the appointment, I'm worried you'll be a target, and—'

'Oh, let's just trust that God can work through it all.' She puts a hand on Virginia's arm. 'I'm sorry. That sounded very preachy! I wish I could tell you everything, but—'

'Of course you can't!' Virginia looks shocked at the very suggestion.

'Anyway, we should have an announcement in September some time, so it's not too long to wait. There's no point fretting until then.'

'She's right, though, Pedro,' says Wendy after her curate has gone. 'A lot of folk are going to be very unhappy. Oh, dear.'

But Pedro is off in dreamland, chasing gulls on an endless Northumbrian shore.

A new choral year looms. Timothy, the director of music, is in the Song School library with a group of helpers, trying to impose order on decades of chaos. The windows are flung wide. Laurence, the cathedral organist, sits quietly in the corner with a rubber, erasing historic pencil marks from a dog-eared set of Stanford in G. Miss Barbara Blatherwick was here yesterday, but is off seeing the consultant about her pesky hip today. In her absence lewd lyrics for 'The Lonely Goatherd' are being improvised.

'A young lay clerk with a bar in his scrote heard . . .' sings Iona.

'Lay-ee-odl-ay-ee!' yodel the others responsorially.

'Apropos of nothing,' says Nigel, the senior lay clerk, 'what's happening with Mr May? Is he locked in his bromance with the bishop's chaplain, or is he moving on to the Close?'

'Giles says the canon treasurer has agreed to take him in,' says Timothy from the top of a ladder. 'God! This dust must be an inch thick!' He brandishes his ostrich feather duster.

'You can't touch those cobwebs, Mr Director!' cries Nigel. 'They have a preservation order on them!'

'Look, we never sing matins any more,' says Iona, 'so I vote we chuck this whole lot into the skip.'

There is an outcry at this dangerous heresy. It is tantamount to burning books, and only Nazis burn books. And so the *venites*, the *benedicites*, all the beloved settings of yesteryear, are allowed to crumble until some dim future when choirs carry smart tablets and paper is no more.

The funeral is over. Father Ed leaves the graveyard at Gayden Parva. The tumbled monuments are properly roped off now. A stone angel lies flat in the long grass. Ed pauses near the cross by the ancient yew. *God is Love*. Someone has strimmed the nettles at its foot down to stumps.

In my dying moments, what will still matter to me? he wonders. Will *proving my point* feel important? Or will love be all that remains of us? All I want to do is pledge myself to you, Neil. For better, for worse, richer, poorer, until it ends – as it surely must – here. At the grave. That is the only point I want to make by marrying you. It should be about you and me, not bishops and archbishops.

Or was that just selfish? Ed feels his toes curling in his black funeral shoes at the thought of 'a feature with Roddy'. Having to be photographed in the too-sharp bespoke wedding suit Neil would bully him into. Then afterwards, the whisky-soused night that would end in Neil and Fallon playing atheist Top Trumps (which non-existent God is viler – Catholic or Calvinist?) and Ed going to bed alone.

God is Love. God is Love.

Ed can still see Bishop Bob dying on the kitchen floor. And Neil fighting to save him – while I stood by wringing my hands and praying. Maybe Neil's right? Maybe we've got to fight? Yes, I should stop being so squeamish. Man up and fight for our legal right to be married.

He gets into his car and heads back home. As he turns down the lane towards Gayden Magna, he passes Neil driving the other way. He blows him a kiss. Neil gurns and sticks two fingers up. Everything is normal.

Martin remains in the chapel of St Michael after evening prayer. He needs to make his peace with Freddie. What happened back there in the office this morning? he asks himself. We've been getting along fine! He's moving out tomorrow. Please don't let it end on a bad note like this.

He tries to humble himself. Yes, I was snippy. Judgemental. I'll apologize. Martin recrosses his legs, violently kicking the chair in front. A tourist jumps, then stares at him. Martin makes a deprecatory gesture, then bows his head again. A fit of giggles seizes him. Did she think I just booted the chair on purpose in a fit of rage?

I *am* angry! Why am I angry?

Because he's doing it again! He's like a silly little boy jumping up and down going, 'Notice me, notice me, Dad!' Martin feels like booting the chair again. Picking it up and hurling it through the stained-glass window, through those silly blonde Burne-Jones angels. Why?

You're older, Martin. You should have more self-control. His mum's voice, when he was fighting with his sister. He flushes. Is *this* what's going on? Some kind of pathetic sibling rivalry? Maybe I'm still just a little boy inside, too?

Martin feels that *clunk* as an inner door unlocks. This keeps happening in family therapy! *Please don't fight over me, darlings.* Martin cringes up inside like a sea anemone as the truth prods him: I behave like a jealous little boy when Freddie's around. Yes, because he's naughty and he blatantly gets away with it! Except he doesn't. No. He's lonely, and I must be kind to him.

Martin gets up and heads back to the palace. He's deep in thought and doesn't see the black Porsche till the last second. Brakes squeal. He leaps back. The car reverses, window down. Martin stares into a pair of mad blue eyes.

'Got a death wish, pal?' With a rude chirp of tyres the Porsche speeds off.

It's dark now. Not everyone is sleeping in the Diocese of Lindchester tonight. The dean keeps her nightly vigil in front of the red N symbol. How tangled everything is. Have we made the right choice of bishop? Yes? No? How can we not think about our persecuted brothers and sisters? Our decisions affect them! Yet it can't be right to try and placate tyrants! Evil prevails when the good do nothing, not when they act. Or does it prevail despite our good actions? Let it not prevail, let it not prevail.

In the vicarage of Gayden Magna Ed is awake. He sits in the dark dining room among the bubble-wrapped sketches – his engagement present! – and cries. Neil is asleep upstairs. Still reeking of Le Male. I can smell him on you. He'd say it, but he can't. Can't. Stand it. Just cannot *stand* hearing Neil deny it. Lie to him. Again.

143

Chapter 18

I present you, reader, with a timeless English scene. It is the last week of August and the early morning sunshine has a smoky quality. Plums ripen. Giant puffballs bulge in dewy meadows. The countryside has harvest on its breath.

A tall, thin figure in clerical black passes through a graveyard and out under the lichgate. Behind him the spire rises classically among copper beeches and old limes as if posing for a watercolour. He walks along the lane towards a lovely Georgian rectory. Ah, look at it! Cream painted, perfectly proportioned. Admire the sweeping drive, the neatly trimmed box hedges, the dovecote, the orangery! Covet those espaliered fruit trees hugging the venerable walls of an unseen vegetable garden! And see: borders full of hollyhocks, like embroidered tray cloths. He approaches the wrought-iron gates . . .

And walks past. Down the lane he goes, towards a grim 1970s house at the far end of what was once the Rector of Gayden Magna's apple orchard, because this is the early twenty-first century, not the early nineteenth.

Oh, well.

Sometimes I wish we could turn the clock back and find a way of not selling off all the lovely old vicarages. Or at the very least, revisit the possibility of building new ones with a bit more flair. Not all the wealth and energy of an energetic wealthy designer could bully this parson-box into a *House Beautiful* (Welsh slate and quarry tiles notwithstanding). The Lindchester diocesan architect back in the 1970s only had one set of plans. I think the idea was that clergy could move from parish to parish happy in the knowledge that their carpets and curtains would always fit perfectly in their charmless new home.

How easily we might improve on the current state of affairs, if we could only rewind and try again! Let's go back and *not* make that stupid decision, then everything will be all right. Let's tell ourselves that hindsight has bestowed fresh information unavailable at the time. Above all, let's pretend we didn't realize back then it was stupid, stupid, thrice stupid, when we went ahead and did it anyway.

'Dude, probably we shouldn't ...?'
  '*Definitely* we shouldn't, you bad boy!'
  'Yeah. We *soooo* shouldn't ...'
  Pause.
  'Och, fuck it. C'mere, gorgeous.'
  'Whoa! Mmmmm, ahh ... Oh, God ... Wait. Lemme just ... 'kinoveralls ...'
  'Allow me.'

But occasionally, when we have barely completed Phase One of Project Stupidity, something intervenes and saves us from ourselves. A phone bursting into the *Jaws* theme tune in a back pocket, for example:
  Duuuuun dun!
  'Gah!'
  'Ignore it.'
  Duuuuuuun dunn! Duun dun, duun dun, DUUN DUN ...
  'Mmm-nngh, please? No, listen. Sorry. Listen. Dude, I should get this ... Ah, nuts.'
  Silence.
  'There. As you were, soldier.' Pause. 'Oh, what? No, c'mon!'
  'Sorry, sorry, sorry. It's just ... I mean, dude, your fiancé? Gah. My bad. Really sorry?'
  'Well, fuck!'

He is more righteous than I. Where was that from? The Good Book, probably. Must have heard it in Sunday School. *He is more righteous than I.*

Nearly a week on, and it dawns on Neil that *this* is why he so nearly bitch-slapped him. Shamed by a wee hoor who rents himself out as topless feckin' cocktail waiter! *Dude, your fiancé?* Ooh.

Neil drums his nails on his First Class table. He scowls out of the train window. Really not liking himself this morning. Away off in the distance he glimpses the cathedral on its mount, spire like a preacher's finger. Not liking himself. At. All. Daft wee stoner, be like kicking a puppy. Bad man. And thank God he hadn't ran that poor bastard over on the palace drive, either! Attack of John Knox-itis on the way home, predictably. But hey, no point hurting Eds by fessing up to something that never even happened, was there? That would be selfish. Here's your engagement present, kiss kiss, love ya, big man!

Then somehow he managed to balls up the sneaky self-medication. Cue the night terrors. It's coming, it's after him, and he's screaming for Maw, but his voice won't work. Fighting, fighting to get out of bed, but something's pressing him down, and Eds has gone, Eds has left him! No! Hunting for him in the dark room, the dark house, room after room, screaming for Eds, not knowing if he's awake, or if this is still the same feckin' nightmare.

'I'm here, Neil. It's OK. I'm here.'

'Don't leave me, don't leave me, Eds, please don't leave me.'

'I won't leave you. Ssh. I'm here. It's all OK.'

And because he was still off-his-tits melted, he only went and told him what he'd done. Nearly done. OK then, fine: *would've* done, but for wee choirslut90 being more righteous than him.

Anyway.

Neil drinks his First Class complimentary coffee. He'd come so close to wrecking everything with that confession. *Of course* Eds read him the riot act. 'Forsaking all others! What's the point, Neil, I mean, what *is* the point? What does marriage mean to you, if it doesn't mean being faithful?' The wedding's still in the balance, but he's going to prove to Eds he's serious about this.

He leans his head back against the white headrest, closes his eyes. Och, if only he'd kept his big gob shut . . . But no, no. This has to be better. To be out in the open at last? No more lying, no more cheating, no more covering his tracks. He's a gritty Scot. He can do this. He can stand out here in a kilt and let the east wind of truth whistle round his baws for once. And in a totally weird way, it feels safer.

Maybe because he knows he's loved? In spite of everything, that good man still loves him.

Freddie May is running, running, running. Reckons he can get a quick 10K in before work. Gah. Still hasn't returned that call. Oh man, total mistake to come out with no music. Coz now the *Jaws* theme's going round his head again. *Dun dun, dun dun* . . . Must ring, must get on to that before Scary Mentor calls again. Or worse, turns up in Lindchester to mentor him in person. No, he wouldn't do that, would he? Oh, Jesus. *DUUUUNNN DUNN!*

Thing is, the very thought of making that call reminds him what a total home-wrecking shite he can be sometimes. What's *with* you? I thought after Paul we were gonna never do this again. No more married guys, spoken-for guys. In the same fucking house even! How bad is that? Oh God, Marty's right, why's he forever hitting on Harry? Wahey! Let's have *another* go at trashing some nice guy's life! Why does he have to be so *needy*? No, to be fair, staying by himself in a big empty house is doing his head in. Yeah, probably that's not helping. But Philip and Philippa will be back from holiday by next week, so he'll have company, and term will start and there'll be like structure to his life again?

I'm sorry, I'm sorry. There's nobody he can say it to. I mean yeah, no, course he said it at the time, but understandably? Neil's not impressed. For one second there he thought he was gonna get his face smacked, literally? Which would *not* have gone well. Oh, man. If he could only say sorry to the fiancé as well, but even he can see that's not a super-smart idea? Dude, I'm so sorry, I nearly did your fiancé, only, yeah, then I like didn't? And he'd be all, what? I don't know what you're even talking about! And what makes it like a million times worse is that he's only just yesterday worked out who the fiancé is? Rector of Gayden Magna? Totally sweet guy.

In the distance the fast train to London slices across the landscape. Silence closes back in. A buzzard cruises over the stubble fields. Freddie's shoulders itch under his vest. New tatts healing up now. Sting of sweat telling him he's alive. Yeah, that's why he's running till it hurts. It needs to hurt.

The totally sweet guy arrives back at the empty vicarage. He's just said Morning Prayer in one of his village churches. Two weddings there this Saturday. Wall-to-wall weddings all summer. He's sick of it. No, that's not fair. It's what comes of being vicar of a photogenic church. He goes to the kitchen and fills the kettle. You wouldn't have thought it possible to spend nearly £200 on a kettle, but Neil kept on going till he found a way.

As Ed stands waiting for the world's most perfect kettle to boil, a phrase from the canticle comes back to him: *In the tender compassion of our God the dawn from on high shall break upon us.* Neil's night terrors, his phobia about being abandoned. A childhood of being passed around the extended family while his mother was 'not so well', or his father was 'away on business'. Tender compassion – that's what he feels for Neil. His heart is tender.

Too right it bloody is! Because Neil has yet again picked up a steak mallet and tenderized it. Ed stares down at the quarry-tiled floor. He thinks of Bishop Bob. Cracked sternum, but – thanks to Neil's ministrations – alive. Yes, Neil is something of a heart specialist. He's fighting to rescue us now, thinks Ed; to rescue our engagement, the marriage. That same Scots terrier tenacity. But will anything really change? This new transparency, this accountability – how long will it last?

'You can check my phone, my emails, any time, Eds. Go on, check my messages.'

Ed shakes his head. 'I'm fine, Neil. I don't need to do that.'

As if you're not capable of deleting stuff, opening a new email account, buying a pay-as-you-go phone. Darling, I don't need to check your messages, I can just check your eyes. After eighteen years Ed can read cheating there as easily as coke or Vicodin. But the sweeties have all been flushed away, Grindr deleted, naughty wee tarts unfollowed on Twitter. Everything will be different from now on.

But *I* haven't changed, thinks Ed. Tenderized? I'm *flayed* by the idea of you with him. I can't look at those beautiful sketches you bought me now. I don't even want them in the house. Jesus, I can't stand it! Him. Moved to Lindchester, with his dirty pretty smile, his trampy clothes, his feral smell. Permanently available, twenty minutes away by Porsche. I can't compete! How can I compete with a greedy amoral twenty-four year old?

Stop, *stop* tormenting yourself! Neil came to his senses in time, didn't he? He chose to walk away from temptation. Yes, draw confidence from that. Marriage, fidelity – they mean something to Neil, they must do. Ed makes his coffee, goes through to his study and kneels. He stares up at the crucifix on the wall. This horrible storm of jealousy will pass. It's like the weather, it will blow over. My heart will mend.

> Jesus, grant me this, I pray,
> ever in thy heart to stay;
> let me evermore abide
> hidden in thy wounded side.

*

It's late afternoon. Miss Blatherwick is in the choir vestry, checking that the boys' surplices have been laundered and ironed to her satisfaction. Why she's doing this, when it's none of her business, is beyond her. Chapter took the decision to employ an ironing service two years ago. This is silly. She's behaving like an elderly busybody who can't retire gracefully.

She sits down rather hard on a wooden bench to give herself a good talking to. The air reeks faintly of historic BO from lay clerk cassock armpits. In her mind's eye the vestry crowds with memories, decades of ghost choristers, flitting through, darting jerkily like a time-lapse nature film of a beehive.

Yes, she sees what's troubling her; what she's trying to put right by ensuring the surplices are kept crisp and white as driven snow. Those boys we so criminally failed. The cathedral laundry! It looks very much as though she'll be required to give testimony next month, and the whole lot will be washed in public court. And now this deeply distressing news from Rotherham. The scale of it! One wonders now if anything has changed, whether in fact things are worse than ever, if all this diligent safeguarding and chaperoning is futile. One is sometimes tempted to think that nothing will ever be learned, other than the depressing lesson that there will always be those who prey on children, and children whose story will not be believed.

No. This won't do. Miss Blatherwick has no time for any weak-minded counsel of despair. However bad things are, one can always do the good thing that lies to hand, however small. She takes her mobile phone from her handbag and composes a text: 'WD YOU LIKE TO COME 4 dinner toñight¿ 7PM BB'

A moment later her phone buzzes in reply: 'HELL YEAH! LOVE YA MISS B Fêâ¿reddie XX'

Miss Blatherwick smiles and gets creakily to her feet. Dratted hip. But she's on the waiting list now, mustn't grumble. She scans the familiar room. That carpet could do with a good hoover. She gathers a couple of dirty mugs to wash and carries them carefully down the spiral stairs to her home.

And thus Miss Blatherwick's heart goes out to this Lost Boy of hers. Freddie's heart goes out to the man he has wronged; whose heart goes out to the man he loves and despairs over. And where does Neil's heart go? Well, I think it creeps by a strange backwoods route to Bishop Bob, not in prayer exactly, but he's like a man pacing to and fro outside a building, nerving himself to go in. He doesn't quite know it yet, but he wants to talk to Bob. About life and death and maybe forgiveness. And Bob — while Janet packs the car to drive them both off at last for a two-week break in the Hendersons' bolt-hole — Bob prays for his brother and stand-in, Bishop Harry, who at this precise moment is praying for Dean Marion, who is lighting a candle at the shrine of William of Lindchester, and praying for her persecuted brothers and sisters in Iraq.

It is gloomy here behind the high altar. As she sets her candle on the stand among the rest, Marion thinks of all the other candles lit at this moment across the globe. All the prayers, all the hearts leaning, yearning, towards some other heart. Linking us. I would like to see these threads of thought lit up across a night-time map, she thinks. A shimmering filigree linking soul to soul. She tries to picture it.

Would it throb with tenderness across space and time? If I could only see that, then perhaps each frail strand of mine would not seem so futile. Saints in heaven, pray for us.

It is Thursday morning. Jane looks down at the bathroom scales. What?! I demand a second opinion, you rude bastard! She gets off and on again. The scales stick to their guns. Right! Time for a run, Lardy Muldoon. She tiptoes back to the bedroom and tries to jiggle the drawer open without waking the large corpse that lies face down across her bed snoring. Broken his iron rule about stopping over, bless him. She can bring him breakfast in bed for once. Come on, open. The drawer jerks right out and tips a tangle of knackered sports gear on the floor.

Bollocks!

But the archdeacon snores on. Poor love. Desperately in need of a holiday. Jane excavates through the fossilized gear of lost eras: Pleistocene sports bra to tether the mighty bazoomers of doom, Mesozoic leggings, Palaeozoic vest. She struggles into them, drops a kiss on the sleeping bald head, and tiptoes downstairs.

Come along, trainers on, you lazy tart. Yay! This'll be FUN!

After a few stretches, Jane puts the door on the latch and creeps out. She skirts round the archdeacon's Mini parked across her drive and sets off at a lumbering pace. It's actually quite a nice day. Red berries crowd the rowan branches. Almost their first anniversary! And they will even manage to snatch a couple of sneaky days away together next week. Jane smiles as she runs. Yeah, life's pretty good right now.

The archdeacon wakes with a hideous lurch, as though he's involuntarily undergone the ice bucket challenge. Crap! He leaps out of bed. No time for a shower even. Flings yesterday's clothes on. Late, late, late! Rings Penelope, tells her to let Harry know he's on his way.

'Janey?' He crashes down the stairs two at a time. She's not in the kitchen. Dammit. He reads her note: *Gone for a run. Pastries when I get back. xx*

Damn, damn, damn! He scrawls an explanation, grabs his keys and hurtles out of the house.

This won't do, Matt. You know this won't do. He has to grit his teeth to stop himself driving like chuffing Jehu. You've got to sort this. Decide if you're going for the suffragan job, and if you are, you've got to tell her. Because you're going to have to choose. This is a fork in the road you're approaching.

No. It's a roundabout. It's a flipping roundabout and I've been driving round and round it for months, trying to kid myself I can go in two directions at once without choosing. I'm a fraud. A big old fraud. And a sinner.

'The archdeacon's on his way,' calls Penelope through the open office door. 'He'll be about twenty minutes.'

'Thanks,' says Harry. He whiles away the time checking the post. There's an envelope marked 'Private and Confidential' addressed to him. He opens it and reads the contents.

'Bishop? Are you all right in there, Bishop?' calls Penelope.

'I'm fine, thanks,' replies Harry. 'Just banging my head on the desk.'

The envelope contains a formal complaint (Form 1a, with written evidence and other documents attached) of misconduct against the Archdeacon of Lindchester, for conduct that is unbecoming or inappropriate to the office and work of the clergy. The complainant is one Revd Dr Veronica da Silva.

SEPTEMBER

Chapter 19

his diocese! Argh! Poor Bishop Harry sat up straight and smiled brightly at Penelope when she hurried in to check that he was all right. Once she was reassured, he scribbled a cartoon of an angry woman priest, and another of a big bald archdeacon. In his mind's eye, he Blu-tacked them to the dartboard he had foolishly not brought with him to Lindchester from his previous job, where it had performed such a key role in stress management.

Ho hum. Sad to say, Harry knew CDM procedures like the back of his hand. The letter of acknowledgement had to go off straight away to the Revd Dr Veronica da Silva. *Not* one for Penelope to handle. Then he needed to refer the matter to the diocesan registrar within seven days, who would get back to him within twenty-eight days to advise whether there were grounds to proceed with the complaint. And in Harry's experience, diocesan registrars seldom earned themselves the nickname Captain Reckless. This thing would have to run its course like some baroque combine harvester scrupulously shelling a walnut.

He looked at his watch. There was time to take a walk and compose himself before Matt's arrival, so that he could act as though he had not just received a letter dobbing him in for shacking up with his girlfriend. He gave the desk one final thump with his forehead and went outside to stroll round the palace garden.

The palace garden! Perhaps this has long been a matter of concern for the keen horticulturalists among my readers. I fear it has been neglected for almost a year now. You may remember how poor Susanna, in her distress, simply let the fruit fall from the trees and rot. The herbaceous borders were not tidied, nor the clumps divided in the autumn. And then along came a vast pathetic fallacy of a gale that laid waste to everything. I am sure that shortly before the new bishop moves in, a task force will sweep through and make things presentable. Whispers continue to suggest that it will be Guilden Hargreaves, but we do not expect an announcement for a couple more weeks, and even then we will still be a long way off the enthronement (or 'installation', if the next bishop is squeamish about pride of man and earthly glory).

I will begin a new paragraph here so that my readers can make themselves comfortable before I launch into another verse of 'Here we go round the ecclesiastical mulberry bush'. Ready? *This is the way we make a bishop, make a bishop, make a bishop!* You might be forgiven for supposing that the process of consultation, mandating, longlisting, shortlisting, interviewing, praying and pondering, and finally choosing a candidate would constitute making an appointment. Not so, my friends! We will pass lightly over the business of DBS-enhanced disclosure and medicals on Harley Street (with mandatory prescription of statins). We will allude in passing to a name going forward to Her Majesty. All of this takes many months, during which time the preferred candidate must maintain complete radio silence. He must have no contact with the diocese and he may not even go and look round the palace he will be living in.

I trust the reader has not lost sight of the fact that there must also be *a process of election*. Dean Marion is standing by to receive a letter from the sovereign instructing her to summon her College of Canons for the purpose of electing a new Bishop of Lindchester. Then comes the second letter instructing them to elect person X. These days person X will be the person the CNC has selected, rather than some foppish favourite of the monarch who nobody wants, and who may tiresomely need assassinating at some future date. Marion will duly summon her canons, and those who fail to show will be declared 'contumacious'. Sadly she can no longer seize their goods (a practice Gene had expressed an interest in exercising on her behalf, having taken a fancy to the prebendary of Gayden Magna's consort's Porsche). The canons will duly appoint X as their new bishop. If they fail to do so, I believe Her Majesty will dismiss the lot of them and appoint a College of Canons who will do her bidding. It is a process of election familiar in many parts of the globe.

There then follows a Confirmation of Election in York. Well, assuming our man is already a bishop somewhere. If not, he'll need to be consecrated somewhere along the way. After this, the new bishop is *officially* the new bishop and may style himself +Lindcaster in his Christmas cards if he is a bit of a ponce. He still needs to pay homage to the sovereign by kissing her hand ('a brush of the lips, not a slobber') and then he may be installed/enthroned in Lindchester and the cathedral choir may sing Parry's *I Was Glad*, as cathedral choirs will under such circumstances, and *finally* there will be a Bishop of Lindchester in place a mere fifteen months after the previous bishop left. Which makes Dr Proudie's elevation to Bishop of Barchester in 185— 'a month after the demise of the late bishop' seem like something from a work of fiction.

The implication of all this for the palace garden, then, is that nobody is falling over themselves yet to weed the borders.

And now it is September. Season of perversely hot summer weather, rendering school playing fields rock hard and skinning knees without mercy during the first rugby lessons of the year. Paint fumes linger in classroom and corridor. Swallows natter on wires. There goes the crocodile of choristers in their cherry red caps filing to the Song School. Aw, look at the tiniest tots, in grey shorts and new blazers, faces a-tremble with homesickness. Freddie May watches them go, and remembers. But I predict that the tots, like most other choristers, will look back on these years and stoutly defend them as magical.

Choral term has not started yet, but the boys must be drilled in their Mags and Nuncs; taught to rrrrroll their Rs and inducted into the mystery of when it is proper to pronounce salvation 'sal-vacey-ohn'. They must get the silliness out of their system and not snort at 'O loud be their trump' or naughtily slur 'our souls' into arseholes. Finally, they must master the Lindchester style of pointing for the psalmody, which is different from that of all other cathedrals, and considered superior; just as other styles are considered superior in other cathedrals, although we know in Lindchester (with a faint smirk) that they are wrong about that.

'She's sent me some rainbow shoelaces!'

'Hello, Dominic! I'm very well thanks,' said Jane. 'I'm just embedding reasonable adjustments into next year's curriculum.'

'Yes, yes, shut up. Rainbow shoelaces!'

'Well, why not? It's an anti-homophobic bullying thing.'

'All the deanery clergy got a pair! I refuse to wear them! It's not a church thing! It's Stonewall and it's football!'

Jane waited until Dominic's rant sputtered out into silence. 'And how may I help you, my darling? Would you like me to hold her down while you garrotte her with your rainbow laces?'

'The letter has the diocesan logo on it, as well as the chaplaincy's and St James' Church. I bet nobody's been consulted. God! It's as though she's the diocesan LGBT officer! And she is not!'

'Take it up with the diocese, then.'

'I will! I hate being bullied and manipulated like this.'

'Yes, it must feel as if she's colonized the moral high ground and now nobody's allowed to query her views without being yelled at,' Jane sympathized.

There was a dangerous silence. 'Meaning what, exactly?'

'Nothing,' said Jane. 'I was reflecting upon the tenor of the Scottish independence debate. You aren't allowed to disagree with the Yes campaign. That would be like questioning equal marriage.'

'And that, right there, is where you ruined it, Jane. That last cheap shot.'

Jane laughed her filthy laugh. 'They should have phrased the referendum question the other way round. Nobody wants to get behind a No campaign, like a bunch of freedom-hating naysayers. We *all* want to say Yes. God, but it's like bloody *King Lear* though, isn't it? All the flamboyant poetry and romance on one side, all the prosaic truth on the other. Hello? Are you still there?'

'I'm strangling myself with my rainbow laces out of sheer boredom.'

'But with pride, I hope. Listen, why don't you complain to Matt about Our Lady of the Laces? She's taking the diocese's name in vain. She shouted at him about women bishops, so he'll be on your side.'

'It's not about taking sides, Jane.'

'Oh. I thought we were talking about the Church of England.'

'Why don't you go and embed some reasonable adjustments up your arse?' enquired Dominic. 'And then do you want to come for lunch?'

'Yes, please.'

'It's only salad and soup. I've had to revert to my fat man trousers.'

'I hear you, brother. I'll bring yogurts for pudding.'

'Oh, joy.'

As it happens, Dominic is not the only one feeling manipulated by the Revd Dr Veronica da Silva. The Vicar of St James' Church, Lindford is sitting in his church office, stunned. The door was slammed shut five minutes earlier by Veronica. His head is still ringing.

All he tried to do was gently press her about it. But the issue shifted from whether Veronica ought to have put the church and diocesan logo on the letter heading, to whether Geoff, by his refusal to support Veronica's campaign, was tacitly condoning homophobia within the Church and, by extension, legitimizing the persecution and murder of gays and lesbians under totalitarian regimes everywhere. What? What just happened there? Geoff closes his eyes. Is it me? He waits in the silence.

Christ in me. Christ with me.

Traffic goes by outside the church. He hears the screech of magpies clashing in the plane tree. There is no reasoning with her. Every time he seeks to clarify something, the goalposts shift. This has never happened to him before; he has never encountered anyone so impossible to deal with! Yes, he's disagreed with people – bitterly, sometimes – but he's never encountered this ... what? This sense of wrestling with an empty coat, not a person. Where, where to find Christ in the experience?

And then there are the apparent discrepancies in her CV. He's been too preoccupied with the CNC process. He kept telling himself the archdeacon's silence must mean that there's nothing to worry about. No, it's no good, he'll just have to hassle Matt again, if only to set his mind at rest.

The Porsche of the consort of the prebendary of Gayden Magna is currently parked on double yellows outside the picture-framing shop near the gatehouse to the Close. Neil has just dropped off the six sketches to get them *properly* framed. (We spare a prayer here for the poor sod who has just blithely said, 'No problem, I'll do that for you.') Neil emerges back on to the street. Shit. It's the wee slut. With *him*, Psycho Boyfriend, from the exhibition. Neil scoots into the car before he's spotted. Heh heh! The *Jaws* tune makes sense now. Not more righteous than me after all – just more scared of his other half!

'Um, dude, why are we ... holding hands?'

'Because I'm your mentor.'

Gah. Freddie's brain is in meltdown. Literally? Barely knows which way they're walking. Mentor's shoes clip along the cobbles. Omigod, omigod, this is totally happening? I'm totally walking along with Andrew Jacks? Like we're together?

'My instructions were clear: to take you in hand and give you a steer where necessary.'

Freddie snorts. 'Ha ha, dude, I think that was like, metaphorical?'

The hand holding his tightens. 'I dare say. But you show signs of flight. Are you scared of me, Mr May?'

'Um, yeah?'

'Oh, good.' They stop. 'Let's try here.'

They're outside a coffee shop. 'Sure.'

A black Porsche roars past them. They go in. A little barista appears, super-excited to see them.

'Hey, guys? How're YOU today? Table for two?' So she's a Kiwi, greeting them like long-lost rellies? 'Wanna stay inside? Or would you rather sit outside on the dick?'

Mentor turns to Freddie, eyebrow raised. 'Would you enjoy that?' Freddie explodes with mirth again. 'Thank you, we'll sit outside.'

He steers Freddie out to the narrow deck looking down over the rooftops of old Lindchester. 'Vowel shift: fascinating phenomenon. What a lovely spot.' He gazes out. 'But then, I am famously fond of decks.'

'*Stop* that.' Freddie wipes his eyes. 'You're a bad man.'

'I have never claimed otherwise.'

They sit opposite one another. Omigod, omigod. Freddie reaches for the menu, so he won't have to look at him. The menu is twitched from his fingers.

'Your full attention, please, Mr May.'

'Oh, God. OK!' He braces himself, glances at those light grey eyes. 'OK. Cool. I'm listening.' Silence. 'Look, about that time you rang me? So yeah, I totally meant to get back to you, only—'

'Ssh.' He waits till Freddie stops squirming and tugging his hair, and manages to hold his gaze. 'Thank you. Rules of engagement. You may trust me one hundred per cent. Anything we discuss goes no further. I am not part of the "How Do You Solve a Problem Like Freddie?" task force. Ssh, don't interrupt. You can say anything, ask anything, call me any name under the sun — as indeed you already did last year. I'm unshockable. Please don't bother being winsome: I have no charm receptors in my brain. No need to impress me, I am already impressed, or I wouldn't be here. Finally, don't lie to me. I will be able to tell, and it will piss me off. So, to summarize: say what you like and I will listen. And then *you* will listen to me and do as you're told. How does that sound?'

Freddie blinked. 'Honestly? Like you're a kind of a bell end?' Whoa. Scary silence. 'Um, you said I could say anything?'

'Ah! I see — you'd finished. I was waiting to be told to go fuck myself.'

'Gah, about that? Really sorry. I just kinda lost it? Only then, later? I tried to, like, take what you said on board, and address it? And not be all, you know? Thing is, yeah? I'm, I'm like, gah, kinda everything's always all—'

He has his hand up. 'I'm going to stop you there, Mr May, as you are no longer making sense. And we need to order.' He turns to the barista. 'Double espresso, and a glass of mineral water, San Pellegrino, if you have it? Excellent. Freddie.'

'Oh, um, yeah, can I get a latte?'

The waitress leaves. Freddie looks out over the town. A seagull comes in, legs dangling, to land on a roof ridge. This is *death*. No, no good. Can't handle this. Got to get out.

There's a hand on his arm. 'Don't take fright, darling.'

Ah nuts, now he's gonna cry?

'What's on your heart?'

'Dude, I like, I just . . . can't do this? I'm a fuck-up, yeah? I fuck stuff up, I can't do this, this, being a grown-up thing, OK?' Are you *mad*? Shut *up*! 'I know it's lame, but I can't handle myself, the money, running my life, the whole, gah, being responsible for shit? I'm trying to be like, organized, but . . . What?'

He laughs. 'Nobody expects you to be organized! You're a divo. Divos have managers.' Freddie stares. 'Be kinder to yourself. We are none of us omnicompetent. Ah, thank you.'

The waitress sets down the drinks. Freddie holds it together till she's gone. Ah, nuts. Like when he was six? Boarding for the first time, Mum's just left him? Can't stop sobbing. Dude just waits, puts a hand on his arm. Then Freddie's telling him the stuff he's never told anyone. Like he's opened that cupboard where he's been hiding junk for years and now the whole fucking lot is falling out, just falling out, falling out.

Yeah. Turns out he's pretty much unshockable.

And then, like three coffees and a million paper napkins later? 'Oh, God. Dude, I am totally in love with you?'

'Of course you are, Mr May. But let's agree to ignore it. Go and wash your face and I'll walk you back.'

The archdeacon is trying frantically to clear his in-box before sked-addling for a couple of days' sneaky holiday. Like painting the chuffing Severn Bridge. New emails pinging in as fast as he clears them. What's this? From the vicar of St James'. Crap. Bit of a heart-lurch there. He never did chase that up. Veronica da Silva. He gets on to it now. Spot of the old detective work. Hmm. Oh dear, oh dear, oh dear. He's heard of this before: 'ordination' from some free independent 'theological academy', then a series of denomination hops, until bingo! Fully fledged Anglican. Definitely worth a conversation when he's back from holiday. He looks at his watch. Better see if he can fix a date before he goes.

'Hello, Veronica. Archdeacon Matt here.'

'You're not supposed to contact me.'

'Excuse me?'

'While the complaints procedure is in train, you aren't supposed to discuss it with me.'

'What?' His heart starts to pound. 'I'm sorry, but I have no idea what you're talking about.'

'I've lodged a formal complaint about you.'

VOOM. Matt's head flames like a beacon. Blood crashes in his ears like breakers in a cave. 'All righty. Well. I was actually calling about something else. Could we fix a time to meet? Some questions have cropped up about your CV that I'd be grateful to chat through.'

'No. This is an attempt to pressurize me into withdrawing my complaint.'

'Sorry? No, it's not.'

'It is. You're trying to browbeat me. I'm making a note of this. Don't contact me again. Goodbye.'

Very, very slowly Matt replaces the receiver. As though one knock might cause his whole world to shiver into tiny fragments.

As though this has not already happened.

Chapter 20

'att. Can you pull over? Here.'

'What, Lindford Common?'

'Yes.'

'All righty.' He turned into the car park. 'Everything OK, Janey?'

'Come on. I want to show you something.'

They got out and he followed her down the track. Pretty torn up underfoot. Spot of illegal quad biking been going on by the looks of it. Used condoms. Knotted dog-poo bags swinging in the branches. Nice. Never could understand that. Why pick it up at all, if you're only going to wang it into the trees?

They were headed for the little lake. He could see it ahead of them, glinting through the trunks. Eerily still today. You could even hear the acorns dropping. But was he going to be able to unwind when they got to the Lakes, with all this crap hanging over his head? Yep, he'd got the mother of all dog-poo bags dangling over him, like the sword of whatsisname.

Jane stopped by the lake and pointed. Matt looked at the white sign nailed to the tree: 'WARNING Thin ice.' He managed a smile.

'I used to bring Danny here,' she said. 'We always found that funny.'

'Hmm. A tad overcautious in the summer months.'

'Except that's how I feel, Matt. Like I'm on thin ice. The whole time.'

Oh, Lord. He said nothing.

'Well? Are you going to tell me what's going on? Something's happened since I last saw you, and I need to know if it's to do with me, or if I'm just being a silly moo. Because unless you talk to me, I'm not going to enjoy this break.'

Matt rubbed his face and sighed. 'Okey-doke. Yep, something's cropped up. I wasn't going to mention it, because it may come to nothing. Right. Someone's whacked in a formal complaint about my . . . lifestyle.'

'What? You've got to be kidding me! Because of *us*?'

He winced. 'Afraid so. Look, no point getting too het up at this stage. Bishop may decide there's no grounds to proceed.'

'Of course there aren't any!' She saw his face. 'Oh, crap. There are?'

He looked away. Stared at the water. Oak leaves and feathers rested on the surface, motionless. 'To be honest, Jane, if a situation like this came to my attention as archdeacon, I'd probably need to look into it.'

'Oh, my God! I thought we were in the clear!' She was standing there, hands spread in disbelief. 'What were you *thinking*, Matt? Were you just hoping we wouldn't get caught? What happens now? You get defrocked?'

'Don't be daft. Worst-case scenario: a formal rebuke.'

'Yes, but after that? We won't be able to carry on as we are, will we?'

'Well, I'd have a spot of thinking to do, for sure. But let's not jump the—'

'Jesus! It's bad enough never being able to live together! This is an *unbelievable* intrusion— *Stop* fucking sighing at me like *I'm* being unreasonable! What right has the Church got to police my sex life? We're consenting adults, we're committed to each other, we're harming no one!'

'I know. I'm sorry. But it's honestly too soon to be fretting, OK? Let's try and put it from our minds while—'

'Who was it? Come on. Which small-minded fuckwit thinks it's their business to go running to the bishop?'

'Um. Probably not a good idea for you to know.'

'Tell me right now!' She grabbed his arm. 'It's someone I know, isn't it?'

'It's not Dominic, if that's what—'

'Of course it's not Dom! Who else knows? Who have you told?'

'Look, you tend to make a fair few enemies in the old archdeaconing trade. Goes with the territory.' He began outlining the complaints process for her, preliminary scrutiny of evidence, possibility of case being dismissed, failing that, his right to respond . . .

Jane narrowed her eyes. 'It's Veronica, isn't it?'

'Jane, look—'

'Oh, my God! How the hell does she know? Has she been *stalking* us? Right. Leave this to me.'

'Jane, no. You absolutely need to keep out of this.'

'I'm already *in* this! Matt, she's a loony from La-La Land! She needs to be stopped. Don't worry, I'll go through university channels. I'll contact HR and we'll soon see if her CV holds up.'

'No!' He cleared his throat. 'Sorry. Didn't mean to shout.' She was staring at him. Tears in those lovely dark eyes. He was a bastard. Owed her a better explanation. So he told her about that little phone call he'd just had. Told her everything.

No, not everything. He did not tell her about the suffragan bishop's post. No point. He'd withdrawn his name. Last thing he'd done before leaving the office. Well, you pray for guidance; you shouldn't be surprised if now and then the Almighty answers with an un-ambiguous thunderbolt.

We must wish them well and wave them off, for their little trip took them beyond the borders of the diocese. The matter now rests with the diocesan registrar, who may ponder the case for up to twenty-eight days. Why does everything take so long in the C of E? Possibly because there's a lot of work involved in being utterly transparent, while simultaneously being fanatically confidential.

How is poor Bishop Harry coping with all this tension? Somewhere along the way I think he must have considered the lilies of the field and learned the knack of not getting stressed about stuff he has no control over. Yes, he prays for Matt and Veronica, but they don't keep him awake at night. I'm glad Captain Harry is in command right now. He radiates calm. More than that, he brings a bit of silliness and fun to the place. And that is something even his worst enemies never accused Paul Henderson of doing.

Tension is mounting. One by one key people are quietly being taken into the inner circle of those who know the identity of the next bishop. So far nobody has blabbed. Nobody needs to blab! Off the record, we all know it's the bookies' favourite, Guilden Hargreaves. Is the Church ready for this? The Archbishop of York, as we know, reiterated the official line that there is nothing to prevent a gay priest in a celibate partnership from being appointed to a bishopric. Nothing, that is, but the hostility of large wealthy evangelical congregations. Sabres have been rattled. Guilden is not sufficiently repentant of his earlier domestic arrangements. Will the archbishop be forced to back down? Those who know Rupert Anderson say he won't be bullied. Will there be blood on the vestry carpet in a couple of weeks?

So I say I'm glad that Harry will be there when the announce-ment is made. I dare say he will be singing his favourite trouble song again. If you went to Sunday School a generation or two ago, you might be able to join him:

> Cheer up, ye saints of God, there's nothing to worry about!
> Nothing to make you feel afraid, nothing to make you doubt!

'That was before climate change, of course, Tarquin,' Harry tells the large pink bear sitting on his desk when he gets in on Monday morning. He looks at the bear gravely. 'I see you've got a new shirt. Penelope?'

'Yes, Bishop?'

'I've spoken to this bear before about dressing appropriately.'

'Oh!' Penelope rushes in. 'That boy!' She wrestles the bear out of his 'Sorry Girls, I suck dick!' T-shirt. 'I'll return this to its owner. Though I've a good mind to put it in the wheelie bin! I'm *so* sorry, Bishop. He must have got hold of Martin's keys.'

'Thank you,' says the bishop. 'Now, if you could put Tarquin on the naughty chair and give him an improving Christian paperback to read, I'd be grateful.'

Lindchester Diocese holds its breath. The landscape itself seems to pause. The pillars climb up from the cloud factory at Cardingforth. Summer weather, yet out of kilter, aslant. Children frazzle in their new uniforms. They peel off blazers and logoed sweatshirts. They loosen ties. Teachers in corridors bark, as they have ever done, 'Tuck your shirt in!' For as everyone knows, untucked shirts are sloppy, sloppiness leads to indiscipline, and before you know it, the entire school is going to Special Measures in a hand basket.

Blackberries gleam fat on barbed stems and the pallid elder leaves are tinged with purple, as though steeped in elderberry wine. The Linden winds slow and lazy between banks crowded with policeman's helmet and the candyfloss of willowherb seeds. Once again Virginia creeper fronds blaze scarlet on Bishop Bob's garden wall, but he is not here to admire them and think sermon-like thoughts about beauty and decay this year. The Hootys will be back next week and Janet will busy herself in the borders. If Bob takes early retirement, it will be her last autumn tending this particular garden. She will want to make sure everything is ready to hand on to the next Suffragan Bishop of Barcup and his wife. Or his celibate gay partner! Or her husband! Goodness, how things change!

Yes, change is in the air. We accelerate towards some hidden eschaton. But can we raise our eyes and greet it yet? The apples ripen. Has the time come to shake the tree? Tree-shaking is a profoundly un-Anglican pastime. If we wait long enough, surely, surely the harvest time will come of its own accord? *All is safely gathered in, free from sorrow, free from sin.* Oh, let the time of fruition come gently, let us all agree upon it, let nothing be bruised or jolted! Let's not be hasty!

But the tree-shakers are in the orchard, like it or not. We hear their feet tramping down below as we cling on up here in the sunshine. What are they about, these madmen? Visigoths and vandals! Or – impossible thought – are they sent by the Lord of the Harvest? How are we to read the signs of the times? If we knew for sure that this was a slave trader and not the ark of salvation, then of course we would give our blessing to the boat-rockers! We wouldn't stand on this deck singing 'Amazing Grace' if we were sure it was the stench of injustice, not the unfashionable scent of scriptural truth that filled our nostrils.

On the wires the swallows gather, and wait for the signal to leave.

The Rogers girls walk to school with Mummy. Little Jessie skips. A new pink Barbie bag jounces on her back. Inside this is a new pink Barbie lunchbox, because that's what little girls are made of, made of. There is a pink aisle and a blue aisle in this world. A princess cupcake pony aisle of lipstick and tiaras, and an adventure pirate dragon aisle of farts and weapons. The divide is policed by the children themselves.

Hur, hur, Leah Rogers is wearing BOYS' TRAINERS!

Leah Rogers is indeed wearing boys' trainers, because there are no *children's* trainers at Clark's (and it must be Clark's, or how is Leah to thank her mother when she's forty and still has nice feet?). As you enter the mystic shopping portal to happiness, childhood bifurcates. You must choose: Girls or Boys. Poor Leah just wanted black trainers. Is that too much to ask? But black trainers for Girls all have purple or jade or pink embellishments. This is important. Should gender confusion strike during PE, a girl needs to be able to glance at her feet and reassure herself that all is well. Look: it is possible to be sporty *and* pretty! I'm still a real girl! Yay!

Leah's Boy trainers are black and white. No good will come of this! She will never grow up to be a happy, well-adjusted adult consumer if she can't decide which aisle she shops in. Oh, and it gets worse! Her new karate backpack is black and white too! Is it a *boy* bag or a *girl* bag? Her karate kit is white,* and one day she will get a black belt and be as awesome as F— M—, whose name she cannot even whisper in her head, in case anyone suspects, and says, 'Hur, hur, you fancy him, you've gone all red!' Which is so not true, she doesn't *fancy* him, she *respects* him, which is totally different, but the pink princesses at school don't get this, because they are IDIOTS, always squealing and texting the entire whole time and going, 'OMIGOD, don't look, he totally looked at me just now!' Plus they

---

* It is true that pink karate kits do exist, but only when some numpty washes it with a red belt.

think everything is about sex, like who even *cares* about sex? They are so immature.

Leah is now in the top year of juniors. This time next year it will be Big School. And *puberty*.

Shut up, *shut up, SHUT UP*!

As she walks to school she practises her blocks and snap punches, because she's got her next grade in three weeks. The poor girl respects F.M. so much she aches. Just *aches* to see him again. She has stopped moaning about boring, boring Fridays, when they have to wait in the office after school for Daddy to finish work. Oh, *why* did Daddy have to go and get that stupid new job? Because after Christmas they won't need to come to the office and wait ever again! There are only four months left!

Every Friday Leah does *pinan nidan* and *pinan shodan* on the palace drive. Over and over. All the grown-ups are impressed. 'Goodness, she takes her karate seriously, doesn't she?' they say to Mummy or Daddy. 'Duh, *obviously*. Coz I want to get my black belt,' she tells them. That's the reason. The reason is not in case *he* comes and joins in again on his way to choir practice and says, 'Hey, you rock, girlfriend!' Tuh! That would be lame.

And anyway, he never comes.

Honestly, this is the last straw! To come in late from a meeting to *this*. Father Dominic screws the letter up, drops it, stamps on it. He rings Janey. No reply. He checks his watch. It's getting late, but he rings Ed. 'Hello, Father.'

'Father! Hello! How are you? How was France?'

'Lovely, thanks. Listen, Ed, is now a good time?'

'It's a perfect time. I'm walking home along a country lane from a harvest supper planning meeting. We're going to hold a beetle drive. A beetle drive!'

'Oh, you country parsons! *We're* having a global food banquet for Back to Church Sunday. Because we're all urban and edgy, so there. Look, can I pick you brain for a moment?'

'Of course.'

'Thanks. Listen, have you been approached to take part in any "shared conversation" thingies?'

'Oh, God. Those. I had a letter, but it wasn't from the diocese, so I binned it.'

'Oh, goody-good! It was from the Reverend Dr Veronica da Silva? Have you actually met her yet?'

'Oooh, you've got your hatchet-job voice on, Father. She's Wendy's curate, isn't she?'

'No, no! That's Virginia. Veronica is the ubiquitous self-appointed chaplain of everything. She's trying to annexe us gay men to her empire, Ed!'

'Ha ha! I'd like to see her annexe Neil!'

'You laugh! Seriously, I can't remember when I ever hated someone this much. I literally cannot be in the same room as her! My head feels like a computer with a great big magnet stuck on the hard drive, or something.'

Silence. 'Hmm.'

'I hide when she calls round, Ed. Literally hide. I screen my calls. Am I going mad? Maybe I'm going mad!'

'I doubt it,' says Ed. 'You poor darling! I'm really sorry to hear this. You're not obliged to have any formal dealings with her, though, are you?'

'No, but I'm Rector of Lindford, and she bobs up *everywhere*! She's on every committee! Honestly, she's like some demon-possessed cuckoo-clock. "Cuckoo! Father Dominic!" Argh! I'm not even convinced she's ordained, frankly. Remember that guy, Wallace something, in Cambridge? Who'd been a mercenary and a diamond miner?'

'Ooh, one of *those*! Well, in that case, though I'm not a *huge* fan, I'd say the archdeacon's your man. He'll be all over her like a rash.'

'You'd think! But he says he's not in a position to do anything for a month or two, and to take it up with diocesan HR manager, for God's sake!'

'Ah, la belle Helene! She's Kay's other half. You know, Kay, Vicar of St Andrew's, Barcup?'

'No! Kay Redfern! No! Well, I never knew that.'

'Sssh! Don't tell Veronica, or she'll annexe them as well!'

'I'm not sure she's interested in dykes, Father. They won't adore her the way we gay men always adore straight women.'

'So why don't *you* adore her, then? You're a closet straight, aren't you? Admit it, Father!'

'Talk to me again about adoring her when you've met her! But thanks, Ed. Good to get that off my chest.'

'Any time, Father. Go and open a bottle of Prosecco.'

Jane checks her phone. Missed call from Dom. Nothing from Matt. If she'd got a job in New Zealand, she'd be enjoying her mid-semester break now. Like Danny, off in Queenstown black water nude bungee-jumping, or something equally mental. She'd be approaching the home straight, not bracing herself for the start of a new year.

Oh, God. Was that the wrong call last December? Gambling everything on Matt being The One, assuming it would work out because they were both wild about each other. If I'm going to be miserable, wouldn't it be better to be miserable in Middle Earth? No, this was cheap escapism. Let this clergy discipline thing run its course. Things may yet work out. She texts him: 'Miss you. Jxx'

Father Ed arrives back at the vicarage to find another silver Skoda parked beside his. Even before he's got the front door open he can hear Neil laughing in the kitchen.

'Eds? C'mere, big man!'

Uh-oh. That'll be the U'Luvka speaking. He goes through to the kitchen to rescue the poor guest.

'Where've you been? I'm 'splaining the YES campaign to Ronnie, here. You know each other?' Neil waves the bottle towards a woman dressed in black. 'Ronnie, Ed, ma fiancé. Ed, Ronnie. Fuck, I'm pished.'

She bounds forward, like a tarantula pouncing. 'Hi, Father Ed!! I've heard *so* much about you from Dommie!!'

Chapter 21

'**M**cIvor,' said Father Ed to Neil. 'McIvor called.'

Neil froze. Went scarlet.

Ed turned to Veronica. 'Really sorry. Bit of a crisis. Oh, dear.' He looked helplessly at his watch. 'Um. Sorry to do this, but if you could, ah, leave us . . . ?'

'Oh, I todally unnerstand!' A compassionate hand gripped Ed's arm. 'That's cool. I hear you. My heart so goes *out* to you guys and your situation? If there's anything I can do? I'll come back at a better time. Neil, thanks for the drink, I'll be in touch, darling. Anon for now.'

Darling! Ed apologized her to the door, expertly shielding himself from a deluge of future commitments with the umbrella of English uselessness. Finally the silver Skoda pulled away. His heart was pounding.

By the time he got back to the kitchen Neil had unfrozen. I'll say! He'd passed from solid state, through liquid, and was now vaporizing.

'Excuse me? *Excuse me?* Did you just *safeword* me?'

'Yes. Yes, I did, Neil.'

'What the actual fuck, Eds? That's not what it's *for*, you bawheed!'

'Really? I thought it was for when you're doing something I'm really not enjoying and I need you to stop *now*, without arguing.'

'*In bed!* It's in bed, not, not, tsh!—' He rapped his knuckles on Ed's forehead. 'Not *socially*, it's not an *in conversation* thing when there's feckin' company here! Christ! Do you even know how embarrassing you are, Vicar?'

'I couldn't think how else to shut you up. Shall I explain what's going on?'

'I would love that, I would *love* you to explain on what planet that is acceptable behaviour— McIvor? I'll give you McIvor! Aye, and another thing, why's Ronnie gone, eh? You threw her *out*? What's that all about? She's the one person who can help us here with, with, strategy, with the media and legal, she's the LBGT, LG, och, the *thing* chaplain. *And* the union rep. Why aren't you in the union, Eds, eh? Anyway.' Neil folded his arms with laborious flamboyance. 'Go on, then. Explain away.'

It should be noted that Neil was not at his most receptive. Ed did his best to convey that Veronica was *not* their friend and ally, that there was no diocesan LGBT officer, that she was not the diocesan union rep; but this was waved aside. Father Dominic was dismissed as 'that wee nellie' and his concerns ridiculed. No, it was pointless to argue tonight. Ed settled himself to endure. An unfocused rant against the Church followed, interspersed with what 'Ronnie' proposed to do to aid their cause, doubling back periodically to McIvor. Ed let it run its course. Neil's drunken discourse resembled a mad wind-up toy that threshed hysterically round your ankles until it finally twitched into stillness – only to clatter back to life if you foolishly poked it. He'd moved on to Scottish independence now. Ed's eyes watered from stifled yawns.

'Don't fall asleep on me, you bastard!'

'Sorry, but you're having a *Braveheart* moment. I lost the will to live.'

Neil punched his arm. 'And *another* nother thing – yon archdeacon, he's been suspended. For shacking up with his missis. Aye, I thought you'd be interested in *that*.' And off he went again: bastard bishops, Yes campaign, Tory bastards, McIvor! Why's Ronnie gone?

My readers may be relieved to learn that the archdeacon has not, in fact, been suspended. I will seize the opportunity offered by Neil's disquisition to bring you up to date. The diocesan registrar has done whatever registrars do in the privacy of their chambers under the heading 'Preliminary Scrutiny' – pondered and stroked his chin? turned cartwheels in his twinkly shoes? we may never know – and has submitted his report to the bishop. Briefly: there *is* sufficient substance to the complaint to justify proceeding with it. Just as Bishop Harry predicted.

Those of you who are interested in the minutiae of such processes may download the document entitled Clergy Discipline Measure 2003 Code of Practice, and consult it at your leisure. It is available on the C of E website, because it is our joy to be transparent. Admittedly, the C of E is occasionally transparent in the manner of a net curtain: you can see out perfectly well. Seeing *in* may be altogether more baffling.

Bishop Harry, were he Bishop of Lindchester and not merely a retired acting bishop, would have dismissed the complaint as 'probably not grave enough to merit a formal rebuke under the Measure'. But there we are. Matt has been officially informed and sent a copy of the registrar's report and the original complaint. He now has twenty-one days to provide a written reply.

Ah, what a dull document to scoop up so much human suffering! Here is the first port of call for complaints about everything from cocking up the interment of ashes, via snogging your youth worker, through to systematically abusing choirboys. The process seeks to deal fairly, kindly and consistently with all: the victims, the wrongdoers, the innocent, the misunderstood, the weak and hapless, and the criminal. Let nothing be swept under the vestry carpet ever again! Unfortunately, the Clergy Discipline Measure also presents itself as a handy tool for malcontents. If you don't like the cut of your vicar's jib, if you take agin a member of the senior staff, here's a way of making life difficult for him or her. The Measure is not designed to deal with 'minor complaints and grievances'; but hey, it's worth a shot. In a previous era all you could do was rattle off a green ink snorter to the bishop. Now you have Form 1a.

But to return to our friend the archdeacon: he has not been suspended. Suspension is not automatic when a complaint is being investigated. It's up to the bishop to decide. So where did Neil get hold of that idea, I wonder? Perhaps the complainant herself is circulating the rumour? For some people, the border between wishing something to be the case, and it actually being the case, is not properly policed. In their inner landscape no armed guards patrol the barbed-wire edge of truth and demand to see visas. Such people wander from fact to fantasy as unconsciously as we (currently) cross from England to Scotland on a hike in the Borders.

We will rejoin our friends in the vicarage at Gayden Magna, where Neil is now striving to articulate to Ed how much he really, really loves him. He has not, for example, tweeted, emailed, texted or in any way contacted yon wee slag in the choir, Eds can check his phone.

'Seriously, I'm serious, check, check it now.'

'I don't need to, Neil. Look, it's late. Let's go to bed.'

'Lis'n, he's hot, fair enough. But it's you I love, big man. It's just, och, he came on to me, Eds?'

'So you said.'

'Seriously. Before I could ... I tried, but there he was, snogging the gob off me.'

'Yeah, thanks. You said.'

'Got this tongue stud?'

'*Thanks*, Neil.'

'Yeah, only then his feckin' phone rings, and *pff!* It's all, "Du-u-ude, your *fiancé*!" Ooh. Nearly smacked him. 'Kin tease. Telling you, *so* close to smacking him.' There was a silence. Neil frowned. 'Said that, did I?'

More silence. 'No. No, you didn't, actually.'

'No? Oh, yeah.' Neil knuckled his temples. 'Wasn't gonna tell you, was I? Ah, shite. I'm so *dumb*. Are you mad at me? Please, don't be mad at me, Eds.'

'Come on. Let's go to bed. We'll talk in the morning.'

And in the morning you'll deny you ever said it, thought Ed. Neil was now snoring beside him. I *knew* there was something you weren't telling me! I should be mad at you; but no, I'm not, you twat. It was almost funny, actually. Phone ringing. Hah. Far easier to believe this version of events, than that you suddenly remembered our engagement and came to your senses. Ed sighed. Well, he'd got the whole shabby truth at last. Curiously, it felt reassuring.

But it was going to tarnish the unambiguous pleasure of hating that tramp Freddie May.

How is that tramp getting on, you may be wondering? At this precise moment he's peeling his shirt off for Totty.

Hmm. I need to back up a little here. Let us (in a metaphorical and scriptural manner) run and never be weary all the way from Gayden Magna, through the days and miles, to the house of the canon treasurer, Philip Voysey-Scott, on Lindchester Cathedral Close. I will fill you in as we go.

Freddie has been lodging with the Voysey-Scotts for a month now. To start with – owing to a silly misunderstanding – he was acutely lonely and miserable. The Voysey-Scotts, you see, had assumed Freddie valued his privacy and independence and that he'd prefer to make his own eating arrangements. Freddie assumed the Voysey-Scotts hated him. It was Pippa Voysey-Scott who took him by the scruff of the neck and shook some sense into him. They now eat together after evensong every night, and Freddie is as utterly devoted to Lady Totty as a newly hatched duckling that has accidentally imprinted on a Range Rover. (Freddie is right: she does sound *exactly* like Lady Campanula Tottington off *Wallace and Gromit: The Curse of the Were-Rabbit*.) Pippa/Totty is a physiotherapist, and she has just ordered Freddie to remove his shirt so she can take a proper look at his shoulder, which is troubling him. We will creep into the sitting room and spy on them.

'Wings! Hoo, hoo, hoo! What a hoot! You've got wings! Pip, darling, come and look! Little Freddie's grown wings!'

'Gah!' Freddie hid his face in his hands. 'You're embarrassing me, Totty!'

The canon treasurer stuck his head round the door. 'Great Scott, man!' he cried (in the voice of the canon precentor). 'Those tattoos are a liturgical *nightmah*! It's not the Feast of Michael and All Angels till the end of the month!' He vanished back to his study.

'Well, you're bonkers, darling,' said Lady Totty, 'but I suppose they're rather sweet if you like that kind of thing. OK, give me your hand. Relax.' She began putting Freddie's right arm through some gentle physiotherapy paces. 'Hurts when you lie on it?'

'Yeah.'

'Can you raise it above your head?'

'Yeah – ow!'

'Do you play squash?'

'Nah.'

'Tennis? No? What about weights?'

'Well, duh, girlfriend? Hafta work out to look this hot.'

'You're overdeveloping those pecs.' She flicked a nipple ring.

'Get off!'

'Common cause of shoulder trouble in gym bunnies. You need to stretch your chest out properly afterwards. I'll show you some doorframe exercises. And you need to make sure you're developing your upper back as well, or you'll end up round-shouldered. More pull-ups, young man.'

'Hnhh. I'm thinking it was maybe painting ceilings? In the school that time?'

'Ah! That when it started? Yah, it can be caused by adopting some unaccustomed posture.' She paused and peered into his face. 'What?'

'Nothing.'

'Hoo, hoo, ha ha ha! Freddie's blushing! Had your arms up over your head for a prolonged period, hmm?'

'No, yeah, *painting*! I was painting! Shut *up*!'

'Diagnosis: BDSM-related subacromial bursitis! Hoo, hoo, hoo! What a scream!'

'*No!* Listen, it was the— Oh, I'm not talking to you. God, you're so mean to me.'

'Sorry. I've stopped. Aw, poor angel! OK, sit yourself down. Come on. Let's have a bash at untangling those feathers for you.' She went to work on his neck and shoulders. 'Seriously though, yah? You should find yourself a nice man to look after you properly, Freddie.'

'Like I'm not looking? Mmmm. Oh, that's good. Oh, God. That's so good. Oh yeah, Totty!'

'Are you two having sex in there?' called the canon treasurer.

So yes, apart from a sore shoulder, all is well with Freddie May. He has attended services and rehearsals punctually and in a godly, righteous and sober manner. He has sung beautifully and conducted himself reverently in the cathedral church of Lindchester. He has been polite to all in authority and helpful about the house for Totty. Above all, he has never worn brown shoes with his cassock. All this indicates – to those who know Freddie well – that a major act of self-sabotage cannot be far off.

And indeed, trouble is a-brewing. The canon precentor discusses it with the director of music after evensong on Thursday.

'As his line manager, Timothy, I think *you* are the right person to raise it with him,' Giles is saying as he opens a bottle of Riesling. The 'no booze on school nights' rule has given way to the 'I try to get through to Thursday' rule; as it so often does on a Thursday. Especially when Freddie May is doing the precentorial head in again.

'We-e-ell,' says Timothy, accepting a glass for much the same reason. 'I was wondering if it might be better coming from *you*, as canon precentor . . . ?'

'No, I think not,' says the precentor. 'You need to remind him of the importance of discretion in conduct and behaviour. That, and the fact that he's still on probation.'

'Damn. He won't take kindly to my raising it, Giles.'

'I dare say not. But I don't take kindly to a cathedral lay clerk selling his services as a topless cocktail waiter, frankly. Have you seen his Twitter account? Look.' Giles hands over his phone.

Timothy looks. 'Oh, God.'

'Exactly. Matron caught the boys sniggering over it last night. This can't be allowed to continue.'

'No, clearly not.' Timothy took a large swig of Riesling. 'Oh, but can't we get his mentor to do it?' he burst out.

'I already asked,' admits Giles. 'Dr Jacks wishes it to be understood that he does not discuss his mentee with anyone, or take instructions from me, and if I don't like this, I may swivel on it.'

'Well, that's helpful.'

'Yes, he always won the Helpfulness Cup at school. Look, set up a meeting with the two of us and Mr May. If he has a tantrum, we'll get the archdeacon to read the riot act. I know Matt has no *official* role here, but he does have advanced tart-wrangling skills.'

'I thought he'd been suspended?'
'No, that's just a rumour.'

Poor Matt. The rumour has been doing the rounds. How is he faring? Oddly enough, he is energized by the situation he finds himself in. That's what comes of being an archdeacon. So much of your time is taken up with troubleshooting and crisis management that you become a bit of a white-knuckle junkie. It takes a right old catastrophe to make you feel fully alive. He did not waste time wishing he'd responded to Geoff's email all those months ago, tipping him off about Veronica's creative CV-writing. He obediently got into his black Mini and drove to see the Bishop of Another Diocese who Harry had designated to give him pastoral support. He's now cracking on with writing his response to the complaint.

What will he say? He will confess. Yep, out of order. But he will outline the mitigating circumstances. Give due credit to Janey's ideological objections to marriage, his respect for her conscience, their devotion to one another. It riles him no end to know that anything he writes will be read by Veronica. He's not going to muddy the water by suggesting that this whole complaint is basically malicious. A pre-emptive strike to head off the disciplinary procedures he was about to instigate against *her*. Not the time or place for that. Yet. The archdeacon is a patient man. He will be getting to that, all right. You'd better believe it.

And when all's said and done, he *is* in the wrong here. His relationship with Janey *is* disorderly. He's got to man up and take the consequences. Funny how it's a bit of a relief to be caught. Said as much to the bishop. He can look God in the eye again. For a second the archdeacon almost glimpses an expression on the good Lord's face. *Come on home, Tyler, you numpty. Stop trying to hide from me.* He blows his nose and carries on with the old Form 2: 'Clergy Discipline Measure 2003, Respondent's answer to a complaint'.

Meanwhile, Jane is doing her best to keep out of it. Induction Week is under way at Poundstretcher. She runs the gauntlet of leaflet distributers as she heads for the Fergus Abernathy building. Freshers herd round the campus with new Poundstretcher cloth bookbags. She tries to distract herself with historic departmental feuds and not go over and punch the Revd Dr Veronica da Silva as she bounces in her dungarees on the chaplaincy stall, handing out rainbow shoelaces.

'Well, Deanissima, the Union is safe,' said Gene on Friday morning. 'You will not need to repatriate your left leg, or whichever quarter of your person you designate McPherson.'

Marion smiled. 'Yes, I'm glad. Although there's going to be a lot of heartbreak today.'

'Let's hope that Whitehall keeps its promises to the Scottish people!' said Gene brightly. 'Betrayal would be too much, following so hard on the heels of Culloden! I must say, I'm rather impressed by the SNP. A *leetle* naive, perhaps. They need to take a leaf out of UKIP's book if they want to capture the true spirit of nationalism. They ought to cast their net wider. As far as I can see, they only really hate English Tories, not queers, yids, sluts, scroungers and anyone from Bongoland. Still, early days. Ooh, talking of queers – when's the big announcement? Can you tell me yet?'

Marion took a deep breath. 'It's next Friday. But, darling, we need to talk about that. I'm afraid it's not Guilden Hargreaves.'

'Ah.' There was a very long silence. 'Now *that*, as the actress said to the bishop, is very disappointing indeed.'

Chapter 22

'**S**o who *is* the new bishop?'

'It's the Area Bishop of Aylesbury, Steve Pennington,' said Marion.

'Who? Never heard of him. Which tribe does he belong to? Is he another Evangelical? Oh God, he is. Another sodding Steve-angelical.'

Marion sighed. 'Well, that didn't take long to come up with a nickname, did it?'

Gene quite literally bit his lip. He raised both hands like an unjust judge trying to placate a gaggle of importunate widows. 'How very lovely,' he said eventually. 'I'm trying really hard not to vent my spleen on you, darling; because I'm sure you did what you could, and that there are sterling reasons for this appointment. And a whole load of cock that you probably can't tell me about.'

'That's about the size of it,' said Marion. 'Basically, the bishop needs to be a focus for unity in the diocese.'

'Focus for unity! Exquisite! In other words, some tiny-minded prehistoric homophobes on the CNC kicked off and blocked Guilden. Or was it the archbishop? Yes, all right, sorry.' Gene raised his hands once more and made tempest-calming gestures. He paced the dean's study in nothing like his usual sinuous saunter. 'My, we live in interesting times, don't we? How are you coping, Deanissima?'

'I'm fine, thank you.' Just for a second Marion's lip trembled. She took a steadying breath and smiled. 'The CNC was unanimous in thinking that Steve will be excellent for the job. He'll be very good for Lindchester. I warmed to him very much on interview.'

'Second-choice Steve!'

'No. Don't you dare repeat that, Gene. Seriously.'

'Oh, come on, everyone knows Guilden was tipped for the job!'

'No, they don't *know* that. The CNC's discussions were confidential.'

'As you wish.' He bowed. 'And I suppose Steeeve is a married gentleman?'

'He is. His wife's called Sonya. They're big in the New Wine network.'

'That means nothing to me.'

'Well, I'd describe him as Charismatic stroke Open Evangelical.'

'I would *never* stroke an Open Evangelical.'

'You say that now,' replied the dean with a smile, 'but you haven't met Sonya yet.'

'Ooh! Is she a looker? Will I like her?' He got out his phone and began googling.

'You'll meet them both on Thursday evening.'

'Oh, lucky, lucky me.'

'We're hosting a welcome dinner in a private room in the Lindford Excelsior.'

'There's glamour.'

'Look, stop being so snooty. The idea is that Steve and Sonya get to meet the senior staff team and their spouses before the announcement on Friday morning. I hardly need say it, but this is all still embargoed, Gene.'

'I'm as mum as a home-schooling Evangelical wife. Here we are. Well, hell-ooo, Mrs Pennington! My, my! She looks like an air hostess in a seventies porn movie. Does she bake? I'd eat her muffins any day!'

'There. I knew I could count on you, my darling.'

'Ooh, and get *you*, Bishop Steve! Isn't he the dapper dog! Heavens to Betsy! He almost out-Gilderoys Gilderoy in the floppy hair department, doesn't he? I *wish* I could rock the ageing *Brideshead* look. Ah well, at least his hair is gay. That's something, I suppose. Ooh, I wonder if he'll be needing a chauffeur? Or, indeed, a topless cocktail—'

'NO!'

'Still not funny?'

'It will *never* be funny.' The dean frowned him into submission.

'And now I urgently need to open a bottle of something *old*. A nineteen-eighty-four Chateau La Lagune? Yes. Because, as the Good Book says, no one after drinking old wine straightway desireth the new. New Wine! Sweet suffering middle-aged Jesus in five-oh-ones!'

'That's right.' The dean squeezed his arm. 'You get it all out of your system, darling, and then you can behave on Thursday night.'

Gene laid a hand on his heart. 'You may rely upon me to do everything that is proper in a dean's husband. And afterwards I'll come home and drown a litter of kittens to balance my chakras.'

And so, dear readers, welcome to the inner circle of those who know the identity of the next bishop. I must ask you to be discreet, no matter how strongly you feel on the subject. Don't talk to the press. Don't sound off on Twitter. It is vital that the news does not get out before the official Downing Street announcement. If Steve's name is leaked, that's seven years' bad luck, and the culprit will have to go and stand in the corner wearing a label saying 'I'm a tit'. Happily, the members of the CNC have taken their vows of confidentiality seriously. Nobody has gone home and offloaded on spouse or colleague, tempting though that will have been. They have been careful not to leave top secret emails open on their desktop. No nods, winks or hints have been issued, and nobody has prattishly gone out and had a flutter on Steve Pennington at Ladbrokes.

This, then, is the net curtain transparency of the C of E that I referred to earlier. We know who the CNC members are, and where and when they met. But we will never know what went on in those – we must imagine – anguished discussions that led to their unanimous decision to select Bishop Steve Pennington for the See of Lindchester, and dash poor Guilden's hopes, just as his mother had warned back at Easter.

The archdeacon, when he heard the news, was not altogether surprised. Probably still a tad too soon for Guilden to get the job. It would only take one member of the CNC to have grave concerns ... And Matt knows the local ones, so he can hazard a guess. Still, it's not going to be too long before Guilden, or someone gay and out, is made bishop. Within a year or two, Matt was thinking. Unless the wind changed. Probably be in a less trad diocese than dear old Lindchester, where some folk were still needing a little lie down after getting a woman dean! No, most likely be a more hip urban diocese. Plus you had to bear in mind the pressure on the archbishops to appoint an ultra-conservative bishop ASAP, to placate the hardliners, who were feeling like a persecuted minority as well. What a mare. Here's how Matt read the situation: three on the shortlist – Guilden, Steve, and Revd Conservative. Which meant it was a no-brainer. There was only one of that line-up who could provide a focus for unity in the diocese. Shame, as he'd got a lot of time for Guilden, and it was about time we chuffing sorted ourselves out on the gay issue. That said, Steve was a good thing, easy guy to warm to. More of the common touch than Paul, had to be said. Plus he's not going to derail the diocesan growth strategy.

The members of the CNC have done their work. For better or worse, they have made their choice. Geoff returns to the parish office after the asylum-seekers' drop-in session. He is still coming to terms with the decision. Had they played it too safe, and valued unity over the prophetic? Is there ever a good moment to turn over the tables in the temple? Ought he to have pressed the point? He'd vowed after Veronica's appointment he'd always voice the unpopular view. No, this was different. He heard no alarm bells over Steve. But Veronica! It's like living in a permanent fire drill. If only he could see an end to it! How much is now just paranoia? He can no longer tell. He's lost track of how many times he's changed his computer password. And he has no real reason to think she's ever snooped.

All across the diocese Michaelmas daisies are in flower. Railway sidings and embankments and derelict sites are a haze of mauve, as if the waste places of Lindfordshire have broken forth into purple to herald the advent of the new bishop this Friday. And still the landscape seems to hold its breath. The driest September since records began. Silence. Like the silence in heaven when the dragon fought with the archangel.

There are clouds of incense at solemn evensong in Lindchester Cathedral for Michael and All Angels. And Freddie May, though his wings are tucked under his cassock, still sings like an angel (*Dum committeret bellum draco cum Michaele Archangelo* . . .), little knowing that tomorrow after evensong he will be hauled up in front of the director of music and the canon precentor and challenged about his use of social media. And all hell will break loose.

The door crashed shut. They waited till the footsteps had pounded off into the distance.

'Well, I think that went off rather well!' said the precentor brightly.

The director of music had his head in his hands. 'Oh, God. He's going to go AWOL now, isn't he? Well, at least tomorrow's dumb day.'

'Which Mr May will doubtless keep in his customary manner, by doing something spectacularly dumb. I'd better text Philip and Pippa to alert them.' Giles got his phone out: 'Tart crisis. Stand to!' He stacked his papers and got to his feet. 'Anyway, this is why I thought we'd better brace him today. There's at least a chance he'll have cooled down by Thursday.' *No booze on school nights. No booze on school nights* . . . 'Well, we should both write up an account of this for HR.'

182

'Yes, will do. Honestly, though, I really think his mentor might step in here. Isn't this exactly the sort of reason we set that up?'

'I tried! I *begged* him to join us for this meeting. But Dr Jacks is a law unto himself, I fear.'. *No booze on school nights.* 'Wine?'

'God, yes. Thought you'd never offer.'

Freddie May is incandescent. Fuck this. He is totally heading off to London *right now.* Well, after dinner. Rude not to turn up, coz Totty's expecting him.

He flings himself on his bed. Giles and Tim have no right to judge his private life! This is nothing to do with the choir! Why does this *always* happen? This *so* wouldn't happen if he was straight! Just when things are starting to go right, why does someone always have to get on his case and totally judge his lifestyle like this?

'Yoo-hoo! Freddie?'

Ah cock, now Totty's calling him? He blots his eyes on his hoodie sleeve. Please let him keep it together till after the meal? He heads downstairs. Turns the landing corner, and—

No! I don't *believe* this, they've only called his fucking mentor in to carpet him as well? For one dumbass moment Freddie nearly turns and sprints back upstairs. What – like he's gonna jump out of the back window and escape? Fucksake.

Dr Jacks beckons like a ref about to give a red card? Yeah, so much for not fucking discussing me with anyone, asshole! Freddie storms on down.

'Mr May. I was hoping to catch a word in private.'

'Yeah, I *know* why you're here—'

'In private, Mr May.'

And he only gets him by the arm and steers him to the sitting room – un-fucking-believable! So Freddie kicks the door shut and goes into Total. Fucking. Meltdown. Judge me, you douchebag? Total betrayal, running to Giles, two-faced, I *trusted* you, man! Told you everything? Behind my back? You slut-shaming, arrogant, up yourself— And all the time Jacks just stands there, bored, like this is some aircraft fucking safety announcement he's doing here!

'Well, *fuck* this mentoring shit, I'm through with it.'

Silence.

It goes on wa-a-ay too long.

Oh, man. The psycho stare? Like he's wondering what you'd look like without skin?

'Thank you for your candour, Mr May. All very instructive, but that's not why I'm here, actually.'

'Yeah, right. Like Giles hasn't—'

'Ssh. I swung by to drop off a tail suit, because you told me last time that you don't own one. You may thank me once, and once only, then I want to hear no more about it.'

'Wha-a-a'?' Nooo! Freddie wraps his arms round his head and shuts his eyes. Kill me now. 'Gah! Seriously? You're not here about . . . ? Oh, man. Listen, I am so-o-o sorry? Only—'

Jacks has his hand to his ear, waiting.

'Oh! Ah, thanks. But . . . yeah, no, listen, that's really nice of you, but you can't just like *give* me stuff?'

'I'm not. It's called "paying it forward". You're familiar with the concept? Good, because I expect my mentees to do the same. And this is all about you creating a professional impression. Being nice is not my forte.'

'Yeah, but no, listen, sir— Gah! I just called you sir! I totally did that! Dr . . . what am I meant to call you?'

'"Sir" is fine.'

Freddie hesitates. 'You're . . . kidding, right?'

'Oh yes, I'm a real kidder.' He glances at his watch. 'May I raise one quick thing, Mr May? I tried to make it clear from the outset that I never discuss my mentees. Sadly, this hasn't prevented Giles from ringing me up to complain about you. So if *anything* occurs to you that might prevent this happening in future, I'd be grateful.'

'Gah, I get that you're totally pissed at me? I am so, *so* sorry?'

Dr Jacks inclines his head. 'Thank you. Then I'll be on my way.' He pauses. The icy eyes do another nad-shrivelling scan. 'Unless, of course, you'd value someone older and wiser telling you what to do?'

Freddie tugs his hair. Hugs himself and shivers. 'Oh, God. Yeah, no, yeah. Probably you should do that?'

'Excellent. Then let me just ask: do you nurse any ambition at all to be taken seriously as a musician? Because on the strength of your online presence – speaking here as a choral director of some standing – I certainly wouldn't hire you.' He leans close and whispers: 'You have a very nice bum, Mr May, but I believe the whole world has now seen it. You can safely delete the pictures.'

'Nng.'

He pats Freddie's face like some scary Mafia boss. 'Sort it out, Choirslut-Ninety. Ciao, ciao.'

Dr Jacks cuts across the Close to pop in on his old friend Bishop Harry, before shooting off up to The Sage. Sir! He shakes his head. Idiot child. Finally he permits himself a smile. Yes. It is true to say that a nobler man would not be enjoying this quite so much.

*

Preparations are under way for the welcome dinner. Penelope has booked the top secret private room at the Excelsior and issued everyone on the guest list with top secret directions. Poor old Steve and Sonya. Pity them just a little, dear reader, as they approach this ordeal. Everyone will behave well, and give them a warm Lindchester welcome, but there is inevitably a tiny undertow of antagonism when a new bishop is presented, as a *fait accompli*, to close colleagues who have had no say in his appointment. When we find ourselves powerless in important matters, all that remains is to sweat the small stuff.

Thus the dean weighs the merits of clerical garb against Diana von Furstenberg wrap dress. Gene goes to London and buys the most viciously purple shirt ever encountered outside the pages of a vestments catalogue. Martin books Freddie May to babysit his girls (they will have a mammoth pillow fight throughout the entire house that Martin will never find out about, and Leah will secretly break her heart all over again). Ah, and lovely Bishop Bob is coming to the meal – his first official outing since his heart op – though he and Janet may slip away early if he gets too tired. Bishop Harry's wife Isobel sends her apologies. The precentor's wife, having seen a photo of the new bishop's wife, has been out to buy a new posh frock. Not that it's a competition, of course. Totty will fling on pearls and LBD at the last minute. The poor chancellor's wife will try to locate *something* that still fits and doesn't have historic puke on the shoulder.

And what of the archdeacon in all this spousely malarkey? Everyone knows about his situation now. Not like the disciplinary process is a secret, is it? Cheers for that, Veronica. So, is he going to make a stand and invite Janey along? Or would that be a bit of a distraction from the main focus, which is to welcome Steve and Sonya to the diocese? In the end, he rings Janey. Tells her how matters stand. He hears the filthy laugh that always makes his heart turn flic-flacs. 'An evening with the diocesan stuffed shirts of Lindchester? That's very sweet of you, Mr Archdeacon, but I think I'll pass.'

It is Wednesday evening. The diocesan communications officer cracks his knuckles. He goes over the schedule for the umpteenth time. Welcome dinner tomorrow night. Bishop designate to attend Morning Prayer in cathedral on Friday, followed by press conference (seen a copy of Steve's speech, all OK, ditto Bishop Bob's, to be read by Bishop Harry), meeting with civics, visit to Lindford Food Bank, chance to meet key business/religious leaders. Local radio interview. He scans on down the list. Yup, yup, yup. Lunch over in Martonbury with Bishop Bob. Chance to look round palace. Press release ready to go live on Friday morning, just after Downing Street announcement. He needs to make a couple more phone calls, but basically everything seems to be in order. Quick check on Twitter to see if anyone had got a whiff. Seems unlikely, but—

You probably saw @roderick_fallon's tweet yourself: 'New bishop of #Lindchester is @BishopAylesbury Steve Pennington.' With a link to Fallon's feature in Thursday's *Herald*, exposing the CNC's decision not to appoint the openly gay Principal of Barchester Theological College.

OCTOBER

C. Lydon

Chapter 23

A voice sings in the darkness.

> When the house doth sigh and weep,
> And the world is drown'd in sleep,
> Yet mine eyes the watch do keep,
> Sweet Spirit, comfort me!

Almost midnight in Lindchester Cathedral. There has been much sighing and weeping tonight. Marion kneels in her stall and listens. Outside the wind rushes. *Comfort me!* The last echo fades. She hears someone whisper, 'Jesus.' Footsteps come towards her down the quire.

'Freddie?'

'Omigod! Mrs Dean! I'm so sorry, didn't know you were there.'

'How did you get in?'

Pause. 'Oh, right, yeah, I kinda . . . yeah? Just wanted to be here and like, y'know? Sing? The acoustic? And because, God?'

A pale gleam from the floodlights seeps in through leaded glass and casts patterns up on the vaults. Like moonlight rippled on water. And the quire is the seabed of this sleep-drowned world. Above in the crow's nest Marion hears the muffled chimes of the clock strike midnight, like a ship's bell – like Herrick's passing bell – and the wind washes in restless waves. Freddie seems to sway there on the current, a ghost fish.

'Have you borrowed Philip's keys?'

'Ah, right, about that. I'll totally put them back? Hhnn. Probably I should've asked first?'

'Oh, Freddie.'

'Sorry, Mrs Dean.'

She sighs.

He steps closer. 'Mrs Dean? Are you OK?'

'Not really, if I'm honest. I've got rather a lot on my mind.'

'The new bishop thing? Yeah, saw that on Twitter just now. Can I . . . do anything?'

Yes, you can stop adding to my problems, you feckless dummy. 'Not really, thanks. Unless . . . Would you sing that anthem again? It's beautiful.'

'Hey. You bet. Cool. So we always sang it back in the day? When I was a chorister? Back then I was, yeah, yeah, Hurford again. Kind of, it was just part of the repertoire? But now, when everything's fucked— gah, sorry, Mrs Dean! When things are like . . . complicated? Still sometimes I . . . coz, yeah, I mean the words? And then it's like, y'know? If that makes sense?'

Marion shakes her head and almost smiles. 'Well. In a way, Freddie.'

'Awesome.' He walks back to the far end of the quire. And then his voice, that bright dark-edged voice, shucks off its earthbound stumbling and soars:

> In the hour of my distress,
> When temptations me oppress,
> And when I my sins confess,
> Sweet Spirit, comfort me!
>
> When I lie within my bed,
> Sick in heart and sick in head,
> And with doubts discomforted,
> Sweet Spirit, comfort me!

Marion – sick in heart and head at what has happened, and at what must come – lets the tears fall quietly, knowing they are hidden by the dark.

That was last Wednesday night. Since then, as you may well imagine, there has been much soul-searching and not a little recrimination over the leak. Some very stiff emails were sent. But so far nobody has confessed. Fallon, of course, refuses to name his source.

Marion – as chair of the Lindchester CNC – has been testing the truth of Kipling's 'If' poem to its limits. She has kept her head while all around were losing theirs and blaming her. The truth she has spoken has been twisted by knaves to make a trap for fools, and she has endured that. She will not, as a result, attain the ultimate dignity of becoming A Man; but in due course I hope she will be a bishop. Frustratingly, she is powerless to correct the impression Fallon's piece created, because to do so would involve revealing the confidential discussions of the CNC. While intolerant views – no, *homophobic* views – were aired, that was not the full story. But on the whole, Marion, Bishop Harry and the diocesan communications officer, along with Bishop elect Steve, have handled the flak deftly. Completely off the record and for your ears only, the communications officer did console himself by composing a spoof press release that Gene himself could scarcely have improved upon. (' "I'm not a bigot. Some of my best friends are shirt-lifters," says Lindchester dean.')

It will blow over. Marion knows it will. But right now she's still smarting. At night she cannot prevent the merry-go-round of suspicion setting off on another mad twirl. Who was it? Which member of the CNC had spoken to Fallon? One by one she calls the local members to the stand and cross-examines them. Nobody cracks. She'd swear to their innocence. They are good folk! Fallon, the key witness in the case, thwarts her by claiming his right to silence. It's clear he's seen at least one crucial email. How much more does he know? Maybe it was a member of the national CNC? But why, why? Surely it served nobody's interests, advanced nobody's cause. Because the whole process of senior appointments has been held up for ridicule. Yes, the system's not perfect, but it's an improvement on what went before!

Ah, leave off your fretting, Marion, she chides herself. Hush that fairground in your soul. The cathedral clock chimes. Two a.m. The wind sighs and the deanery windows rattle. Hush, my soul.

But no! The jangly music starts up, and off we go again. Could it have been Guilden himself? Every instinct rejects that idea. *Of course* he will be feeling crushed and disappointed – as everyone does, when they are shortlisted but don't get the job! There's no way he'd want to be dissected in the press, or have the world's nose metaphorically pressed to his windows! Besides, he will have known from the feedback what happened, that Steve simply performed better. Can she acquit herself? Did they just use the Diocesan Growth Strategy as an escape route from bitter division? No! Yet she cannot deny the secret relief. Oh, leave it. Leave this pointless picking over the bones. *Comfort me . . .* Outside the clock chimes three. *Sweet Spirit, comfort me.*

Yes, it will blow over, just as other catastrophes have done. In the meantime, things remain pretty grim. My readers will no doubt remember that Roderick Fallon has a spot of previous with Lindchester. Almost a year ago he experienced the chagrin of watching the most stupendous episcopal catch of the decade twist off his hook and vanish into the weeds. It is not the purpose of this tale to suggest that journalists are driven by vengeful malice, any more than we seek to imply that canons curse and precentors like their tipple. However, I hope I may persuade you that Roderick Fallon, when he opened this particular can of CNC worms, was energized by more than a simple journalistic desire to expose institutional homophobia and see truth prevail.

At a local level Fallon shot himself in the foot. His piece belittled the Lindchester CNC members. This is like belittling a family member. While we reserve the right to abuse our mad aunts and surly teens in whatever terms we choose, we don't take kindly to a stranger wading in. Thus colleagues, sniffy about having yet another Evangelical thrust upon them, had to execute a swift about-turn. Perhaps Fallon was on the side of life? I leave that to my reader to determine. But moral rectitude is seldom palatable when dished up with a large side order of obnoxiousness.

The top secret dinner was therefore much more convivial than it might otherwise have been. I am pleased about that, for Steve is lovely too, and Sonya is not a nightmare. There is no tick beside Steve's name on the Senior Appointments list in the 'WI' column. ('Wife Impossible'.) So the meal was lovely, lovely, lovely. Perhaps a *little* too much wine was drunk? That is not for me to say. At any rate, not a whiff of Poppinsical disapproval was detected on the face of the bishop designate. He laughed very hard at the canon treasurer's impersonations. Yes, provided Steve is biddable in matters liturgical, the cathedral canons have high hopes that this might be workable.

And he will be biddable! Unlike Mary Poppins, he *gets* cathedrals and the choral tradition and knows his place. During the meal it emerged – gloriously! – that Steve had actually been a chorister at another cathedral in his youth, back when he was still called 'Stephen' (or Pennington Major), and before he tragically went off on some summer camp and fell into the clutches of the evanjellybabies. Such a man was to be pitied, not reviled; much as one might pity someone who, through no fault of his own, had lost an arm in a baler. These were the sentiments laboriously expressed by the precentor in the taxi home. '*Du hast gesoffen*, darling,' observed his wife.

Meanwhile, back in their little vestry, the vergers have been congratulating themselves once again on issuing Fallon with a ticket last year when he parked in the Close. He was not specifically targeted. I can vouch for the fact that, in a completely even-handed way, the vergers of Lindchester Cathedral will ticket *any* illegally parked convertible, be it Audi, Merc, Porsche or BMW. Another time it will be personal, though. I am sorry to say that Gavin has even been speculating about how much damage a carelessly driven cherrypicker might do to an S5 Cabriolet if it happened to be left on yellow lines.

October has arrived, bringing with it storms and rain and hail. But today it is calm. Freddie May is out running. You may already have inferred that he did not flounce off to London, get off his tits and paint ceilings. Instead, he remained in Lindchester, where he amended his life according to his mentor's word. His online presence is now impeccably professional. After a night of heart-searching, it came to him that there *might* be a helpful distinction to be made between getting picked on for being gay, and getting picked on for being a dickhead. So the following morning, without even being prompted, he sent grovelling emails to the director of music and the canon precentor, in which he lamented his hissy fit, his indiscreet use of social media, and begged to be given another chance. Happily, the director of music and the precentor were inclined to mercy. What role the new tail suit had in this, I cannot say: but it hangs on the back of Freddie's bedroom door like a mentorly presence, where it sternly monitors his every move.

Totty (to whom Freddie's heart is open and from whom no secrets are hid) very much admired the suit. She stood over Freddie (as Miss Blatherwick had done when he was a chorister) till he'd produced a proper handwritten thank you note like a well brought up boy. 'Yeah, no, he'll go mental, he said I could only thank him once?' Freddie protested in vain. 'Rubbish! He'll be expecting a thank you note,' said Totty. And Totty was right, for the letter prompted a reply, beautifully handwritten in fountain pen: *You're welcome, sweetheart. A x*

OMFG! Freddie had no words to express his feelings on reading this, just a shaken Scrabble bag of letters. Nor can I easily articulate them. I would need to gauge star height and take ocean depth soundings in order to calculate just how much in love poor Freddie now is.

And so he goes out running. The world is fuzzy-edged today; it is all padded and wadded with mists and old man's beard, with thistledown and willowherb seeds. High wisps of mare's tail clouds and vapour trails drift in the blue. Come with me now, and we will fly from Lindchester out along Freddie's long punishing route towards Cardingforth. Look, a golf course down there, pearlized in dew, the greens frosted like sage leaves, like sea glass. Velvety brown fields have a watercolour wash of winter wheat. It rained in the night, and now the roads are blinding. Sheep graze in faded water meadows. How green it all is, the trees still in leaf – in October! Oh, uncanny. Where are the frozen puddles of childhood, the red noses on the way to school? Look at the Linden! It lies a ribbon of mirror as Freddie pounds along the bank.

We climb, then swoop, then climb again – ah, how our DNA knows the art of flying: we come from the birds! – and below we watch Freddie pass under a graffiti-tagged bridge, and then for a straight mile the railway unspools beside the river, sunlight wincing along the tracks as we fly. Pylons play like giants across the landscape, cat's cradle, French skipping. They stride massive, yet invisible to the human eye trained only to be offended by wind turbines. Magpies in pairs swirl between ash trees. Joy, joy! And there's a jay on a fence, dandy flash of chequered turquoise, like underpants glimpsed over waistband.

That is Carding-le-Willow below us now. See the houses backing on to the railway line? Little conservatories and plastic gutters tick softly in the sun's warmth. Brambles tangle up an embankment where old sofas have been toppled over the back fence, out of sight, out of mind.

Freddie runs on. Distant spires rise from clumps of trees, the parishes of rural Lindfordshire, the old prebendal lands, all Gaydens great and small, and the wise and wonderful Itchington Episcopi. Cardingforth is a mile off now, with its Cotman idyll of a humpbacked bridge: the halfway point. Steam ascends to heaven from the cooling towers, so quiet, so benign, so unlike the mushroom clouds that menaced the edges of our childhood.

On the other bank a white-haired woman walks in her floral wellies, with a three-legged greyhound on a lead. The leak has been weighing heavily on Father Wendy's mind too. I dare say the reader is anxious to be reassured that she kept her oath of confidentiality, and has spoken to nobody about the deliberations of the CNC. Alas, I can offer no such consolation. Wendy has blabbed everything. There is nothing that Pedro doesn't know about the affair.

'Oh, Pedro, Pedro, Pedro! What a mess this is. Poor Marion! I'm trying my hardest not to think unkind thoughts about whoever talked to the press. Why do you suppose they did it? Oh, you're right, it must feel like a life-and-death matter, mustn't it? It *is* a life-and-death matter! We only have to look at what's happening to gays and lesbians in other parts of the world. Oh dear, Pedro! If only Guilden had interviewed better! But he just *doesn't* find the diocesan growth strategy congenial, does he? With the best will in the world, he *wasn't* going to be able to take

Lindchester forward. Whereas Steve . . . Yes. He'll do the job, won't he? Yes?'

But Pedro has seen something. Moorhen? Moorhen! There, emerging from the rushes on the path ahead. He tugs on his harness. Wendy laughs. 'Not yet, darling, I'm sorry. We'll take you back to Northumberland in half term, I promise. And you can chase seagulls to your heart's content.'

So who did blab? Was it Geoff? No. But a chill crossed his heart when the news broke and the angry emails exploded in his in-box. He *felt* to blame. Why? He hadn't spoken to anyone, he'd taken no phone calls in anyone's hearing, he'd never left important emails open and unattended.

But had he been sufficiently careful? He can't prove anything. Can't even ask, because that would unleash a tidal wave of toxic counter-accusation. He tries to imagine going to Marion and saying, 'I think it may have been my colleague checking my private emails without permission.' No, he can't, he just can't.

And now Fallon expertly re-stokes the fire with another feature, this time upending a vat of scorn on the House of Bishops and their deliberations on 'Facilitated Conversations'. He expatiates on hypocrisy and double standards. He alludes to cases where senior church figures are sitting in judgement on gay priests who want to marry, while they themselves are subject to disciplinary procedures for conduct that is unbecoming or inappropriate to the office and work of the clergy . . .

The communications officer gives the archdeacon the heads up. Matt reads the piece in his office. Ooo-kay. Looks as though Fallon's got him in his sights. No prizes for guessing who his source is. Matt drums his fingers on his desk. He has not yet sent off his respondent's reply. He's playing the waiting game because he's a bloody-minded sod when his chain is yanked. And it's been well and truly yanked now. You bet your rainbow laces it has.

Father Ed doesn't see Fallon's article till that evening. He's just finished reading it when he hears Neil's key in the door. Neil (still in disgrace for his overcompetitive behaviour at the Harvest Beetle Drive) sweeps in with a blast of London. Kiss, kiss, c'mon, let's eat out, big man.

Ed taps the page. 'I don't suppose you know anything about this, Neil?'

'Me? No. Not read it.'

Ed stares into those wide, honest-as-the-day baby blues.

'Oh, what?' Neil gets his U'Luvka out of the freezer. 'Och, it's just Roddy doing his thing.'

'I thought you hadn't read it,' says Ed. 'Please tell me you didn't put him up to this?'

Neil pours a shot. 'Yes, well, and *why* hasn't the recycling been taken out?'

Chapter 24

I t's Friday. Ed sits in his study and emails his spiritual director:

Dear Father Malcolm,

Can I arrange to see you very soon, please? I find I'm not coping. If it isn't possible to meet this week, please pray for me. Briefly, the things I need to talk over concern Neil. I am finding his behaviour impossible to deal with. I can't seem to get him to understand how deeply what he's doing distresses me, and how talking to journalists impacts on my role as priest in the diocese. Sometimes I cannot see a way forward for us at all.

If you can make time this week, I'd be most grateful.

Ed

In the next room, Neil drafts a letter to Bishop Bob:

Dear ~~Bob Bishop Robert Right Reverend Sir Lord~~ Bishop,

~~You probably won't remember me Just a note to say~~, I hope you are ~~recuperating~~ on the mend now. ~~Ed and I are~~ I was wondering whether you are ~~up for~~ feeling well enough yet to receive visitors, as I would ~~very much~~ really ~~appreciate value~~ appreciate the opportunity to ~~visit~~ come and see you some time ~~to talk through some issues just to say 'Hi' just to introduce myself and~~ FUCK WANK.

Neil starts again: 'Dear Bishop, ~~I was wondering if~~ WANK!!!!!'

Neil gets in his car and drives to Martonbury. Ed hears the Porsche snarl off into the distance. Where is Neil going now? Ed never asks any more. It is either something perfectly innocent (so why check?) or Neil will lie (so why check?).

The email is sent. There's nothing he can do now but wait. Father Malcolm might be busy, he might be away for a few days, on holiday for two weeks. Ah, God! What is Ed going to do with himself? What is the point of bothering to take a day off any more, if he and Neil can't seem to be in the same room without fighting?

So Ed gets out of the vicarage and walks for miles in the rain. From Gayden Magna to Gayden Parva. From Gayden Parva to Itchington Episcopi. I am the vicar here. And here. And here. I am a priest, a clerk in holy orders and prebendary of Gayden Parva. This is what I am. From Itchington Episcopi to Turlham. He walks and walks. As if this is Rogationtide and he's beating the bounds, beseeching, begging for mercy. Help me, help me. From Turlham back across more prebendal acres to Gayden Parva again. Along lanes where, since Anglo-Saxon times, priests innumerable have trudged, trudged, ridden their horses, driven their carriages, their Austins, Fords, Skodas. Under Midlands skies, in Lindfordshire rain and Lindfordshire mud. Loving the people, hating the people, blessing them, baptizing them, marrying and burying them.

I really don't matter, thinks Ed. I am just passing through. He pictures his name on the long, long list of incumbents, from Walter de This, Henry de la That, through plain English names, John Wyatt, Richard Graves, down the list, down past Reformation, Protectorate, Restoration, through plague, famine and war, and again war. And today the vicar is Father Edward Bailey. And after him, what? A handful more? Are these the twilight years of the parish system that has shaped our inner and outer landscape all these centuries? He looks up at the spire of Gayden Parva church. Will its significance one day be as obscure as stone circles?

Rain drips from the yews. Ed walks under the lichgate – the corpse gate – and along the gravel path to the west door. In the distance he can hear footsteps on the road, someone out jogging. *Tick tick tick* of trainers on tarmac. The feet turn and enter the churchyard. The lichgate clatters. Ed can hear panting now. The runner passes him and jogs into the church porch and grabs the handle, like a fugitive claiming sanctuary. Ed hurries to catch up. Young man, black running skins, green beanie. He's bent over, hands on knees, panting.

'Did you want to go in?' Ed feels in his pockets.

The figure straightens up. Then he flinches. Tugs the hat down lower, looks away. 'Nah, I'm good, thanks.'

'Don't worry, it's not a problem. I'm the vicar.' Ed fumbles in another pocket. 'Damn. Actually, I'm really sorry, I seem to have come out without my keys.'

'Hey. No worries.' He turns to leave. Ed glimpses a strand of blond hair, gets a whiff of sweat. And Le Male.

'Freddie May.' The runner freezes.

'Yeah. Um. Hi.'

'What are you doing here?'

Silence.

Suddenly it falls into place. Ah, Jesus! He's *still* seeing him? 'Waiting to meet someone?'

'Wha'? No! God, no!' He reaches, touches Ed's arm. Ed shakes him off. 'Listen, ah nuts, it's just . . . Man, this is gonna sound really lame. So I sing in the cathedral choir? I'm like the lay clerk of Gayden Parva, or I will be, if . . . yeah. Um, so the other day, yeah, in evensong? I was suddenly: you know what, I have never even *been* to Gayden Parva? And just now I'm like, why not? Why not swing by and see the church? That's all. Swear?'

'Right.'

'Gah. You don't believe me? This blows. I honestly, honestly— there's nothing— Listen, I'm sorry.'

'Just leave. Please.'

Ed knees buckle. He sits on the stone ledge in the porch, head bowed. The lichgate clatters again. The footsteps fade, *tick tick tick*, off along the lane. Rain drips. He raises his head and stares at the notices. The Harvest Supper and Beetle Drive poster is still there. He should take that down. But he just sits. How long before he hears the sound of the Porsche approaching? Is he just going to wait here till Neil arrives?

Somewhere a robin sings, tender and heartbroken.

Neil frets as he drives. Maybe he should phone ahead? I mean, what if he's out, or it's not convenient? He should ring. But no, he's too chicken, he wants the option of baling if he finds he can't quite get his nerve up to knock on the door. He should definitely take something, though. Flowers. Is there a decent florist in Martonbury? Not like you can give a bishop a bunch of turquoise feckin' chrysanths from the garage forecourt.

There! Roadside stall. He squeals to a stop. Reverses. Nobody about. Just a table in the rain. Free range eggs. Plums. Bunches of dahlias tied with baler twine. Random assortments just grabbed and bundled together. He gets out of the car and examines the bouquets. Tight little pom-poms, great shaggy globes, like footballs a Rottweiler's got hold of. Neil picks through. Autumn rusts, and purples. White, cream. Shocking scarlet and then a single acid yellow bloom shoved in. Total mishmash thrown together by a visual illiterate. He considers untying them and making a proper coherent bouquet; then again, maybe they're charming just as they are? In an unforced retro way? Like a symbol of something. Humanity? Eds would know, he'd put it in a sermon. Eds, Eds.

Och! Ssh, Ferguson, you big jessie. He sniffs, wipes his eyes, then gets out his wallet and leaves a tenner in exchange for a dripping bundle of dahlias.

'Obviously, I don't believe any of it. No offence, Bishop. Mind you, I was sent to Sunday School. My auntie packed me off every week, just to get me out of her hair, coz I was a wee shite— sorry. And Boys' Brigade. And that meant church parade once a month on top of Sunday School. You weren't meant to turn up for BB if you'd not been to Sunday School or church parade. "Sure and stedfast" was the motto. Aye. We used to sing the BB song, "Will your anchor hold". I can still sing it. Never forget stuff you learn as a child, eh? "Will your anchor hold in the storms of life! When the clouds unfold their wings of strife?" Ha ha, I'll spare you. And Scripture exams! The memory verse. John 3.16. *For God so loved the world*. And sword drill! Bible under your arm! And temperance exams! Temperance! Can you credit it? Anyway, as I say, I'm not a believer, Bishop.'

Bishop Bob bows his head in acknowledgement.

Neil can't stop himself. He blethers on, like he's explaining to the bishop why he *is* a believer, not why he's not. He tries to focus.

'Aye, well, anyway, in the end, these Christians, they're all hypocrites. BB Captain, och, he was the biggest hypocrite of them all! Always telling us we were sinners, on to us to invite the Lord Jesus into our hearts in case we fell under a bus and it was too late, and sinning meant swearies, and nicking stuff from the shop, smoking, and playing doctors and nurses. Or sneaking into the back of X films, saw *Last Tango in Paris* and *The Exorcist*, scared the living shit out of me, but anyway – him! *He* ups and leaves his wife for this wee lass, wee bit of a thing, seventeen, she was. A Salvationist. With the bonnet and the tambourine. Timbrels, is that what they called them? Aye, timbrels. With the ribbons? Seventeen! Looked more like fourteen. Like a wee mouse. In my class at school, never even knew she was there, you know the kind. So what I'm saying is, on the Last Day – which I don't believe in, but on the Last Day – there'll be two queues. And the Christians, the respectable folk, will be in the heaven queue, and I'll be in the other queue, with the queers and alkies and all the other sinners. And I wouldn't have it any other way. Why? Because I don't want to spend eternity in any heaven that's got God in it. No offence, Bishop. Not that I believe in God, obviously.'

Bishop Bob smiles and bows his head again.

'Aye, well, so that's a bit of background. That's why it's important to me to get married. To make a stand against hypocrisy. Half the bishops in the C of E are in the closet, for f— for God's— anyway.

That's what my journalist friend tells me. Not yourself, Bishop, I don't mean. *Some* of the bishops. I mean, hasn't there been this "love letter"? Urging them to come out? I keep *telling* Eds, unless we're prepared to stand up and be counted, the status quo will just continue. C'mon! The law of the land says we can marry! Don't get me wrong, I know it's hard, God knows, I'm not saying it's easy coming out – mind you, it's not as hard as it was. To be *gay*? Nu-uh. That was *not* an option in my mind when I was growing up. Not even an option. I was the *opposite* of gay. Proving myself. Being gay was the worst thing, *the* worst thing that could ever happen to me, until finally, I had to admit, OK, this is what I am, and you know what? It's not actually the end of the world. So don't get me wrong, I can sympathize. Or I *could* sympathize, if they didn't keep voting against equal marriage! Sorry. Running ma gob again. Motormouth, always was a motormouth.'

Bob nods. There is a silence. Outside a different robin sings the same sad sweet song. 'Thank you for explaining.' More silence. 'Can I just go back a bit? You say you don't want to be in any heaven that has God in it?'

Neil's throat tightens. 'Nope.'

'Because I'm not sure God feels the same,' says Bob. 'I'm not sure he'd think heaven is quite complete without his Neil.'

And Neil, big jessie that he is, bursts into tears.

Freddie May fights back tears as he heads to Lindchester. Oh God, gonna have to get a grip before evensong. Guy hates me. Literally? Oh God, what had Neil told him? Had he actually confessed, or had Ed just worked out they'd got it on that time? *Kinda* got it on. Oh shit, what if Ed hadn't actually known anything, and Freddie accidentally confirmed his suspicions back there, by acting guilty? Gah, I am so dumb! No, don't start crying, you'll trash your voice. Ah nuts, what am I gonna do?

Yes, there have been a lot of tears in the Diocese of Lindchester recently, I'm afraid. My readers may be wondering about Jane. I have not forgotten her. She has been exercising considerable restraint in these first weeks of term. She has done her best to keep out of Veronica's way. But Veronica has done her best to cross Jane's path. She appeared on the back row of one of Jane's lectures, and Jane very publicly ejected her. Veronica very publicly confronted Jane about this in the bistro later, and Jane very publicly ignored her, despite Veronica pursuing her through the crowded atrium to the lifts, still loudly haranguing her for her unprofessional and non-collegial attitude.

Ignoring the bejesus out of someone is very much part of Jane's skill set; but Jane has a range of other transferable skills from rugby days she was just longing to deploy. Yes, she has exercised considerable restraint.

And now this is taking its toll. Unlike Matt, she is ill suited to playing the long game. It's Friday afternoon. The evil timetabling genius of her nemesis Dr Elspeth Quilter has foisted a 4 p.m. lecture slot on her. Jane didn't complain about this; she would not dream of giving the Quisling that satisfaction. And it has to be said that the current warfare with La-La Loony makes the decade-long spat with Elspeth seem like a squabble over who gets to draw the hopscotch grid on the playground.

Jane opens her window on Floor 6 of the Fergus Abernathy building. It doesn't open far. Traffic noise rises like fumes. Student voices. A train coming in to Lindford station. It's stopped raining now. Matt is sending off his respondent's reply today. Jane has cast her eye over it. The tone is pared down, non-defensive and factual. Nonetheless, it sticks in the craw that Verruca will be copied in, and will shortly be able to read all about Jane and Matt's relationship.

Her office faces south. Oh, for the wings of a dove. South, that's the direction she'd be heading in. To the other side of the globe! Where summer is approaching, not winter. The bishop will read Matt's reply, and decide what action to take. Probably no action, Matt thinks. And then, just for the sheer hell of it, Verruca will appeal against the bishop's decision. Yeah, and once again flap her big gob to Roderick Fallon, no doubt. Fallon! Pah, Jane remembers him from Oxford days, though Fallon would not remember anyone as insignificant as a big lumpen comprehensive school Christian Union girl from the illiterate wastes of The North. And to think, she could have clubbed him over the head with an oar and dumped him in the Isis in 1982 and spared the world all his toxic waste.

And baby's coming home in just over a month. The whole of Lindford swims. Stop it, not now, you silly mare. Jane sniffs back the tears. She's been kidding herself she'd got used to the idea of not having Danny around. But oh. Later. We'll wallow later.

But this woe is just the antechamber to more woes! Slam the door, we have a lecture to deliver. Matt, what am I going to do about you? How can I go on expecting you to damage your reputation, violate your conscience, bollocks your career prospects? He hasn't said it, but Jane fears he will resign from his post rather than end their relationship. Because they clearly can't carry on with this rubbish compromise that has set tongues wagging.

Face it, you grumpy old tart, your view of marriage is outmoded.

She swats Dominic's voice away. Mentally hangs up on him again, like she literally did when he told her that last week. How she misses those old-fashioned receivers you could crash down into the cradle to make your point!

If marriage is inherently unequal and repressive, why the hell do you suppose we are campaigning so hard to be allowed to get married?

Shut up, shut up. She leans her forehead against the glass. Is it time to rethink, though? Is there any room for manoeuvre here?

Somewhere in the mayhem down below, in some tree she can't even see, a robin starts to sing.

Ed gets back to the empty vicarage. He checks his emails to see if Fr Malcolm has got back to him. He finds this message waiting in his inbox:

> Dear Ed,
>   Really sorry, but autofill has sent this to me. I'm afraid I didn't spot it in time, and read on. I will now delete your email and will treat it as forgotten. But if there's anything I can do to support you, do get in touch.
>   Blessings,
>   Matt

No! No! This is a paper cut to the heart. But before he can even begin to process his anguish and rage, Ed hears the Porsche arrive. And now they must have one more horrible confrontation. The last one. For surely this has to be the last betrayal he can stand? Even Neil must see that. He goes to the door to meet him.

In far-off London town, Roderick Fallon belatedly acts on a tip-off. He gets on Twitter and searches once again for @choirslut90. Nada.

But wait a moment! @FreddieMayTenor. O-ho. Cleaned our act up, have we, Mr Lay Clerk at Lindchester Cathedral? Fallon enlarges the photo. Yep, it's him all right. Nice try, choirslut. I think another trip to choral evensong is in order. Thank you, Neil Ferguson!

Chapter 25

Once, when he was six years old, Ed visited a farm with his parents, and was charged by a billy goat. It butted him smack in the chest and knocked him flat. He remembered this when he opened the vicarage door and Neil hurled himself into his arms with a howl.

Oh, great. Once again Ed's pain was eclipsed. Like an actor about to open his lips to deliver a soliloquy, when a blood-stained tenor in full aria bursts on stage from the wings.

'Eds! Eds!'

'Just stop it!' Ed tried to peel himself away. 'You went to see him, didn't you?'

Neil nodded against Ed's chest. 'I *had* to, Eds.'

'Had to!' Ed wrenched free. 'After everything you said! OK. That's it. I can't take any more, Neil!'

'I'm sorry! It was unfinished business. Eds, please!'

'No. Get off me!'

'Listen, he's a sweet guy—'

'*Shut up!* How's that supposed to make me feel? Why do you have to torture me like this? What do you want? You want to force me to say I hate you? Is that it? Shall I say it? Shall I? Then you can tell me you knew all along! You're mad, Neil! I won't do this any more!'

'No, no, you can't be like this!' He got hold of Ed's shirt front with both hands. 'He's invited us for a meal!'

'A meal?! Fuck off!'

'Yes! A meal. With Janet.'

A gap, like sudden deafness, like the roaring seabed. 'What are you talking about?'

'Janet! His wife. They've invited us for a meal. Eds, c'mon.' He gave him a shake. 'Please?'

Ed could see the words. Each one. They hung like beads in the air. But strung together they made no kind of sense. 'Janet.'

'Yes, *Janet!*' Neil shook him again. 'I'm telling you. The Hootys. They've asked us to dinner. Hello?'

'Oh, my God.' Ed's hands flew to his head, as if to check everything was still intact. 'You ... went to see the bishop?'

'That's what I've been trying to get through to you!'

Ed sat down on the hall chair and put his head between his knees. 'Oh, my God.' He began trembling. He felt Neil rubbing his back.

'What's wrong? No! You thought I'd gone sneaking back to blondie from the choir? You didn't! Och, Eds!'

'No, I'm sorry, but he was there. Today. At the church. Gayden Parva church. He turned up.'

'And you thought—? C'mon! Are you daft? Shagging in the kirk? With Mr Jesus watching?'

Ed laughs. Then weeps. 'He said he's lay clerk of Gayden Parva and he just wanted to see the church.'

'Eds, you weren't mean to him, were you? Och, Eds!'

'I just asked him to leave,' protested Ed. 'I don't think that's unreasonable, given the history. Mean! And, frankly, I didn't believe him. It sounded so dumb.'

'Aye, well, he's a few sandwiches short. That's the wacky baccy for you.' Neil tutted like a maiden aunt who'd warned you not to run with scissors. 'Screws adolescent brain development, they say.'

Ed straightened up. 'You're unbelievable. Can you actually *hear* yourself, Neil?'

'Oh, what?' Neil knelt in front of him. Raised both hands, showed the empty palms. 'Didn't I promise? No meds, no boys, no nothing. Just you, big man. Swear to God.'

Ed stared into the maniacal blue depths. 'OK. I believe you. Sorry.' He closed his eyes and waited. Neil would rap on his forehead, knock the fact of his innocence in like a nail. Cheating? Me? As if!

'Och, well,' Neil muttered. 'Given my track record, I'd suspect me.'

Ed opened his eyes. Neil was scowling at his fingernails. The admission was a frail thing. A breath would blow it away.

'God, I need a manicure.'

'So how was Bob?' Shrug. 'What did you talk about?'

'Nothing. Never you mind.' The scowl deepened. 'My feckin' hands look old! I've got crone hands. Do they look like crone hands to you? And another thing: I do not *torture* you.'

'Yes, you do, Neil.'

'Huh. Yes, well. Maybe it's because I can't torture God. Did you ever think of that? Because the bastard doesn't exist! Anyway, they've invited us— You big jessie, Ferguson.' He wiped his eyes. 'So. Are we saying yes to dinner, or what? And it's not like I *enjoy* it, Eds! I hate myself, I don't *want* to hurt you, but I just can't stop doing it. That's why I went to see Bob, OK? When we're married, maybe I'll feel safe and, I don't know, maybe I can stop treating you like shit? Och, never mind. So, I'll email him and suggest some dates, shall I?'

'If that's what you'd like.'

'I would.' He hesitated, then gathered up both Ed's hands. 'Listen. Are we OK?'

Ed sobbed. One sob, like a stray hiccup. Were they? He felt like a man who'd steeled himself for execution, and then the firing squad had produced bananas and shouted 'Bang!' instead.

Neil squeezed Ed's hands. 'Listen. I'm sorry for running my big gob. I get that it makes things hard for you. I mean the whole Roddy and Veronica thing. So I'll tell him to get back in his basket, we'll not be doing the interview. OK?'

'I'm sorry – what interview?' Silence. 'You promised him we'd do an interview?'

Ed watched the lie forming. Like a big blatant bubble, right in teacher's face, while denying he had any gum. I'm sick of being the grown-up in this relationship, he thought.

'Course not! It's just . . . He *may* have that impression, is all. Oh, fine then, fine. I'll *un*-tell him. I'll cancel. That's what I'm saying.'

'Please do that, Neil.' The grip tightened. 'Oh, God. Now what?'

'Um. Listen, you know I told you I saw Roddy in London – no? Oh. Well, anyway, I did and we got to talking over drinks? Well, he was ranting about the scoop that got away – you know what he's like – the last bishop, the one there was all the talk about? Well. Thing is, I might've given him a wee tip-off there. About who might know. And now I'm thinking we should maybe warn . . . him?'

'Who? Oh, God. Not Freddie May?'

'Aye.' Neil winced. 'And I was *thinking*, maybe it would be better coming from you . . . ?'

'No. No! I hate him. You can't ask me to do this, Neil.'

'But I promised you I'd never contact him again! Please? I feel really bad, big man. Roddy'll eat him and spit out the feathers, poor wee daftie.'

'No. I'm not doing it.'

It's Monday morning. The pest control man flies his Harris hawk round Lindchester Cathedral Close, to keep the pigeon population down. Round the spire, off, off forth, over rooftop and chimney pot, striding high there, out across battlement and wooded slope, then back to the falconer's call, jesses trailing (oh, my chevalier!). But there is no gold-vermillion moment for the pest control Harris hawk. It is never allowed to make the kill. The public doesn't like to see that. So the falconer feeds it a defrosted turkey poult, and puts it back in its cage. He is still loading the cage into the back of his van when the first pigeon sidles to the edge of the roof, cocks his head and peers down with a bonkers eye. *It's all right boys, he's going.*

It was the dean who went to find Miss Blatherwick first thing this morning, and told her that the court appearance later in the week – for which she had been preparing her soul for so many months – would be cancelled. The accused died in his sleep last night. Peacefully in his sleep.

Miss Blatherwick sits now in the choir vestry, in the armpitty smell of ancient cassock. There's the familiar choral detritus of scores, folders, half-eaten packets of Polos, and wind-up racing nuns. Well, there will surely now be an enquiry into how the cathedral and diocese handled the business all those years ago. Aged bishops and deans (as well as aged matrons!) will still have to endure seeing the behaviour of the 1970s scrutinized through twenty-first century lenses. None shall escape; except the former chaplain who slipped away last night. Or will he? Was that departure *actually* peaceful?

Miss Blatherwick is not a universalist. She believes that it is possible to reject the grace of God. It *has* to be, or whither free will? If grace were inescapable, and all are tumbled into heaven, willy-nilly, then how is one to justify this appalling charade of human suffering? What is one to say to those little boys whose presence she can still sense here in this room? Never mind, dear, it's just a theological experiment, and in heaven all tears are wiped away?

And yet one longs to be a universalist! For not a single soul, however corrupt, to lie beyond redemption. And indeed, how could there be limits to grace – or whither God's omnipotence? Well, well, finer minds than hers have puzzled over this old chestnut. The question now was, what one ought to do? She had been all prepared, as it were dressed up in Sunday best, and now there was no court ordeal to be faced. What is she to do with this surplus energy?

But this is to wallow in self-absorption. As if she mattered! How must the victims be feeling? Cheated; how could they feel anything other than cheated? Perhaps this feels like the ultimate in closing of ranks, that the Almighty himself is now collaborating and moving the perpetrator on one last time without bringing him to book! Fanciful? Perhaps. But how one clings to the notion of judgement!

Surely death is not a getting off the hook, but a calling to account! It is not so very long now till Advent. She can almost hear a voice singing at the dark west end of the cathedral. *I look from afar, and behold I see the power of God coming, and a cloud covering the whole earth* . . .

And it will not be long now before Miss Blatherwick herself will be called to account. Without being morbid, she's had her three scores years and ten. And when that day comes, what can one do but throw oneself on the mercy of the court? And find it in abundance, one hopes. As one must hope the chaplain had done, although every instinct cries out for vengeance.

Perhaps my readers are hankering for justice to be done in the matter of the Revd Dr Veronica da Silva? I know I am. I chafe with Jane and Matt at the thought that she is now privy to an account of their relationship. I long, as Jane does, to deck her in the student bistro, when she comes and sits near Jane's table and stares at her. Jane knows perfectly well that Veronica would love nothing more than to provoke a confrontation, but I'm glad to report that Veronica has underestimated the ocean depths of Jane's counter-suggestibility. No bathysphere can plumb those dark fathoms, where eyeless bio-luminescent monsters pulse, and extremophiles unknown to science seethe in boiling sulphur vents.

Bishop Harry has read over Matt's response and today he will decide that this offence does not merit a formal rebuke. And yes, Veronica will contest this decision loudly, and I dare say she will get on the phone to her new best, best friend, Roddy (she *adores* Roddy). Neil is no longer answering her calls, for some reason.

I ought to take you, reader, into the consciousness of the Revd Dr Veronica da Silva. I promised at the beginning of this tale that no doors are locked to the long inquisitive nose of my narrative. And yet, I must confess I balk at the idea of voyaging deep into the terrain of Veronica's psyche. I have no maps, and all the agreed landmarks of human interaction shift as I approach . them. The best I can do is direct you to the internet with the hint that you might search 'personality disorder'. I am with Dominic on this one: I can't bear to be in the same room as her. Perhaps this tells us something? I wonder whether something intolerable happened to her as a small child. Something which no decent, kind person could look upon. We sense in her some unnamed *thing*, some suffering creature, flayed, nailed to a wall and still alive, but way beyond our ability to save. Sadly, this does not make the day-to-day business of loving Veronica any easier. We are deflected from pity by all the manipulation, the gob-smacking confabulations, by her ravenous attention-seeking; and in the end we must flee, because it feels as though we can barely save ourselves – let alone her – from the monster.

Anyway, Jane has other things to occupy her. She cannot expunge Dominic's accusation from the blackboard of her brain. It stands in chalky block capitals for the whole class to see (Jane's brain hasn't yet adopted interactive smart boards). *YOUR VIEW OF MARRIAGE IS OUTMODED.* Naturally, she has had many arguments with him since he told her this, arguments in which he was trounced and made to whimper like a pup. Admittedly, these arguments have only taken place in Jane's head. She reflects on this with her usual academic rigour: why haven't you pursued this conversation with Dom, eh? Afraid he's right? Dammit. Yes, I'm beginning to wonder. My students don't seem to have any hang-ups about marriage, do they? Heck, they don't even seem to have problems with becoming Mrs Husband's-Name, for God's sake! Maybe I should talk to them about this? Or preferably to some other paid-up Young Person not attending Poundstretcher. Well, Danny would be back soon. And there was young tarty-pants. Not seen him for a bit. (Pang of displaced maternal guilt.) Hope he's getting on all right, and not putting too much lay into his clerking. Maybe she should hunt him down and get his opinion on all this marriage business.

And that is why Jane was found in Lindchester Cathedral on Thursday for choral evensong. She lurked in the nave, rather than rushing to bag one of the prebendal stalls in the quire, like a normal cathedral Anglican. This meant that she was cut off from the liturgical action by the elaborate quire screen; but she rather liked that sense of watching from the outside. As though there were indeed another realm where angels ascended and descended, and went about the business of heaven without Jane Rossiter having to conjure it all into existence by the sheer force of her faith.

Purcell setting. She'd narrowly missed Day 15, with its psalma-thon. The familiar collects slipped past. *Lighten our darkness.* How it brought back memories of gear-crunching in Book of Common Prayer term at theological college. Father, Son and Holy Spost. Now came the anthem. Brahms. *Wie lieblich sind deine Wohnungen.* Ah, there was Freddie's voice, unfurling the tenor line like a shining ribbon of gold. She smiled. How effortless he made it sound.

Jane didn't bother standing when the service was over and choir and clergy processed out. Freddie caught her eye as he passed, so she could just wait here till he'd got his kit off.

That's when she spotted him: Roderick Fallon, coming down the quire like an animated angle-poise lamp. Ooh, little speed-bump of dread under the wheels there! Why was he sniffing around? He couldn't be after Matt, could he?

She watched as he approached, secure in her middle-aged invisibility. Not that Fallon had ever had an eye for The Ladies. Yes, not hard to do a reverse ageing process and discern in this middle-aged man the lanky undergraduate she had hated. There was still something of the etiolated ugly-pretty boy about him, the big mouth, like Mick Jagger racked in some dungeon till he was six foot two. Fallon was obviously waiting for someone. Maybe Jane should go over and ruin his day?

She was pondering how best to achieve this when Freddie appeared. Oh well, another time. Jane grabbed her bag and got to her feet.

But Fallon stepped forward and intercepted Freddie.

Uh-oh.

But never fear. Our good friend Father Ed – because he is so lovely – did get in his car and drive to the Close to warn Freddie last Friday after all. (No, Neil does not deserve him.) The result was that Freddie recognized Fallon at once, and launched the most spectacular short plank offensive that Jane was ever privileged to overhear. Would you like to listen in?

'Excuse me. Freddie May?'

'Ohh, hey! Well, hey, *you*! How're you doing? God, how's things?'

'Um, not sure we've met, actually. Roderick Fallon.'

'Oh, thank God for that!' Radiant smile. 'Thought we'd fucked and I'd forgotten? No offence.'

'Right. I'm a journalist. You may remember tweeting me last summer?'

'Yeah! Actually, no? I tweet a lot of guys? I mean, a *lot* of guys?' Tongue stud.

'I'm sure. This was in connection with Paul Henderson.'

'Hnn. Paul . . . ? Ohh! Bishop Paul!'

'Yes. Bishop Paul Henderson.'

'Bishop Paul.' Long boss-eyed pause. 'Awesome.'

'Yes. Do you remember tweeting me, to say you could tell me a lot of things about Bishop Paul Henderson? Late last summer?'

'I did? Hnn. Maybe?'

'You have no recollection of that?'

'Nu-uh. Maybe I was off my tits?' Big happy grin. 'Happens.'

'Am I right in thinking you were his chauffeur?'

'Yeah.'

'And you lived with him?'

'Yeah. Him and Suze. Totally love those guys!'

'Well, maybe we could talk? Can I buy you a drink?'

'Yeah, we should totally do that some time, but right now I'm meeting my aunty? Hey, Aunty Jane!'

Aunty Jane does a little finger wave.

'Can I have your number, then?'

'Hey, you *so* can, only, thing is? Lost my phone?'

'Have you now. Well, here's my card. Ring me, and we can fix a time.'

'Awesome. Catch ya later ... I wanna say ... Roger? Roderick! Cool, I'll ring you sometime, Roddy?'

I regret to say that when Roderick returned to his car, he discovered that the vergers had given him another ticket, even though he was legitimately parked this time.

Chapter 26

There. Jane deletes her browsing history. Those searches never happened. She did not just go on the Church of England website and force herself to wade through the marriage service with its smorgasbord of prefaces and declarations, vows and proclamations, blessings and registrations. No, siree. Nor did she go on gov.uk and familiarize herself with registry office Marriages and Civil Partnerships to find out all about Giving Notice At Your Local Register Office; or calculate that if she got a move on, they could theoretically get it done and dusted while Danny was in the country.

Nope, Jane did none of these things.

It is now half term. The cathedral choir is on vacation. The canon treasurer and his wife have nipped off to Norfolk for a clan gathering. Friends of Freddie May – aware that the devil finds work for idle tenors – may relax. He is not rattling around that big house all by himself. No indeed; Freddie May has been invited to join the Dorian Singers (omigod, only the actual Dorian Singers?) to record their Christmas CD. The director has looked with favour on Freddie's sanitized online presence and rewarded him with paid work. They will be recording in some secret location with a fabulous acoustic in the far north, where we, alas! may not follow. I'd say Freddie is excited and terrified in equal measure. Dr Jacks stalks the corridors of his brain like Professor Snape, wand raised to perform the *Humiliatus* curse. But recently he has started to appear in the guise of Mr Darcy as well: In vain I have struggled, Mr May! It will not do. You must allow me to tell you how ardently I admire and love you!

Well, the truth will probably lie somewhere between these literary paradigms. At any rate, Freddie will gain some valuable experience singing with this group of top-notch musicians. If he's lucky he may also get to carry Mr Dorian's music case, and be suffered to hang around and adore him in whimpering inarticulacy. So Freddie packs a holdall and heads for Lindchester station. Yeah! *Finally*, he's got his shit together, his dreams are coming true?

Uh-oh. Was that the gun-foot klaxon going off again?

I dare say the reader is hankering to know about Jane and Freddie's discussion, the one that led to all the internet browsing Jane is now pretending never happened. Come with me, back to last week, and we will hover in the October dusk, and watch them as they leave the cathedral. There they go now, arm in arm across the Close (while over on the far side Fallon, like a gangly Rumpelstiltskin, stamps on his parking ticket so hard I'm afraid his leg will go right through the cobbles). Freddie and Aunty Jane pass under the gatehouse and down the steep street to Lindchester's Oldest Pub. Or perhaps this one is the Smallest? Most historic English towns boast a couple of each. Anyway, the pub in question has a fine selection of locally brewed ales, and that's what's important here. Watch them enter the King's Head, or the Caput Regis, as it is waggishly known in choral circles. And now we glide down to street level, fold our viewless wings, and slip in after them.

'So, I imagine you're all in favour of marriage, little nephew? Cheers.' Jane raised her Old Lindcastrian Gold.

'Course. What's not to be in favour of?' He clinked his Peroni glass against her pint. 'Why? Has Matt popped the question? Omigod! He has! You're blushing. That is so sweet! Go for it! Ooh, want me to sing during the signing of the—'

'Hold your horses, sunshine. Nobody's getting married.' Jane took another pull of her pint. 'No, I'm ... simply trying to understand what the big love affair with marriage is, all of a sudden.'

'Ha ha ha! Sure you are, Jane.'

'Shut up, this is purely academic. Yes, so speaking as a hairy-legged old feminist, I've always viewed marriage as an oppressive institution.'

'Wha-a-a'? No way! Oppressive how? Seriously, Matt's gonna, like, *oppress* you? God, I'd marry him in a heartbeat if he asked me.' He stroked her arm. 'Aw, c'mon, Janey, why don't you guys get married?'

Jane cantered him through a brisk little history lecture, footnoted throughout by a Marxist-feminist interrogation of the institution as she understood it. He listened meltingly, shaking his head, as though she were his granny grumbling on about why she couldn't be doing with Kindle, she liked the feel and smell of a proper book.

'Yeah, no, I get what you're saying, only it's not like that any more?'

'Oh? What *is* it like, then? Go on. Elucidate.'

'So yeah, it's more . . . Um, y'know? He's my everything and I'm his? For better and worse? For ever?' He began tugging his hair and fidgeting. Classic body language of the student who has not familiarized himself with the set text. 'Hey, would you stop with the whole bitch-tutor from hell thing?'

'Sorry. But can we focus on the question of whether everyone's just mesmerized by the shiny twenty-thousand pound *wedding*, for a moment? Because my concern is—'

He sighed. 'God, you're so . . . explain-y. You sound like a biologian, Jane!'

She laughed. 'I think "biologist" is the word you're after, sweetums.'

'Whatever. Like Dawkins? Einstein-evolution-genes-science. Boom! NO GOD, religious dickheads! And I'm all, whoa, but what about in your actual soul? Where you can literally *feel* God? Like, look, listen.' Freddie sang her part of that evening's anthem: *Mein' Seel' verlanget und sehnet sich nach den Vorhöfen des Herren.* 'Make sense?'

'Lovely, but what's all that got to do with marriage?'

'So yeah, I'd give anything to marry the man I love? My soul longs. To be joined, in the sight of God and yeah, everyone?' He spread his hands. 'I don't know what else to tell you.'

'Well, sorry to piss on your bonfire, but you're still just trying to map yourself on to the Hollywood romance narrative, like a good little consumer. You say you'd give anything to marry to the man you love. And who is that, eh? You don't know, you've not met him!' Freddie flinched. 'Well, sorry, but that's not a million miles from my starry-eyed undergraduates, who tell me they've got their entire wedding planned. They aren't even in a relationship, and they've already chosen the fucking bridesmaids' shoes, for God's sake!'

Freddie picked up his glass and drank. His eyes were bright. Was he going to cry? Oh, Jesus. But she was right, wasn't she? Yes? Argh.

'*A* of all, how do *you* know I haven't met him, Jane? I might've. And *B* of all, what the actual fuck? Why's it all so *left brain* with you? What if maybe marriage is the house, yeah? And that's where you live, and that's your home, your dwelling place, and it's all like . . . this shadow? Of . . . As in, I'm so homesick, I just wanna go home? To be with him for ever?'

Jane narrowed her eyes. Was that a will-o'-the-wisp of coherence glimmering in this wombling morass? 'What are you proposing here, exactly?' she asked. In her left-brainy bitch-tutor from hell kind of way. 'Is this a plea for a more metaphorical type of discourse?'

'Yeah!' The radiant stoner smile. 'God and marriage and everything all one? The New Jerusalem? It's all, I dunno, like one awesome metaphor?' Pause. 'Except *technically*, that would be a simile?'

She stabbed a finger at his chest. 'You, my little friend, are a whole lot brighter than you let on.'

'Hnn? Me?' He grinned and rattled his tongue stud round his teeth.

Yeah, you. Only you're wired for an off-kilter brilliance that school never managed to fire up. 'Was that it, or is there a "C of all"?'

'Yeah – C of all, Janey, Janey, Janey.' He stroked her arm again. 'Don't you wanna be with Matt?'

It was her turn to pick up her glass. Probably her eyes were bright too. 'Yep.'

'Then maybe just get over yourself, girlfriend? You can commit feminist hara-kiri after.'

The clocks have gone back. Dark evenings swoop at us on Halloween wings. The tail end of another hurricane lashes the country. Afterwards, in Lindford and Lindchester, Martonbury and Cardingforth, the streets are graveyards of trashed umbrellas. Spokes jut from muddy grass like pterodactyl fossils. But *still* it is warm. No frost has nipped leaf from twig yet. Sumachs and cherries blaze in astonishing Neverland splashes of colour. True, under the knobbled, crippled urban planes you will see yellow leaves the size of dinner plates gathered in gutters, and the sound of the leaf-blower is heard in the land. But for all these wild winds, most of the trees are still in leaf and many are still green. In this uncanny unlooked-for clemency, something overshadows the heart. Why, this is judgement, nor are we out of it.

There is movement in the palace this half term week. If we wander casually past – I know, let's pretend we are off to the cathedral shop to buy Advent calendars – we may glimpse the bishop elect and his wife measuring up for curtains. The clerk of works and the diocesan finance officer accompany them, to salute and say, 'New wet room? Yes, Bishop, how wet do you want it?' (The Penningtons are old hands – they know how to get most of what they'd like without looking acquisitive or high maintenance;

which is lovely, because they really *aren't* grasping, difficult people.)

Let us press our faces against the dining-room window, where the 'sold' pictures from the *Souls and Bodies* exhibition were temporarily stored, and an act of greedy concupiscence was averted by a ringing phone. Bishop elect Steve is taking photos of the off-white walls and oatmeal carpet with his iPad. Mrs Bishop elect Sonya holds a trade paint palette, like a massive unwieldy fan. It is so comprehensive in its fractional tint gradation that every single Farrow and Ball colour can be perfectly matched. Mrs Pennington is minded to have a red dining room. We will permit her a red dining room (though Neil would tell her that these have had their day) because a new bishop's wife must be allowed to put her stamp on her own home. She needs to demonstrate in a bold splash of Rectory Red (or rather, 07YR 10/489) that she is *not* Susanna Henderson. If she had private means she'd have the Aga replaced by a smart electric range cooker with a gas hob. The Aga has to stay, but by golly, there will be real colour in the palace in the new regime! Pale pistachio, farewell! Faded raspberry, adieu! I'm sorry to say that Sonya's taste in interior design was forged in the furnace of the 1990s and has not evolved since then. We may look for a lot of bold Victoriana and/or adobe-style rusticity when Steve's reign begins next year.

There will be other changes when the Penningtons arrive. Oh, Penelope! Your boss-to-be looks like a smooth outward-facing high-tech networking operator, doesn't he? More so than Paul Henderson, even; and heaven knows, Paul's mitre appeared above the diocesan waves like the first laser shark in a dot matrix sea. And although you know the ins and outs, the quirks and oddities of the diocese like nobody else, Penelope, you are part of a bygone era. In short, you are a lovely, lovely, old style bishop's PA. I'm afraid that a little conversation will happen soon after Bishop Steve is installed. He will sit down with you and wonder aloud whether this is really working? Whether you'd be happier in another role?

I wouldn't like my readers to think that the new bishop is a monster. He is a really nice guy. But he is slick. Not too slick, not quite. He has a slickness rating of 6.2 (on a scale where 7 starts to curl toes, 8 deserves a smack, 9 is Tony Blair, and 10, the antichrist). So you will understand that Steve is going to need the right kind of PA. In fact, he might even need a EA, an *executive* assistant; which is like a PA, only you mustn't call them that to their face. Nobody likes sacking lovely people. But Steve has learned that sometimes it has to be done. And if it's got to be done, it's worth grasping the nettle right at the start.

Oh, dear. I fear the reader is now predisposed to hate the next Bishop of Lindchester. Perhaps it would help if I told you that there is one person who would wholeheartedly endorse his trenchancy on the matter of PAs. A surprising person! It is our good friend the dean. Yes, if Marion could have her time over, she'd get rid of her inherited PA right at the start. Honestly, how can you have a dean's PA who exudes the impression that she'd be able to do her job so much better if the dean didn't keep coming in and making demands on her time!

Poor Marion is still under a lot of pressure. Let us rejoice with her, then, that the cathedral's bid for a chunk of the £20 million First World War commemoration pot has been successful. That £270,000 will knock a bit off the £7.8 million needed to prevent the steeple toppling. She does rejoice, of course she does; but there's been another flurry of unhelpful speculation about Who Will Be The First Woman Bishop, after the passage of the bill through the Commons. Inevitably, the CNC debacle was raked over again, and the suggestion lingers that Marion is either a closet homophobe, or a lily-livered liberal who gives way to bullying conservatives. It will pass. Marion tries to school her soul into accepting that there may be no closure, she may never learn the truth. How foolish to let her sense of self become defined by this! And yet the process lingers in her mind like a play missing the last act, a jumper pulled off the needles without being properly cast off.

I'm pleased to say that there are people looking out for Marion. Bishop Harry is a steady confidant; he soothes her with his unflappable good humour, his eye for the big and lovely picture of grace. And her Chapter colleagues support her in every way they can. They do their own jobs well, they eschew all moaning of a non-essential kind, and viciously impersonate any member of the cathedral, diocese or Close community who steps out of line. Miss Blatherwick, spotting the culinary chasm left by the departed Susanna, bakes Marion a batch of parkin. And that sweet dozy Freddie May always asks Mrs Dean how she's doing after evensong. But these good folk are only an ad hoc company of foot soldiers. Where is the general, with his maps and fiendish acumen?

O-ho, Gene is on the case, don't you worry. He rightly identifies the lack of closure as the thing that most torments his beloved deanissima. He concedes that while it would undeniably be fun, it is sadly not possible for him to make a little late-night call on each member of the CNC in turn, with his ice hockey mask and electric drill. So he focuses his ingenuity elsewhere, and books a table for four in a swanky Michelin-starred restaurant – the sort of place where you are served an *amuse-bouche* of snail foam on clam fudge – midway between Lindchester and Barchester. He sets up a meeting. Happy are those called to that banquet!

I would love to book the table next to theirs and eavesdrop – and pretend in a genteel English way not to have recognized Perdita Hargreaves – but there are narrative rules, reader. We must adhere to them, or I would end up having to mediate between you and the entire Anglican Communion worldwide. One small diocese is doing my head in, frankly. And besides, I can't afford to eat in places like that. As a small concession, we will join Marion and Gene on the way home, as their car approaches Lindchester the following day.

'Well, thank you, darling. That's set my mind at rest. He's such a lovely man, isn't he? I knew I was being daft imagining that he blamed me.'

'Has he bounced back, or has he got something else lined up, do you think?' says Gene.

'We-e-ll, I did wonder.'

'Ooh! Where? Which other sees are vacant at the moment?'

'The answer is a Google search away, darling.'

'You know, but you aren't telling me!'

'I don't know anything. Like you, I'll just have to wait and see.'

'Talking of vacancies, how goes the lady bishops' race?'

Marion sighs. 'It's not a race.'

'I like to think of it as a race. Tits first to the palace. I'd back you to win any time.'

Marion leans forward and turns the radio on. Some beautiful piece of Elizabethan polyphony pours out of the speakers. She leans forward again and turns it off.

'Yes, a bit of a busman's holiday,' says Gene. 'Shall I sing to you instead? I do a fine Peter Pears impression.'

'That would be lovely.' Marion closes her eyes and laughs, while he warbles his way decorously through an unspeakably filthy English and Afrikaans rugby song recital. It lasts till they are safely back in the Close. Yes, she thinks she can probably let the CNC go now, closure or no closure.

The Vicar of St James' Lindford peers into the church office. Thank God, Veronica is not there. He unclenches a little and crosses to the computer. It's turned on. He moves the mouse. Oh, Lord! She's forgotten to log off. *Doosh, doosh.* Geoff's pulse sloshes in his ears. He could check everything. All her files, her emails, her browsing history. He looks round in panic. Listens. Silence, apart from the traffic, and the sound of metal shutters dropping in shops nearby.

Do it! He grips the mouse. Quickly!

No, I can't. Can't stoop to this.

As he dithers, *ping!* a new email arrives. The small box appears in the bottom right-hand corner of the screen. Then fades.

Roderick Fallon
　　RE: Some More Information – Thanks for this, Veronica, I'll . . .

Chapter 27

hat would you do if you found yourself in Geoff's position? Would you open the email and devour the entire thread in a welter of righteous indignation? And then would you swiftly forward it to yourself, CC-ing the archdeacon, the dean, the acting bishop, the Archbishop of York ...

His hand hovered. Go, Geoff, go! Use a bit of worldly nous for once. Surely this opportunity has appeared, gift-wrapped, an answer to your prayers? Seriously, Geoff, you are innocent here. She left her account open – perhaps at some level she wants to be caught out? You have a *responsibility* to do this: to your fellow CNC members, to Guilden! Now's your chance to set the record straight, right a few wrongs.

And to get rid of her ...

BOOM! A firework went off right outside the church. Geoff leapt out of his skin.

Slowly he moved the mouse –

Click –

And logged off Veronica's account. The last shutter came clattering down outside. Silence. He stared at the screen. What had he come into the office to do? He couldn't remember. Oh yes, the order of service for All Saints. And the street pastors' rota. But he continued to stare, as stray fireworks shook the dusk.

What? you cry. Does vengeance not belong to the godlike narrator? Could you not have compelled Geoff to dob Veronica in? Of course I could. But then he would no longer be Geoff. I'm very sorry about that. I know that you have been longing for Veronica to get her comeuppance. Geoff acted in accordance with a lifelong habit of trying to do the right thing, to steer his little canoe by the Pole star, however lost and far from home he might feel. He thinks he's a coward, of course. But the same habit of integrity will later make him challenge Veronica about what he saw, and require an explanation from her about her email correspondence with Roderick Fallon. He will not relish that encounter, but he will do it nonetheless. No, he's not a coward. Bravery consists in overcoming fear, not in being fearless.

It is early evening on Wednesday. There's singing in the vicarage at Gayden Magna. Ed pauses to listen. Neil has a surprisingly nice voice, bold and tuneful, if untrained. With an extensive pop diva repertoire at his fingertips, he's never bashful in a karaoke session. But Ed has recently discovered – to his vast amusement – that Neil also has a secret stash of Sunday School choruses hidden away in his memory banks. Ed is saying nothing. He doesn't want Neil to get self-conscious and stop.

> I met Jesus at the crossroads,
> Where the two ways meet!
> Satan too was standing there and he said come this way!

Ed stifles a laugh.

> Lots and lots of pleasures I can give to you today!
> But I said 'No!' . . .

Ed shakes his head and goes back to composing his Rector's Letter for the church magazine. Sometimes it feels as though Neil has a more full-on relationship with his non-existent God than Ed has with the maker of heaven and earth, whose existence he daily affirms.

> . . . There's Jesus here, just look what he offers me . . .

Neil's footsteps approach the study. 'What d'you think, big man? Does this tie work better?'

'I've told you, it's informal, Neil.'

'And are you wearing your dog collar? I rest my case.' He stands on tiptoe and checks his reflection in Ed's little mirror above the filing cabinet. 'Down here my sins forgiven, up there a home in heaven! Praise God, that's the way for me! Well?' He wheels round. 'This one, or the other one? Come on, focus!'

'That one. Definitely.' He watches Neil's face for a clue. 'Or maybe the other one. Yes, the other one.'

Neil folds his arms. 'Uh-huh. Describe the other one.'

'Well, it was different. In some important aesthetic way, it was subtly different.' Ed flings his hands up in defeat. 'I honestly have no idea, Neil. Wear what you like. I'm guessing the Hootys' good opinion is based less on your snappy dress sense than on the fact that you saved his life.'

'Och, don't start that again.'

'Besides, you're hot whatever you're wearing, darling.'

'And?' Neil rolls his hand. 'Keep going.'

'You are hotter than a hot thing. You're smoking hot.' Hand roll. 'Piping hot. God, Neil, you are hotter than Satan's crumpets at high tea in hell! Argh, my retinas just melted! I can't—'

'OK, fuck off now. You've spoilt it.' He consults the mirror once more. 'Well, I'll wear this one, then. Oh, and I've ironed your black shirt, by the way. That's seriously your best shirt? How old is it? Twenty years?! You need some new ones. Yes, you do. The collar's worn out.'

'I'll touch it up with a black marker pen. It'll be fine.'

'Marker pen?!' utters Neil in Bracknellian tones. 'I'm buying you some new ones. Pssht. Don't argue. Now, go and get changed. Chop chop.'

It's still a good hour until they need to set off for supper at the bishop's, but Ed discerns it's no use arguing.

All Saints Day, and the cathedral choir are still on vacation. On Sunday a visiting choir does the honours. They tick that most important of boxes: they are in tune. They are also audible, and they don't come a cropper by over-reaching themselves. (O visiting choirs, I charge you, fling away ambition! By that sin fell the angels.)

Why, then, is our friend the canon precentor in such difficulties? He stands rigid beside the dean at the altar. He maintains the *orans* position stiffly through the preface, hands lined up with nipples like the rubric states, and braces himself for the Sanctus and Benedictus with gritted teeth.

Here's why: the choir contains one of *those* sopranos. You know what I mean. Perfectly in tune, but incapable of blending in. Her reedy tones stand out the way middle C on the Song School piano would, if you were to stick a drawing pin into the hammer – as a certain chorister from hell demonstrated a dozen years ago.

> Sanctus, Sanctus, Sanctus,
> Dominus Deus Sabaoth ...

Probably the soprano was rather an accomplished singer in her prime. But yikes. If Giles were this choir's director he'd have her humanely put down.

Giles thinks that's what he'd do, but in reality, it's never that straightforward. There are many reasons for not getting rid of screechy sopranos. Compassion, denial, stark terror; or the choral table of kindred and affinity, which forbids the sacking of close relatives or spouses. We must not blame the singer too much. Perhaps she wonders, perhaps she even asks her fellow choir members whether she's still up to scratch. And they, being English, speedily reassure her, and continue to moan behind her back for many years to come.

Ah, the gulf that still exists between us and the kingdom. We are four Sundays from Advent. O Radix David, open wide the door to the heavenly quire! From east and west, north and south, let them come; let every voice prepare a song, ready to enter that gate and dwell in that house where there shall be no tone deafness nor virtuosity, but one equal anthem.

Eschatological visions aside, the visiting choir was a far cry from the high professional standards of the Dorian Singers. But I will admit that these are so stratospherically high that ice crystals form in your ears as you listen. Their Christmas CD, *Realms of Glory*, will zip up through the Classical charts like a Category 4 aerial shell firework and stun us all. We must expect their trademark technical wizardry, combined with an accessibility that jealous rivals will again disparage as 'dumbing down'. Nip into any cathedral bookshop and buy a copy, if you are the sort who prefers the feel and smell of an actual CD. Otherwise download it like a normal person. In particular, do listen to the third track: 'What wondrous love is this, oh my soul?' I'm telling you, your withers will be wrung. It's a heartbreakingly beautiful folk melody arranged for solo tenor. It's performed here by a talented young man whose light, pleasing voice seems made for English art songs. So no, we are not talking about Freddie May, (whose timbre has a distinct whiff of the night about it). Freddie was lined up to do it, but . . .

Look, I'm going to level with you, reader: Freddie does not feature at all on this CD.

Oh, Freddie, Freddie, Freddie! What have you done now? Don't tell me you were packed off home in disgrace, as you were from choir tours in your chorister days!

No, it was nothing like that, I'm relieved to say. Freddie managed to arrive sober at the right place, at very nearly the right time. The rehearsals went well. On two separate occasions Mr Dorian said, 'Oh, very good, Mr May!', and on another, he all but smiled at him. Then, just as the sound levels were being checked prior to the recording, *whoosh!* Freddie had one of his spectacular nosebleeds.

An hour later, when all the usual tricks had failed, poor Freddie was put in a taxi and sent up to the nearest A & E. I will spare you a detailed account (in any case, this all happened outside the Diocese of Lindchester) and simply report that an excruciating nasal cautery procedure put an end to any possibility of Freddie singing that week.

To say he was majorly disappointed comes nowhere near describing Freddie's feelings. He was *distraught*. But he knew that a noisy public display of wretchedness would not commend him to his mentor. To be needy, as well as a total flake? No way. Totally killed him, but he reined it in? Any case, he was shit scared that crying would trigger another nosebleed. Consultant was literally threatening him with surgery to sort out his busted septum, if the cauterizing didn't work?

So Freddie is not on the CD.

Actually, I tell a lie.

'That's you! In your nuddy pants! Ha ha ha! What a hoot!'

'Totty— Gah! It's not— I had my jeans on?'

'I'll take your word for it. Aw, he's blushing! Poor angel! Hoo, hoo, hoo!'

'Shut *up*, Totty! Listen, it's, it says something about the incarnation, OK? Power and weakness, yeah? The juxtaposition of . . . Hnn. Wait, human vulnerability, in, y'know, the shoulder blades? Plus the whole archangel . . . wing thing? What? That's totally what he said!'

'Who?'

'Nng.'

'Ha ha! The great man himself! A bit rich after all his lectures! Next minute he turns round and says, "I know, let's put a hot bod on the CD cover and sell shed-loads of copies!"'

'Hey! Out of order! It's my shoulders, not my ass! I'm so not talking to you, Totty. Gimme that.' Totty held the CD out of reach. 'You're making out it's inappropriate?'

'Let me look properly.' She popped her reading glasses on and studied the black and white image. A figure – radiant, bleached-out – in a stone archway. It might almost be an image from the *Souls and Bodies* exhibition. 'All right, Freddie-bear, it's very tasteful and arty. Not porny at all. And you can't actually tell it's you.'

'Mm, they kinda like photoshopped it to death?'

'So how did Mr Dorian know about the tattoos, hmm? Or should I not enquire . . . ?'

'I wish! So I had this massive nosebleed? Had to change? Well, hey girl, never pass up a chance to get your shirt off in public. That's totally my motto.'

'Hoo, hoo, hoo! Bad bear!'

Talking of bad bears, the large pink teddy in the bishop's office is currently sitting in the window, looking out across the car park. He's wearing the archdeacon's pork pie hat. Matt left it behind last time he had a meeting with Bishop Harry. Such are Matt's levels of distraction, he hasn't had time to work out where he last saw it. In fact, he's barely registered his hatlessness.

The battle with Veronica is now in the endgame of Phase One. The complainant has exercised her right 'to request the President of Tribunals in writing to review a dismissal under section 11(3) of the Measure'. Well, he'd seen that one coming. It's a time-wasting resource-wasting bit of bloody-mindedness. Harry's decision can only be overturned if the president believes that the bishop was flat out wrong. It will drag on for another month, six weeks, max.

And after that, Phase Two. When the archdeacon will be calling the shots. He has all his ducks in a row. A spot of digging around in the Revd Dr da Silva's CV has thrown up a whole bunch of inconsistencies. A couple of trips to previous workplaces and a few off-the-record chats with former colleagues proved, shall we say, enlightening? He's been in conversation with the legal team who steered him through the employment tribunal malarkey.

And then what, Matt? whispers his conscience. Is there a Phase Three? What about the big picture? What about Janey?

Fair enough, fair enough. He'll get to that. Right now he's focused on the short term. He'll sit tight in his bunker for the next few weeks, then he'll be strapping on the archiepiscopal gun belt and adjusting his Stetson.

Talking of which, where the chuff has his hat got to?

Halloween has been and gone. Father Dominic doled out sweeties and Bonfire Party invitations once again to callers at the vicarage. It was 'Blended Learning Week' at Poundstretcher, and young female undergraduates, had they been willing to learn from Dr Jane Rossiter, might have interrogated the messages about women underlying the choice of fancy dress on offer. Slutty nurse, slutty vampire, slutty witch, slutty cat. Oh, for fuck's sake. Maybe if I publish enough and my funding bids are all successful, one day I'll be a slutty professor! And think: we can even have slutty bishops now! Yay equality!

Uh-oh. Looks like I haven't managed to blend my learning with a sense of humour, thought Jane. She was holed up again, not answering her door to the stream of trick-or-treaters. I just don't get that it's *ironic*, do I? Just because my boobs are saggy, obviously I'm jealous of young attractive women who want to have fun getting their tits out for the boys. Why don't I go and hire a slutty feminist outfit, instead of judging other people's lifestyles? *Stop ringing my doorbell, you slutty sluts, or I'll show you empowerment!*

Was it possible she'd drunk a wee bit too much Malbec? Yeah, that was just about possible, given the bottle was empty. Oh Lordy, drinking by yourself, Rossiter. What's the world coming to? I've been doing too much of everything by myself. Still, Danny will be home in three weeks.

Jane hugged one of her manky cushions so tight it was ... whatever. Tight. Like her. Oh Danny, I remember when I used to sit you in the laundry basket and wedge you upright with these very cushions! I used to let you suck bunches of keys and eat file paper, just so I'd get half an article read. I was demented with boredom all the time you were little. But now I'm sobbing into a filthy tartan cushion, hugging it and wishing I had my baby boy in my arms just one more time.

Hah, you maudlin old bag. If you told Danny any of that, he'd probably wedge *you* in a laundry basket with a manky cushion, just to prove he was a grown-up. He's going to come back for three weeks, then he'll be off again. You've got to move your life on, gal. Get over yourself, girlfriend.

It's Friday. It's meant to be Matt's day off, but he's at his desk trying to keep on top of the old email in-box. If he can get it down to under seventy, maybe he'll ring Janey and— His phone bursts into 'Lady in Red'. He smiles.

'Hello, Janey.'

'Where are you?'

'At home.'

'In your study?'

'Yep. Um, are you mad at me, Jane?'

'No.'

'All righty. Only you sound a bit mad.'

'That's as maybe. Have you got a utility bill to hand?'

'Probably. Why?

'Find one. Passport?'

'What's going on, Janey?'

'HAVE YOU GOT YOUR PASSPORT?'

'Flip! Yes, I've got it here somewhere.'

'Find it.'

Pause. 'OK. Got it. Now what?'

'Pick them both up and come out of the front door. I'm in my car on the drive. Bring your wallet with your driving licence.'

'Ooo-ka-a-ay. Are you going to tell me what's—?' He stares at the phone for a moment, as though an explanation is going to appear on the screen. He scans his inner world to check which metaphorical loo seat he's left up this time. Working too hard? Ignoring her? Yep, that would be it. Unless . . . Oh Lord, was this showdown time? She was never expecting him to put a deposit on a house with her?

He pulls the door shut. There she is. He gets into the passenger seat. Looks at her face. Yep, it's judgement day, all right. 'Janey, where are we going?'

She takes a deep breath. 'You are only allowed to say one thing, and that is "Thank you, Jane". We're going to the register office to give notice.'

He stares. 'I'm sorry, what?'

'Of our intention to marry, dickwad!' she shouts.

Like the rising of the sun in the east, like a bridegroom coming out of his chamber, like a strong man rejoicing to run a race, that is how the smile appears on the archdeacon's face. 'Thank you, Jane.'

NOVEMBER

Chapter 28

onfire Night! Smoke broods in strata above the Diocese of Lindchester, and everywhere, in parish and deanery, in back garden and public park – fireworks. BOOM! Far off, near. Ah! Look at the fire blossoms, how they melt to smoky dandelion clocks in the night sky. Then comes a fierce crackling, like the flash frying of recusants. Listen to those screaming fireworks. Don't they put you in mind of the squalls of live cats in burning effigies of the pope? But perhaps you didn't know they did that, our forebears? I believe it amused them. But then, the public hanging, drawing and quartering of traitors counted as a fun day out, too. Yes, yes, but the cats, though, the poor cats! Fighting and screaming in terror as they burn! Odd how that detail has the power to trouble an English temperament inured to the fate of Guy Fawkes.

How can it be a whole year? thinks Father Dominic. He mops the muddy footprints from the vicarage kitchen floor after the last guests have gone. Lord! What larks, trying to explain to his Farsi-speaking congregation what Bonfire Night is all about. Until this year, Dominic has stubbornly contemplated gunpowder, treason and plot through the nostalgic haze of childhood bonfires. It has always smacked of toffee apples and sparklers for him. But now he's viewing it through the lens of current events. Terrorism. Political instability. Beheadings. Islamophobia. War. Maybe he ought to be glad that Guy Fawkes' night is being edged out by the commercialized mission creep of Halloween?

He squeeges the mop and tips the dirty water away. All his kitchen surfaces are cluttered with leftovers from the bonfire feast. Cold sossies for lunch tomorrow. Goody-good. Project Clingfilm is under way when his doorbell rings. It's Jane. With a bottle of posh Prosecco.

Ooh, Lord! There go the good intentions. Well, never mind; Wednesday is day off eve eve. And it falls within the octave of last week's day off, doesn't it? Not forgetting that Prosecco goes very nicely with cinder toffee.

'Well, chin chin, fatty,' says Dominic. 'What's the occasion?'

Jane scowls. 'There's no occasion. Why does there have to be an occasion? Oh, I know – what about, because it's Guy Fawkes' night? Yes, let's drink to the hideously protracted torture and death of papists and other traitors to the Crown. That's the occasion. Or because I haven't seen you properly for ages. In fact, what's not to celebrate? Apart from Ebola and UKIP, obviously. And ISIS, global warming, welfare cuts—'

'You're blethering, darling.'

'True. Cheers.' They clink glasses.

Silence.

Dominic gives good pastoral silence. He knows perfectly well Jane is working up to something. A horrid thought assails him: never say she's emigrating to New Zealand? No! You can't abandon me! He arranges his expression into selfless sympathy.

'Oh, stop doing your "Trust me, I'm a priest" thing,' she snaps. 'Yes, you are – you're tilting your head. You look like Susanna bloody Henderson.'

'Eek!' Dominic straightens up. 'Come on then. Out with it, you old tart.'

'Very well.' Jane takes a dignified sip of Prosecco. 'Now, I'm going to ask you a question, and you're to answer calmly and sensibly, without screaming. Because it's really not a big deal. OK? Good. What are you doing on Friday the twenty-eighth of November, at ten a.m.?'

'Well, nothing as far as I know. It's my day off— OH! Omigod!' he screams. 'You're getting hitched! You're—'

'I *said*, no screaming! It's not a big deal.'

'Omigod, omigod, omigod! You're actually getting married! This so is a big deal! Oh, congratulations, darling! Mwa, mwa! Let me see the ring. What?! Why haven't you got a ring? Can I be your flower girl? Oh, please? All right, can I give you away, then?'

'NO! Just shut up, you big ponce. Listen. No, listen to me! Matt and I are entering into a legal contract. That's all. A legalized partnership. No rings, no flowers, none of that oppressive patriarchal bollocks.'

'Yes, yes, but what are you going to wear?'

Jane hesitates.

'Why don't you turn up in your fat bloke trackie bottoms and rugby shirt?' he asks. 'If it's just a legal contract.'

'Fuck off.'

'You fuck off. Oh, this is so exciting! More Prosecco?'

'Yes, please.'

'What about that red dress?'

'No! I can't possibly wear that. I wore it to Danny's dad's civil union, for God's sake.'

'Oh, and I thought this wasn't a big deal. Silly me.'

'You're being very tiresome, Dommie.'

He seizes her face in both hands and plants a smacker on her lips. 'Oh, this is wonderful, Jane! I'm really, really thrilled for you both. Oh no, I'm welling up!' He fans the tears back into their ducts. 'So, it's at Lindford register office? Do I have a role, or shall I just sit and cry happy tears?'

'We'd like you to be a witness. But it's a very small low-key private thing, so don't tell anyone.'

'Of course not, darling. Do you want me to suit up?'

'Wear what you like. I really don't care. But if you show up in a vicar jumper, I'll kill you.'

The question of what to wear is a daily dilemma at the moment. All around the Diocese of Lindchester people come up with different solutions. Some consult the temperature and go about in sandals and summer tops. Others cling to the notion that this is November, and don their boots and scarves. You will see both these extremes – and every possible expression of the sartorial *via media* – represented on the streets of Lindfordshire's towns. You will also encounter the full spectrum of explanation, too: from 'the overwhelming scientific consensus for human-induced global warming' to 'that volcano in Iceland'. I mean, can't we just enjoy the lovely weather without all this doom-mongering? Live in the moment. That's all we have. Don't waste the precious moment worrying, what if by some perverse twist of fate the 97 per cent of serious scientists turn out to be right after all? What if, on some cosmic November 6th, our planet orbits silently on without us, and we are just charred sticks and empty cardboard after our brilliance has burnt out to nothing?

Still, autumn slowly advances across the landscape. Father Wendy notes its progress on Thursday, as she walks towards the Linden with Pedro. Leaves are finally starting to go now. Her floral wellies scrunch through all the toffee shades: tablet, butterscotch, treacle, liquorice. She raises her eyes. Bare trees on the rim of the field there, with dark clots of magpie nests; although the poplars are still silver-topped and the beeches gold.

They reach the bank. Moorhens flick their tails and scurry to the river. Among the neglected coppicing to her left she sees a stretch of bright rippled water, like sunshine through a 1960s bathroom window. There's an alder full of goldfinches tara-diddling softly among themselves. Is anything so green as English grass in the low winter sun, with strands of gossamer criss-crossing from blade to blade? The leaves have all gone from the hawthorn, but every bush is stippled over with wine-coloured berries. She passes under the echoing arch of a bridge where a lane crosses the Linden and a cutter munches its way along the hedge.

Out on the other side lapwings lollop and pheasants wander in stubble. Pedro leans on his harness.

'Sorry, boy. Can't let you run here.'

On they go, past pigs in humpback corrugated iron sties against the backdrop of cooling towers. Behind her she can hear a runner approaching. There's a blue tractor parked in a field of green; then newly ploughed acres, all blackish brown like moleskin. In the distance a flock of starlings hurls itself up into the sky. It lassoes out, comes sifting, sifting down, then flicks back in like a fish tail.

'Look at that, Pedro!'

But Pedro has seen another pheasant. He darts—

It happens in a flash. Pedro yelps, the runner goes headlong.

'Fuck!'

'Pedro! Oh, I'm so sorry!'

The runner rolls like a ninja, and he's on his feet. 'Oh God, I'm—' he gasps for breath.

'Are you—'

'Sorry – is your dog—'

'—OK?'

'—OK?'

The runner stands there panting. He grins. 'Whoa! That was mental. Muscle memory?'

'Are you sure you're all right? I'm so sorry.'

'No worries, I know how to fall.' Then he squats by Pedro. 'Hey boy, c'mere. It's OK, c'mere, dude. Yeah, that's it.'

She watches, jittery with shock. Then the penny drops. 'Oh, it's you!'

'Huh?'

'I've seen you out running lots of times. I'm the local vicar.'

'Oh wait, you're Wendy? Hey, Wendy. Awesome!' He smiles up at her. How radiant he is, how beautiful! 'I helped paint the curate's house that time? Matt, like, sent me? Last summer?'

'Oh, that was you!'

'Yeah, that was me.'

He's that naughty boy who drove Marge mad! But there's something else, some problem, a smear of rumour – what is it? His smile dims. He drops his eyes. Fondles Pedro's ears. 'Hey, boy. Hey, it's OK.'

'I always pray for you,' she hears herself say.

A quiver crosses his face. The long lashes flutter. Trouble. He's in trouble.

'Cool. Hey. Catch you later, Wendy?'

He's on his feet and away before she can say anything. She watches till he's out of sight. Her prayers follow, follow after.

Father Wendy's pastoral antennae were correct. Freddie is in trouble. He has his hands up his sleeves, playing air guitar on that fretboard of scars on his upper arms.

Helene, the diocesan HR manager, turns over another sheet on his file.

Gah, here it comes.

'Well, Frederick, given that you admit the offence, and that there's probably enough evidence for a realistic chance of a conviction, I think you'd do well to accept the police caution.'

'Cool. Yeah. Totally. Probably I should do that?'

'I think that would be wise.'

'But it's totally not a conviction? It won't go on my record?'

'No, it's not a conviction. But it will form part of your criminal record, for the purposes of any DBS check. For six years.'

'Ah, nuts!' He bites his lips. ''Kay. Thanks, Helene.'

'You're welcome.' She closes the file. 'Is there anything else I can help you with?'

'Yeah, no, um, oh God, can they like fire me for this? Gah, I was so close to the end of my probationary period! I was gonna be installed in, like, two weeks? Man, I'm such a numbnuts.'

'Far be it from me to disagree with you, Deanissima,' said Gene the following day, 'but a police caution for flouting the Firework Code seems a little draconian to me.'

'Gene, he was firing roman candles at people.'

'Tush, pish and nonsense! They all were! It was a game, an upmarket snowball fight. You make it sound as though he was gunning down innocent passers-by.'

'It was stupid and really dangerous. It's a mercy nobody was hurt. I can't let this one slide. What kind of role model is he for the choristers?'

'Is this the end for the lovely Mr May?'

The dean scowled. 'No. Giles and Timothy are going to extend his probationary period for another three months. But I don't care how brilliant his voice is, this is absolutely his last chance.'

Gene inclined his head. 'You are both wise and merciful, O queen. One more small question and then I'm done. I saw at least half a dozen young scallywags out there. Why is poor Freddie the only one being punished?'

'Because poor Freddie was the only one up on the cathedral roof!' exclaimed the dean. 'And as usual, poor Freddie was the only one stupid enough to get caught!'

'Ah, but poor Freddie wants to get caught, surely?' said Gene. 'If you're never caught, you can never be forgiven. I offer you that little theological insight from the vast storehouse of my intellect. And I see you are not impressed, so I offer you the wealth of my wine cellar instead.'

I think Gene is right. And I think that Freddie himself is closing in on this idea. He sits at the kitchen table writhing under Totty's watchful eye as he tries to compose a letter to his mentor, explaining why his installation as lay clerk of Gayden Parva has been deferred. He absolutely must write this letter now, before Giles gets on the phone and complains about him again. Or worse, Dr Jacks – having condescended to rearrange his diary in order to attend the service – arrives to finds it's not happening, hunts Freddie down, and turns the mentorly stare from stun to kill.

Oh God, oh God.

Dear Dr Jacks. I'm an idiot, I fucked up. No, can't put that.

He tosses down the pen and grips his hair in both hands.

What were you thinking?

I seriously don't know, Mrs Dean, I'm so, so sorry?

Man, that's what *everyone* asked. Like, the precentor, the police, literally everyone? That's what they always ask, and know something? He can never answer. It's not like he's all, hey, here's a really dumb thing, ooh, shall I do this really dumb thing? Whoa, let's run this one by the frontal cortex first, guys? No, it's *boom*. Ri-i-i-ght. Yeah, that was pretty dumb.

Oh man, he should totally stop doing this? He's gotta move his life on, it's like he's stuck in some permanent dumb-fuck loop at fifteen years old.

So write the fucking letter, OK? Dude, it's not that big of a deal. He picks the pen up again. Seriously, you do not want Dr Jacks pissed at you.

Or wait. Does he? Maybe he kind of does want that? Coz that way, at least he'll have his attention. Hhnnh.

'How's that letter going, Freddie bear?' asks Totty.

Freddie jumps. 'I'm all over it.'

Perhaps the reader's thoughts have turned to another character now, who unlike the luckless Freddie May has so far been too clever to get caught. I refer, of course, to the Revd Dr Veronica da Silva. She escaped justice when Geoff proved himself to be too noble to read another person's private emails, even though that person had almost certainly read his, and used the contents selectively and tendentiously to cause mischief and mayhem in the Diocese of Lindchester and beyond.

It is fortunate for Veronica that the archdeacon and Jane currently have other, more interesting things than retribution to absorb their energies. Perhaps she thinks she has neutralized them by winding up the clergy discipline measure and pointing it in their direction? That would be foolish. She made herself a couple of heavyweight enemies there, and like crocodiles they may yet slip into the water, though they are currently basking on the bank in the sunshine of their imminent nuptials (even if it's not a big deal).

She certainly has nothing to fear from her vicar Geoff. Geoff is no crocodile. If we were obliged to select one of the animals featured on Geoff's Noah's Ark stole to stand as a metaphor for him, we'd probably fix on the giraffe, generously eating only the topmost leaves the other animals can't reach. But this gentle herbivorous vicar must invite Veronica (whom we will characterize as a dangerous rhino) into the parish office and confront her about that email exchange with Roderick Fallon (a hyena, definitely). Oh, dear! My heart is starting to pound as though I'm watching a nature documentary. This cannot go well.

Unless there's a ranger with a tranquillizer gun in the corner.

'Hello, Veronica. Thanks for coming. This is Helene, the diocesan HR manager. I've invited her to sit in on our meeting today as an observer.'

'Hello, Veronica.'

Ah, Helene, you are magnificent! How the light of justice glints off your metaphorical weaponry! Veronica sees it, and blinks. There is a pause while the goalposts are swiftly disassembled and replaced with a basketball hoop.

'Hello, Helene!! I'm real glad you're here today! Geoff, this is really sweet of you to fix this meeting up! Because it'll save us all time, and hey, I know just how busy you are right now! Helene, I was gonna email you to ask about giving notice? The ins and outs, the legalities. Because, long story short, I've been offered a new post, and I've accepted. I start in January.'

'Well,' says Geoff. 'That's rather sudden. Um.' The landscape reconfigures around him. For a moment he cannot get any bearings. 'Will you need me to give you a reference? Because there are a couple of things—'

'No, they've already taken up my references, but that's real sweet of you to ask. No, it's all in train. Just a few loose ends to tie up at the uni end of things.'

'Yes, but – um. I still need to ask you something, please. I was in the office, working on this computer. You'd left your email open, and a message arrived from Roderick—'

'Geoff, if I can just break in.' Veronica laid a hand on his arm. 'Are you accusing me of something? Because I'm feeling harassed here. If you wanna make accusations, then I'm not prepared to have this conversation unless I can have my union rep and legal advisor here.'

'What?' Geoff pulled his arm away. 'Look, we've got the diocesan HR manager here! Surely that's—'

'Oh, Geoff, Geoff! Don't let's do this, OK? We've worked real well together, don't let's end on a bitter note, OK? Let's just get through these last weeks as friends and co-workers in the gospel. Bless you, now.'

Helene and Geoff stare at the door as it swings shut.

So Veronica is off. In general we have little reason to place confidence in what she says, but on this occasion, she is telling the truth: she has a new job. And I dare say she has judged rightly, and Geoff won't bother pursuing the matter of the emails.

Has she escaped scot-free? I leave that for the reader to determine. Her new post is in the Diocese of Sydney.

Chapter 29

oppy petals fall like red snow. Listen, as they whisper down on to the crowds in front of Lindford Town Hall. They brush the upturned faces, the berets, epaulettes, vestments, snagging on medals, perching on hat brims. Down, still they whisper down, until they come to rest on the road. Red confetti. Blood running down gutters. A hundred years since the outbreak of the First World War.

The crowd stands motionless. Shoppers pause to stare. Of course, Remembrance Day. They hush their children and tiptoe by. Christmas trees wait in sockets on shop walls. Unlit lights hang poised across mall and street.

As soon as thou scatterest them they are even as a sleep, and fade away suddenly like the grass. All our sons, borne away on the ever-rolling stream. Long ago. A century ago. But a hundred years in thy sight are but as yesterday gone. *O Lord, thou has been our refuge from one generation to another.*

Eleven a.m. The Last Post sounds in Lindford. It sounds in Lindchester Cathedral, in Renfold, Cardingforth and Martonbury. A young cadet, shaking with nerves, puts bugle to flaky lips in the churchyard of Gayden Parva. The small crowd bears him through it in a tight-knotted net of good will. They stand there among the roped-off dangerous monuments, the poleaxed angels and headstones lying flat. Gayden Parva, where the names of dead sons line the pretty lichgate (so photogenic for weddings), the corpse gate. Those village sons, no older than this boy bugler, gave their today that tomorrow's lads might face no worse an ordeal than this – the one he's bungling his way through now.

And the final broken note fades. The cadet gasps in a desperate lungful. Silence. Well done, it's over now, lad.

At the going down of the sun and in the morning, we will remember them. Rest in peace, Jack and William, sleep, sleep, all you

Johns, and Henrys, mown down like Normandy grass, all the Thomases, Herberts and Walters of Gayden Parva. You shall not grow old. Rest in peace, and rise in glory.

In the silence – in the sorrow and the remembering and the waiting for the Reveille – a flutter of wings. A robin lands on the stone cross by the ancient yew, and sings.

This is where we all stand, between Last Post and Reveille, between All Saints and Advent, first and second coming. We are in the tail-end of the church year now, the home straight. Our eyes turn east and hunt a black sky for that first gleam of tender compassion, of the promised dayspring.

> In the darkness of this age that is passing away
> may the light of your presence which the saints enjoy
> surround our steps as we journey on.

In these weeks great swathes of apocalyptic weirdness are read in public worship. Beasts and dragons, horns and eyes, angels, scrolls, plagues, fire, blood and horsemen. And always, at every turn in the road: a choice. To do justly, or not. To be faithful unto death, or not. Wise virgin, foolish virgin. The bridegroom is coming. Stay awake, therefore. And that Great Day – is it light, like lightning coming from the east? Or dark, very dark with no brightness in it? Judgement or mercy: which? Or is the mercy of God a kind of judgement? Might judgement be merciful? Can anyone escape judgement? And those who escape, will they ever know mercy?

I wonder. I wonder about Veronica. I know my readers think that by skedaddling to Australia she has evaded the comeuppance she so justly deserved. But if we were to study Veronica's CV – as Helene is doing even as I write this – it would betray that she is a woman on the run. All her adult life, every year, two years, or at best three, she has moved on and reinvented herself. She can never rest. She must always run before the truth catches up with her.

I admit: justice has not been done. But I would call escape a merciless process all the same.

Freddie May, by contrast, whose strategy is flagrantly to court retribution, has perhaps fared a little better. That apology he was writing to his mentor last week went from one degree of garble to another, till in the end he tore it up and bolted from the kitchen table and out from under Totty's stern gaze. He crossed the dark Close and sat shivering on a bench – the very bench from which he once tweeted Roderick Fallon in a fit of rage. He got out his phone this time too, cursed himself, wept a few tears, then screwed his courage to the sticking point.

With how sad steps the full moon climbed up above the palace roof opposite!

'Mr May. How lovely. Are you well? How's that deviated septum?'

'Yeah, it's fine, thanks. I'm good.' Pause. 'Actually? No. Not good. Really not. I fucked up majorly?' Silence. Oh, God. Please say something?

'On a scale of one to six – where six is "you've brought about the end of Western civilization as we know it" – how major is this?'

Eesh. Put like that? 'Ah . . . um, maybe like . . . one point eight?' More silence. 'Or one point seven?'

'You didn't burn down the cathedral, or take someone's eye out?'

Shit! Giles phoned him! 'No, but—'

'So in fact, you really only fucked up *minorly.*'

'Yeah, but no, yeah, listen, here's the thing, my installation's been postponed? And I know you, like, rearranged stuff and everything, to be here? So yeah, sorry to mess you around.' Silence. 'Oh and yeah, you should probably know I'm on totally my last warning now? Giles and Timothy? They've like, extended my probation for another three months, but if I, like, fuck up again, that is literally it, game over? Coz the dean—'

'Thank you. I get the picture. Would you like my advice?'

'Mngn – kinda? Yeah.'

'I suggest you avoid another fuck-up.'

Freddie waited. That was it? Jesus. 'Ri-i-ight. Thanks.'

'You're welcome. Was that everything?'

'Um. Nearly. So just to give you the heads up, I got a police caution, and—'

'Yes. I know. How do I know? Because once again the precentor rang to complain about you. Can I be candid? I'm finding you rather tedious, Mr May.'

'Sorry, sir— Gah! *Keep* saying that. I'm really sorry, Dr Jacks?'

'Let's skip the breast-beating. The only thing that interests me here is whether you've learned anything. Anything at all.' Silence. 'Well? Come along. Don't play with fireworks? Never get caught?'

Freddie bit his knuckle. Forced himself. 'Yeah, OK, I'm probably gonna start crying here, but whatever, here goes? So I'm thinking part of me, like, does this on purpose? Fucks up, just when every-thing's on track? Coz then, you'll have to pay me some attention?'

'Aha! Now you're interesting me. Go on.'

'Right, so it's like, if I get my shit together, then everyone will be all, finally! Freddie's got it together, he doesn't need help any more, and then I'll be like, on my ... gah, all on my own? Ah, nuts. Told you I'd— God.'

'Freddie, I'm not about to abandon you, never fear.'

'Oh, God. Sorry. Thanks, Dr Jacks.'

'Would it reassure you to know you already have my attention? Remember the mentoring ground rules? No need to impress me. I've been interested in your progress for years. Ever since you were a brilliant boy soprano hanging around me at the Three Choirs Festival.'

'Omigod! No way! You actually remember that?'

'Oh, I remember.'

'Whoa! I'm— Seriously? Um, but can you remember what you ... said?'

'Piss off, kid?'

'Ha ha, no. You were all ...' Freddie's voice went tiny. He tugged his hair. 'You said, "Come and find me when you're grown-up"?'

Semiquaver rest. 'And I still very much look forward to that.'

'Na-a-aw!' Face-palm. Laid yourself wi-i-ide open to that one.

He laughed. 'Well, Freddie, you've done some hard thinking, and this sounds to me like progress. Anything else to report? No more nosebleeds?'

'Nah.'

'Then keep up the good work. I have every confidence in you. Ciao, ciao, darling.' He hung up.

Freddie pressed the phone to his pounding heart. Please. Please. Let him ...? Oh, please?

The moon looked down. How silently, and with how wan a face!

The precentor's wife, Ulli, is kneeling in the utility room sorting laundry. Her son Felix is nearly eighteen, and that's far too old to believe in the Magic Washing Machine. Yet he still drops his dirty clothes in front of it, and lo! They still reappear in his bedroom clean and ironed. It is a maternal truth universally acknowledged that last-born sons get away with murder.

Ulli checks all pockets for plectrums, thumb picks, Rizlas, crumpled A-level notes, mobile phones, cash, school ID cards, tissues (bastard sodding things) and Bic lighters. She makes a pile on the machine top. Any cash she finds is hers. That is the rule of the Magic Washing Machine. She stuffs the clothes in the drum. Stops. Examines a black hoodie. Is that a hole? A hole burned through the sleeve?

Was hat sich hier ereignet? She sniffs. No! That stupid firework battle last week! She slaps the washing machine hard. What had Felix said, exactly, when Giles confronted him? Something like: I can't believe you're even asking me this! Do I look like I want to get my head blown off? Yeah, thanks for displaying your trust in me there, Dad!

Oh je. Felix Joseph Littlechild, you little weasel! She can't let him get away with it, not after all the trouble Freddie May caught for this!

Can she?

Quickly, she shoves the hoodie in and slams the machine door. La la la! Freddie May has a tongue in his head, *ja*? He could have bloody told the dean and the police who the other culprits were! Of course, she must talk to Felix and tell him to own up. Yes, yes. But what if *he* ends up getting a police caution too . . . ?

Ach, Gott! She sets the machine going and hurries off to give the choral scholars their weekly lesson. And if the four of them weren't also involved in the firework fiasco, then Ulli will eat her broom. There's no way *they* are getting off if her son's going to catch it! And Freddie May is much older, come to think of it. He's nearly twenty-five now, for God's sake! The ringleader ought to take the rap!

She jabs the Song School door keypad (1-6-6-2) and lets herself in. They are late again, the little sods. Bet they're all crapping themselves in case Freddie turns them in. Hah! They won't do anything so daft again in a hurry! So maybe she'll just scare Felix a bit, and tell him he can bloody buy himself a new hoodie. Yes, that might be the best thing.

There. What did I tell you? Murder. They literally (in the Freddie May metaphorical sense of that word) get away with murder!

It's Friday. All around the Diocese of Lindchester laundry is being done. Traditionally speaking, Friday is not washday. But washday no longer exists in this age of automatic washing machines. Every day is washday now. Jane reflects on this as she crams in a load of cushion and sofa covers that have never before been washed in all their twenty years. God, she's a slut!*

Jane can remember Mondays when she was a child. The electric boiler with its hose, the blue-marbled rubber mangle on top. And the spin dryer Jane used to sit on (nose in book) to prevent it trundling round the kitchen widdling water as it went. Her only useful contribution. Lord, how domesticity used to eat women alive! Wash

---

* Not in the Freddie May sense of that word.

on Monday, iron on Tuesday, bake on Wednesday. Jane grips her ancient trusty Zanussi's sides. Thank you, old friend! A whole day just for washing. Lugging heavy cotton sheets out to the line in the big wicker basket. Despair and rage if it rained unexpectedly while the washing was out and you were a mile away in the library. Winter days of steaming clothes racks round the fire. No wonder Mum swapped to Bri-nylon sheets. And brushed nylon nighties. Ooh, those secret lightning storms under the covers! Oh, the eiderdowns, the candlewick, the sides-to-middled sheets of the pre-duvet era! Tuh. Say that to the young people nowadays, and they don't know what you're talking about.

I don't want to shock you, reader, but Jane is spring-cleaning this morning instead of responding to her emails, updating class registers, reading minutes and agendas, or any of the work cobblers that make cleaning behind the fridge a tempting displacement activity. Danny will be home in a week. Not that she went in for much housework when he was still living here, but his stepmother keeps the house spotless. It's not a competition, and Jane does not have any sense of personal worth bound up in her kitchen surfaces, obviously. But viewed with a little detachment, she concedes that the place is a total disgrace. Furthermore, *if* she's going to rent it out in the New Year, and move in with Matt ...

Aargh!

Or possibly, *Yay!*?

Jane tries them both. She has to confess, *Yay!* seems nearer the mark. And financially speaking, it's daft to run two separate households. Oh God, is this the slippery slope, though? Will she end up morphing into a Stepford clergy spouse like Susanna Henderson? What if the new bishop's wife takes it upon herself to call round and give Jane some friendly advice, and Jane is obliged to punch her lights out, and it all ends with the police, prison, tabloid headlines and messy divorce?

Or alternatively, what if she stops being a silly mare, and instead contemplates waking up every morning for the rest of her life with that good man beside her? Do you, Jane Margaret Rossiter, take to this idea? I do. I rather think I do. Jane puts on rubber gloves and an Ella Fitzgerald CD and starts cleaning the stove. She's got rhythm, music, her man. What sane woman could ask for anything more?

Across in his pad in Lindford, our friend the archdeacon is also doing some laundry. He's just whacked in a load of brand-new bedding to soften it up a bit. He knows his stuff, does the archdeacon. Knows that even the most undomesticated woman in the world (and his

Janey has to be in with a shout for a medal here) appreciates a nice bit of Egyptian cotton sheeting. Pig to iron, mind you, but definitely worth it. He pours in a shot of Summer Breeze fabric softener, and away she goes.

Ha. Just can't get the big soppy grin off his face for any money. He'd love to tell the whole world, but he wouldn't put it past his chum Veronica to lodge a legal objection to their marriage just for the hell of it. The notice is on display in the register office, but it makes sense to keep schtum. He sticks The Proclaimers on and does a spot of cheeky internet browsing, the details of which the reader is at liberty to imagine for themselves. Too right, he's gonna be the man who wakes up next to her.

The Vicar of Gayden Magna is not doing any washing today, because he cannot be trusted to do it properly. A few strategic displays of tissue-related incompetence on Ed's part mean that laundry is now Neil's fiefdom, and no challenge will be brooked. Still, there are always plenty of other things to quarrel about in the vicarage at Gayden Magna.

'Neil, look, why don't I go on my own to pick up the sketches?'

'What if he still hasn't done a proper job?'

'I'm sure it'll be fine. Anyway, they're supposed to be a present for *me*, so surely I get to decide if they're properly framed.'

'You! You'd be happy if they were Blu-tacked to the wall like a student poster! No, I'm going. He made a dog's breakfast of it first time. I don't trust him.'

'Oh, for God's sake, Neil, they looked absolutely fine! Why do you always have to make difficulties about every—'

'McIvor.'

Ed gaped. Then he clamped his mouth shut. Exhaled through his nose. 'Neil—'

'Bu-bu-bu! Psht! You're doing something I hate, and I need you to stop now, without arguing.'

Ed gritted his teeth and managed to incline his head.

'Yeah, that's better. Listen, big man, this is me, this is what I'm like. Got that? I'm a perfectionist. So we'll hear no more about it, if you please.' He picked up his keys. 'Coming?'

On the way they quarrelled about speed cameras, tyre air pressure, whether that large bird of prey was a buzzard or a red kite, how to pronounce 'vulnerable', and if it was worth risking a ticket by parking on double yellows outside the framing shop. Neil was satisfied he had won every round. Ed had to be satisfied with knowing he was right.

The six newly framed sketches were produced by the long-suffering framer.

'Actually, I've come round to your view,' he said, as Neil checked them one by one, front and back, mitred corner, bevelled edge, glass, string, hook. 'They do look better with a slightly darker mount. It lifts them.'

'What did I tell you?' Neil bent to examine the last picture. 'Customer's always right, pal.'

Ed caught the framer's eye over the top of Neil's head. He met Ed's gaze blandly. You haven't changed the mount at all, thought Ed. He looked away, loyalty to his fiancé battling with profound sympathy for his victims.

'Happy now, big man?' Neil asked as they drove home.

'Yes, absolutely. They're perfect.'

'No, they aren't.'

'Why not?'

'Because the wee bastard didn't change the mount at all.'

'Oh.' Ed blinked. 'I'm sure he—'

'Och, I'm not blind. I know the difference between deep cream and sand! And it will drive me mad every time I look at them. But I know you hate making a fuss.' He wiped his eyes and sniffed. 'That's what really matters to me. That you're happy.'

Ed reached out and laid a hand on his knee. 'Thanks.'

'Aye, well. And another thing, that was definitely, but definitely, a red kite.'

'It was a buzzard, Neil. It didn't have a forked tail.'

'It was a kite!'

'Buzzard.'

'McIvor.'

Chapter 30

I t comes to Miss Blatherwick, over her bowl of porridge, that she is part of the problem. All these years she has quietly believed that she is able, in some small way, to offer solutions. To dispense kind, sensible advice and practical help. To sort things out and brook no nonsense. In short, to carry on playing matron.

And this, it now strikes her, necessarily requires Freddie to continue in the role of naughty chorister. And this can't be good for him. In fact, it may already have done damage. For if she had not chivvied him into applying for the lay clerkship here – where everyone remembers a hundred and one harum-scarum escapades – Freddie might by now be standing on his own two feet as a responsible adult. In another cathedral people would not see and indulge that little tinker still misbehaving on *dec*; they would see Freddie as a man, as the man he is. Yes, without her intervention there would be none of this Peter Pan nonsense he is currently enacting. Playing pirates and redskins around the Close with his band of Lost Boys!

But this in itself is a piece of vanity. As though she were the sun around which Freddie orbited! Countless other bodies exert a gravitational effect, and – Miss Blatherwick discards astrological imagery here in favour of grammatical – Freddie is the subject of his life's sentence, not the object. He is active, not passive.

Nevertheless, it is high time she adjusted her behaviour. She's holding him back. She must stop indulging herself by treating him as a ten-year-old scallywag who still needs his Miss B.

Sunlight slopes into her kitchen from a high window. Dust motes glint; tiny but astonishing flashes in that slanting beam. She has never noticed before – but how beautiful they are! They float, scintillate, turn, fade. Bits of dust, nothing more. They must all settle and be swept away in a duster in due course. But at this precise moment, picked out there by the sun, they seem absurdly glorious and worthy of attention.

And so our steps journey on through the darkness of this passing age. Blossom sugars the winter-flowering cherry branches, where here and there bright leaves still cling. There is a chill in the air now. Sometimes we wake to find a fur of frost on car roofs of a morning. The canonical houses grow cold and canons come in sight, like the poor man of the carol, gathering winter fuel. Years after they have moved on to warmer accommodation the urge to skip-dive for firewood will remain strong.

Leaves limp across roads like wounded creatures. The wind rattles in the lime trees of the Close. In the deanery garden, the palace garden, and behind the Choristers' School, the holly and the ivy wait to be harvested by the flower guild. Pink berries, snowball berries, orange, red, yellow berries decorate hedges again, and under the urban sycamores and planes, leaf stamps mark the pavements like dinosaur footprints.

Dawn is coming. High up on Lindford Common a lonely figure battles uphill through the mist towards the rising sun. He weeps as he runs because he cannot see how he will ever change, ever move his life on, how he will ever grow up enough to win the one he yearns for. *Love me, please love me.* All the other guys? Nothing. Just shadows of you. Because it's you, you I've been looking for? For like, my entire life?

But even if one day his love is returned, Freddie knows deep down that this beloved will fail him, turn out not to be the answer. But that's why he yearns for him! Around, beyond this bright-edged shadow he glimpses, sidelong and refracted, the Beloved – dear desire of every nation, joy of every longing heart. Oh, he will never get home and be safe! Oh please, oh please. His soul is nothing but an aching O of longing. O Oriens, O Emmanuel. O come. O come.

He crests the hill, lungs bursting. Behind him his long shadow stumbles after like a poor rickety giant. For an instant, though he doesn't see it, a halo of rainbow light gathers in the mist round his shadow's head, and he is touched with glory.

'All right, then, Mr Archdeacon. It's not important, but I thought I'd just ask: what are you going to wear on The Day?'

'I don't mind, Janey. What do you want me to wear?'

'I honestly don't mind either.' Pause. 'Are you hiring a flash suit?'

'If you want me to hire a flash suit, I'll hire a flash suit. But it'll make me look like a rugby player up for Sports Personality of the Year. What are you wearing?'

'I don't know. What do you want me to wear?'

'Oka-a-ay ... I'm going to opt for "whatever would make you happiest".'

'Answered like a sensible man! However, I note with interest that the thing that would make *me* happiest is now tangled with what would make *you* happiest. So feel free to tell me. Whereupon I will call you a sexist pig.'

'All righty. In that case, I'd love you to buy yourself another knock-out sexy dress. Red. And tight. I like a sexy tight red dress on my woman.'

'You sexist pig! OK. I'm on it. And feel free to buy yourself a non-flash suit. Ta-ta for now.'

Dean Marion is away for the first half of this week. She's at General Synod, where among other weighty matters, they will be asked to vote 'That the Canon entitled "Amending Canon No. 33" be made, promulged and executed.'

I hope, O pedant reader, you did not get excited there. 'Promulged' is not a typo, it's an archaic form of 'promulgated'. We like our archaisms here on Planet Anglicanism. Where else does one encounter the words 'apparitor' and 'porrect' (which pleasingly, spellcheck wishes to correct to 'correct')?

So: you say promulgate, I say promulge, let's call the whole thing off. Fortunately, it won't come to that this time round. Arguments are done and dusted, as far as General Synod goes. The relevant website notes: 'This will be the final rubber stamp on the legal process permitting women to be ordained as bishops. The vote is a formality.' We are, of course, permitted to wrangle about this unofficially for as many decades to come as we care to; but the serious combatants are now hunched in their bunkers strategizing for the next battle. Having disappointed the media by our inability to tear the Anglican Communion into ribbons over women, doomy predictions are now focused on the gay issue.

Will the Most Revd Dr Michael Palgrove be the captain at the helm when the good ship Anglicanism finally gets scuttled by its warring crew? But that is to adopt a very Anglo-centric view. The Anglican Communion worldwide is more a flotilla than a ship, and the Most Revd Dr Michael Palgrove is perhaps better viewed as the admiral on board the titular flagship. He may lead, but he cannot compel the fleet to follow. The captains on board the GAFCON vessels have long been tapping their compasses, sending up distress flares and semaphoring, 'Ahoy! Check your readings! Is north no longer north on board the *Canterbury*?'

Has our destination changed? Or are liberal instruments more finely calibrated, better able to discern true north amid the distortions of culture, the warping shash of context?

But anyway. Let this not blight our celebrations. Huzzah for General Synod! We can now, for the first time in history, officially appoint women bishops. In the C of E, I mean. There have been Anglican women bishops elsewhere in the Communion since 1989. The sees currently vacant may now engage in a seemly scramble behind the scenes to appoint England's First Woman Bishop. Stealthy manoeuvring has already begun, in the manner of rush-hour commuters trying to steal a march by suavely positioning themselves on the platform where they believe the train doors will open.

If you wish, you can nip to the bookies and have a flutter on Dean Marion. Unless you come from a Nonconformist background, and even a church tombola still smacks of Satan (who with bath salts and York Fruits seeks to lure you down the slippery slope to gambling on the Sabbath). I have been told that the odds on Marion Randall are rather good.

From all over the diocese, clergy – or lay readers, or churchwardens – drive to Lindchester to buy Advent candles from the cathedral shop, where sales of the Dorian Singers' new CD are brisk (word's got out: it's Freddie May in his nuddy pants on the cover). Well, I say they drive to Lindchester, but that is to gloss over the increasing numbers who adopt the dastardly practice of ordering their Advent candles online. But however they are purchased, five Advent candles are required: four for the Sundays in Advent, one for Christmas Day. Depending on churchmanship, that's one white, one pink, three purple; or one white, four purple; or one white, four red. Artisan, smokeless, beeswax, pillar, tapered, large, small, oil-filled, 'natural candles that visibly burn down', 'nylon candles that eliminate wax spills'. From choice overload and micro-decisions: Good Lord, deliver us.

Advent rings are fetched out of vestry cupboards. Advent wreaths are bought, or dug out of lofts and garages. Advent carols are rehearsed. In traditional parishes, fruit and suet are laid in ready for the making of Christmas puddings on Stir-up Sunday (aka the Sunday of Christ the King).

Before long the gigantic cathedral tree will arrive in Lindchester and be dropped into its socket on the lawn in front of the west end, right in the middle of Gavin's labyrinth. He's mowed it flat now in readiness – to the dismay of little Chad William, the chancellor's son – but from high above, the stone saints, the gargoyles and pigeons, the pest control man's Harris hawk, the masons and naughty lay clerks up on the scaffolding may still trace the faint pattern if they wish.

Only four more Fridays. Leah has worked it out. Only four more Fridays-after-school spent in this office. Ever. Daddy's new job starts in January, and from then on Mummy will drop her and Jess off at his new office in Lindford, which is a lot closer to school. Oh, it's so convenient for everybody, Mummy doesn't have to use so much petrol and Jess won't get car-sick. So everyone's a winner!

Like Leah cares. Tuh.

Last Friday Bishop Harry and Penelope were saying to Daddy, 'We need continuity, can you give us one day a week until the next bishop gets here?' Leah prayed with her fingers crossed: *Let him say yes, say Friday! Say yes, say Friday!* Right, like prayer ever works. Because they decided Wednesdays. So this is the last four Fridays left. Whatever. Like who even cares?

Leah sits at Daddy's desk and does her maths homework. Jess is under the desk playing with lame-tastic Barbie. If you stay really quiet, grown-ups forget you're there. They think homework uses up your entire whole brain, so there's no brain power left over to listen to what they're saying. Seriously, who needs an invisibility cloak? Grown-ups are so dumb.

The archdeacon is getting married next week. Massive big secret. And the woman priest who everyone hates is going to Australia, and now she's off with stress. Massive big secret. And Bishop Bob might be going to take early retirement. Massive big secret. Do they seriously think Leah can't hear them? Maybe they think she's as dumb as Jess, who can't even crack the grown-up so-called 'code' of leaving gaps, and going 'hmm-hmm', and saying 'You Know Who', like they are talking about Voldemort. What kind of a duh-brain do you have to be, if you can't work out who A Certain Lay Clerk is? (Next year she is *so* going to get some roman candles and fire them off like a gun in the back garden.)

But today nobody is talking. It's boring. Why does everything in her life have to be so boring? She might as well be DEAD. She gives a push and the office chair spins. Someone has put a mitre and a bra on the big pink teddy bear, which is really inappropriate and childish. The clock says 4.20. Quickly, she fills in all the gaps on the sheet with random numbers, coz who cares about stupid maths? Oh, look, I got zero out of twenty, that is very disappointing, I am very disappointed, but I tried my best, Miss, that is what counts.

It's cold and it's getting dark, but Leah goes outside and does kata on the palace drive. Because she's working towards her next grade, obviously. Not because she might see the choir men going to their practice soon, or anything.

Gah! Face-palm. Friday. She's there again, poor kid. So Freddie heads round the Close the long way. Still, come the New Year, Marty will have started the (ha ha ha!) BLO job in Lindford. Maybe Freddie will swing past the palace on the last week, do a farewell kata with her? Yeah, be good to do that. He jogs to the Song School. Totally reminds him of himself back in the day? Three Choirs, hanging around Dr Jacks, all notice me, notice me!

And it totally kills him to think: that poor kid out there going through her moves in the dark? The one who can't see it's never, ever gonna happen? Honestly? – that's him.

So, that woman priest everyone hates is 'off with stress'. Do we believe her? Do we heck. Still, from Geoff's point of view as her clergy colleague, it is a huge relief. He will not have to stand at the altar with her, pretending that her dagger handle is not jutting between his shoulder blades. Geoff has been cited as one of the causes of her stress. To my mind, this is a bit like all of the other reindeer filing a complaint against Rudolph for bullying in the workplace. With his sensible head on, Geoff knows this: but it still distresses him out of all proportion, and though he knows it is out of proportion, this doesn't assuage the distress. Only time will mend this one. Time, and the absence of Veronica.

Why should she be allowed to get away with this? The tendency of this narrative is to imply that ultimately, there is no getting away with things. That is why we strain our eyes to the east in Advent – with all the yearning of a mother at the arrivals gate at Heathrow, straining for the first glimpse of her great shambling ogre of a son, back from New Zealand after nearly two years of absence. We watch and wait and long for the coming judgement. Or the coming mercy. Are they one and the same? Two sides of the same coin? Two different coins as far apart as the east is from the west? But by that, do we mean sunrise and sunset, or the Greenwich meridian? Maybe justice and mercy are divided by the entire universe, yet paired;

quantumly entangled in ways the non-physicist cannot comprehend, so must humbly accept?

I will abandon this argument. Because right now, in the vicarage of Gayden Magna, a less metaphysical conundrum is being teased out, as Ed and Neil try to hang the six newly framed sketches in the dining room without killing one another.

'I'm telling you, that looks fine to me, Neil.'

'It's not straight. No way is that straight.'

'Well, it's straight enough. Oh, for God's sake, Neil!'

'I'm downloading a spirit level app.' He hums while he waits. Another old Sunday School chorus. 'Mercy there was great and grace was free. Here we go. Ha! See there? See? I was right. Move that end up a bit. Not *that end*, you tool! Hey! Where do you think you're going?'

'Call me when you're done, Neil, and I'll come and admire it.'

'Hello? We were supposed to be doing this together. As a couple? And another thing!'

Ed sighs. 'What?'

'Listen, I want Bishop Bob to marry us.'

'Neil, he isn't allowed to, and we can't ask him. It's not fair on him—'

'I know that! What, do I look stupid? Do you think I want to give him another heart attack? If I'm honest, I'm thinking with hindsight you were wrong to drag him out here to meet us. I mean, you weren't to know, obviously.'

Ed gawps in disbelief. 'That was *you*! You insisted on it!'

'Well, we'll not argue. I'm thinking he's not long off retiring, is he? Can he maybe marry us when he's retired?'

'No! Get it into your head: C of E clergy are barred from conducting same-sex marriages. If you insist on Bob doing it, you'll have to wait till the legislation changes.'

'Och, well. Maybe we should get civil partnered while we wait? Then we'd be *something*. I hate all this . . . this no proper status thing, Eds. Think about it? I know you're dead set against it, but will you at least consider it?'

'What? What are you on about? I'm not dead set against it. That was you, remember? You're the one pushing for—'

'Well, you're wrong, but we'll not argue. Psht! Stop arguing. Just promise you'll think it over?'

'I don't *need* to think it over! I'd do it now, Neil.'

'Aye, you say that, but I mean, do it *soon*. ASAP. Before—'

'You're not listening!'

'I *am* listening! Ssh! – before Christmas. Coz we could, our notice is still valid. That's what I'm saying.'

'And I'm saying *Yes*. Idiot! YES, let's do it! Shall I ring the register office now?'

'Och, no need. Way ahead of you.' Neil grins. 'Wanna get hitched next Friday, big man?'

Chapter 31

ake, O wake! with tidings thrilling
The watchmen all the air are filling,
Arise, Jerusalem, arise!

Jane watches her sleeping son. He lies on the sofa under a nice cuddly red throw. Jane bought the throw when it became clear that no amount of brute force was sufficient to cram the sofa cushions back into their shrunken covers. Danny lies like a felled pylon, face down, snoring. Jane remembers how you lose sleep at university, then spend the rest of your life trying to catch up. And if you go on to become a mother, that second tsunami of sleep deprivation means your infrastructure never fully recovers. And this is why I am such a grumpy old cow, my darling boy. I blame you. She strokes the mane of black curls back from his face. He doesn't stir.

Bookends. Those choo-choo train bookends. Where did they get to? Jane can picture them. Handmade, wooden, brightly painted. A gift from Paul and Susanna Henderson, the closest Danny had to godparents. Bookends and an illustrated Children's Bible. Packed off to the charity shop in some purge or other, probably that time she humanely culled the menagerie of soft toys. Oh dear, and that Mother's Day necklace, wooden beads from a car-seat cover, strung on an orange bootlace. Should've kept that. I could've worn it to my – argh! Deep breath and say it – WEDDING.

This is a bookend moment. The close bracket round Danny's childhood. There was a life before Project Motherhood, and there will be life beyond. Two decades ago – straight out of hospital – she'd sat by his cot (reeling, schnockered with exhaustion!) and watched her little curled-up dab of a thing, burrowed face down into the sheet, black wisps on his head, bum in the air. This is it; from now on, the wheels on the motherhood bus go round and round. I've got to drive safely, keep you alive and drop you off in adulthood in one piece. Brahms' 'Lullaby' tinkling in the background. Garish yellow activity bear clamped to the cot bars.

Totally *verboten*, allowing your babe to sleep face down, but no matter how dutifully I put you on your back, you ended up on your front. Ha, my first insight into your sweet stubbornness. And now I'm watching you again, fast asleep, aged nearly twenty. Knowing full well that there's no way you're going to come clothes shopping with me today. No, sadly, I can no longer chop you in the back of the knees, fold you into your buggy and strap you firmly in place.

Look at you! You big, funny, kind man. You'll make some lucky gal very happy. Or guy? Probably gal. Flashback to Christmas before last – the icy heart-stopper of surprising Danny under the palace mistletoe with young tarty-pants. A game of 'gay chicken', it turned out. Lovely. And did you not clock that Freddie's probably going to win that one, son? Yes, but The Dare, mother! The Dare is sacred! Oh, the strange Samurai mentality of teen boys. And the hetero-normative knee-jerk reaction of even the most liberal of mothers ...

Jane kisses his sleeping brow and gets to her feet. No, she'll bully Dom into shopping with her instead. His line's engaged, so she leaves a message.

Poor old Father Dominic. In the midst of dry-mopping his pale oak laminate kitchen floor, he finds himself in a *Groundhog Day* moment:

'Oh! Omigod! You're finally, finally getting hitched! About time too! That is *so* exciting! Oh Ed, I'm so happy for you!'

'Thank you, Father.'

'Can I give you away? Can I be your matron of honour? Or shall I just sit and cry happy tears?'

'We'd like you to be a witness, but please cry. I'm counting on you to cry, in the absence of any mothers of the groom.'

'Oh, I won't fail you. Buckets of happy tears guaranteed, Father. I'm so excited! But I thought you were planning on getting married, not civil partnering?'

'Yes, well, this is a staging post on the way to marriage. A holding position. While we wait for some change of heart in the House of Bishops.'

'Really? But I thought ... Neil ... ?'

'Ours is not to reason why, Father. Mr Ferguson has decided.'

'I see. Well, goody-good.'

Pause.

'Look, I'm not hen-pecked, Dom.'

'Of course not! Neil's not a hen. He *can* be a bit of a—'

'Yes, I see where you're going with the poultry imagery, there. Moving on. It's just a low-key private thing. The big fat gay wedding is deferred till further notice.'

'Well, that will give Neil lots of time to plan everything properly, won't it?'

'Jesu mercy! I mean, yes, yes, it will. So, Lindford register office, this Friday at eleven o'clock. OK?'

'OK. Wait! *This* Friday?'

'You're shrieking in my ear, Father.'

'Omigod, omigod! This Friday, as in the twenty-eighth?'

'Yes. It's the only slot they had left this side of Christmas. Is that a problem?'

'No! It's— Eek! Short notice, that's all. Eleven, you said? No, no, that's absolutely fine. I'll be there, ha ha ha! So! What's the dress code?'

'The dress code is: "Tell him not to dress like a wee nellie vicar".'

'Oh, thanks a bunch! I've actually just bought a very suave new suit, I'll have you know.'

'That sounds perfect.'

'And just for the record, your fiancé's a cock.'

Ed laughs. 'That's never been in any doubt.'

Poor Father Dominic hangs up and has a little weep. Then he wipes his eyes, picks up his fluffy dust mop, and waltzes round his kitchen doing his best Lily Morris impression. 'Why am I always the witness, never the blushing bride?'

Oh, oh, oh! How ghastly – but how hilarious! Ed and Neil following hot on the heels of Jane and the archdeacon! In the same register office! Oh, Lord – the bridal parties are going to tangle in the foyer, aren't they? He pictures old Janey, emerging with a face like thunder – having endured the patriarchal bollocks of marriage – and bumping into Ed and Neil, as they arrive to make do with the staging post of civil partnership. The scene unfolds like a Whitehall farce in Dominic's imagination. Because – help! – Janey has invited the blond mantrap to come and sing during the signing of the register. Oh no, oh no! Is it Dominic's place to say something? He knows Ed can't stand the sight of Freddie (no explanation necessary *there*, Dom has known Neil for years).

No. Stop fretting. Not my responsibility. We'll muddle through. That's all we can ever do, thinks Dominic. Live generously, muddle through. Keep on walking towards the light, beckoned on by little glimpses of glory, until finally we arrive home. And then the meaning will burst in on us. Oh, it was you, it was you all along! No more marrying and giving in marriage. Everything will be scooped up, everything will marry up. Everything in heaven and on earth. And no one will be left outside weeping any more.

Well, well, it's early Advent. Each year he longs for it more. The New Year. A chance to recalibrate the heart's instruments, get his bearings, and set out once again on the right path. Dominic abandons his beloved music hall repertoire in favour of *Wachet auf* and – like a virgin wise – finishes mopping his floor:

> The Bridegroom comes in sight,
> Raise high your torches bright!
> Alleluya! The wedding song swells loud and strong:
> Go forth and join the festal throng!

*

Bookends. I fear that before many more years have passed they will become an oddity. Like paperweights and blotters, they will join the paraphernalia of period drama. Discarded bookends will clutter up charity shop shelves among the ashtrays and videos. But for now, a set of bookends still has enough resonance for me to venture upon an extended metaphor. We began this narrative with a question: who will be the new bishop? And now, as neatly as the other bookend, our tale ends with the answer: on Monday, in York, the Confirmation of Election took place of the Rt Revd Stephen Henry Pennington as Bishop of Lindchester.

Although our rules forbid us to join the select throng gathered in the Minster, I can assure the reader that everything was done correctly. A confirmation of election is essentially the medieval equivalent of an ID check. Is this the real Steve Pennington? Prove it! The process is no longer conducted in Latin behind closed doors, but it retains a medieval theatricality. Anyone blundering in might wonder whether they've interrupted a D'Oyly Carte rehearsal. There's a pleasing amount of poncing about in wigs, with apparitors, letters patent, advocates submitting that 'all the matters set forth in these exhibits respectively were and are true and were done as therein described', and proctors stating, 'I porrect a definitive Sentence or Final Decree in writing which I pray to be read and declared.' After a great deal of quasi-medieval frolicking, the definitive Sentence or Final Decree is read, declared and signed and – phew! – Steve Pennington is now officially Bishop of Lindchester.

Huzzah, huzzah, huzzah! My days, that took long enough, didn't it? Of course, Steve and his fragrant wife won't actually move into the palace yet. Goodness me, no! Quite apart from the fact that the new wet room isn't finished, nor the oatmeal carpets banished and every trace of the last regime purged, we haven't had the service of installation yet. And although that won't take quite as long to plan and get perfect as a big fat gay wedding, we are unlikely to receive our invitations till next year. If Dean and Chapter get a move on, the new bishop might be installed by Easter.

In the meantime, Bishop Harry will continue holding the fort. After Christmas our good friend Bishop Bob will be back at work full time. He is easing himself in now, taking it steady, aware every hour, every minute, of his patient, faithful heart; still beating (still beating!), conscious all the time how he carries it in the crib of his chest, carefully, carefully, like a newborn, not jolting it (hush, it will be all right). And how it carries him.

The archdeacon has survived his stag do. He was taken paintballing by his stepson-to-be and young tarty-pants. Jane's fear that the two of them would gang up on her beloved was not misplaced. But Matt proved the truth of the adage that age and treachery always overcome youth and skill. He also underlined a piece of ancient church lore: Never piss off an archdeacon.

Nobody dared suggest a hen do.

And so The Day arrived. Black Friday – that bacchanalia of acquisitiveness. The scope for mordant humour was not lost on Jane. She battled through shoppers and arrived at Lindford Town Hall in her long knock-out sexy red frock and black velvet opera coat. Yes, carrying a fecking bouquet, because Dom had bought her one, and she didn't want to hurt his feelings. And anyway, it gave her something to do with her hands, other than box people's ears or strangle herself. Long-stemmed red roses, a mere thirty this time, trailing black organza ribbons. Pah.

There was Dom in his new suit and pointy shoes. Danny in a new shirt and clean jeans to be a credit to his mum and to adorn the office of witness. Freddie in tight black with almost as much cleavage going on as the bride.

Up the steps. In through the doors. Jesus. I can't believe I agreed to this.

And there was Matt. New suit, charcoal grey. Red rose in his buttonhole. Accessorized by a smile wide, wide as the ocean. Don't bloody smile at me like that, you bastard, I'm not happy. I'm not. Ha, all right then, I am. Oh, I am so happy!

Well, it all went swimmingly. In the absence of real clergy, the registrar adopted such a portentously Anglican intonation as would not have disgraced a trained actor playing the rector in a costume drama. The bride's voice was squeaky with tears, the groom blotted his eyes, one witness sobbed happily, the other witness rolled his eyes, and Freddie May sang like an angel. 'The Lark in the Clear Air' (Matt's choice) and 'Now Sleeps the Crimson Petal, Now the White' (Jane's choice).

> So fold thyself, my dearest, thou, and slip
> Into my bosom and be lost, be lost in me ...

Aw, bless. Bless them one and all.

They will be coming out soon. We will mount up like feral pigeons, and perch wherever we can, wherever the town council has failed to put spikes, and watch greedily, hoping that rice will be thrown. Here they are! But no rice; red rose petals swirl in the breeze. They settle on the steps where, only a few weeks before, the poppy petals whispered down. In the distance a band oom-pahs some carols, and the world's worst violinist scrawks out 'Jingle Bells'.

A black Porsche pulls up and parks on double yellows. It's the next couple arriving. Out they get. We stay aloof, up here among the hostile spikes, and watch as the tall woman hurls her bouquet. It flies as if she's hoofed a high Garryowen, up, up, then down, like a pimped warhead trailing black streamers. The receiver stands firm in his kilt, calls his mark. Catches it, thorns and all.

'Oh, ye-e-e-e-ah!' He strikes a *Braveheart* pose, bouquet-broadsword in hand. Then he and his man mount the steps as the last handfuls of red petals swirl, laughing as they go.

And so, Jack shall have Jill, and Jack shall have Jack. I cannot promise you that naught shall go ill, dear reader. But I believe we can say that this Black Friday was not all darkness and gloom, with no brightness in it.

Dean Marion is in her garden on Saturday. She is admiring her new beehive, bought for her by her husband, tireless in his pursuit of deanissima's happiness. She will not be the first woman bishop in the C of E. No, a whisper about this has reached her, and of course it's a relief! She needs no consolation prizes.

O, reason not the need! He has bought her a beehive anyway.

'But I know nothing about beekeeping, Gene!'

'I shall be your keeper.'

'Thank you. Do we buy bees? How does it work?'

'Oh, we lure them in, Deanissima. With sweet aromas. Or we steal them from other hives. I see it as a paradigm of the Diocesan Growth Agenda.'

The little white wooden house stands in the lavender border. 'Maybe they will just come. Out of the blue, one June day. Like they did this year. Maybe they will just appear, Gene.'

'And this time we will have a home waiting for them.'

'Yes, I hope they come. Like a gift of grace. "Drop down, ye heavens, from above",' she quotes.

' "And let the skies pour down righteousness",' he warbles in his Peter Pears voice. 'Did you know that in the winter the worker bees all huddle around the queen, and shiver in order to keep her warm? She will be quite safe until her hour comes.'

'Thank you, darling.'

'Come, let's go and find a last-wine-before-Advent treat.'

They go back to the deanery and close out the November dusk.

Advent Sunday. Darkness into Light. The cathedral is a hive of liturgical activity. The choir rehearse. The early birds have already arrived to bag the best seats. They show their Teutonic roots by putting coats on empty seats as flagrantly as any lounger-bagging German by a hotel pool. Stewards stand on chairs and gouge old wax out of candle sockets with screwdrivers. We will look away and not ask about risk assessment. The candles are all pre-lit, then snuffed, to ensure that they will light first time and darkness proceeds into light with military precision. The tapers are ready. We still shudder in Lindchester when we recall the Bic lighter fiasco of 2007, when the nave resounded to a tattoo of frenzied clicking.

Up in the organ loft the organists practise *Wachet auf* and make sure they are ready to train their cockpit camera on the sleepiest person in the quire, so they can wet themselves laughing when an unexpected crescendo in one of the carols jolts some sleeper awake.

Evening services across the diocese will be sparsely attended tonight. Lo, from the north they come! From east and west and south! This is one of the highlights of the liturgical year. Here is our lovely friend Father Wendy. Ah, and our good friend Geoff. Let's hope the service knits up the ravelled sleeve of Veronica-related care for him. Here is Dominic. Goodness, is that Jane with him? It is! She is being a clergy wife for the very first time! Golly, I hope the sign in her reserved seat doesn't say 'Mrs M. Tyler'!

The reliable soprano with a straight voice climbs up the stairs to the triforium, to sing the O Antiphons again. Our two lovely bishop friends, Harry and Bob, gently quarrel over who must have the place of honour at the back of the procession. See how determinedly they strive to out-defer one another, until the precentor appears, knocks their mitres together, and orders them to walk side by side. The choristers are demented with excitement. Candles! Darkness! Fingers crossed they don't set fire to themselves. Lay clerks in their red cassocks flit about on errands.

Well, well, well. I do believe that I just spotted the great Mr Dorian himself gliding in and insinuating himself into one of the best reserved seats in the house, front row, nave, next to the Lord Lieutenant. He has come to hear his mentee sing that solo Freddie should, by rights, have performed on the Christmas CD. 'What wondrous love is this, O my soul?' After all, he wrote it for Freddie. With hindsight, *not* clever to phrase it like that just now, though: 'I wrote it for you.' Rather than: 'I had your voice and its unusual timbre in mind when I arranged this piece.' Hmm. He rather feared the subsequent clarification was lost on his smitten mentee.

The lights dim. The dean mounts the pulpit steps and makes her announcements.

Still, not a problem. Mr May would grow out of it soon enough. That said, it would be idle to pretend that a smile could not light up a lost lake in the soul. Where a thousand lilies had just unfurled without permission. Ah, well.

Silence. Darkness. In a moment a lone voice, like one crying in the wilderness, will sing. But for now, we wait.

Outside on the Close the wind *shh-shhhes* in the empty lime trees. A robin flutters up to the old-fashioned lamp post. Perhaps it is the same bird who built its nest behind the high altar? In the silence he starts to sing. Perhaps, poor thing, he is deluded, and mistakes the lamplight for the dawn?

Perhaps. But he will still be awake, singing – whether at midnight, or at cock crowing, or when day breaks.